VOID
STAR

VOID
STAR

·

ZACHARY
MASON

FARRAR, STRAUS AND GIROUX   NEW YORK

Farrar, Straus and Giroux
18 West 18th Street, New York 10011

Library of Congress Cataloging-in-Publication Data
Names: Mason, Zachary, 1974– author.
Title: Void star : a novel / Zachary Mason.
Description: First edition. | New York : Farrar, Straus and Giroux, 2017.
Identifiers: LCCN 201603324 | ISBN 9780374285067 (hardcover) |
    ISBN 9780374709822 (ebook)
Subjects: LCSH: Artificial intelligence—Fiction. | Memory—Fiction. |
    BISAC: FICTION / Literary. | GSAFD: Science fiction. | Dystopias.
Classification: LCC PS3613.A8185 V65 2017 | DDC 813/.6—dc23
LC record available at https://lccn.loc.gov/2016033247

Designed by Jo Anne Metsch

Our books may be purchased in bulk for promotional, educational, or business use.
Please contact your local bookseller or the Macmillan Corporate and Premium
Sales Department at 1-800-221-7945, extension 5442, or by e-mail at
MacmillanSpecialMarkets@macmillan.com.

www.fsgbooks.com
www.twitter.com/fsgbooks • www.facebook.com/fsgbooks

1 3 5 7 9 10 8 6 4 2

Contents

VOID
STAR

1
·

Floating World

elow her are the lights of the valley, like burning jewels on a dark tide. The Bay is a negative space around them, its leaden ripples picked out in the moonlight. There is, Irina realizes, a pattern in the flawed latticework of lights, something deeper than the incidental geometry of buildings and streetlight, to which the city has, unwitting, conformed itself, and, with this revelation, what she had taken for single lights expand into constellations, and each of their lights is a constellation in itself, luminescent forms in an endless descent, and the city is like a nebula, radiant with meaning, and this is how she finally knows she's dreaming.

She is aware, now, that she's on a plane, her forehead resting against the window, is aware of her slow, even breathing, of the awkward abandon of her legs skewed out in front of her. She caught the last shuttle from Los Angeles to San Francisco, leaving after midnight from a terminal abandoned by everyone but the drones scrubbing the floors. Now, twenty thousand feet in the air, she is alone, the plane following the sky's ley lines of its own accord, like a mute, friendly animal that knows the way home. Even in the dream's residue this gives her pause, automated commercial aviation only having come about when she was a teenager, but she thinks how, with access to the eyes of satellites and databases of the windforms and cloud-forms and aircraft in the sky, the plane can see all the night at once.

She remembers the camera set unobtrusively into the seatback—perhaps in some distant darkened office-park there is an attendant, bored, lonely, her fingernails digging crescents into her coffee cup, face awash in LED glow, who is watching her, and worries, briefly, at her stillness, but is reassured by the motion behind her eyelids, and does the attendant feel some vast compassion for her charges adrift in this dark gulf of sky?

The plane banks and she comes fully awake. A loudspeaker offers muffled advice that she automatically ignores. Out the window she sees the imbricated panels of the wing shift slightly, the airflow whitely visible. Below her, the Bay and the ragged scrawl of lights, but now they are entirely legible and entirely banal—the glitter from the spires of the new down-town, the shoals of the office parks, the favelas glowing like cyclopean piles of cinders. She feels lighter, now; she is descending.

2

·

High Playground

The stinging impact of Kern's palms against the cool concrete and he's up and off again, flowing over the rooftop jumble of the favela's density. The night's celebrants and their predators have dispersed, and the workers are just stirring, so his progress has no witness but the flags and laundry shivering in the wind.

A canyon opens before him, a gap in the fabric of the rooftops— discipline requires that he never break stride, so he gauges his footing and leaps, glimpsing balconies below him, the cables criss-crossing the void— the momentary coldness of the rift's exhalation. Landing, he's grateful for the concrete's roughness, its traction, how it makes the favelas his playground.

A drone like a bulbous, dog-sized ant methodically deposits a new layer of concrete on the wall before him; it slowly lifts its mauve plastic head to scan him but he is up, over and past. Illegal, that kind of robot; their hum, ubiquitous this time of day, will be gone by the time people are working. Another night and whatever it's building will be finished, its weight added to the ever-burgeoning city.

The concrete seems to give, slightly, under his feet; perhaps an illusion, born of his speed, or perhaps this block is overbuilt, and unstable. He has seen the sinkholes, the fractured declivities, the rubble intermixed with splintered furniture, scattered clothes, all the sad relics of ruined private lives. He has explored the settling ruins of recent collapse, remembers the cramped incidental geometry of the unplanned mazes, the terror of masses shifting above him. He runs faster, as though pursued, breath steaming, feet seeming barely to touch the ground.

Now the rooftops slope down and he is infused with a terrible lightness as he leaps over prisms of broken concrete, the slope reminding him that there were hills under the favelas, once, and he wonders if the favelas' broken contour mirrors the hills' hidden swell. He has never found bare earth, there, just tunnels, tiers and old rooms ever deeper, and below them the ancient buildings, the basements and sewers, the forgotten warrens in the dark. There were wonders down there, they said, if you knew the way— a brothel in a long room lit by a single bulb, a secret club where men played chess and no one ever spoke, a swimming pool full of seawater, tiled in lapis.

Before him is an aluminum water tower, once a chemical tanker, protruding from the roof like an egg set on end. He gathers momentum and launches himself up, its crudely welded ladder creaking as it takes his weight, and then he is perched on top, the tanker shifting, vibrating with the slosh of its thousands of gallons. As his breathing slows and his sweat dries he takes in the pale moonlight on the water, the silver clouds enveloping the bridges, traces with his eyes the map of his secret byways through San Francisco. Something about the light on downtown's towers makes it seem remote, incorruptible, a place outside of time.

3

·

Oculus

Thales stumbles, catches the wall, clings to it, suddenly woozy.

He looks over his shoulder at his brother Helio, sees his dawning horror, realizes this might be serious.

His upper lip is wet. Touching it, his fingers come away red, but taking his hand from the wall was a mistake because he loses all sense of where he is in space until he finds himself on the floor, which is covered in wet sand, coarse and cold against his cheek, reeking of ocean.

They're in a tunnel from the beach, under the corniche. The seaward mouth is an oculus of variegated blue. The tunnel's acoustics make the wave's crash ring.

Black wave of nausea, then he's vomiting. Gouts of red darker than blood should be. That's bad, he's thinking, as the spasm climaxes.

"We need some *help* here," Helio is shouting to the bodyguard who is also, Thales remembers, a nurse, and who, from the footsteps, is coming at a run.

Shadows kneeling around him. A needle pierces his shoulder.

"This will help you breathe," says the bodyguard-who-is-a-nurse, his voice too calm, it seems like he should be more upset in honor of the occasion, and then a plastic mask is pressed over his nose and mouth.

Black military boots by his face. Beyond them, white lines slide down the glowing circle of celestial blue—waves, perhaps—but they won't come into focus, so he looks at the weave of shoelaces, the scuffs and scratches on the black leather, the grains of sand stuck to the rubber sole. His implant will record this moment in every detail, as it records every moment, so perfectly he's come to feel that nothing is lost to time.

Oxygen hisses into the mask, chills his lungs.

"Medevac drone incoming in . . . ninety-one seconds. Eighty-nine," a bodyguard says hoarsely.

A girl in a crocheted bikini has stopped in the tunnel mouth, her fingertips at her lips, like she's just seen the saddest thing in the world. The men kneeling around him are like statues, immovable and remote. He tries to roll to face the wall but they hold him down. I don't want to be here for this, he thinks, and retreats into his implant's memory.

The tunnel and his pain dissolve, and there's the recollection of the last two weeks, there in their entirety, sharp and undecayed. He skims over the surface of the hours—there's the clinic, the beaches, the many books on the theory of numbers, the freeways of Los Angeles as seen through the hardened windows of the armored town car—and finally alights on the first moments of the implant's record, when he was waking up in a hospital bed in a room he didn't know. A window framed the early light on a strange sea—it wasn't Leblon, maybe not even in Rio. His mother, looking haggard, was drowsing by the bed; waking, she crushed his hand in hers, bent to kiss his cheek and, he thought, breathe in his hair. Beside her sat a stranger, tie but no jacket, perhaps a doctor, immersed in his tablet.

Something was stuck to Thales' chest—his fingers found a thick pad of gauze, and another on his forehead—had he been injured? He couldn't recall, and he couldn't look away from the restless sea, because, incredibly, its changing shapes persisted in his memory, a new memory, another memory, and every moment as though immured in glass, as clear as the little poetry he had by heart, and he wondered if it was a hallucination, or the side effect of some drug.

"How are you?" asked his mother, her voice thick, smoothing back his hair, careful of the bandage, and he saw her relax when his eyes focused on hers. There was the memory of his words, and the memory of the memory, and then the memory of that, echoing on until his attention shifted.

"What happened?" he asked. A beat of silence while his mother worked out what to say, which meant it was bad, which was, come to think of it, obvious.

"There was an attack," she said. "An assassination. You were wounded, and your father was killed. It was political." He reached for sadness but felt only surprise that the old man had run out of tricks; he wondered if his father's demise would turn out to be staged, if, like Sherlock Holmes, he was not dead but just in hiding, waiting for the right moment to dramatically reappear. "Rio was untenable," his mother went on, "and the doctors you needed wouldn't come to Brazil, so I brought you here, to Los Angeles, with your brothers. We'll leave for the U.S. proper once we get visas and you're well enough to travel."

"I was hurt?"

"A sniper fired armor-piercing rounds at your father's car," the stranger says, standing. American, with an intensity and an absolute confidence, his cologne redolent of river water and orchids. "You were hit twice. You suffered a pierced lung and major cranial ablation. You've been in an induced coma for three weeks. I operated on you for twenty-six hours." The surgeon's motions seemed excessively controlled, as though he refused to let his fatigue show.

"I'm *remembering* things."

"That's your implant. It's about two inches under the bandage on your forehead. It took over the function of the unviable tissue, and so saved your life. The expanded memory is a side effect, a kind of bonus." The surgeon looked at his tablet and smiled, the first crack in an otherwise impenetrable professional facade. "The installation was . . . complex, but I'm happy to say it's working perfectly."

Thales had read about memory implants, had wondered what it would be like, had never thought to learn. "But those never really worked," he said. "The memory thing worked, but the people who got them usually died."

Impassive, distant, compassionate, the surgeon said, "There is absolutely no doubt that the implant will improve both the quality and the duration of your life."

And then he's back in the tunnel feeling like he's choking as someone stuffs a glove into his mouth and now he's biting down on the leather and cotton as a lozenge of white light—reflected from someone's watch?—skitters across the ceiling. His muscles are trembling—is he cold?—and someone is holding his head on their lap, and he wants to say he's going to be sick again but the tunnel is dark and its roof seems far away and as though from a distance he hears Helio say, "You're going to be fine!"

Someone is complaining that the medevac has been delayed by two minutes, its flight path went over the wrong neighborhood and someone shot at it, it's rerouting, fuck LA, in Brazil they'd know not to fly over the fucking favelas.

His awareness narrows to a single mote of light, the implant diligently recording.

Then it's time to let go of everything, and then he does, and the implant quietly turns itself off.

He wakes up in a hospital bed in a room he now knows well. Out the window the early light shines on the Pacific. Through the window he sees the sun shining on the sea and is aware of the rules of light's motion through space.

He touches his upper lip—his fingers come away clean. There are gauze bandages on his chest and forehead.

The sea heaves and shifts but its shapes slip away from him. He wonders if the implant is broken, and what happened, and, confusedly, if this is anesthesia annihilating time.

His mother isn't there, but the surgeon is sitting by the bed; he looks up from his tablet and says, "We need to ask you some questions."

4

•

Negotiable Sense of Place

Whatever liminal grace informs airports—some sense of perpetual arrival and departure, of being in an anonymous crowd united in separation from their proper lives—is absent now; the terminal stinks of disinfectant, and stalls blink garishly, trying to sell her perfume, T-shirts, duty-free alcohol, things Irina could not ever imagine wanting, and she has a sudden and overwhelming sense that the trip was a mistake, that she does not after all need the money, and wishes with all her being that she hadn't come.

The terminal funnels her to the entry checkpoint; they make you go through security again, when you get off a plane from LA, an uncomfortable reminder of how bad things are in that city. On the customs card she lists her profession as "computational translator," as accurate a description as any. This late there's only one guard, who stops reading the news on his phone long enough to take her card and wave her through the humming scan tunnel but she stops, says, "I have an implant," fishing through her purse for the letter on FAA letterhead certifying that, yes, she has a cranial implant, yes, it is the legal kind, no, it is not construed as a munition. With it, she forgets nothing. Only a few dozen people ever got her kind, less than ten are left, and she dreads questions. (Even the simplest implants are getting phased out—you used to need one to be a combat officer in the Marines, but the technology never really matured and now no one much uses them.) The guard reads the letter, eyes her skull with professional interest (she always wears bangs, against this very eventuality), and says, "Is it one of those direct connections to the net?" As he seems kind, and is without swagger, she delays her course toward hotel and sleep long enough to muster a smile and say, "It's memory," then retrieves the letter in the same motion that carries her into the scanner. The screen of the guard's laptop is reflected in the chromed walls; she sees herself as a ghost, walking, bones and the hardware in her bag glowing slightly, as does the arc of the device just behind her forehead.

As she rides the conveyor belts past empty storefronts, a closed Koffee Kiosk senses her gaze and illuminates itself, its marquee displaying helically frothed cappuccinos twirling through an abstract mathematical space. A direct connection to the net, she reflects, feels like an airport at night (the implant has this feature, but she almost always keeps it turned off)—something about being bombarded by sterile, impersonal and ultimately vacuous information, though part of her wishes that the Koffee Kiosk were open; she briefly considers turning on her wireless, cracking the Kiosk's security as she would an eggshell, making it give her coffee.

Finally, the double doors to the outside, their surfaces glowing with a last, desperate attempt to sell her discount fares to Gdansk, Helsinki, Reykjavík, and then they whisk open. As the cool outside air envelops her, the sense that place is fundamentally negotiable—endemic, she suspects, to airports—departs.

On the curb, she smells the chaparral in the hills, the fog, and knows where she is. As though in acknowledgment of this, a drone cab pulls to the front of the empty taxi queue. It's painted bright green, marking it as robotic. She gets in and a video screen on the inside of the door lights up; a software agent appears, a sort of sexy cartoon librarian who says, "Welcome to . . . the San Francisco Airport! Where can I take you tonight?" and beams. Her business being the inner lives of AIs, she knows exactly how little this one has, and touches the small button on the screen that dismisses the friendly interface. "Destination, please," says a calm, genderless voice. She finds the option that brings up a keyboard on the screen and types in the name of the hotel.

The cab winds its way through the labyrinth of over- and underpasses that lead out of the airport and onto the freeway, where it pulls into the designated drone lanes. A semi barrels past, its hood a prickling, insect-splattered expanse of stubby antennae, cameras, other protuberances that she can't identify but that must be sensors of some kind; she can't help but read the windowless cab as the face of a blind man with his visual prosthetic. The tank rushes by and she glimpses colored stickers indicating a payload of extreme toxicity. She feels a stab of pity for the people who once drove trucks long distances, how boring their lives must have been. There are stories, probably urban legends, about drone trucks disappearing, usually in the fog, in the mountains where radio signals get distorted, their cargoes of industrial solvents, Italian shoes, heirloom tomatoes surfacing in distant markets. Myths, most likely, grounded in occasional database errors, and in the slight eeriness of the things, roaring through the night with their sightless faces.

A drone Mercedes passes her, the light of streetlamps revealing a middle-aged suit looking absurdly vulnerable as he nods over a closed laptop. There was a psychological shift, with drone cars, that made people act less like they were in semipublic and more like they were in their bedrooms. She often saw people getting dressed, men bucking in the confined space to get their legs into pants, women putting on makeup or stockings, anonymity substituting for privacy. Now there's a car full of kids, the boys drinking whisky from cans, the girls' faces glowing, laughing at nothing, off on an endless cruise through the night, converging, briefly, at bars, but always believing that the final destination, some desirable center, is elsewhere, a promise never realized, and so, with blood alcohol no impediment to motion, they are, with each arrival, already preparing to disappear; she wants to disappear with them.

Waking, she stumbles out of the cab into predawn fog and the smell of the sea; the hotel, beige and sterile, is entirely devoid of a sense of place. This quiet hour, she thinks, of fatigue poison, suicide, ghosts.

There's a guard in a little booth by the concrete planters that keep anyone from driving too close to the hotel; he ignores her, and at first she thinks he's breaking down his rifle but then sees that he's watching television on its display. She has a vision of rounds raining down on the hotel while the indifferent guard flips channels.

Although she is not a gun person, at all, she recognizes the guard's rifle, an anti-armor Heckler & Koch, the same weapon used on the virtual battlefields of her most recent contract; she'd spent a week trying to persuade the house AI of a Santa Monica defense firm to take an interest in a tactical simulation, and then, interest taken, to make its army win. Surprisingly, the simulation was beautiful, with the bright arcs of missiles, the airborne drones like flocks of easily startled birds, the strike zones of the weapons satellites like cloud shadows scudding over the hills.

In the empty lobby the lights are dimmed. Her phone shows her the way through the corridors.

Her room is the color of the dry grass in the hills. She checks mail on her phone. Inevitably, there's a reminder from her agent about her meeting at Water and Power Capital Management in now alarmingly few hours. She drops the phone on the floor.

She looks out the window—there's a sense of glittering immanence, of menace, almost, over the salt flats—then regrets not brushing her teeth as she shrugs out of her clothes and falls into bed, glad of the silence and of the guard, out front with his gun, keeping the world at a distance.

5

·

Working

The concrete is still cooling under Kern's back when the moon starts to set. Under the faded sky the favelas' rooftops are a plain of undulating shadow, fractured by the glowing faults of the alleys and the streets. Lifting his head, he sees the Bay and across it the firelight flaring among Oakland's ruined towers. The wind brings cooking oil, sewage, the sea. Ear to the concrete, he hears music's muted subterranean pulse.

His phone chimes as a text arrives. Phone framed on pale night, the message one word: *Working?* The sender is anonymized, but only Lares has the new number. Tempting just to lie there, and watch the night progress, but his restlessness is growing, so he texts back *Yes*, and an instant later gets another message with an image of the night's mark and his latest GPS.

Corded muscle on the stranger's arms, billowing thunderheads tattooed on his shoulders, a studied gangster's gravitas. Another text: *Touch him up and bring his phone to me.* He memorizes the GPS, then deletes all. Springing to his feet, he stretches through the moment's dizziness and then lopes off across the rooftops.

A vertical plane of light rises from a wide fissure in the concrete before him. He starts to sprint and as the fear rises he launches himself from the edge, floating, for a moment, and in the light rising from the street below he casts a skyward shadow, and then the balconies of the far wall are rushing toward him, then the shock of impact in his palms, knees and soles, his eyes just inches from the stratified concrete, and then once again he's pushed off into the air.

He lands running, stumbles, jogs off the last of his momentum, unscathed, euphoric, though the descent is easy, on these surfaces, if you commit yourself, which he's done now many times. (The first time, when he'd only seen it done in videos, it had taken an hour to work up to the jump). As he wasn't hurt, he won't be hurt, and for tonight he is invincible.

The pulse of the music is louder on the street. It's a carnival night, which he likes, for the shattering music and the fires and the strobe lights that make a strange country of the favela's familiar mazes, and because there will be crowds, mostly drunk, making it easy for him to fade away. Lares, who is particular about words, says it's not technically *carnival*, but more like this *floating world*, which Kern first thought referred to the levels flooded by the Bay—he's found basements where you can hear the tide race—but it turned out to be Japanese; he forgot the details but retains a sense of lantern light and sake jars, of hot water clattering into tubs, of ragged samurai walking through the cold mud singing, and as the bass vibrates in his bones he's floating over the surface of things, exultant and detached as he closes on his victim.

Dank corridors with closed doors, mulched paper squelching underfoot, reek of urine. A family place—mothers had their children piss in the throughways to keep the working girls away. An old man with a too-wide grin, dressed as though for church, calls out to him, full of unctuous concern—is he entirely well—is he hungry, perhaps? Kern shakes his head just perceptibly and the old man laughs, says he's sorry, he hadn't recognized him, would never have spoken so to a resident of such standing. Go with him and you'd get a meal, fall asleep, wake up in a brothel. It didn't seem fair, kids making it this far just to be picked off by a pimp who seemed to think that it was funny. The gang kids hated people like that, caught them and hurt them whenever they could, prone, afterwards, to sentimental monologues on sisters disappeared.

A momentary silence, shocking in its suddenness, ringing in his ears. It passes, as he moves on, but there are places like that, here and there, islands of quiet, implied by the ways that shape warps sound. They move, as people build, and he imagines the silences projected from high above, like spotlights roaming the surface of the city.

The sky is intermittent strips of indigo, and the street—dark even in the day—is lit sporadically by bioluminescent strips stuck to the walls. He dodges into the gaps in the gathering crowd, making a game of it but one with an urgency, and someone shouts "Woo!" as Kern slips by, not touching him but passing near enough to feel his heat, and he knows he should slow down, avoid notice, but needs to be in motion.

He rounds a corner into a wall of darkness and deafening sound and then a blinding flash of light. The music is from everywhere, the stereos built into the walls and the floor—there are guys who are into that, who spend weeks and their own money getting it just right. Every strobe flash brings a static image of the dancers in their ecstasy, like a sequence of luminous stills, and he retains details that would otherwise be lost—the hair of a girl in mid-jump splayed out like a corona, her eyes shut tight, her smile raw, inward, somehow like a child's, the skinny shirtless boy turning to watch her, the beads of sweat flying from his forehead. On a concrete stage there's an elfin-looking girl screaming into a microphone and she has black lipstick and black eyeliner and a torn, sweat-stained army T-shirt, and she can't weigh more than ninety pounds—she's what Kayla would call one of the banshee cases—and it's like she's been possessed by something terrible that's working out its pain through her disintegrating vocals. A pulse of darkness, like going into a tunnel, and then the next strobe shows the way.

He checks his position on his phone, scans the teeming faces when the next light comes. So many, and though it's only been minutes the mark is surely gone, but the mass of dancers opens up and there he is.

Kern pulls on the thick leather gloves he got from a gardener for someone's credit card and reminds himself to breathe. There are brown stains on the knuckles that won't scrub out. Remembering fragments of jumbled meditations, he tries to slow his heart.

The music is the soundtrack for what he's about to do and he must be near a speaker because the noise is on the verge of obliterating his consciousness, and no one is really watching and no one will really care but still he finds he doesn't want to hurt this stranger, not really, and he stands there foolishly, pulling at his gloves, but then he remembers a story he read on his laptop, one from Iceland about men who had the souls of wolves, berserkers, they called them, and they were usually soft-spoken and unassuming till they went into battle and then something shifted deep within them and their mouths foamed and they chewed the corners of their shields as the wolf rose up through them to swallow their hearts and their pity and the last vestiges of their fear. *Come,* he thinks, calling to the wolf in the music's barrage, even though he knows it's just a story, but then it comes, and he is ravening.

Hands shoved in pockets, eyes lowered, he advances on his victim. Now his heart is calm and his fear has become something poisonous and almost like affection. Annihilating echoes roll between the concrete cliffs in the periodic dark. The mark glances at him, but Kern is staring off into space, not even a person, just so much empty air.

The mark's loneliness is evident in the way he watches the girls, and how he doesn't know what to do with his hands. There's something in one of the mark's pockets and for a moment Kern worries it's a gun but it's too bulky and then he notices the paint on the mark's shirt and realizes he's a tagger, that it's a spray can in his pocket. Kern sees him decide to leave, start shouldering his way toward an alley, and knows his moment.

Music so overwhelming it's like silence as he runs through the momentary darkness, leaps on the strobe flash, and as it ends drives his elbow down through the space where the mark's skull was, but hits nothing, lands kneeling, and holds the position—though it's not necessary, is even self-consciously cinematic—until the next flash shows the mark, eyes wide, hands raised, backing away.

They run flat out and when the dark comes Kern feels he's standing still. The next flash shows the mark losing ground, and with the next he's gone but Kern intuits that he's slipped into another, narrower alley, and the next flash shows him pressed against the wall, and in his momentary glimpse of the mark's face Kern sees his decision to stand and fight.

Pain blooms in Kern's hand as the mark's orbital shatters, and then the mark is on the ground, Kern astride his chest, throwing punches unimpeded, and the mark's face is like an outraged child's, successive strobes revealing his progress from shock to misery and finally to a blankness, almost an abandonment, and then more bone collapses, which is probably enough.

Leaving the alley with the mark's phone in his pocket, he sees men rushing toward him, mouths open and teeth bared as they shout things he can't hear. He turns to meet them, flooded with rage, welcoming death, knowing that he won't lose, can't lose, will live forever, but then he recalls his discipline, and with it reason, and with the next strobe he runs at the wall, finds traction, jumps, grabs a balcony, is up, vanishes.

6

·

What Forgetting Is

rina dreams of blue rubber gloved hands, the rush of pure oxygen, and
the pain, perceived through the shock and anesthesia as a terrible cold, a
continent of ice afloat in dark water.

She wakes, and that numbness is still with her, as is the exact record of
her restless sleep: the rough silk of the hotel sheets, the weight of the duvet, her sporadic motion as the hours passed, the novae bursting and
fading behind her sleeping eyes.

She sits up, sees her clothes draped on the distressed leather of the club
chair across from the bed, the sort of chair that serves only as an im-
promptu clothes rack or a place from which to watch one's lover, sleeping,
if one has a lover, which she does not, nor has for some time, a line of
thought best abandoned.

The hotel room is podlike, expensive and forgettable. The open cur-
tains frame a view of the whitely glistening salt; beyond them, in darkness, the Bay. Her phone blinks, probably with queries about wake-up
calls, morning coffee, but she ignores it, stares out the window, noticing

once again how this part of the world, where so much has happened, looks like nothing in particular.

She only watches television in hotel rooms, needing to fill their chilly banality with any kind of human noise. The wide black rectangle of screen shows a rubicund Japanese politico insisting that Japan has the right to deploy missile platforms in space, three coyotes padding through the empty streets of Santa Fe, a hotel burning in the atolls that are all that's left of that peninsula that used to be a state, and a South Korean official attributing the disappearance of one of their newest drone submarines to a software error—the ship is considered lost at sea. The missing ship appears on screen—it's black, seamless, somehow cetacean-looking.

The salt flats look like plains of snow and she thinks of her childhood, obliterated decades ago on an icy Virginia road. She remembers the car's terrible rotational velocity, her mother's hand on her father's shoulder; then lying on her back in a room without windows, listening to her respirator's hiss and sigh. There was nothing to see but the white ceiling and, sometimes, the nurses leaning over her. She found she remembered everything—how the light changed on the ceiling, every little sound from the corridor, how the nurses looked every time she'd seen them; she could tell how long they'd been on shift from the darkness around their eyes. When the blue-eyed nurse took the tube out of Irina's mouth she started talking: "And she's powered up. Are you sure? Is the implant working? How's her EEG? It's all good—we're recording. Is she awake? Not yet. Can she hear what we're saying?" The nurse's blue eyes widening.

The possibility of sleep is gone. She kicks back the duvet, on the theory that the cold will make bed and sleep more appealing, and goes to stand by the window, cradling her forehead in her hand. A ship's light out on the Bay. What good this ship, she thinks, this salt, this restive night, and is on the verge of wiping them away from her other memory, but she hesitates, then saves the indigo of the Bay, the chill, her melancholy.

7

.

Discipline

K ern's laptop bleats, and in the moment of waking he is up, though
his body aches, as it always aches, for to hesitate is to risk losing the
day. Dizzy with sleep, he is stretching his shoulders when, at the
laptop's signal, the espresso machine—spoil of an unlocked condo—winks
on, huffs loudly and begins to steam.

The low room is dark but for the faint glows from the light well and
from his laptop's screen, just enough to illuminate the espresso frothing
into his one chipped cup. The room is cold, this early, except near the
space heater, salvage from the landfills, wired to a fuel cell with a shiny
spot where the serial number once was, the severed stubs of steel bolts
gleaming rawly.

He sips coffee, tells himself it makes him feel more awake. The phone
he took from the mark is on the floor by the laptop. He dreamed he heard
a voice from it, perhaps a woman's, but it's not possible—there's no signal
this deep under the surface. Later, when the sun is down, he'll run it over
to Lares, get paid.

Before he's ready, his laptop chimes, and it's time to work the heavy bag. The bag hangs from the ceiling on a rusted chain, swaddled in silver duct tape, mottled with dark stains, a mass of shadow. He circles it, poised on the balls of his feet, hands by his temples, his weariness subsumed in the familiarity of the stance. The laptop chimes again and he shuffles his left foot to the side and pivots on its ball as he turns his hip and throws his right leg at the bag, his technique unfolding effortlessly. A moment of sweet stasis, awareness of the bag's mass, the room's emptiness, his own exhaustion, and then when the kick lands the bag spasms, and there's a sharp pain in his shin, but less than there was a year ago, and the books say that in another year the pain will be gone. He's just recovered his stance when once again the laptop chimes and once again he kicks.

The room was on the surface when he found it, years ago, abandoned in an epidemic's wake. He hadn't been strong, then, as he's strong now, and was able to hold onto it only because so many had died. He'd been shivering with fever in his huddle of blankets when a paramedic in scarred blue armor eased his head in through the door, wary kindness in the blue eyes above the dust mask, a muddy jail tattoo on his neck. He'd said something in English, which Kern had barely understood, then, and left in moments, leaving two bottles of water, vitamins, and an octagonal green pill he'd swallowed less in hope than resignation. Now the room is buried under new construction, some fifty feet below the surface, and the light well, once his preferred route of access, has become occluded, tortuous, and too narrow for his shoulders; to reach the outside, now, he has to navigate a warren of tunnels and lightless stairwells in the dark. It's better that way, he finds, a safe feeling, and the other residents must agree, because no one has put up even the cheapest bioluminescent strips.

Through the light well he hears a woman gently scolding her children, who will be late, she says, for school. Farther away, another woman sings a song he almost knows, and for a moment he thinks of home. As he strikes the bag again a breath of wind brings frying dough, cooking oil, coffee, the day.

Yet another chime. He remembers Kayla singing to him. Is she still up, he wonders, and does she have a new lover, and does she ever think of him? He wrenches his thoughts back, chastising himself for wasting even a moment, and for having failed already, so early in the day. He kicks the bag hard enough to crush a rib cage—his shin feels shattered, but the bag caroms into the wall.

Five hundred and ninety-six kicks later, his vision greying, his breath ragged, the laptop chimes twice. He staggers away from the bag, but neither sits nor puts his hands on his knees. He doesn't feel like vomiting, this time, which is progress. When he can breathe through his nose again he scrapes himself dry with a towel already stiff with dried sweat.

Eyes closed, he runs through the move in his mind, correcting the subtleties of balance, the nuances of technique. Soon the laptop will chime again, and again he will attack the bag with a narrow technical ferocity, coming another step closer to total purity of spirit and keeping out the void that's all around him.

8

·

Unreal City

Thales' chair is on the edge of the terrace, inches from the empty air. Far below him, waves bellow and dissolve into foam, sometimes so loud that they keep him from sleeping. He wonders where his mother is—there's no railing, and it would be easy to take a step forward and go tumbling into space. The coastline is concave here and across the water the surf shimmers before the grey masses of the beachward favelas, where the poor dwell, where he has never been, a ghost Los Angeles shimmering in a heat haze below the real city.

The breeze catches the awning above him, its shadow undulating over the Cartesian grid of the black basalt tiles, and he thinks of the equations describing its rippling curve, the elegant entanglement of position and motion. With an effort, he pushes mathematics from his mind, as the surgeon says he must, if he's to improve, and focuses on the world: the weave and texture of his white linen trousers, the Corbusier table beside him, the water beading on the heavy crystal tumbler, its wedge of lemon entombed in ice.

He closes his eyes, and the details of the water glass have already vanished. This is how it was before the implant, he supposes, though in fact the memories of that time are scarce—he looks down at the water, sees the orange surf buoys bobbing in the swell, remembers how, the last time he saw them, he'd thought of their house deep in the Amazonian jungle, the river flowing past it in full flood; swimming in the "safe zone" denoted by buoys, the prehistoric menace of the crocodiles sliding down the muddy bank into the tea-colored water.

They're in the rooftop suite of the St. Mark Hotel, which his mother had said was the best that was practical but even so leaves him feeling exposed, with the constant hum of drone traffic overhead, and the lines of sight from the terrace to the rooftops of distant buildings, like an invitation to a sniper's bullet; he misses the sense of hermetic insulation of the family compound in Leblon and the hotels they'd stayed in when they still had money. Since his father's death and their flight to LA he's overheard his mother on the phone trying to arrange high-interest loans secured on frozen assets in Rio, on the house she built in the mountains around Los Angeles, and even to get new architectural commissions, though she hasn't practiced in many years, but he's made a point of pretending not to notice.

His brothers, Helio and Marco Aurelio, will come and find him soon, and greet him with back-slapping false bonhomie. (He suspects they're glad to be out of Rio, regard LA as an adventure—Marco Aurelio had been expelled from his college for choking someone half to death at a party, and Helio had been brought up on rape charges, though they'd soon been quashed—a columnist who'd said the family was Brazil's answer to the Julio-Claudian dynasty had never worked again.) They'll see the book beside his water glass—*Ramanujan's Analytical Theory of Numbers*—and look disconsolate but say nothing as they take him away from the hotel and out into the city, and the day will be the same as every other. He'll pass the morning in the humid jiu-jitsu studio of the Malibu Athletic Club, watching them roll on the blue mats in white gis. In the afternoon he'll wait in the dunes wishing he had his book with him as his brothers ply the waves on their longboards, and when the sun sets their friends will gather, the cauliflower-eared jiu-jitsu players and their slim-waisted girls, and all watch the fading light through a serene cannabis haze. His brothers pity him, but take pains to hide it; he accepts their charity without resentment, for to him they are no more than vacant, handsome animals, moved solely by instinct, blind to all the beauty of mathematics and the world.

A wave closes with the shore, and as it approaches the narrow beach below the cliff its vitreous curvature furls and collapses, and the equations of hydrodynamics rise in his mind, but the white foam is unanalyzable; the world around him shivers, then, and fractures into a meaningless chaos of atoms and light. Where the water glass was there's an illegible confusion of reflections; he sees the warped light of migraine, and closes his eyes.

Luminous patterns burn inside his eyelids. He opens his eyes onto a blur of pinions, white motion, refracted light. The headache intensifies, and he starts to panic, but he's going to the clinic in the evening, and the surgeon, a competent man, will help him; he draws a deep breath, focuses, and the blur resolves into a gull hovering over the table, its churning wings glowing in the sunlight, red eyes on the untouched omelette on the rough porcelain plate.

9

·

Matches

The match flares and fades, and then the next, and the next. The face of the man flicking matches into life and tossing them into the darkness is that of her first surgeon, and Irina is calm, lost in the slow sequence of conflagrations, and she thinks she'll be content to watch forever but then the surgeon says, "These are the seconds, you know, burning away," and lights another. In the dream she laughs and says, "Nothing is lost, or ever will be," and summons forth all the recent images of the matches burning and fading out, delighting in her power, but the surgeon shakes his head and points at her stomach and looking down at a point just above her navel (she is naked, now) she sees a black spot so tiny it ought to be imperceptible, and as she tries, futilely, to scrape it away with her fingernails she can feel the tainted cells' surging reproduction as they boil outward into clean tissue. The black spot widens before her eyes—it hesitates, as her immune system rallies, then surges again. As it reaches bone, she feels cold.

She sits up in the hotel bed and turns off her phone's alarm; the sound of waves hissing over sand stops abruptly, leaving only room tone—voices reflected down corridors, the hum of the air-conditioning, distant traffic. In her bag are pills that offer sleep, or worse than sleep, but she's already late, and the client pays well, and more years of life come dear, so, moving herself like a marionette, she gets out of bed.

Brushing her teeth, the little lines around her eyes are a legible fraction of a millimeter deeper, the visible consequence of another bad night, and what other, less obvious damage has her restlessness caused, damage not reparable by any decent plastic surgeon. "So get to work," she tells her reflection.

In the early light the hotel lobby seems oddly tragic, suggesting a valiant determination not to waste the morning. Other souls rush by, coffees in hand, immersed in their phones or having energetic conversations with the air. Most are younger than she is, bustling young things from the vast reaches of the middle middle technocracy; a pretty, somehow Midwestern-looking girl with roses in her cheeks, clad in the Armani of seasons past, is all but hyperventilating as she berates a cloud of invisible subordinates who have apparently failed to establish a link between networks in Reykjavík and Poznan. Irina tries to imagine feeling so much emotion over infrastructure, thinks that, medical bills or no, she may have to be less frugal about hotels.

In the cab, the fog glows with diffuse morning light, a migraine light, and she puts on her sunglasses, closes her eyes. Her face, reflected in the chrome of the cab's dash, looks closed, remote, arrogant, a mask formed over an interior darkness. She tries a smile, convinces no one. They'll see her essential strangeness, but let them; her mind turns to the cathedral vastnesses of the AIs' memories.

She dozes, soothed by the rush of tires, opening her eyes as the cab ascends an overpass and there, slipping by, are the favelas, like concrete termite nests on a monumental scale, if termites were inclined to cubism and many balconies. Occasional windows reflect the morning sun; squinting, she imagines she's looking at geology, the product of a chthonic upheaval in the faults beneath the city, but, no, the favelas are actually like a Lebbeus Woods drawing she saw in an architecture textbook for half a second twenty years ago, and these things are, of course, what she always thinks when she sees favelas. Her other memory stirs—she has thought these thoughts two hundred and nineteen times, now two hundred and twenty.

Like sculpture, the favelas, but she reminds herself that, avant-garde rapture notwithstanding, they're sinks for all the saddest ugliness in the world, that to set foot in them is to step back decades, or even centuries; they're the last bastion of the old, bad kind of HIV, and have little law but the gangs in their various and occasionally lurid plumages—even the cops won't go in except in armor. She's read about refugees starving slowly, unlicensed dentists with third-hand tools, child brothels moving from room to buried room.

Childish, she reminds herself, still to expect to find wonder in cities, especially when it's elsewhere, and just under the surface of things. She remembers the Metatemetatem, an AI that makes other AIs, owned by a Vancouver research lab from her last gig but one. Metatemetatem is a name given to a class of AIs that burn through trillions of possibilities a second in search of the shape of their successors; every Metatemetatem had been designed by its predecessor for some thousand generations and ninety years. There must have been some definite moment when they'd passed beyond the understanding of even the subtlest mathematician, though when this happened is a matter of debate—all that's certain is that no one noticed at the time. Now most of the world's software, and, lately, its industrial design, comes from machines that are essentially ineffable, though only a handful of specialists seem to realize this, or care, the world in general blithely unaware that the programs and devices that mediate their lives have emerged from mystery.

She drifts off but comes back enough to open her eyes to slits as the cab rushes through a canyon between buildings, and she could be anywhere, or nowhere at all. There's no one else around, but every few seconds the cab passes through the shadow of the SFPD drones hovering at intervals over the street, which is a kind of company.

She wakes again when the car stops and the door clicks open; she steps out onto a vast too-bright field of concrete before what must have been a naval air hangar once, the Bay glittering beyond it. The hangar's hull has weathered beautifully, the gradients of lichen on the ancient aluminum cladding streaked with ocher and rust. What is now much too much parking lot, bounded by distant chain-link fence and concertina wire, must have started as an airfield, or perhaps a spaceport, but she doesn't think they had those, really, when the hangar was built. Cracked white lines on the tarmac denote parking stalls, swallowed by the scale of the place, magic diagrams to ward off air and emptiness. The few dozen parked cars seem forlorn, huddled around the hangar against the morning. Gulls circle; the wind brings her the Bay, the tang of iron, the smoke of the fires in the cities to the east. She shivers, checks her phone; this is the place. She turns to watch as the cab pulls away.

In the hangar's shadow, she feels calmer. She picks her way among the cars, which look mostly new, and mostly expensive, except for a handful of white fleet vans. A few workmen in paper overalls stand by low double doors set in the monumental wall, face masks around their necks, their eyes powdered with white dust; seeing the cigarettes burning between their fingers, she stops dead, intensely aware of the hours burning off of their lives; she'd once seen a video of a lung cell, in vitro, exposed to nicotine smoke—she remembers the cascading mutations, the computer model of unraveling DNA. The one nearest the door, an older man with an air of bemused dignity, smiles at her with yellow teeth and grinds out his cigarette on his calloused palm; in the face of his kindness, she is abashed to be read so easily, and to think that the lost time won't matter for them anyway. He says something in Russian, and the others laugh and saunter away from the doors, indulging her. She'd once read a Russian dictionary, and the definitions of his words rise up in her mind, so many ragged chunks of disconnected meaning, but she pushes them away, as reminders of the distance between language and the world.

The doors open as she approaches, bringing her the high whine of power tools, an exhalation of cold air. Within, the space is vast, underlit and vertiginous; looking up into the shadows, she expects to see the gently bobbing ghosts of dirigibles past. Some workmen are grinding up regions of floor with industrial sanders, throwing up clouds of sparks and dust, others, with tablets, observing. The actual offices appear to be built onto the sides of the hangar's interior; the effect is of mass-produced pueblos clinging to the walls of an Industrial Age canyon. A pause in the sanding; she hears the muted hubbub of voices, footsteps, their echoes, all illegible, and somehow comforting; the concrete under her feet, cracked and indelibly oil-stained, is covered with a thick, hepatic varnish.

No one challenges her, or even seems to notice her presence. Before her is a rising sweep of concrete that will be a reception desk, probably, when all's done, but is, for now, abandoned; behind it is a huge, hollow globe, the diameter of a bus—the continents are iron, the seas absences and the major rivers are traced in blue enamel; the mirrored rectangles must be the great dams. She wonders if there are firms specializing in the sculpture of hubris, and do they ever build heroically scaled, improbably muscular statues of their older, more literal-minded clientele? It was the sort of thing they'd have had in Dubai, when it was a city-state, back before it was a ruin beloved of documentarians with its toppled spires, cavernous drowned malls, iridescent fishes schooling in the atriums of what had been hotels, would soon be reefs.

"Those are good boots," says someone, a man with a tablet, older, but his face has the polished, windswept look of the better plastic surgery. She looks down at her boots—an entire commission blown on them, the best thing out of Milan some five seasons past; they have the matte gloss of old black clay, and, however sleek, have a hint of blockiness, the barest suggestion of engineer's boots, which saves them from being at least a decade too young for her. "Let me guess," he says. "You're here with the travertine. Am I right?"

"No," she says, wonderingly. "No travertine . . . marble?"

"But you looked like you must be the travertine," he says. "The serpentine then?"

"I have no stone at all," she says, showing her palms. His expression doesn't change; superficially his outfit is corporate-neutral but the materials and the details are very good—he's probably some kind of creative. "I'm here to visit with the house AIs. What's the travertine for?"

"Flooring! At least, a judiciously calculated part of the flooring. It's the most remarkable thing. Himself has commissioned us, us being Applied Structures Incorporated, to retrofit this hangar into viable office space that will last for the next one thousand years. Literally, the next one thousand— it's in the contract in triplicate, in italic bold. I've spent the last two months measuring the rates of erosion of flooring materials, and having my little team of quants model traffic. It has to look the same in a millennium as it does now, he says, though he *has* conceded that it *may* take a patina."

"All this toward what possible end?"

"Far be it from me to examine the motives of such a consistent patron of the applied arts. After all, the very rich aren't like you and me."

"No, they have a great deal more money," she murmurs.

"Exactly! Anyway, this is nothing—we're also building him a house to last *one million* years. We hired seismologists to find a stable site, someplace that won't be subducted the next time Pangaea rolls around. We're building on the top of the Rocky Mountains, which is almost not isolated. It's an absurd project, but it has a certain grandeur—we hired evolutionary biologists, for heaven's sake, to get ahead of the adaptations the bacteria will make to the cooling system. I can only imagine he's obsessed with his legacy." His eyes go to the tablet in his hands. "Materials crisis. You must excuse me. Good luck!" He smiles at her, is off into the hangar's distances.

She stands there, emptied of all volition, watching the workmen grind the floor down as the seconds pass. A chime from her phone as a text arrives, joining the confusion of the echoes in the space, but she ignores it, and the next one, and the next. When she looks, finally, she sees it was Maya, her agent. *You're on-site?* she's written, and *Hello?*, and finally, *They're waiting for you upstairs, dear. Go Now. Do Well. Call Me Later and Tell Me How It Went.* XXOXOX, and then she is walking toward an elevator bank, grateful that Maya is there, unseen and far away, to push her through the world.

As the elevator rises she turns on her implant's wireless, is instantly aware of the presence of the Net, its vastness and sterility. There was a time when she did the background for a job before she was in the elevator, watching the ground floor recede. (*But you can get away with it,* she thinks. *You can get away with almost anything.*)

She sighs, then reaches out, lets the company's data come flooding in, filling the shallows of her other memory with websites and SEC filings and all the articles in the trade press and the blog posts and the records of old offices and learned articles on dead platforms and generations of annual reports and every mention in every public document. Fragments of text flicker through her awareness—". . . closing its Manhattan offices in favor of Northern California . . ." and ". . . predicting energy consumption in major metropolitan markets . . ." and "Water and Power Capital Management LLC, an innovator in AI-driven resource arbitrage and medical engineering . . ." and ". . . James Cromwell, serial entrepreneur, founder and majority shareholder"—and in all of this there's a sadness for there can be no doubt that Water and Power, the focus of the lives of its thousands of employees, is essentially the same as all the other trading houses owned by all the other stridently aggressive suits, and in fact she could just walk out, and be damned to no money and the marred reputation and the dwindling options and presently the doctor's face a mask of seriousness as, with practiced gentleness, he tells her that it's time to make her preparations and before he can finish she'll turn away and stagger out of his office, full of the terror of the nearness of the end. She thinks of the chill outside, the blue of morning. The lift stops. The doors slide open.

"Irina?" says a slight, almost plain woman, smiling, somehow birdlike, head cocked to one side. "I'm Magda. I'm so glad you could come." Her ensemble is, Irina thinks, an Asano, and, as such, gorgeous, her blouse like fires flaring on a black patch of night, but she seems uncertain in her finery, and Irina wonders if she's some sort of partner, perhaps newly minted, to be able to afford a designer she associates with maturing starlets, less formal cabinet ministers and, regrettably, minor royals, and she is expecting offers of coffee and the usual chatter to which she need not attend but Magda says, "Come with me—he wants to meet you."

She duly follows, smiling woodenly, though she hates it when they want to meet her, as the questions are always the same, and, unless they're very well bred, they'll *peer* at her, fascinated by her difference. She thinks of her minute fraction of celebrity, centered on a handful of university departments, mostly brain science and AI, places she makes a point of avoiding.

Corridor upon corridor, none finished but all the same, loops of cable hanging from the ceiling like jungle vines, and she wonders what it would be like to be able to be lost. They come to a wide interior courtyard of bare concrete, stark in the muted light glowing through the tinted glass ceiling. Like winter, in that grey light. On each of the four walls is a sheet of canvas, ten feet across, restive in the air-conditioning; the canvas before her ripples, seethes, reveals a few inches of something spray-painted, complex, maybe some kind of writing? She wants to run her hands over the smoothness of the polished concrete, then take the rough canvas in her hands and yank it hard so it comes down in a billowing cloud to reveal . . . what? "It feels like a gallery," she says, her voice reflecting off the walls.

"It will be," says Magda. "When we're done. It marks the transition to the inner offices."

"What's behind the canvas?" Irina asks.

"Nothing we're ready to show yet," says Magda with stagy regret and a false smile and Irina is surprised to find herself feeling like an unwelcome guest in another woman's home. "He's waiting," Magda says, turning to lead her away.

They come to a massive steel door whose overengineered solidity speaks of bank vaults and a kind of vanity, but no, Irina reflects, that's the mentality of a past time. She thinks of the LAPD (now reborn as the Provisional Authority), frantic and militarized, how you need the right ID, now, to get up onto Mulholland, how the drones scour the wastes through the night, like lethal constellations floating over the hills, visible from the flatlands, both reminder and warning. Metal groans at middle C as the door's lock releases.

Darker than expected, within, a narrow room walled with bookshelves. There are fossils on the shelves, ammonites and trilobites and a carnosaur's fanged grin, and butterflies pinned in display cases. At first it all reads as a set designer's take on a Victorian naturalist's study, but then she sees the books' spines are broken, mostly, that they run to novels, number theory, card magic, recent history. The only light is from the far wall's high windows, the dusty glass panes framing nothing. Cromwell sits at his desk, backlit and obscured; as he closes his laptop, there's a momentary glow on the lenses of his glasses. The suits who've been waiting on him— attorneys, most likely—turn to regard her with glazed hauteur, unable to place her in any hierarchy, but she takes no offense, for, however well-paid, they're essentially servants, and in any case her eyes are drawn toward Cromwell's desk by a flare of dream-blue like the wing of a *morpho*.

The iridescence is from a jagged shard of metal as long as her hand, its surface comprised of tissue-thin membranes whose tiny convolutions remind her of disinterred cities, and these in turn comprised of other cities still; the purity of the blue is remarkable, a blue to disappear in, and as its forms fill her other memory the fugue stirs, which she won't permit, not in company, so she looks away as she sets down the shard, which she has, she finds, picked up. The attorneys must have excused themselves. Behind his desk, Cromwell smiles up at her.

He's younger than she'd supposed, but no, that's just the quality of the work. He presents as a man whose age is just starting to show, his temples greying, the crow's feet around his eyes concessions to the expected presentation of an alpha male. No tie with a dark suit whose very simplicity suggests considerable expense, like a kimono reinterpreted through bespoke Italian tailoring, and she sees how intently he's watching her, and has the sense that she interests him, which is rare, for his kind, and she wonders if she was right to preemptively dismiss him. "It's a computer," he says, nodding toward the shard. "We think. Unfortunately, it doesn't work. It seems to be an improperly assembled prototype. Certainly designed by AI. Beautiful, no?"

"Beautiful," she says, the word hanging there as she tries to put the blue from her mind, clear her other memory. She's seen AI-designed computer hardware, but nothing like this. "Why this blue?" she asks, still shaken, feeling a little like she's asked a question about the reason for the sky.

"The physicists haven't been able to figure it out, though they seem to find the problem a compelling one," he says. "In fact, I was hoping you could tell me something about it. Bright as they are, my researchers, they're not . . ." He makes a gesture perhaps meant to indicate that she's something else entirely but he's too discreet to mention it.

She looks back at the shard, like a window on another world and a lovelier one, then quickly looks away. "It'd be hard to say with a microscope, much less with the naked eye. The AIs' designs tend to be impenetrable. Sometimes I think they're just addicted to complexity."

"I've often said as much," says Cromwell, eyes shining, and he has a friendliness, even a latent giddiness, that she doesn't expect in Big Money. "It sometimes seems to me that trying to talk to the AIs is like trying to read the future in the clouds, or flocks of birds. Do you think we'll ever really be able to communicate?"

It's the right question—usually CEOs ask her when AIs will be able to predict the stock market, or when they can get a robot nanny (or, god help them, mistress). The bright young university men seem always to be claiming that true communication is just ten years away, but it's been ten years away since before she was born. Cromwell's interest seems genuine, even acute, so she says, "No, because there's no common ground, and there never will be. We're primates, evolved to live on Earth and pass on our genes, and this has given our thoughts a certain shape, but the AIs have nothing to do with these things, and their thoughts are shaped differently. Terrestrial matters are as counterintuitive to them as tensor algebra is to us. For them, the physical world has a kind of ghostliness, if they're aware of it at all. Some of them don't even know about time." It's the set piece she'd give to strangers at parties, years ago, before she stopped talking about her work, but who knows, it might strike Cromwell as profound.

"But surely there's some way to bridge the gap. Maybe if they had enough information about the world."

"They've tried that," she says, trying to conceal her boredom, and not to remember how many times she's had this conversation. "In fact, someone rediscovers that idea about once a decade, and has for more than a century, but no matter how many encyclopedias or decades' worth of newspapers you put in front of the AIs, they still see nothing but confusion."

It's a commonplace, known to every grad student, but Cromwell seems rapt and says, "But it *is* possible, to connect with them, at least to a degree. I mean, that's what you do. From what I've read, it's practically who you are."

Exhaustion washes over her, and as her will to speak fades the room starts to seem remote and unimportant, and Cromwell must have felt a door close because he says, "Forgive me. I'm too personal. A bad habit— one of the disfigurements of influence—it makes one unfit for decent company. I'll let you get to work, but first is there anything I can tell you about the job?"

In fact, she hasn't read her contract, or the email that Maya forwarded with the project précis, and if she checks email now there will inevitably be a new message from Maya reminding her of where she's supposed to be and what she's supposed to do there, carefully worded to suggest a subtle compassion and entirely conceal any impatience or disgust, and though she won't want to read it and be exposed to these unwelcome emotions she knows she'll do so anyway so she says, "Why don't you tell me about it, from the beginning? It's always better to hear it in the principal's own words."

Cromwell appears to accept this—in fact, the gambit has yet to fail— and says, "I have a pool of in-house AIs, all custom-made. There's one that does resource arbitrage. It's one of my biggest earners, but lately it's been noticeably off. I don't want to prejudice your judgment, so I won't tell you much more, but I'd like to know what you make of it." He seems momentarily uncomfortable, apparently in the belief that she's capable of caring about his company's secrets and failings.

"So it's not working as intended?"

"Not exactly."

"Could it be a virus?"

Slight hesitation. "No. I think not."

"If it's some kind of exotic virus, you need to hire someone else. That's not what I do, and I don't want to waste your time or money," she says, wearier than ever.

"I know! I assure you, I'm aware of the parameters of your expertise," he said, smiling. "This is of some importance to me, and my talented young men are getting nowhere, though I didn't really expect them to." In a lower, more inward voice, he says, "It's hard to find the right people. Only the brightest, the nearly autistic ones are any use, and they mostly want to collect stamps and solve Hilbert's problems," and she thinks of the rare, talented, incomplete boys who sometimes come close to doing what she does, how, in the technical world's uppermost reaches, autistic symptoms have a certain cachet, ambitious young men affecting the inability to look one in the eye and a total innocence of the world.

Fathomless blue in the corner of her eye, pulling at her, and then an irresistible flash of intuition. "Is your problem AI running on hardware like that?" she blurts, pointing at the shard, and a beat of silence tells her she's been impolitic.

Cromwell is about to speak but Magda turns to him and says, "Don't you have a ten o'clock?" with such a studied professionalism that Irina turns in time to catch their shared look, and she realizes that they're lovers, and probably new ones, and don't wish to have it known, and she watches him as he assents, and it's the combination of his intensity and his sincerity and the fact that he's chosen this nervous, unfriendly woman in lieu of whatever model or actress or pediatrician she'd expect to find in a rich man's bed that makes her interested enough to turn on her wireless again and run a search on him.

She finds the public records of his purchases of server farms, decaying factories, abandoned cities in Costa Rica. It's been decades since he's spoken to a journalist but fifty years ago, during the second AI bubble, he founded a sequence of start-ups, all long since acquired or dissolved, and his interviews from that era boil past, his remarks comprised of the usual founder's boilerplate about striding boldly into bright futures, all of them forgettable, almost conspicuously vacant, though she senses an undercurrent of irony that suggests an awareness of playing with a form. Not long after the last start-up exited he'd bought a majority stake in ReTelomer Inc., an early player in genetic life extension, which later did very well; a forty-year-old editorial in *Harper's* inveighed against ReTelomer for making long life available only to the rich, and she takes a moment to pity the writer as she would a child first encountering the hardness of the world. A website dedicated to the meticulous and fawning investigation of the higher *beau monde* asserts that Cromwell is much richer than is generally supposed, that most of his gains have been hidden from public view over the last generation, that he's approaching the point of being a state unto himself, less like Leland Stanford now than some rapacious Borgia prince. Recent photos show him beside senators at fund-raisers and an older photo, in which he looks exactly the same, shows him drinking in a dive bar with a then-young actress who was famous about the time Irina was born; the oldest photo of all shows him in late adolescence peering at a computer screen beside an older, bearded man whom she realizes was a founder of one of the first googles, which puts Cromwell's age at at least a hundred and fifty, an incredible figure, old even by the standards of the stratospherically rich—he must be one of the oldest people living, though he is, she believes, approaching the limit of what life extension can do. She wonders how all the years have shaped him, what desires survive.

On the periphery of the mass of data she notices that in his days collecting art he briefly owned *The Physical Impossibility of Death in the Mind of Someone Living,* which she saw once, years ago, in the Louvre, back when she'd meant to see and so hold forever everything beautiful in the world. She remembers her jet lag and sense of dislocation as she wandered into yet another room in the sprawling postcontemporary wing, the shock of the sight of the shark floating in the green fluid glowing in the glass-walled tank in the otherwise empty gallery, the shark's jaws gaping, like its relentless forward motion had just then been arrested, and, as the words of the title had shimmered in her mind, tank and shark and text fused to become an image of a blind rage for more life, and the wrinkles incised in the shark's face seemed to imply great age and an absolute and unthinking cruelty. Strange to have run her fingers down the cool glass of an artwork that had passed through his hands, though she supposes that's what happens, with time, with those rich enough to be, in some way, central to things, and, of course, to survive.

And now a second has passed, and a new one is starting, and Magda is turning toward her, and before they can notice her abstraction she stands and says, "Let's go wherever's next."

10

·

Laptop

Kern's laptop chimes twice and he stops mid-punch, the bag swinging crazily till he stills it with his palm, then sits cross-legged with the laptop in front of him.

He's found that it's best to read one book at a time. This month it's Penjak Tharanawat's *Radical Thai Boxing*, in an English translation now ninety years old. He's on the chapter about elbow strikes, how to use them to inflict hematoma and concussion, or to cut the skin over the occipital ridge so that blood will blind his enemy.

As the laptop wakes he remembers the years when its game was the focus of his life, and once again regrets that he came to the game's end. Even now he sometimes hopes that there's another game, held in reserve, so far, but about to be revealed, but if there is, there's no sign of it today, just the usual hierarchy of the folders of the laptop's library, which is infinite, or might as well be, containing, as far as he can tell, just about all the media that had been published as of sixty years ago.

There's a samurai manual that has the maxim *While you sleep, your enemy trains*, and for a moment he's afraid he's being lazy and should go back to the bag, though his hands and shins are an agony, but no, it won't do, hard training is one thing but overtraining is another; the laptop has documentaries about professional fighters reaching back centuries and he's seen what can happen when they spend every waking hour in the gym, how their bodies stop working and in the ring they're slow and stumbling and they end up sitting on the curb after their fights wondering how they could have lost when their commitment was total.

Before returning to Tharanawat, he indulges himself by bringing up a video clip, apparently made by a tourist a century ago, of a waterfall in the forest on a mountain in Japan in whose icy flow Miyamoto Musashi had once meditated. Musashi was a ronin, without teacher or attachments, and flawless, fighting sixty duels without losing once as he wandered penniless through the wilds of ancient Japan. An ascetic, Musashi, beyond fear or desire, indifferent to women, money, even survival. As the clip plays, Kern tries to clear his mind, imagine the force of the waterfall's torrent.

He'd found his laptop in a landfill some six years ago, not long after coming North, in a deposit of fragmented wine bottles, its black plastic chassis held together with frayed translucent tape. He'd slid it under his shirt, before any of the other pickers noticed, and slunk back to his room to cherish it.

The letters were worn off the keys but the screen was intact, and a hand crank unfolded from the laptop's side at the touch of a button, which was fortunate, as it was difficult, in the favelas, to steal electricity.

The old owner's files were still on the disk. The emails were indented rows of symbols without meaning but there were also photographs, thousands of them, flash-frozen moments from decades of a life. The photos were dated, and Kern, able to read numbers a little, figured the owner, who'd been adult, white and apparently rich, must have died at least thirty years before he, Kern, was born. It was eerie, somehow, thinking of all these images sitting there on the disk as the years slipped past.

There were loving shots of a bright red antique sports car and a big house standing alone in a desert. There were snapshots of street corners and signage, probably in San Francisco, that he could almost place. There were groups of beautiful people smiling in the refracted bottle-light of bars and he wondered if their gaiety was affected, a reflexive reaction to the camera's stare, or if there really was some stratum of existence where everyone was always this happy. Some of the photos showed women alone, abandoned to sleep under rumpled sheets, drinking coffee, standing at the rail of a boat. Sometimes they were naked, sometimes inviting, but it was never the same one for long, except for one, a blonde, who went away for years at a time but always came back, while the others went away for good, and he wondered what she'd been to him. One photo, the only one that had its own folder, showed the blond woman's naked back as she waded into a dark river, just starting to look back, the densely tangled trees on the far bank reflected in the black water around her waist.

After an hour the laptop locked him out. He hit keys at random, hoping to get the password by luck, but on his tenth try the screen went dark. The injustice was galling—the laptop was fair salvage, its owner long dead, and he'd never find another. He wondered if it could call the police to report itself stolen, if they'd make an exception, for it, and come to the favelas. There were garbage pits nearby, or he could sell it, if he moved fast, but the laptop's screen flashed, faded, slowly brightened—a gesture he'd come to recognize—and then it launched the game.

He played a small child walking through a dark forest. The eyes of animals gleamed in the shadows and when he approached them they would speak, but never in a language he understood. He found a glowing deer who spoke English, which he barely knew, then, and he couldn't tell what it was saying. Finally he found an eagle sitting on a tree branch who greeted him cordially, said that it had prepared another world for him, and a better one, and to enter it he had only to walk around the tree three times clockwise and then climb up into the branches. (For a long time afterward he questioned the surface of things, hoping to find secrets by touching worn spots on high walls, turning silently in place when no one was looking.)

Clambering up, he found doors set in the trunk. There were other branches, higher up, but just out of reach—the eagle told him there were more doors there, but those were for later, and for now he had to do what was before him. Behind the first one he found a huge cave where brightly colored crystals cascaded in pulses down the slick wet walls from the darkness of the heights. *We are here to learn the secrets of number*, said the eagle's disembodied voice. He learned by trial and error which keys meant which numbers, pressing them to match the number of crystals rolling down—bells rang, high and clear, when he got it right. He knew from the chimes high above when the crystals were released, and was waiting, poised, when they came clattering down, subsuming himself in the pattern and rhythm. The light well off of his room was brightening by the time the eagle told him that it was time to go, that he'd learned all he could there, but he was happy, in the cave, and the eagle said nothing as he played on until his eyes finally shut.

He woke to afternoon light with the laptop in his arms. He wasn't hungry, and in any case it was safer to scavenge after dark. He found the child lying on a tree branch, kicking his legs, the eagle hunching his wings beside him. The next door had writing on it and wouldn't open so he passed it by, the eagle watching wordlessly. The door after that opened onto a sharp jag of rock protruding out into a void of storms. Vast shapes coalesced in the cloud mass—letters, he thought, and when he pressed the right key the child on the precipice had to grip the rock against the surge of wind as someone spoke the letter's name in a voice of thunder and the cloud shape flared into fire that turned to smoke and drifted away.

The next door opened on tree roots like long hills, rivers winding through the valleys between them. Craning his neck, he saw the trunk rising up forever, its higher branches fading in the blue of distance. There was a road carved in the bark, and ladders when the way turned steep, though by then it was evening's last light and he could barely see the way. There was a wooden bridge over a canyon between immense roots and on the floodplain far below he saw the lights of distant houses.

He came to a cirque with a stone well from which there came a blurred muted song. A bent old woman emerged from the shadows, her face concealed in a black cloak, and as she approached the well the world darkened until they were alone in a circle of dim, sourceless light, the great tree gone, the night inky. *This is the naming,* said the crone, throwing stone tiles onto the well-mouth. Light rose from the well—peering in, he saw brightness occluded by rapid dark cloud. The tiles had shapes on them, letters, and made sounds when he touched them. He moved them, tentatively, considering— when he got the arrangement right the old woman said *Sun!* as a brilliant star shot out of the well, hung in the air, filled the sky with light.

He and the old woman called forth the world. Moon, clouds, stars, planets roared out of the well and took their places in the sky. Next they called up mountains, seas and forests, and animals to live in them.

The next door opened onto winter. Snow encased the trees, and smothered the hills, and the rivers were quartz. The silence was stifling. The stones of the path just protruded through the white. Nothing moved; he saw a deer, shining with frost, motionless. The wind, stilled, was a white scrawl in the sky. He found the old woman waiting by a waterfall frozen into intricate columns of ice. *This is the changing*, she said, and cast a handful of bright sparks into the air among the motes of snow. She showed him how to shape the sparks into letters of red firelight; when he'd finally arranged them into a word she said *Break!* and the ice shattered, its fragments falling down through the air. The waterfall's roaring, the frigid water pouring by.

They set the flowers growing, the deer running, the wolves hunting. They made the sun rise and fall, and unlocked the wind.

San Francisco's billboards and video screens had been masses of symbols without meaning, their pulses catching and holding his eye, but now he saw that they just wanted him to buy things. There were abandoned shipping containers by the Bay, with long chains of stenciled white numbers that seemed to float off of their aluminum hulls, and these numbers stayed with him, for it seemed they must be a code that would tell him where the containers came from, what cargo they'd carried through the world, why they were left baking in the sulfurous mud.

Graffiti was everywhere, all the gangs' marks of territory and memorial. In the buried levels his flashlight found blocky, diamond-eyed skeletons clawing their way out of the wall, bony fingers stained with blood, uttering spiky words that, he found, proclaimed the valor of the Downtown Aztec Kings, which had a sadness, the Kings having been wiped out years ago in their war with MS-13, which had itself crumbled before the waves of new arrivals all determined to seize a piece of the limited markets in drugs and girls.

He dreamed of letters black as embers, crawling with red light, coalescing into words or forms with words' sweep. At night he swarmed up the new walls to the empty lunar surfaces where no one had been but the drones who had built them; he wrote what he remembered of the dream's afterimage with scavenged spray paint under wind-driven fog. The favelas were always rising, like hard clouds of grey stone billowing up, and he knew his work would be buried soon, but he liked to think of it, down in the concrete, abiding.

The locked door with the writing read *Knock three times and enter*, so he did, and stepped out onto the upper branches where the eagle was waiting. There were more doors there, and the child, who seemed a little older now, opened one onto a huge room where a fire burned in a hearth big enough to hold a car. The eagle said, *This is the ancestors' hall*, and he saw that there was a thickly branching tree incised on the stone floor. A mirror rose up from the flagstones and the eagle asked him to write his name in its fog, but he stood there with his arms folded. Then the eagle asked for his mother's and father's names, but tentatively, and seemed unsurprised to be ignored. Finally it gave him a book of names from which he chose *Kern*, for its harsh foreign sound and because it meant "warrior" in the dead language of a cold island somewhere far away, and choosing a name seemed like a magical operation, as though his choice would give him strength.

The next doors opened onto games. There was one where stuffed animals chopped carrots and peppers and dropped them in pots boiling on a stove while a grandmother rabbit watched them from her bed. There was a garden out back with rows of flowers and vegetables. The grandmother seemed to be sick—the blankets were pulled up to her chin, and her voice was kind when she asked him if he'd like to help them make dinner, but he was already backing out of the door.

The next game was about designing clothes and making outfits, and the one after that was about digging tunnels in a mine; his attention was wandering and the outside world seemed closer but then the next door opened onto a steaming, snake-infested jungle where he picked his way down vines thick as cars to a derelict spaceport. Moisture dripped from the roof of the hangar onto the husks of shattered aircraft, covered in moss, long left to ruin. White orchids drooped from cracked fuselage. The steel blast doors were black and twisted, the concrete seared as though in unbelievable heat. In a corner of the hangar, under a thick growth of red bromeliads, he found an armored transport, treads melted, hull intact. The ancient metal clanged hollowly as, using the flowers for handholds, he clambered up. The hatch was sealed, but by it was a black plate with the outline of a hand—on impulse, he pressed his palm to it—the hatch sighed open.

Within the transport was a cavity full of shadows, rotten seats of padded fabric, and a crate painted in black-and-white camouflage. On the crate's side was a long chain of stenciled alphanumerics, just like the shipping containers, and he wondered if they shared some secret affinity. Inside the crate, fitted in molded foam, was a gun—oiled black steel, the grip deeply textured, an old one, its mechanism so simple he could see it with his eyes—and a tablet computer in layered black armor. Machines within machines, he thought, and, perhaps, machines within those, and so on forever, and for a moment he remembered that he was playing a game, but then the tablet woke to life. *We're dying*, said an old man with cheekbones, a soldier's haircut and a fierce intensity. *We're dying, but there's hope. If you've found this, if you have the courage to take up the gun, then we can still break the Shadow Clan, save everything, bring the war to the final chamber. Even if the spaceport can't be saved*—outside the transport the wind howled through the pierced, listing hangar—*even if our army is scattered*—birds called brightly in the jungle's distance—*victory can be ours—yours—if only you have the discipline.*

There were explosions where the old man was, the lights flickering as the walls shook, the recording momentarily fading out, but he never stopped speaking of survival, of the need to improvise, how everything would be against him, how the Shadow Clan ninja were ubiquitous, unspeakable, an enemy out of nightmares. *Find the final chamber*, he said, *and everything will be explained*, but then there was shouting, commotion, a horrible metallic hissing—the old man turned, reaching for his sidearm, his face a mask of hateful determination, and the video turned to static.

He hunted them unseen through steaming deltas, glittering temples full of chimes, the ebb tides of flooded cities. The Shadow Clan, complacent, thought their enemies long gone. Their installations were like seashells, vast and full of symmetry.

The tablet guided him to long-abandoned vine-entangled depots. He levered open the sealed doors and found water, medicine, and, best of all, weapons, baroque and glorious, the neodymium laser and the Higgs cannon and the phased accelerator reflex rifle—he murmured the names, shivered at their power. They were finicky, though, hard to repair and harder to customize, their manuals in a dense, technical English that he spent hours picking through with the tablet's dictionary.

He was holed up in a ruined military base by the sea, trying to make a water purifier out of scavenged parts, when the old man spoke from the tablet. *There is no room for mistakes*, he said. *You're hopelessly outgunned and have virtually no resources. The only one on your side is me, and I'm dead. God help you, boy. You've got the one chance, so make the most of it.*

The old man's gravity shook him. He hid the laptop and went out into the favelas but another epidemic must have come and gone because the boys he'd known had vanished, replaced with pinch-faced children who spoke in the voice of the deeper south.

The Clan's ninja loved the dark so the dark became his hunting ground. Their grace was inhuman, fluid, wholly jointless. They turned to ash when they died, so he didn't get a good look at one until he shot down a hovercraft and found the pilot trapped in the wreckage—its body was strangely formless, like a viscous mix of oil and coal; the jewels that were its eyes tracked the barrel of his gun.

He shot the struts out of bridges, loosed viruses in their reservoirs, launched missiles into the power plant on the cliffs above their city. With great effort he taught himself the mathematics needed to decrypt their archives, and then nearly despaired, for he found that he'd only been killing servants, that the Clan lords dwelt up the gravity well in eternal night and silence, their satellites an archipelago rising away from the Earth. The last and most remote, the Void Star, was the only point of light in a blank span of sky. The final chamber was there, he read, as he might have expected. It was a long way away, but at least he knew where he was going.

He stowed away on a Clan shuttle headed into low Earth orbit. The battles in the satellite's cramped tunnels reminded him of the favelas' density and confusion. In the satellite's robotics dump he found power armor; its hull was cracked, but the tablet taught him how to weld it.

On the next satellite he met his first shadow lord and killed it in the dark. He took to waiting for the shuttles out on the satellite's hulls, at home in his armor, staring up at the galaxies glittering coldly, the empty space where the Void Star glowed. By the tenth satellite he'd found his rhythm, though there was always an eeriness about them when everyone else was dead. Now and then the old man spoke from the tablet, but where at first he'd been encouraging now he was full of rage and obscenity, railing at him to purge the world, and finally Kern stopped listening.

In the penultimate satellite he stood on the thick glass of a porthole, looking down past his feet at the Earth, a brilliant coin in the night. His Gauss rifle clicked as it cooled from burning out the hive/core. He hated his enemies for dying and leaving him alone, but by then there wasn't far to go.

The last shuttle was cramped, its elliptical walls complexly incised, as though it were purely ceremonial and never intended for use. He felt like he was falling as his destination approached.

The last lord of shadows stalked the empty corridors of his island in the night, howling to itself, raking the walls with its claws. When he had burnt its body with napalm (the lords, he had discovered, were prone to resurrect), he set himself to hunting down the surviving ninja—he found and killed the last one in a vicious struggle in the shuttle bay, and that was that.

The shadow lord's jangling severed steel claw was the key to the lock in a wide spiral door that opened onto rickety stairs rising in the empty spaces between the station's walls. He knew it was the end, and time to go for broke, so he dialed the Gauss rifle to MAX-AUTO as he crept up the dusty steps past structural beams. He was expecting to find a last horror lurking but the stairs ended under flickering fluorescent lights before a disconcertingly ordinary-looking laminate door on which was taped a piece of paper where *The Final Chamber!* was written in black marker. He gingerly took off his helmet, pressed his ear to the door, heard what might have been laughter.

He went in hot, bursting through the door, firing everything he had, or trying to, but his guns had become lifeless, and his missiles didn't launch; he glided to a halt in a conference room in the middle of an applauding crowd. Thin carpet, office furniture and out the window blue sky and white thunderheads. Impression of men, white and Asian, and dressed formally, as though for an occasion, except for a few shaggy ones in T-shirts and sandals. From the ceiling hung a banner with CONGRATULATIONS! next to a logo like a stylized centaur. The old man was there, clapping steadily, but he seemed calm, and wore a suit like all the rest. The old owner, the man from the pictures he'd found so long ago, was there, too, looking decades younger.

He tried to draw his pistol but his weapons had vanished and so had his armor. A short man in a dark grey suit stepped forward and said, "This world was created for you, but now it is ending." He explained that they were engineers who had designed a laptop to save children in the far reaches of the world. It was meant to be their school, to teach them everything, to draw them in and hold them while they grew. It would make poverty unimaginable, the relic of a barbarous past.

They told him their names and their titles in turn; it took a long time, but they seemed to think it was important. "Aaron Levy, data architect," said the laptop's former owner, who was handsome and distant. "Sol Eagleman, Chief Psychology Officer," said the old man, smiling.

The short man said, "Keep the laptop for as long as you need it, but when you're done with it, please give it away. It's made to last, and it's always looking for the next child to help. Meanwhile, there is a last gift, the final thing we have to offer."

A door opened—beyond it were books, shelf upon shelf of them, receding into the distance. He said, "It's all the libraries in the world."

11

•

Theater

Irina follows Magda through the labyrinth of W&P's offices, aware that Magda is glad to be getting rid of her, glad herself that she can soon be alone, lose herself in the machines.

Magda gestures to a door, smiling falsely. "Let us know if there's anything you need," she says with a slight involuntary bow.

The theater is a steep slope of black seats descending to the white screen that spans the wall, like a rich man's private cinema, though the space evokes tactical briefings more than film. Clean and quiet, here. Irina closes the door behind her and sits, aware of the empty space, the silence.

As the houselights fade Irina's heart rises. Her other memory is full of the last day's imagery—sun glare on asphalt, her hotel's existentially sterile lobby, the sudden chill of conditioned air as she stepped from the Santa Monica heat into the defense contractor's office—which she now deletes, and those hours, briefly reprieved from oblivion, vanish for good, leaving an ache like a word just forgotten. (But even now new images accumulate:

the flash of her phone as it acquires the local network, the smooth leather under her hand, her declining tension.) Like a sun slowly rising, the screen begins to glow.

Static, then, bright and churning. She watches intently, sifting the white noise for structure, but finds no more than the faintest ghost traces, always dissolved before she can give them a name. Her thumbs move in the air over her phone's screen, changing the filters, upping the resolution and intensity, and for some reason she sees herself as if from a distance, a woman sitting alone, staring wide-eyed at the screen's entropy, this most abstract of all possible cinemas. And then, without warning, the static is gone, and the AI's thoughts are there before her, manifest as a dully glowing nebula, riddled with storms, roiling sluggishly. Her other memory floods with its geometry and shadows.

Zooming in, the storm's surface becomes glyphs flowing in waves over the screen. The glyphs are intricate, radiant with significance that she can't quite articulate. Like rain, she thinks, on a clear day, seen over miles of ocean. Like ideograms distended in a black hole's gravity. Like thick filaments of DNA, fraying before her eyes. This is what she always thinks, on seeing the glyphs, and then, as always, she remembers that language won't suffice here. She remembers rain blatting on the bay windows of a high room in a good hotel rising over the surf of the South China Sea; her lover, a mathematician, whom she never saw again after that night, had asked her to explain a glyph, just one, the simplest, fully, and she had tried, as the hotel swayed, just perceptibly, in the wind, offering analogies, at first, and then, when that failed, reciting the glyph's structure in a child's singsong, her voice rising and falling, and as she wound on and on she lost track of where she was, seeing blurred shadows of glyphs in the rain channels on the glass, and then of time, until, finally, he stopped her with a finger to her lips, and moved her hair aside to kiss tenderly her forehead's faded scar. She cranks the resolution, then, and the glyphs seethe, splitting and fusing, burning off into nothing, her face flickering in the violence of the light. Her perception vibrates as her other memory churns, searching for pattern, vainly, and the moments pass, and still she can make nothing of the glyphs rushing by.

She knows, then, with an absolute and dismal certainty, that her gift is lost, that the machines' luminous otherness is closed to her for good, but then the fugue hits, and her breath catches. The theater is gone, and she's somewhere else, bodiless, lost in the light and motion of the transit of Los Angeles.

She knows the temperature, the wear and slickness of every meter of every highway in the Inland Traffic Authority. She hears all the chatter of all the surveillance drones hovering high in the amber smog, and sees, through their cameras, tens of thousands of taillights receding. She sees all the cars' positions and their velocities and the spectral probabilities of accident and delay overlaid on the interchanges, the overpasses, the long desert straightaways, and the patterns implied by these trajectories, beyond number, without meaning, rising up endlessly, like thermals shimmering over the freeways, pulling at her attention as they form and disperse, and there on the coastal highway where the ocean roars under raw cliffs a new BMW's steering fails catastrophically, and three lives and the car's computer blink out for good, and in that moment seventeen more cars merge onto the freeway, and she is grateful, almost, for the accident that marred her life but brought her this vision.

Time falls away, and she would linger there, in transit's endless present, but she reminds herself that she is not the sum of all velocities, that she is, in fact, alone, somewhere, in a theater, staring at its screen, her neck aching and her eyes dry, that she has work to do, a question to answer, that the AI isn't doing what it should.

The filters change—somewhere, she is changing them—and in rapid succession she knows the mass of the water behind the high desert dams, the number of solar cells turned like silver flowers to the sun, the blue Chartres glow of Cerenkov radiation in the coolant tank of a desert fission plant, the kilojoules of power humming through the high-tension lines strung over the desiccated mountains, through the exurbs, pouring current into the Los Angeles sprawl. A sense of pressure, then, and heat lightning flaring at the edges of her vision, and the machine is with her, vast and slow, less persona than weather.

She'd been diligent, once, in trying to know them, but that was long ago, and now it's enough to look, as others look at the stars. The machine lacks all human feeling, and all human meaning, but somehow feels close. Its thoughts pour over her—it's like trying to read letters written on turbulent water—and it's beyond even what her other memory can hold, so each moment, as it passes, is lost for good; she is acutely aware of leaving a strand of old selves behind, like brilliant pebbles on the timeline, of falling, headlong, into the future. This, she knows, is how other people always experience time, and she wonders if they notice.

She wills herself to passivity, letting the torrent of its thoughts roar around her, like an infinite flock of birds always exploding into motion, and is drawn up with them, through layers of abstraction, and at first there are glimpses of meaning—transient correlations between delays in coastal traffic and the dry mountain wind, strange spikes in power usage repeated at intervals of years—but then there's just form, beyond words, and her mind is a cloud dissolving in the wind.

Abruptly, the maelstrom crystallizes as the machine's focus narrows onto the Santa Monica coast, the fortress enclaves of the rich behind the high walls glittering with jagged broken glass. Its thoughts slow as it runs over and over the long chain of causes whose sole conclusion is the shadow of a probability that they'll burn the lights a little longer, tonight, in those high rooms over the sea, and Irina sees that, for all its intricacy, it seems to be performing exactly as intended.

The machine starts buying up futures contracts, wringing all the value from its sliver of prescience. *What now?* she thinks, as its millions of micro-trades pour out into the markets, and she's tired, and ill at ease, though she's just been sitting still—the fugue flickers as her focus wanes. She wonders if it's lack of sleep, then realizes she feels watched.

There's a sense of decreasing pressure as the machine turns back to its work. It's sublimely complex, but somehow empty, and she feels certain it doesn't know she exists. Could she have been wrong? No—there's something else, barely there, and now, just like that, vanished. She adjusts the filters, eliminating the flows of energy and traffic, and now the city is gone, leaving her floating in an empty neutral space.

She looks out into the dark. Nothing, and nothing, and nothing without end. *I know you're there*, she thinks, trying to persuade herself, and there, like she's willed it into being, a distant phosphene shimmer. Gone already, but she pursues it, and yes, there it is, receding. (She's aware of following it off of W&P's servers and out into who-knows-where—she feels like an explorer in a lightless country.) Will it always be like this, she wonders, though it's only been seconds, chasing this fleeting sense of presence, never giving up or getting closer. She stops abruptly, because there before her is another machine, like a turbulent ocean of pale light.

It's fathomless, crystalline. Rapt, she drifts closer. It's the biggest AI she's seen by far, bigger than she'd thought was possible. Its surface is golden, seething, is already closer than she thought, and now she's in it.

Sense of rushing over the sea at dawn, and then the paper-lantern glow of the glass and steel towers of a city rising from the waves, rising up without limit, its heights lost in cloud and the blue of distance, and there, up at the apex, something is hidden, and she can't quite bring it into focus . . .

Hard transition to a road through the desert under a dust-cloud sky, empty except for a girl driving too fast in a car that isn't hers, and the girl is leaving everything behind, and Irina pities her, for she's lost, though the road lies straight, and doesn't know where she's going, and now the road is gone and there's a screen shimmering with static in a steep room full of black seats where a woman sits alone holding her phone in both hands, looking old and tired in the half-light and staring at the screen as though it hid her salvation, and she thinks someone says, *It's you.* In the voice she hears distance, and surprise, and maybe wonder, and she starts to speak, though she doesn't know who will hear her, or what she's going to say, but everything is collapsing, and as the fugue dissolves the houselights rise and she hears the projector's whine as it powers down. She's clutching her phone too tightly; deliberately, she unclenches her hands. The back of her shirt is damp with sweat but she shivers in the cold of the theater.

12

·

Clinic

The interior of the town car is dark as a cavern, cramped by the thickness of the armor of the hull. No sound, there, but for the muffled creak of leather as Thales shifts in his seat. The windows, set to black, don't show him his reflection.

As the car accelerates, the crash seat folds itself around him with a ginger, almost maternal, precision. The map of Venice Beach on the dimmed seatback display shows him leaving the hotel's garage, passing beyond the last of its defenses—there's a faint vibration as the car's weapons come online. There will be other cars, he knows, pulling out beside him, empty and identical, a fleet of sacrificial distractions, and in each, he imagines, there is a false, other Thales, bound for someplace else.

His father died in a car like this, Thales in the seat beside him. He tries to summon the memory, but of course there's nothing, just an absence, and images from after the fact, which is probably a kindness. That car's armament was the same as this one's, but his mother says the risk is less, with his father gone, that now his uncles are the focus of the violence. (Even so he feels her constant tension, her new fear of strangers.)

In the weeks after the attack, she'd barely let him leave their suite, had
spent all day reading to him and holding his hand; once, when he was
having a clear day, she'd taken him to a tiny, beautiful house she'd built as
a young woman in the mountains over LA, back when she still worked as
an architect, but recently she's been staying in her room—he suspects she's
been drinking—and once again he's going to the clinic alone. He doesn't
have his math book, so he closes his eyes, sinks deeper into the seat, wonders what the odds are that he'll reach the clinic whole.

He wakes with a start as the car turns and the mini-fridge clinks. Opening it,
he finds two splits of champagne, one open and half-empty, its carbonation
fading—his brothers must have been using the car. As he shuts the fridge
the car stops, the door sighing open onto too much light, and as he covers
his eyes he's momentarily convinced that he's denying himself the specifics
of his death, but in fact there's no ambush, just the clinic's courtyard.

The car is parked in a garden of raked sand and a few irregular stones,
placed with studied randomness, and low pines whose wind-bent forms
suggest endurance in the face of extremity. The curved walls are high and
sheer, defining a cylinder of air and light; he looks straight up into dust
motes burning in the sun. Behind the car, the foot-thick steel gate closes
soundlessly, sealing him in.

A girl in clinic livery approaches—young and pretty, he notes
distantly—her posture conveying both welcome and submission. He
wonders if the better clinics have always been modeled on elegant hotels,
perhaps to conceal their underlying horror.

Within, the clinic is cool and dark and the girl says they've lowered the
lights for him, to minimize the potential for—she frowns—disturbance;
she looks him full in the eyes and her face, which might hold pity, is a
landscape of uncertainty and of a significance into which he feels himself
falling and though he looks immediately away the migraine flickers and
he finds himself staring into a twisted blur of curvature and fangs but he
exhales carefully and stills his mind and the blur ripples and resolves
into a white porcelain vase with blue Chinese dragons on its stand by the
reception desk.

The girl sends him down a corridor alone and he starts to feel steady,
almost poised, probably capable of facing the morning, and this isn't least
because the tessellations of the floor's tile are predictable without being

intricate or even interesting and then, deep within the clinic, he opens a door onto an office as enshadowed as a tomb where the only color is the muted red of a Persian rug on the weathered hardwood floor. His surgeon is there, behind his desk, perfectly still, studying his phone, and Thales notes the clarity with which the little light picks out his features.

"Is it more physical therapy today?" Thales asks, feeling edgy, trying for a weary familiarity.

The surgeon says, "Actually, I have some questions for you." The lack of greeting or preamble is off-putting, somehow worrisome, and then, like a conjurer, the surgeon produces a handful of small metal objects and sets them on the table. Their surfaces glitter in the narrow halogen beam, their faces reflecting the room, and the other objects' reflections, which starts to draw him in. When the physician says, "What do you see here?" he rallies and says, "The platonic solids, cast in metal, maybe tungsten, each about four inches on the longest axis, about the length of the last two joints of a finger."

"Good," says the physician, and Thales scans him for signs of hope or satisfaction, but he remains impassive as he puts a tablet on the desk. He says, "I need you to interpret this for me," and plays a video.

It shows a close-up on a woman—handsome, young, or actually not young but young-looking—and she's sitting in some kind of sloped theater by herself, her phone in her hands, her thumbs moving. She has a thousand-yard stare, or perhaps a million—it's a private face, and a vulnerable one, reflecting an absolute immersion, and the light playing over her is so bright it looks like she's in a cinema, and if she is then what's the film that's gripped her so completely? He could try to explain all this, but he's tired, and he wants to go home, to the hotel if he must, ideally to Rio, though the Rio house won't quite come to mind. Nothing much is happening on the screen, though for some reason it's hard to look away, perhaps because of the tension in her face. For a moment he wonders if this is meant to be art, though it seems way beyond the surgeon's likely tolerance for the avant-garde. He rallies, finds words, and with an effort says, "She's in a theater. She's maybe about forty. I don't think she knows that anyone's watching."

"Why is she there?" asks the surgeon, with an irritating serenity that reminds Thales of the Provisional Authority immigration police. "What does she want?"

"I have no idea," he says, as politely as he can, and he's ashamed of his evident petulance as he says, "Maybe you could explain to me why you're asking me these questions?"

"I'm evaluating your prospects."

"Prospects?" Thinking how his father had wanted him to study law instead of math and physics, which he'd said were respectable but essentially middle class.

"I need to assess the severity of your impairment. Your implant saved your life, but created new problems, and we've come to a crossroads in your treatment."

Thales tries to interrupt but the surgeon talks over him. "There are two protocols. In one, we wind down treatment and transition you back to a fully independent life. Unfortunately, this option is available only to the rarest, highest-performing patients. The other option, the one for most patients, is, in essence, to keep you as comfortable as possible through the course of your decline, so please do your best in the testing today."

It's absurd, and so sudden—he wants to call his mother, get a second opinion, maybe even call the family counsel, who must have offices in the U.S., though in the stress of the moment the firm's name eludes him, and why in god's name haven't they told him this before? He immediately sees that the answer is that they didn't want to worry him in vain, and so, in the space of this brief and quiet chat, his life has been transformed, and to resist already seems as futile as throwing punches at the wind. The surgeon says, "Here's the next one."

The tablet plays a clip showing an old man sitting at a wide desk. It's shot from above, backlit, low-res, maybe from a security camera. The old man reminds Thales of his father's political friends with their immaculately cultivated health, his age less in his face than in his stillness.

A woman enters the frame, very slight, her hair long and dark.

"It looks like you're going to make it," she says, sitting on his lap, but he says nothing.

"It looks like you're going to make it," she says again, coaxingly, as though trying to persuade a child to accept good news. "Are you happy?"

The old man says, "Once upon a time there was a king who owned everything but was afraid to die. But there was an angel, who lived far away in the northern aurora, and one night it spoke to him from the dark, saying it could grant eternal life, but its speech was all but unintelligible, less like speech than the Arctic wind. The king found a seeress who, having passed through the kingdom of death, spoke the tongues of both angels and men, for he didn't know if the angel was from the hosts of the righteous or the fallen, and he knew he would need her when it came time to enslave them. The king and the angel bargained, and it finally gave him what he wanted, taking, in its avarice, half his treasure, for the angels spun palaces of molecular gold in the high empyrean. The king thought, *Now, finally, I alone of all the men who have ever lived need not fear time.* Replete in this knowledge, he closed his eyes and slept, unworried, for the first time since he'd been a boy. Waking, he found that everyone he knew had died. Looking out the window of his tower he saw that his kingdom was buried in ice."

Thales draws breath to start to try to unpack the parable but his eyes are full of golden filaments hanging in the sky and the seeress hovering at the doorway of the kingdom of death, and that, he thinks, is the gate I have passed through, but, far from speaking the tongues of angels, I can barely speak the tongues of men, and he imagines himself turning and going back through the doorway while the seeress watches with jaded curiosity, and all the while the angel is trying to ask him if the king can be trusted but can't find the words.

The surgeon is watching him so he tries to find something to say but now the tablet glows with migraine light, as though revealed in its insubstantiality, and the couple's faces have become membranes without meaning. He's going to plead for more time or another chance or try to invoke his family's power but the surgeon says, "No," shaking his head, and Thales can already see that his resistance is futile, and then the surgeon says, "But you're not alone."

"You know, I think I am," says Thales, trying to swallow his tears.

"I want you to succeed," the surgeon says. "I'll boost your working memory. Let's see if that helps."

"Through my implant?" Thales says as the surgeon's fingers trace patterns over his tablet's screen.

The glare diminishes, but Thales says, "Everything feels the same."

"Look again," says the surgeon, and when Thales looks back at the screen the video is playing again and he finds he feels more awake and sees the significance of all the details, in fact it's almost pressing at him how she clings to him, how he's adjusted his legs to accommodate her weight, how two of his fingers have found the exposed skin of the small of her back, how plain she'd be but for her clothes and the tenderness in her face when she touches him.

"I'm so sorry you won't be with me," the old man says. "I *did* try."

"Maybe you'll figure it out."

"I refuse to proffer false hope."

"Well, I'm happy," she says, but like he's the one who needs comfort.

"But how shall I get along without you through all the time to come? How shall I ever find anyone as dear?"

"I'm not going anywhere."

"But you are, and in about ten years," the old man says, making an effort to say this matter-of-factly.

"Ten years is a lifetime," she says.

"Ten years is an eye-blink. It will pass, and then comes the next thing."

"For you, there will always be a next thing," she says. "It's what you wanted."

The old man stares into space, then says, "When I was a young man I went to Iceland. I had no real reason—I just wanted to go—I liked their poetry and I wanted to see the world. It was the end of the season, the summer fading, and I rented a car and left Reykjavík, the city, their only city, then, behind. Now to think of Iceland is to think of software but back then there was nothing, just the empty island and the glaciers, remote and menacing, the waste at the heart of a place no one went. It was already evening and I didn't know where I was going, didn't even know where I'd sleep, and I was afraid, hurtling along the ring road, as I lost the light. I hadn't even remembered to bring a coat. It was painterly, the graded shadows of the mountains, the color of distance, the ghosts of shape."

"Now you can go back."

"That Iceland is gone. It's arable now. Cultivated. All tourist traps and code factories. But that's not the point. It's how I feel. This future I'm approaching."

"I've stood between you and the world for a while now," she says, "and I'd do it forever, if I could, but soon enough you'll have to get along without me."

"The world doesn't suit me."

"Then you'll reshape it."

"And if I can't, then that other door is open."

"Other door?"

"Pills. Heights. I don't much like guns. These are the doors that lead out of eternity."

"I don't like to hear these things," she says.

"I didn't tell you, did I," the old man says, recollecting himself. "They've changed the terms. Akemi no longer suffices—now they want Ms. Sunden too. Not what I had expected to come of her visit, and I can't imagine she told us much of the truth, but it doesn't matter. There's just the one game in town, so I'll touch my cap and hop to it."

"Your good friend Irina," the woman says bitterly.

"She's interesting. Unique. An intermediate kind of thing. You can't begrudge me my interesting friends—I've been collecting them since before you were born."

"Wonderful. She can keep you company through the ages." Her voice sounds toxic and artificial.

"We'll see. She's essentially mercenary, and her price is within my means. Hiro keeps encouraging me to take more direct action, but I'm not yet prepared to accept his standard of ethics. I haven't told you about Hiro, have I? He handles my disavowables. His résumé is a demon's. You'll never meet him. In any case, most likely that will work out, one way or another, and most likely Hiro will get the phone, last night's debacle notwithstanding, and soon after that I'll have no real limits. I'll hold more power than any one man since, oh, Genghis Khan. I'll be able to make things whole, and I'll have everything I've ever wanted, except for one thing."

As the old man grips her hand the scene and in fact the clinic seem to be floating away and Thales realizes how tired he is, more tired than he's ever been before, and the migraine is coming, and though he knows he should keep fighting to try to make an impression on the surgeon it's no longer in him to act and he slumps in his chair feeling that the clinic and the surgeon are remote and insubstantial and have nothing to do with him.

Somewhere, the surgeon is saying, "I need to make changes but I'm not sure where."

Thales is distantly aware of the surgeon doing something on his tablet and then, spontaneously, Thales vividly recalls the evening light on the brick wall of an empty storefront on the Westside. The surgeon does something else, and Thales recalls the shifting weight of a glass of water in his hand.

"What did you experience?" asks the surgeon.

"A wall. A glass of water," Thales says, surprised out of his torpor. "What are you doing?"

"So that was episodic and sensory memory. Let's try again."

The physician does something else to his phone, and Thales curls up in his chair, wholly spent.

"What was that like?" asks the surgeon, but Thales has pulled his knees to his chest and now sees nothing but black and grey moiré patterns and in fact feels nothing but a flicker of interest in the logic of his dissolution.

"There," says the surgeon. "Maybe that's it. Let's see if it works."

Thales is suddenly wide awake. "What did you do?" he asks, though in the moment of asking he knows, in fact it's obvious that the surgeon is accessing his thoughts through his implant, and in his clarity he realizes that his clarity is new, and presumably artificial, and he wonders how long he'll get to keep it.

"Good," says the surgeon. "I've locked it at high activation. Now we can work." Thales nods and forces himself to smile, the better to conceal his burgeoning anger at this casual manipulation of the structures of his innermost being, though perhaps this is mere petulance and he should tolerate what's necessary for his recovery, but now in his acuity it's like his thoughts are tumbling forward and he sees that the surgeon's story doesn't hold together—the protocols amount less to treatment than to a veiled threat and if the videos with the strangers were part of a clinical test they'd probably feel anodyne and as though they'd been scripted for some particular purpose instead of essentially opaque and highly specific—and Thales feels like he's become a detective sifting the evidence of the world as he searches for a plausible motive behind the surgeon's actions; it seems like the surgeon wants him to be biddable and inclined to answer questions but the only things that are certain are that information is still missing and that the surgeon has lied.

13

•

Secret Book

t's a front," Irina says. "Your arbitrage AI. There's something else going on underneath."

They're in a conference room of perfect neutrality. Neither Cromwell nor Magda appeared for the debrief; her interlocutor, Martin, some flavor of quant, is scowling at his tablet while scribbling notes. According to his class ring, he's a newly minted Ph.D. from Toronto; he looks like he learned how to knot his necktie on the web. It's clear he finds it necessary for her to know she doesn't impress him.

"A front for what, exactly?" he asks. She freeze-frames his expression—false smile on the lips, eyes narrowed in fear, hostility.

She remembers the high city and the girl—eurasian, probably a teenager, how her car's windshield was webbed with cracks and looked like it was last washed a thousand miles ago. She's on the verge of explaining, or trying to, as in duty bound, but she doesn't like him, and in the absence of sympathy it's hard to communicate subtle things, and she thinks he'd relish the chance to play interrogator. "It's hard to say just what it was hiding," she says, as neutrally as she can.

"And why is that?"

"Well, I suppose it's because the AI was *hiding* it," she says. She re-members the AI's vastness, and shivers as its echoes press at her.

"That's a very strong claim," Martin says, looking up, fingers poised over his tablet. "I assume you can support it with evidence?" He's in his late twenties, and has that slightly fussy programmer diction—his sense of his manhood will be tied up with his technical skills, and this must be his first job, so he'll be more invested than he needs to be. She urges herself to meet his hostility with compassion. Fails utterly.

"It's too complicated for me to try to convey the details," she says. "My job is to provide an outline of what's the case, not to convince you of anything."

He half-sneers, half-laughs, but before he can speak she says, "I have another appointment," and rises. She hasn't read her contract with W&P, but knows that in it, as in all of her contracts, there will be a clause cap-ping the debrief at half an hour—she reserves the right to answer further questions over email—it's something she usually uses to fend off clients who become fascinated, and want to linger.

She's already turned away when she hears his phone get a text and he says, "Wait. Please don't go." His tone is different, supplicating. She turns back, finds him looking alarmed. "We'd really like you to stay. I'm autho-rized to offer new and favorable terms."

She wonders what could have changed so suddenly. Not that it matters, as in her heart she's already gone.

She says, "You've got my agent's number."

Afterwards she always needs to be alone.

She squats by the wall outside the hangar, pulling her jacket close against the cold wind from the Bay, wishing she still smoked, letting her-self attend to the echoes of the machines.

Her mind is aglow with power grids, the ley lines of the freeways, water in free fall in the dark. She reminds herself that these are the machine's thoughts, not her own, and that she must let them go, but still they whirl in her memory. She inhales the sharp salt reek of the wetlands, watches the planes' choreography in the airspace over SFO; the fugue stirs, not far from the surface, and she has a sense that planes and bay are shadows and symbols whose true significance is hidden but that revelation is close. Her hand finds a stone on the asphalt, grips it—she grinds her fingers into its surface, savoring its texture, reminding herself that she is here, in this morning, in the world, not lost in the pages of some vast and secret book. She thinks of coffee, its heat and bitterness. Breathe, she reminds herself, staring blankly at the Bay's glitter.

14

·

Ghost

The favela's rooftops are slick with rain but Kern runs flat out, lost in his velocity. The mark's phone is in his pocket, and Lares' place is close, but he wishes it were farther so he'd have reason to maintain his reckless forward motion.

A gap in the fabric of the rooftops before him, and as he accelerates toward the jump his foot slips. Momentary free fall, and through it an awareness of the approaching abyss, but he catches himself, jarring his shoulder, and stumbles off the last of his momentum before reaching the edge.

At the gap's edge, he looks down into emptiness, sees how it's full of rain, the strangers passing far below. He crouches there, panting, the humidity such that his sweat stays on his skin. His shoulder aches but all he regrets is the loss of his sense of flow.

At least now I'll have money, he thinks, touching the phone in his pocket, listening to the buzz of the drones flying by. One is close, coming closer; he can't see it clearly—it's a shadow on the grey sky—but it lacks the red fore and aft lights of the SFPD ones, so he hesitates, though now it's practically on top of him, and then there's a spotlight in his eyes and a muffled squawking—"*SFPD sit the fuck down and stay where you are!*"— but it's a lie, it's obviously a lie, and once again he's off and running.

He thought he knew the rooftops and the secret ways across them but the construction drones must have been hard at work because it's like a nightmare where familiar things have turned perilous and strange, and he almost misses his footing when a berm of wet concrete rises before him where nothing ought to be. The buzz of the drone is close behind him, and if he twists an ankle it's over, but now atop the berm he sees the city glowing through the fog and there across the rooftops are figures running toward him—they are many, but their hesitations tell him that they don't really know the way. There's a stairwell nearby, or was, so he breaks for it, as though he knows for a fact that it isn't built over, and then he's in the air over the stairs and then the shock as he hits the landing.

The stairs descend into the darkness of the favela's interior, which is good, because flying drones won't go into confined spaces, and as he runs down flight after flight he's wondering who he attacked last night and thinking that he's always known it would end like this, that he'd offend the wrong person and resources would be brought to bear against him such that all his hardness and his will and his incessant training would be meaningless, and leave him without defenses, and he'd thought he was invincible but in fact he's just a nobody and no one important has ever cared enough to put him down.

He comes out onto a street full of stalls where they're just putting up awnings against the rain. Peripheral flashes of lurid video game posters and glowing neon signage and hand-drawn menus over the food carts. It feels better to be around people though he knows they won't help him but if he's going to die at least he won't be alone. He slows his pace and makes himself breathe through his nose, though his lungs are burning, and he takes out his phone to give himself a countenance. A man with a shaved head and a cheap shiny leather coat is coming toward him, in a hurry to get somewhere, and he realizes he's holding the mark's phone when from it a girl's urgent voice says, "He's one of them."

Kern watches as the man reaches casually into his coat, as though for a pack of cigarettes, and takes out something the size of a phone but from the way he holds it Kern knows it's a weapon.

In the laptop's library, there's a video, very grainy, at least a century old, of an old man with white stubble on his cheeks explaining the secrets of fighting with knives. Kern guessed he was in his eighties, and his accent was southern, possibly Argentine, and he seemed like any other dumb old hick until he spoke of fencing, at which it was as though he were illuminated from within. *If your adversary is unskilled,* he'd said, *then, even if you're unarmed, his weapon is most dangerous to himself.* Kern had studied this video for weeks, practicing its moves to the exclusion of all else, and now he slips to one side, just a little, the way the old man said—*Get out of the way but stay close enough to hurt them*—and he feels the motion of the air as the weapon, a taser, passes through the empty space where his abdomen had been; he notices the taser is a uniform matte grey, probably fabbed. *Get the knife,* the old man had said. *Let him hit you a few times if he wants to, but get the knife.* And then he's got the man's wrist, and is prising his fingers from the taser, and as it clatters away his fear flowers into rage.

For a moment they sway in close embrace, and at first it's like holding a lover—he's aware of every shift in the stranger's body, his rough cheeks, rank armpits, floral cologne—and then it's like fighting a child, for, though the man is determined, he has no art, really none, and it's only seconds before Kern has the clinch, his forearms trapping the man's neck, his palms cradling the back of his skull, pulling him in. The man tries to duck out of it, a beginner's mistake and a fatal one, and Kern, full of joy and a sort of technical pride, drives his right knee into the man's face, and then the left, and then right again. He finds himself supporting the man's limp weight, hesitates, and then, putting all his weight behind it, spikes the man's skull onto the concrete floor, and screams, though he hadn't meant to, a raw cry, torn from within, and the paroxysm seems to last a long time, but when it ends the vendors are just turning to look, and he picks up the phone as tears wet his cheeks and walks away.

It's like a cloud has settled on his mind and he keeps laughing a little to himself as he takes turns at random, putting the fight into the past, and he knows the body will be gone soon, taken to some out-of-the-way place and picked over by scavengers, and if the man was in good health and not important enough to register his DNA then his organs will be harvested for the open market and whatever's left will disappear into the cold water flowing out through the Golden Gate, and he thinks of the sharks there, swarming in the deep channels, how it's said they've multiplied since the

ocean got warmer, and then the street turns again and widens into a labyrinth of low, rebar-studded concrete barriers leading circuitously to the
gate in a breach in the favelas' walls, and beyond the fence is the wide
unbuilt cordon of cracked earth and dried weeds and rotting garbage and
then the city.

There's a marine in armor watching people trickle in, a white kid with
a buzz cut and bad skin, not much older than Kern, his helmet retracted.
They're not picky about who comes into the favelas but getting out can be
trickier—they'll usually let you past the checkpoint in the mornings, if you
don't give any attitude, and say you're going to a job, but if you get the wrong
soldier you can get arrested, maybe not come back. The marine is staring
into space, and seems not to have seen him, and Kern hears bass-heavy red-
neck music rumbling from his armor, and then he remembers the phone.

He puts it to his ear and the girl says, "Listen to me. Please just listen.
Don't close the line."

He raises the phone to chuck it but stops when he feels the marine's
eyes on him, remembers how nervous they can be, how they'll light up
anyone they think might have a grenade, or even a stone, and the phone is
still close enough to his ear that he can hear her shouting, "No, don't do
it, don't leave listen to me I can help you you need me *please*," and she
sounds young, younger than he is, and the rawness of her panic seems
unfeignable, and for some reason he's reminded of the desperation of the
dead, how they say that ghosts linger in the world looking for someone
who will listen.

He puts the phone back to his ear and says, "Who is this?"

"Okay. Good," says the ghost, composing herself. "So the first thing is
to not get caught. You want to leave the favelas right now."

"I'm good here."

"They can fly drones there. No one cares what they do there. In the
city the cops control the airspace. You're not getting away if they have air
support." Kern eyes the checkpoint doubtfully and the ghost says, "Go,
now. They'll be coming."

Kern doesn't like soldiers, and there are other, safer ways out of the
favelas, but the checkpoint is right there, and his fear pulls him down the
winding path between the barriers. The marine looks down at him with
blood-shot eyes, and he hears the rush of the suit's air scrubber, then smells
the pot. "Go on," the marine croaks, uninterested, dismissive, in a Spanish

so heavily accented that Kern wouldn't understand it if he didn't know English too, and it's clear that the marine thinks it's better to be high and peaceful and watch the evening go by than to waste time harassing some punk favelino, and Kern accepts this and goes on.

On the worn track over the open stretch of earth he feels exposed, like he's about to be shot in the back, and it's a relief to reach the asphalt road, dodge between the cars, go in among the buildings whose age and rectilinearity tell him he's not at home. He glances back at the favelas' outer walls, the only surface there that never really changes, its graffiti a solid mass, and in it, for a moment, he sees a greater shape, as though the writing had come in waves, and the waves frozen.

Surprised still to be alive, he walks away quickly. He remembers how he'd felt the first time the laptop started, and he wonders if this, somehow, is the game's next chapter; the last five minutes have had the same sense of wonder, dislocation, shocking arbitrariness. The sidewalks are crowded now, the blank faces of the houses giving way to restaurants whose windows frame candlelit tableaux that have nothing to do with him. He puts the phone to his ear and says, "What is this?"

"I did you a favor, right?" she says. "I've established that I'm your ally? All I had to do was nothing and you'd already be dead."

"That's true," he admits, imagining the taser's prongs hitting his chest, then convulsions, helplessness, the unrecoverability.

"For now will you take my word for things so we can get down to business?"

"I'm listening," he says, poised to hear the new game's terms.

"We have to get you out of town. You're already lucky to have lasted this long."

He thinks of his room, his espresso machine, his two other shirts, and most of all his laptop, and it's like she's been following his thoughts when she says, "They've probably found your place by now. Whatever you had, it's gone. You need to let it go."

"Who are 'they,' and why are they after me?" he says, trying to rally, wanting to argue her into admitting that nothing has really changed. "Did I touch up someone important? So look—I'm just hired help. I could just go wait it out till this all blows over."

"Who they are is a private hit squad, and the phone is a prototype, something special—I think it has to do with encryption. I know their boss, and he's not going to give up. If you stay in San Francisco, you'll die."

It feels like he's always been in San Francisco—Kern knows he grew up in a different country, but barely remembers it—and leaving seems unimaginable. He wonders how long till new construction seals his room off, and if he dies will his spirit return to work the heavy bag there, forever throwing combinations in the dark? He tries to accept this, but finds himself saying, "But what if I just gave them the phone? I could just leave it somewhere and they could take it and they'd never have to see me—"

"You're not going do that," she says. "Okay? They'd kill you just the same." Her voice sounds flat and hard and younger now, less educated, more of the country's burned-out core. "They don't allow loose ends. Better that a thousand innocents should die than that a single enemy go free. Okay? Do you understand that you can't negotiate?"

He doesn't say anything, in fact his mind has gone blank, but then, more kindly, she says, "The phone has an earpiece with a camera—why don't you put it on?"

He studies the phone, finds the button that detaches a whorl of more-or-less flesh-colored plastic with a tiny lens at one end. When he puts it in the ghost whispers, "Now we share a perspective," and he feels her presence twining around him.

"Look around a little, so I can orient," she says, so he duly peers around the street, feeling like a tourist. "I think this is the lower Mission," she says. "God, it feels like a long time."

"Why help me?" he blurts. "Whoever you are. I mean, why bother? Why not just let me die?"

"Would you say you're a man of a grateful spirit?" she asks, and he thinks, *Here it comes.* "Because if you are, you could do me a favor, because I'm trapped here and I need help getting out."

"Trapped where?"

"I'm locked in an empty house," she says. "There's a computer, but no net—all I can get is the phone you're on. There's a window overlooking mountains and a pool of black water, but otherwise it's just stone. I think I'm near LA. So how about it: if I get you through this, will you help me?" Fear in her voice, though she's trying to hide it, because this is her big pitch, and he realizes that if he were inclined to negotiate he'd have a lot of leverage, but he's not some grasping businessman, and he owes her, and moreover it looks like he has nowhere else to go, so he just says, "It's a deal."

"Okay. Good," she says. She'd seemed omniscient at first but now her evident relief makes her seem smaller. "You should wait till they've given up trying to find you, but we'll find you an out-of-the-way place to lie low. So, first things first—let's have a look you." He focuses on his reflection in a plate-glass window, tries not to worry what she'll think of him, but what does it matter, they've reached an agreement. He'd forgotten what he was wearing, but it turns out to be a sleeveless soccer jersey made of light synthetic—it dries fast and doesn't smell after he sweats in it—and cargo pants, loose enough to kick in, once white, now soft and grey. The fresh bloodstains on the knees signify his recent, violent victory, though no one else will get it, they'll probably think he tripped.

"Damn, boy," she says, "work out a little? You look like you live on protein and Zen Buddhism. I guess I might have known. Anyway, you look like a favelino street fighter, which I'm guessing is more or less what you are, but that stands out here, and we have some business in the city, so we're going to need to change your look. How much money have you got?" When he tells her, she says, "Constraint elicits creativity."

She takes him to a street where rain patters on the awnings between the rooftops and there are too many people drinking in little bars and browsing in the stalls. A woman bumps him with her handbag and he knows exactly how he could pivot and shatter her jaw with his elbow but he does nothing and forces himself to wear a blank mask. Even so, the ghost says, "You can relax a little. Look up," and he does, sees the SFPD drone hovering there, thirty feet overhead, its red lights shining through the rain, its props' hum audible.

She takes him to a stall where old clothes are stacked on plastic crates. The proprietor, an elderly black man with bushy dreads, is either staring straight at him or watching TV on his sunglasses—in any case, Kern is careful to give him an unobstructed sight line as he picks through the stock. The ghost finds him a hooded leather jacket, glossy with use, worn through at the elbows, and a black T-shirt with *Desolation Angels* emblazoned in white letters over an out-of-focus white dove, and the words and the image have an eeriness that grips him.

"It was a band," the ghost says. "They were big, in their niche, in the day, which wasn't so long ago. Not your demographic, which can't hurt."

He's aware of a muted ripple of interest in the crowd as he swaps shirts, and wonders if you're not supposed to do that out here.

"Now you look a little more like you belong," she says. "The next things are money and a passport. I'm going to guess that you haven't got one?"

He's heard of passports, knows you need one to travel between states now, and even to get into some cities. He thinks of Lares' brisk trade in server intrusion, stolen credit cards, fraudulent documents. "No, but I know someone who makes them," he says. In any case Lares owes him an explanation for the last job. "But it's expensive." Strange to need a passport, like suddenly needing a necktie or a pram.

She says, "Awesome. So, money first," and though he has many questions he feels that there will be no answers, that the harder he struggles, the less he'll finally know. This is the logic of dreams, he tells himself, not of waking life, but then he's letting her guide him deeper into the city.

15

•

Future Shift

rina tells the cab to drive at random through the city. As it's a drone, there's no one to ask why.

The streets slip by, and the sullied marble facades and the spotlit couture and the sidewalk crowds, whose faces will be with her forever, like a haphazard catalog of the dead-to-be, all the same as every other city, forms repeated without end.

She lies down on the backseat and, as though by magic, the city vanishes, replaced by a narrow view of blank walls and fragments of signs and sun glare on the glass of third-story windows. She thinks of childhood car trips, wishes she could remember them better.

She'd meant to stay another night but decides she'll leave that hour. There are outstanding bids for her time in Tokyo and Stockholm, Maya's said. Tokyo, then—she likes flying west, how it draws out the day. She'll go straight to the airport, have the hotel send her bags.

Her phone chimes. She's expecting Maya but the text is from Philip, her friend, whom she hasn't seen in years. A *little bird told me you're in town today. Thanks for keeping me informed! Dinner? Tonight? Unless you were blowing me off for reasons of real personal significance.*

It's three years since they've spoken but with the one text those three years seem to vanish. *Yes,* she texts back. *Good. Sorry. Distracted? Fundamentally a bad friend? Name a time—I'm available then.* She feels the future shift—no vanishing act, then, at least not yet, and no long suspension in the evening.

Her phone rings and she picks up, thinking it's Philip, but Maya says, "They *loved* you!"

"Oh?" says Irina, staring at the cab's ceiling. "How can you tell?"

"Because they made an offer for an option on your time! For the next week you get your hourly for doing nothing, and double that if they need you to come in. Okay?"

"I'm a little surprised," she says, remembering how it feels to speed-walk through the Prosperity Airways concourse, the sense of freedom, almost of release. "And it's not like I accomplished much." She remembers the hidden AI's immensity, its strangeness, but feels helpless to convey it.

"Well, they loved you anyway, and to prove it I just got a request to push funds to your account. Do you want me to accept?"

The cab lurches to a halt. She pokes her head up, sees a trio of girls in front of the cab, high-school-aged, entirely absorbed in each other, seeming not to see her. "Accept," she hears herself say.

A little pause, and she says, "I'm sorry if I worried you this morning. I'm afraid I must be your most difficult client."

"Most difficult? *Ha,*" says Maya, in full ballsy big-time-player mode. "Do you want to know how I spent *my* morning? I have a new client, you might have heard of her, the Korean kid, Sun Yong Min, the one who can sight-read DNA? I had to chaperone her through a meet-and-greet with the board at Biotechnica. Serious money on the table. Sunny is twenty, looks fourteen, and is emotionally about ten. Sweet kid, always smiling, but her parents are fresh-off-the-boat and don't speak English—Sunny's making beaucoup bucks but her dad is too proud to quit his job as a security guard. So I'm standing there on the steps of their black glass office-tower-of-doom for twenty minutes in the rain and texting her once a minute until finally she shows up in a pedicab, which she took instead of a real cab, she tells me, *to save money.* Moreover, she's wearing sweatpants and a sort of furry hat with cat ears and it's immediately clear to me that she has *absolutely no idea* that any of this could possibly be a problem.

"So we walk into the conference room and the CEO is this handsome son of a bitch, he looks like an executive in a commercial, and when he sees us he *freezes*, because he's an important man and there's a way to do business and blah blah blah, but this girl is amazing, and if they don't exercise her non-compete option then they're pretty much bent over, because I packaged her with my other brightest biotech stars, because I am very clever and use y'all's brilliance like a god-damned bludgeon—and I can see him just dying inside as he absorbs this new reality.

"Bless his little MBA heart, he rose to the occasion, and listened for ten minutes while she rambled on about cartoons. He said he liked her hat, and asked if it was Gamba-chan, which is some *kawaii* fuckin' Japanese licensed character that's big with the tweens, and then he told her about getting his daughter the Gamba-chan video game for Christmas."

"I'm glad you could let that out," says Irina.

"Ha!" says Maya. "I know, right? Look at me, crying on *your* shoulder. *Where's your ten percent?* But the kicker is, after Mr. CEO sent away the elegant little gilt porcelain espresso pots and the lox, very expensive, *not from vats*, and had his big-titted mistress-slash-assistant bring Sunny-chan hot chocolate and a Danish, he takes out a tablet and shows her the genome of a bacterium that Biotechnica's so-called alpha nerds designed to eat industrial waste in polluted waterways. Lots of government contracts there, so many it moved the stock price, but she scrolls through it for five minutes and says they made a mistake, that it's going to die in acidic environments. You know me, I'm a jill-of-all-trades, but Sunny talked for two minutes in her squeaky little-girl voice about the implied chemistry of the thing and I was totally lost.

"So. Was it worth it? Yes, absolutely, and in every sense. But you will notice, my dear, that *you* are highly functional even among the high-functioning. You have more fashion sense than even I do, and to my certain knowledge you have had romantic relationships with *actual human beings*. So in answer to your question, no, you are not, in fact, my most difficult client, girlie, not by a damn sight. Okay?"

She remembers Philip, who has worked with Maya, saying she gets clients by hanging around MIT in low-cut blouses. "I suppose the females are more difficult to manage," Irina says, and is immediately ashamed of her tacit malice.

"Hell yeah!" Maya says. "I love my boys to death but they usually think I'm their mom or their girlfriend and they're often starkly in need of both. I used to have a little preciosity about getting them hookers but my god it makes them easier to work with."

"So for me, you're, what, my pretend best friend and confidante?"

"You *are* in a mood!" Maya says blithely, and then, in a fake bedroom voice, "*Baby, I'm whatever you need me to be.*"

"You are aware that technically we have a *professional* relationship?"

"Too late! But, babe, you know I'd get you a hooker if you wanted one. When's your birthday?"

Irina turns a laugh into a snort. "Thanks."

Sober now, Maya says, "Seriously, what I am for you is your friendly little helper who's always there on the other end of the line. I play the clown when you need it, and cheer you up when I can. I'm also the one who helps you monetize your intelligence, which is prodigious, and, as you well know, a bit more than human, but hard for the uninitiated to appreciate, much less value properly. No one else is as good at talking to AIs, which means no one else really gets how good you are at talking to AIs, unless I buttonhole them and spend fifteen minutes praising you to the skies, which I assure you, my dear, is my god-damn stock in trade."

"Thanks again."

"Come on, what else are you going to do? Live in a garret and write a novel about your hurty little feelings?"

"That doesn't sound so bad. Proust's madeleines have got nothing on me. It's madeleines all the way down." She had tried to write, once. It had been almost eerie, every sentence she wrote eliciting thousands of parallels from everything she'd ever read, as though they were just a continuation of conversations between old books for which her presence was barely welcome, or even necessary.

"I get that! The rush-of-memory thing. Cute. Anyway, stick with me and you'll be in a much better class of garret. And *speaking* of, well, money, it's that Mayo Clinic time of year again. After the Water and Power gig, you should have enough saved up for this year's longevity treatment. You want me to book you?"

"Do you ever suppose we should just grow old gracefully?"

"Totally. We should also get fat, have some brats and watch a lot of TV. Maybe wear sweatpants when we leave the house to go shopping. Add a cat-ear hat and you've really got a look."

"Please book me."

Typing sounds. "Done."

"Always a pleasure, Maya."

"Hang in there, I. Let me know about that hooker. Or hook*ers*. Don't be shy, now."

"Goodbye, Maya," she says, and ends the call.

While she was talking, Philip sent another text—they have a reservation at Fantôme, in SOMA, but not for hours, which makes the afternoon a long stretch of dead time. She could probably go hang around his offices but it would be pitiful to be seen to have nothing to do. Tempting to nap there in the back of the cab, like it's a tiny hotel room, endlessly in motion; she'd run up a bill, but the cost would be minute compared to what she's getting from Water and Power, and compared to the cost of the Mayo would scarcely count as loose change.

She remembers her last visit to the Mayo, now ten months past, the long road to the clinic weaving through the green shadows of the wooded plain. Expensively unobtrusive, the clinic, like a boutique hotel in the prairie style. The staff's fathomless politeness and oddly uniform beauty was chilling, somehow, and she never set eyes on another patron, as they call them, supposes they're paying for discretion as much as longer life (and how they pay, and exponentially more as they get older). But however flocculent the towels, however luminous the marble of the tubs, the fulcrum of the trip is the succession of injections that preface the narcotized haze and the febrile days in bed hallucinating mandalas on the whitewashed walls as the tailored retroviruses knit up her frayed DNA, overwriting all the past year's errors and erosion. When she'd packed her bags with shaky hands a girl of the most vivid youth and vitality took her arm and guided her, still nodding, out into the daylight and down the manicured gravel path to the waiting town car and as she helped Irina maneuver her inert limbs into the air-conditioned dark the girl said, "Go in good health, and we hope to see you next year!" the same thing they said every year, and even in her fog Irina sifted her tone for irony, as the only choices are to come back or to decay, and to miss even a single year is to pass the point of no return.

She remembers the TV blaring in the first class Alitalia lounge in London Heathrow—willowy blond Keri Kendrick, last year's cinema darling, faced an unseen interviewer, pale blue eyes widening with passionate sincerity as she said, "It was a deeply spiritual decision. For me, life is a succession of seasons, and right now it's the season of motherhood. I finally realized that I don't need the Mayo to be happy, and I don't care if my decision is quote-unquote 'terrible and irrevocable.'" Put another way, she could no longer open a movie and her alcoholic husband-slash-manager had squandered most of her wealth. That's me, Irina thinks, the first time I have a bad year, and the cab and its pointless motion start to feel like a prison and a metaphor for the vanity of her life. She thinks of all the flights leaving SFO, and how she's now constrained to linger.

Rain starts pattering on the roof of the cab. She's lost track of where they are but knows the favelas are nearby, as though she can feel their penumbra.

A girl hurries by wearing a man's long dark coat with the sleeves rolled up; it looks like it's expensive, or once was—she probably got it from the ebays or a thrift store. She has a frayed ammo bag for a purse, and there are dark rings under her eyes, though she can't be more than twenty, like she's hungover but too young to mind it, and somehow Irina knows that though the girl lives in the favelas she is not of them, a daughter of the upper middle class out having an adventure, and she thinks of her own youth—still there, perfectly preserved—and of her months in Singapore, her own brief withdrawal from living cities and the world.

The girl disappears into the crowd, and now it's raining harder. "You wouldn't believe it, sweetie," she says, "but I used to be punk," then worries the cab will interpret this as new instructions. She checks the time on her phone, though she knows she has hours, and then, indulgently, lets her months in Singapore rise up in her memory.

At the time, the experience had seemed to be one of singular importance; now she preserves the memory, in all its vastness, out of a careful respect for her past selves. Straining a little, she can hold all that summer in her mind at once, as a sort of porous, four-dimensional solid, she and her friends streaks of color twining among the ponderous hypervolumes of the buildings, the sinuous masses of the changing tides. But this isn't how a person should see the world, she reminds herself, and lets the days of that summer play over her in sequence.

She was twenty and Singapore was drowning. Most of the people had left—garbage ran in the tide race between buildings, and Malay looters plied the waters downtown—and the government did little more than post edicts online demanding Confucian fortitude and virtue. Young people from all over had converged there to roost among the sinking towers, that last summer of the city's viability, and, having no need to work, and no ties to bind her, she'd joined them.

Construction drones were just getting cheap and spavined older models were all over the rooftops. She built herself a room on top of an old glass-and-steel skyscraper, its base flooded, her room and the other itinerants' clustered like swallows' nests. The trip was nominally educational— she was enrolled at the national university—but she rarely went to class and someone told her that most of the teachers had left the city.

Such stores as weren't sunk were empty, but a boy on her rooftop had a boat and would take her to the market ships down from Malaysia; the ships' holds, creaking, rusty and as long as a landing strip, were full of multi-colored piles of gemlike fruit, crates of tinned beef, oranges, milk, the dizzying stench of durian. She and her new friends often made grand plans—snorkeling expeditions, trips to the wreck of the Raffles Hotel—but these ambitions rarely materialized; most days they woke in the afternoon and spent the nights at parties on the lowest unflooded levels—dance music and strobe lights, the sweat of strangers, long-haired boys burning marijuana by the bale, the music's pauses filled with the reverberation of the waves.

It was a beautifully disposable youth. When it was time to go, people would just leave, rarely saying goodbye, their rooms left to the next squatter. One girl sealed over the door to her room, forever preserving the wilted Kerouac paperbacks and empty vodka bottles. Irina left the day she noticed that her tower was listing. A few of the kids spoke of staying forever, of founding families among the waves, of building mansions out of concrete and raising them ever higher as the seas rose—a mistake, she thought, as their interlude, like the city, had a term.

She wonders whether her room is above water, still, or has sunk, become the abode of rays and fishes, and lets the tremendous mass of old data sink once again into the dark.

She's kept equally detailed recollections of old lovers. Someday, if she has children, she will edit these, and leave her descendants this eidetic record of her life, and will they be abashed to know her so completely?

Her afternoon with Water and Power is in the periphery of her awareness, there toward the surface of her memory, and she's about to let it dissolve—she'll retain her memories of their AIs, which is technically a breach of contract, but one she commits all the time, and no one has ever been the wiser—but she finds herself disliking Cromwell and Magda more than seems reasonable, given how often she's worked for worse.

She calls up her ten minutes in Cromwell's office, holding all of it in her mind, sees how when she'd walked into his office, he'd looked up from his laptop and for a tenth of a second he had a strange expression comprised of wonder and fear and superiority, like a man who knew a secret.

It could be anything, is probably nothing, but now she is intent, and sees how quickly he'd closed his laptop, the Cycladic figures on his desk, the grey at the great man's temples, the almost tangible light, and there it is: his laptop had faced away from her but there in the antique affectation of his eyeglasses there's a reflection of its screen, and zooming in she sees a browser window, and though most of the text is too small to read there are many sequences of legible numbers, probably GPS coordinates, and above them all is a single word, MNEMOSYNE.

16

·

Circumference

In the town car on the way back to the hotel Thales feels a lucidity bordering on euphoria and his mind is like a searchlight moving over the surface of the city. A gap between buildings frames a rectangle of the dull lunar gold of the dry mountains and the wildfires' swathes of black ash and he remembers their flight into Los Angeles, how the plane had banked over the golden mountains and then the shock of his first sight of the city, the dull glare of the vast plain of concrete and glass, which seemed to have no limit, its far boundary lost in the enveloping smog, and he'd remembered that someone had said God is a circle whose center is everywhere and whose circumference doesn't exist.

The car shudders over concentric rings of fissured concrete characteristic of an exploded IED—placed by whom, he wonders, and what, here, had they expected political violence to accomplish?—and now there's a row of dying, dessicated palms that must once have been meant to evoke a Polynesian tropicality, though Los Angeles has always been a desert, and never more than now.

It's not at all like Rio, he thinks, because Rio is like . . . what? He tries to remember but can only come up with a handful of images—his school, their home, a beach—though he's lived most of his life there.

Another car follows his on the turn off from the freeway onto the surface streets of Venice Beach, and he realizes that it's been behind him for miles, and in fact is the same model as his own, though filthy, like it hasn't been washed in weeks.

The other car pulls alongside. Seconds pass and nothing happens. Heart racing, he's ready to give the command that would put the car on full alert and elicit its focused aggression, but if this other party were really determined to hurt him they could already have started shooting, and he wants to know if they're really following him, and if so why, so even though it's almost certainly a mistake he lowers his window.

His reflection in the black glass of the other car's window and the hot sunlight on his face but as the road turns the light's angle changes and the other car's window becomes translucent enough for him to see that it's probably a woman, on the other side, and then his car makes the sharp turn onto the shielded ramp leading down into the St. Mark's garage which makes the other car vanish.

17

·

Tunnel

Rain washes in sheets over the cab's windshield as Irina opens a map in her other memory. The map shows the whole world but the Mnemosyne coordinates are all in San Francisco, so apparently it's a local thing. Each coordinate has an extra number, which at first leaves her nonplussed, but then she realizes it's probably altitude, which means that these locations are mostly underground.

The closest one is ten minutes away by foot, and several hundred feet down, which must put it in the BART tunnels. The mystery of the thing is stirring. She must be ever deeper in breach with W&P, but that's what lawyers are for. Strangely happy, she tells the cab to pull over.

She turns on her implant's wireless and finds a site called *Urban Underground*, which is an atlas of the spaces below the cities of the world, cobbled together by generations of urban explorers. There's a list of the city's points of access to the subterranean world, and she feels like Alice on the threshold of Wonderland with all its rigors and absurdity (she's always been told she resembles the photograph of Alice Liddell as a young woman in her garden). The nearest is in a restaurant called Boulevardier, which seems to have been around for centuries, and to offer access to the old infrastructure of the city; in its basement bar is a staircase leading down into the BART tunnels, which should put her at the right depth, and about a quarter of a horizontal mile from her chosen Mnemosyne coordinates. The site says the restaurant staff are used to people slipping in and disappearing.

She opens the door and wind blasts rain into the cab, like it wants to keep her there; she takes a breath, ducks into the wind and runs for an awning.

She draws the gaze of a soldier in power armor in the middle of the street. Helmet retracted, he wears a sodden, dripping camouflage hat, and how does he keep the water from getting inside? The armor is wearing him, she thinks, taking in the roses in his wet, sunburned cheeks; barely old enough to shave, and death in the missiles in the pods on his back. With his head protruding from the massive steel body he looks like a parable of masculine insecurity, a boy trying to present himself as robot and gorilla.

Meeting her eye, he flashes his authority-face, and then, reflexively, looks down at her chest; she's wearing a thin shirt of midnight-blue linen, now rain-damp and clinging. Embarrassed, he turns away and makes a show of waving on cars whose hulls seem to vibrate in the downpour, unaware that she's warmed to him, a little, for the humanity of his gesture; she's reminded of an old boyfriend, how, deep in REM, he'd pull her close, stiffen against her as dawn lit the windows.

The rain lags, a gap in the clouds opening onto white depths, a tower of empty space culminating in a blue disc of sky; the air is sweet, now, redolent of eucalyptus, maybe jasmine; there are private gardens on the city's rooftops, though few know they're there—she remembers spending New Year's Eve in one, leaning on the rail in the glow of Christmas lights looking down at the traffic and the revelers crawling by. She feels thankful for the gardens, and for the rain, wonders if without them the city would always smell like piss and decay.

Boulevardier is lit with dim red light and even this early in the afternoon there are pairs of silhouettes hunched intimately over their drinks and when the maître d' accosts her she murmurs something about meeting friends and brushes past him toward the stairs leading down into the bar.

Even darker, down there, and there's a table full of women convulsed with shrill, manic laughter, a reminder of why she's always preferred the company of men. The red velvet and shadows and extravagant deco chandeliers put her in mind of the Paris Metro. There are black-and-white photographs of what must be seraglios, some abandoned ones with pillars crumbling and others populated by fleshy beauties disporting themselves in the bath, and it's all persuasive enough that she can accept the illusion that this place is about absinthe and decadence and sin and not just a basement with a decorative motif.

As per the directions on *Urban Underground*, she finds a closet next door to the ladies'. Taped to the door is a legal notice disclaiming responsibility for what happens to anyone who chooses to go through. Opening it, she finds a narrow and plainly ancient staircase leading down between water-stained red brick walls, the product of some more ancient building code, or perhaps preceding them. It occurs to her that, not trusting her phone's battery, she should go and find a flashlight, but then, as though her thought had called it into being, she sees a heavy-duty industrial flashlight in shatterproof yellow plastic, hanging from a nail driven into the smirched brick wall.

A few steps down, she hesitates, imagining getting lost, inhaling spores or stumbling on a coven of broken people who can't function in the light, but it's a point of pride, now, to continue, and what else could be as interesting, so she goes on into the dark.

The service corridor is ankle deep with crushed coffee cups, papier-mâchéd newspaper, dead leaves, used condoms—she wonders who would find BART infrastructure romantic. The intermittent fluorescent strip-lighting shows a path of crushed litter and bootprints worn down the center of the corridor. The walls are completely covered with jagged overlapping graffiti scrawls, like a continuum of largely illegible words, or of forms inspired by words, and for a moment she fancies it's a mineralogical property of the concrete that, in this darkness, in the waves of pressure from the passing trains, it exude these vibrant, vaguely calligraphic lines.

There's a grating low on the side of the corridor, opening into darkness. She hears the onrushing rattle of metal, and then the train roars by, almost close enough to touch; yellow strobe flashes of its windows and frozen passengers, and for a moment she feels absurdly exposed, but then the train is gone in a gust of ozone and cold earth.

She comes to a round metal door set in the wall, the graffiti warped to accommodate its shape. On the door is a joyfully grinning death's head, apparently recently painted—she's reluctant to touch it, but does, and finds to her relief that the paint's not wet. Under the layered paint, the maker's name, she assumes, is written in raised capitals. She deciphers them by touch: BRAUMANN MANUFACTURING, SINGAPORE.

She expects the door to be locked, and at first it won't move—that's it, she thinks, my journey over—but then it swings open under the slight pressure from her hand.

Dark, within. She fishes the high beam out of her bag, suddenly reluctant to leave the relative security of the service corridor's light. She imagines some morlock vagrant wandering the tunnels, finding the door, locking her in, leaving her too deep for cell service, far from any help. Taking a breath, she ducks through the door, pulls it almost shut.

The high beam picks out isolated graffitos on the rough walls; they're spaced out, here, and seem to have been made with greater care, as though this was the place for the really serious vandals to follow their muse, hidden from the world and the BART police. How did it feel, she wonders, when that farmer first saw the horses in the cave in Lascaux? The dim tunnel recedes in the distance before her.

As she goes on, the graffiti gets less frequent and more baroque; the avant-garde of urban art in this waste below the world. There's a sort of rebus that might be a manticore made out of indecipherable, almost Arabic calligraphy, the monster's smile idiotic and baleful. She almost misses a tessellation of UFOs on the ceiling. There's the story, written in careful lowercase letters bounded by an intricate knotwork, of a maintenance man taking care of his dying and increasingly senile mother.

When she finds it, she thinks at first that it's a water stain running from floor to ceiling. Homogenous from a distance, on close inspection it's a mat of minutely interlocking blue and green spikes, suffused with vital energy, as though it were about to burst apart. The fugue hits her then— she sees desert, empty highways, shallow seas—and then vanishes as she drops her light.

She sits there, rapt in the image, hugging her knees to her chest, scarcely breathing. The stillness is broken only by the Doppler rush of distant trains. The flux in air pressure looses a fine grit that floats down through her high beam as though she were in an undersea abyss. The fugue comes and goes as the light moves with the tremor of her hand; the graffito is a flawed image, but behind the errors, the limited resolution of narrow-gauge spray cans and epoxy pens, the glyphs are discernible, and it has nothing to do with theorem or proof or the AIs' usual concerns but is something like a story. Her other memory flickers with images of wastelands as she takes in the graffito inch by inch, careful not to touch it. She shines the light up and down the pitch-black tunnel, looking for some context or explanation, but besides a tiny line drawing of stylized abstract clouds there's only the bedrock's lunar surface.

It's the voice of the girl, the one on the road, the one who was the focus of the AI's concern—it has to be. She tries out various translations, still bemused to find it translatable, turning and polishing sentences until she gets it right:

> . . . and the last night, driving through the desert. Empty, there, nothing but the cone of light before me, the dust in the light. Deaf to engine's roar, my velocity such that I felt like I was floating. I was out of money, so I didn't look at the fuel gauge, just floored it, red-lining. No one cares what you do, out there. It was like waking, when I rounded that bend, saw the city open up below me, just like that, with the lights of all its highways, right there, finally real, in all its possibility. At sunset, I'd heard, if the light's just right, you can see the reefs, the old city's outline under the water. The car's windows were open, the air-conditioning having died before my boyfriend stole it, my ex-boyfriend by then, I guess, since I'd left with his car, but it hardly mattered, since I wasn't going back. As the road fell toward the light the air changed, sage and dust giving way to something burned, chemical, notes of salt and maybe ether, and I knew that this would be the smell of home. There was moon enough to reflect palely on the loops of road incising the miles of hillside below me, and it was like gravity and momentum were drawing me in, welcoming me, would carry me the rest of the way, like the city wanted me.
>
> I thought of my mother then, the gin empties like votive offerings around the TV, always tuned to the channel of Loving Christ Victo-

rious, and her week-long stupors, and her hysterical prayers. The dust-occluded, fire-colored skies, out there, the shattered skylights in the endlessly branching terminals that used to be an airport. Making love on the cracked tarmac, in backseats, on the floors of boys' squats, once even in the middle of the street, the broken windows of vacant houses staring blindly.

I steered into the first turn and the emptiness, which had always been there, rose up in me, pressing against my skin, burning where it touched, but there was nothing to go back to, and it was the next thing or nothing at all . . .

•

She emerges from a service corridor into the disinfectant reek of Powell Street Station, joining the damp and dark-coated throng around the escalator, trying to present a semblance of composure. It's raining, outside, and harder than ever—it must be the monsoon.

What, she wonders, is Cromwell's interest in this strangest of artworks, and what, if anything, does it have to do with her? In her preoccupation she almost walks into a cab, one with a driver who gesticulates and abuses her in Arabic as he peels away in a fantail of water.

Dazed, she stops at a window display of Japanese prints, tries to collect herself. Peasants in wide hats bent under their loads, struggling over cold shingle through driving diagonals of rain. A fisherman and his son haul on a taut net, Fuji looming across the water. Hokusai, she thinks; the prints' names and histories, glimpsed once in a book, flashing to the surface, drifting away. There's an erotic print—*shunga*, they're called—showing a samurai grappling with a lady-in-waiting, their kimono fallen open. Another print shows the face of a woman, probably a geisha, white-cheeked and doll-pretty, her black hair precisely coiffed.

A light clicks off inside, the prints disappearing, leaving the reflection of a woman peering in, her hair glinting wetly; behind her the passersby are bent against the wind, the sporadic diagonals of rain. She squints, and the image becomes as abstract as a floating world print. As always, helplessly, she tries to find a loveliness in her own image, and when she does to believe it's unillusory. In Hokusai's time, the season of beauty would be passing, would have passed long since, but now, with the Mayo, there's no telling, for her money will get her time, is the key to the kingdom of life and death. She once met a regenerative surgeon, drunk in the bar of the

Chelsea Hotel, who'd insisted he was an artist, *literally* an artist, volubly scorning the mid-market hacks in the strip-mall plastic surgeries; there's always an elegance, he'd said, in the givens of bone structure, cartilage, the chemistry of skin, one that he, and here his hand had brushed hers, would not let fade.

A flash of dread, sudden and staggering, for no reason she can see. She looks back at the last few seconds, and there it is, in the reflection in the window, the lights of a hovering drone, and then another, and her adrenaline spikes as she sees the wet gleam of their lenses, focusing on her, and they then shot up and away, and now an unmarked van with tinted windows is pulling up beside her.

18

·

Essential Hardness

Vast and sheer, the glass facades of downtown's canyons, reflecting the blue of the evening, enclosing him like a trap.

Kern cringes as drones whip by overhead. Glimpses of men in suits seen through windows, a doorman standing before a gilded multi-story mural of the hills. He has the sense that life is flowing out of the city, leaving it to its essential dull hardness. His reflection in the glass wall of a darkened lobby is a stranger staring back at him. "Relax," says the ghost. "You look like you're waiting to be arrested."

The bank doesn't even have a sign—there's just a hand scanner by an armored white door in an otherwise blank concrete wall.

"Are you sure this is it?" he asks.

"This is it. It's a branch of Crédit Nuage Cantonale de Genève. Very discreet, Nuage. There's never any signage."

"Are you a client?"

"Something like that."

"Well, I'm sure not."

"That's less of a problem than you'd think. For one thing, your new look is consistent with family money—you look like you could be slumming it to piss off your dad. For another, the point of Nuage is it's a numbered-account bank—if you've got the account number and the passcode, which I'll give you, they don't care who you are. So if they don't think you're a rich brat they'll think you're running errands for someone important. Put your hand on the scanner and let's go on in."

"Won't that make me findable?"

"Elsewhere, maybe. Here, no. And there's no other option, unless you want to do hits for pocket change until they catch you, which I'm guessing would take about a day."

The surface of the scanner is cool under his palm. A woman's voice, the accent maybe German, asks for the first eight digits of his account number, which the ghost whispers in his ear.

"I don't see any security," he murmurs, stepping into a wall of cold air, the odor of leather from the glossy black couches, a faint floral perfume. "It's hidden," the ghost says as the door locks behind him, sealing off the evening and its melancholy.

He clenches his fists in his jacket pockets, wonders if the bank people have gone home, or if they made him and he should run for it, but then a tall woman in a pale suit emerges from a corridor and from the way she looks past him it seems she must have other business but she says, "This way please, sir"—sir?—in the same voice as the scanner and leads him into a tiny high-ceilinged room with cinder-block walls and not much light and the air conditioner's roaring is so loud that it's hard to hear her as she leans across the table and with absolute seriousness says, "This room is secure. Do you wish to make a withdrawal?"

19

•

No True Security

rina, at the insistence of her insurer, had attended a two-day class on kidnap prevention. Her teacher, a retired army sergeant, had prosthetic legs and, as he'd told her with a kind of schoolboy relish, a lower intestine that came out of a tissue printer. She remembers the chaw on his breath as he explained how most kidnapers tracked their victims with drones in order to find "the random moment of purest vulnerability," a phrase that had struck her as having a certain poetry, and even as she thinks this she's started running.

Faces whip by, eyeblink flashes of dismay, indifference, surprise, and she weaves around bystanders to occlude the lines of sight and fire, and she's grateful once again for never really having aged. *Keep moving*, the sergeant had said. *Don't be predictable, find a strong point to retreat to*, all of it obvious, none of it useful, and now here she is completely on her own.

As she runs she tells herself there's still time to act, doesn't let herself panic, and obliges herself to think of the city, and what it has that she can use. She could try ducking into a bank or a good hotel, but their doors will be locked and it might be seconds before they buzz her in, and the Marine with whom she had her moment is now too far away. There are drones overhead—she could turn on her wireless, seize a few and use them to run interference or, if they're armed, shoot down her pursuers, though she'd thought her days of intrusions were done.

She corners hard, slipping a little, and sprints down the block, aware of the fear in her wake, how the brighter and more careful people are scattering, and then she sees hard-hatted workmen supervising a segmented drone the size of a van, dodecapodal and safety yellow, its nimble forward appendages pulling fiber-optic cables up through the incisions in the asphalt of the street, all under the eye of a trio of cops. One of them, leaning against a parked car in his green slicker, registers her speed and starts to raise his gun as he scans the street behind her.

Maybe she should find cover but she needs to know what's going to happen so she turns, sees the damp pedestrians, the headlights of the cars going by at a rush-hour crawl—no camera drones, no van, no obvious pursuers. The cop is glaring down his rifle-sights now, aiming back the way she came, panning left to right, right to left, but, finding no targets, he lowers his rifle as he turns to her with a look of inquiry. It looks like no one's coming, and in decency she should talk to him and explain but instead she ducks into a cafe.

Inside, she peers out through the raindrops on the windows at the blurred passersby. The cop across the street stares after her, then loses interest—worse things happen all the time.

Her mouth is dry so she orders a sparkling water though she finds it's difficult to look away from the windows. The barista is friendly but his hair is sculpted into planes and spines that suggest nothing so much as a lion-fish, and she feels old because instead of implying some extraordinarily specific cultural fealty his hair just reads as an elaborate waste of time.

She tells herself it was nothing, just another false alarm. Vans are legal, and camera drones are nothing special, especially this close to the favelas—they're probably searching for illegal construction. She's often seen jackbooted cops hassling refugees with their cheap little construction drones, and pitied them, though she's also seen the claustrophobic Piranesi webwork that Jakarta has become, favela clotting all its parks and alleyways and public spaces—she remembers the masses of concrete filling the rail yards, the shadows and confinement of the narrow tunnels over the tracks, grey dust raining down as the trains roared through.

Find a strong point, the sergeant said. On her phone she searches for hotels with five-star security—the nearest is the Doric, seven blocks away. Finalizing her booking, she wonders how she'll get there—it seems far away, and traffic is almost at a standstill, and she doesn't want to walk on the street.

She startles when her phone rings; the hipster programmer at the next table looks like he's going to ask if she's all right but he sees her face and turns back to his computer.

When she picks up Maya says, "I hope you feel like making money tonight, because Herr Cromwell wants to see you."

"Does he."

"Hey, are you all right? You sound like your puppy died."

"No. Yes. I'm fine," she says, unable to bring her voice to life.

"Why don't you tell Auntie Maya what's wrong."

"The afternoon has gotten strange." She wonders if the line is secure, then wonders about the physics of parabolic microphones, if they work through glass. "It's probably nothing."

"What kind of nothing? Whatever it is, I can probably help. The agency has lawyers, coders, contractors, what have you. I think there's even a masseur now."

"In this context, contractor means mercenary, right? Like a hired soldier?"

"Shit, really? You in bad trouble, hon?" Her voice is almost squeaky, like a pubescent boy's. "Do you need some help right away?"

"I might." She feels like crying but she'd lose her self-respect.

"In Northern California we usually work with Parthenon Associates. They're mostly British ex–special forces," Maya says, and Irina is aware that she's trying not to show how much she wants to ask exactly what the trouble is. "They're very good. Pulled any number of client asses out of fires, and they're *extremely* discreet. Would that help?"

"Yes."

Sound of typing as Maya says, "Soooo . . . You now have an account with Parthenon, and as of two seconds ago they've dispatched a contractor to your current location. Any charges go on your tab with us but as of now you're officially their client, so their obligation is to you, and the agency is out of the loop. I just pushed their contact info to your phone. I might add that they have strong ties of reciprocity, as they say, with the state and city powers-that-be, so they're in a position to clean up their own messes, or for that matter most any mess at all."

"Thanks," Irina says, feeling a little better, though part of her questions the wisdom of bringing in shooters when it's not at all yet clear who, if anyone, needs to be shot.

"So anyway. The reason I called. Cromwell wants to have dinner with you tonight at this restaurant, Maison Dernière. Apparently he has an offer for you and wants to make it in person. And since it's short notice and you'll actually be doing something for Water and Power, even if it's just eating breadsticks and listening to him talk about his many achievements, they're offering quadruple time."

The hourly seems high, almost desperately so, but she's not going to blow off one of her few friends of long standing, so she says, "I have plans tonight."

"Philip, yeah?"

"Yeah."

"Tell him I said I love him to death but if he wants his company to grow he has to stop being such a little priss about using me and my people, and accept the reality of TMP's market power. Actually, maybe you could phrase that in a nicer way? And tell him I said I love his tie, because I think he wears them now. Anyhow: Cromwell's people thought you might be busy, but they say it's urgent, and that he really wants to talk tonight, so he's available when you are, and after dinner is fine. I kind of suspect he doesn't sleep much—hell, I don't sleep much and I'm less than half his age. I know you must be tired, and there's whatever else is going on, but money-money-money, you know? So are you down?"

"Sure," says Irina, though the night seems far away.

"Great. And are you absolutely *sure* you don't want to tell me what's up?"

"I'm fine," she lies, sounding annoyed.

"Okay. Well, great, then. Call me if something comes up. Bye, sweetie. Good luck. You've got my number."

At the table beside her is a boy with a bowl haircut, ethnically Korean, wearing a glossy black sweatsuit, rapt in his laptop, and surreptitiously looking over his shoulder she sees he's playing a first-person shooter, though no guns or adversaries are in evidence, and he seems only to be wandering through a dark mansion, going up and down stairs and stopping before locked doors and passing in and out of shadows, and she wonders what the point is, if whatever nameless evil implied by the endless eerie corridors will reveal itself in the end or if finally the game is about boredom and dread and long, fruitless searching.

She stopped playing video games years ago—they're too easy a way to annul her emotions, and there's no getting away from computers—but now she envies his absorption.

A tall rangy boy in a black hoodie comes into the cafe, head down and hands in pockets. He doesn't look posh enough for the neighborhood, but maybe he has a job here, and she's wondering what's keeping Parthenon when the boy stops in front of her, and her momentary terror dissolves when he lifts his eyes and she sees that he's a man—she'd been fooled by the clothes and the body language—blue-eyed, windburned, smiling down at her.

"Parthenon?" she asks, and feels foolish.

"Yes, ma'am," he says, his voice Scottish, sounding at the same time like he's making a joke and reporting for duty.

"Good. So. Thanks for coming out. I won't need you to come very far with me today."

Out on the street on the way to the Doric he seems not to mind the rain and she isn't sure if they're supposed to make conversation. You know you're truly rich, she thinks, if you're used to dealing with private soldiers.

Finally she says, "So is one of you enough to deal with . . . whatever arises?"

"Probably," he says. "I'm wearing armor, so I'm more durable than I look, and in addition to my sidearm I've got a collapsible long gun under the hoodie, which is more firepower than nonmilitary personnel are really supposed to have. And if I fire a shot, or shots are fired near me, then reinforcements come at a run—armed drones arrive in under one minute, and a squad in five, and if at that point there's still a problem, then, well, the escalation is ridiculous, but Parthenon isn't in the business of losing fights." He's both grave and cheerful, and she wonders how he manages such sangfroid in the face of the violence of his profession.

"You don't present as I expected."

"Well, I could dress like a proper bodyguard, but that would just tell the world you're someone worth robbing. Better if I look like no one in particular. They send us to classes to learn how to do that—the costume helps, but, if you'll forgive my boasting, I can look like a nobody even in an excellent suit." He sighs. "You sign up to be a soldier and end up doing amateur theatricals. It's the story of my life."

Silence, for a while, as he slouches along beside her, for all the world like a sullen teenager, until, peering down at her from under his hood, he says, "I don't mean to pry, but the précis was light on detail. May I ask if we're expecting some particular kind of trouble?"

"Kidnap," she says. "I think there may have been an attempt," and tells him what happened, disguising her fear.

"That's probably manageable," he says. "And it might make you feel a little better to know that, while I'm here, I'll fight to the last for you. There's no true security in this world, but I'll do everything in my power for you, and if things go bad and we're going to die, then I'll stand in front of you and die first." He says this casually, like he's explaining company policy, but his tacit conviction is more of a comfort than she'd have expected and in fact there are tears in her eyes.

The silence is benign now, and she realizes that the tension was in her alone, that he's comfortable being quiet with his principal. "How did you come by this level of commitment?" she asks.

"Parthenon is very selective," he says. "I'm under contract not to reveal the specifics, but early on in the selection process they test your dedication in the most revealing ways. And then, it's a way of dealing with fear. We all have to die sometime, and I've chosen to put aside fear in the name of service. It seems like the only way to live with equanimity."

"You sound like a samurai."

"The job does require dedication, and a level of comfort with the nearness of death, but *actually* being a samurai? My god. With all the repression and the social rules and the obsession with caste it sounds even worse than being English."

Blocks later she has the feeling there's something he's wanted to say for a while and then he says, "Do you know who made the kidnap attempt, or do you think it was just speculators?"

"I have no idea," she says, then thinks of Cromwell, the strangeness around that gig, his latest attentions.

"I don't mean to speak out of turn, but it seems like you might have someone in mind," he says. He seems to look for words, then says, "It's evident that you're a decent person, and you might not believe the viciousness you can find in the world. Even the gentlest people are sometimes obliged to take aggressive steps. I note that we will never have any interest in, or awareness of, your private business, beyond the minimum required to do the job, and that after the job's done we forget everything, forever. I also note that we deal in definitive solutions, the details of which needn't concern you."

It takes her a moment to realize that he's offering to find her persecutors and kill them. "Wouldn't that put you at risk?" she asks.

"It's a dangerous business. But if you mean legal risk, well, that can be finessed, especially if one is careful to respect the structure of things. But we're certainly not going to let a client's interests suffer because of a narrow-minded adherence to the letter of the law." She's surprised to find herself already inclining toward the view that the illegality of killing for hire is a burdensome technicality.

"I honestly don't know what's happening. Even *if* anything's happening. Actually, it doesn't matter—the only person I have in mind is rich, like private-army rich. He's out of my weight class in every way."

"This very rich person. Does he know you suspect him?"

Thinks of the information seized from the reflections in his glasses. "I'd imagine not."

"Well, it *would* be expensive, taking care of that for you, but in these matters initiative is everything. You'd just get the one shot, but that's often enough. Like I said, there's no such thing as true security."

It's heady—discreditably so—to think she has only to give the word and her enemy will be annihilated. (But of course Cromwell might not be her enemy, might in fact just be an exceptionally generous and possibly somewhat smitten client—all she knows for certain is that the coordinates from his laptop led her to the glyphs on the wall of the tunnel underground, and that there might possibly have been a kidnap attempt, though it might have been nothing, and if it was something might not have been him.) She says, "Let me get back to you on that."

Outside the Doric the doorman is dressed like some kind of Renaissance courtier, a monocle in one eye, and he regards them blankly for a moment until, presumably, the monocle's facial recognition software identifies her as a guest, at which the massive glass doors swing open and the doorman ushers her in.

The soldier pushes back his hood; his hair is copper in the foyer's light.

He's rolled up his sleeves and she sees a list of names tattooed on his left forearm, some Anglo, some Indian. It occurs to her to ask him up for, as they say, a drink, and twenty years ago she'd have done it, but now it seems too socially complex and like it might strain his sense of correctness and it's probably a cliché for a girl (a *girl?*) to have a crush on her bodyguard and in any case she wants to have a nap and be alone and maybe read before her dinner at Fantôme.

"I never got your name," she says.

He smiles with his eyes, kisses her hand, walks away.

20

•

Fundamental Things
Never Really Change

Waiting in the rain at the checkpoint into the favelas Kern worries that the soldiers will frisk him and find the money in his pocket—more money than he's ever seen in one place before—but they just wave him through.

Inside, he says, "Lares' place isn't far" to the ghost, though others may think he's talking to himself, another of the favela's mad ones.

Everyone hurries through the rain which gives him an excuse to hurry with them. His tension, which had diminished in the city, has returned; he clenches his fists in the pockets of his jacket.

The favela's old men will shake their heads and fret about the drainage but he's always loved the storms' violence, the smell of wet concrete. The music of the water pouring from the ledges reminds him of the light well off his room, how in the monsoon it becomes a cistern, how he could hear its depth in the sound of rain hitting, a sound he'll never hear again, though he could walk there in ten minutes. He tries to feel the force of that, but nothing comes, until he thinks of Kayla, though he's sworn never to see her again, has made it his practice to keep her from his mind.

A woman comes out of an alleyway, backlit, heavily pregnant, her soaked cotton shorts and tank top displaying her body's metamorphosis. His first thought is that she, too, likes the rain and its cleanliness, but then he sees her staring eyes, her wide rictus grin, how she walks by without seeing him at all.

He wonders how she managed to conceive, with her craziness all but palpable, and imagines a pack of boys running her down, their honor dissolved in the group's euphoria. The image of her swollen breasts under the wet cloth stays with him, and he could do what the boys did, and no one would know, for she must be all alone, and he is afraid, then, for this impulse is someone else's, and purely contemptible, and of course the ghost would know, and even if he is a predator—and he is, must be, and the world peopled only with victims—the noble, he reminds himself, do not prey on the weak. (In any case, she'd smell like cold, and despair, and as he pressed her down her black eyes would be windows onto nothing.)

He stops, can't bring himself to get moving again. He gathers his will and takes a few steps but his will fades, leaving him standing there, staring straight ahead. He thinks of Kayla, how she looked when she was sleeping, how she'd promised she'd always care for him. "Everything all right?" asks the ghost as he turns and heads for Red Cloud Street, where Kayla will be dancing in the Club Lazarus's heat and shadows.

From a distance it looks like firelight flickering on the low cloud, and then Kern turns the corner into the glare of video. Thousands of screens are embedded in the walls, the lowest over the bars' awnings, the highest lost in the rain, their light reflected in the puddles, the windows, the wet hair of passersby, and as he stares up into the screens the world falls away, leaving him floating among abstract planes of shifting light, a dream saccading without intent, but then the images, which have been form purely, resolve into the shapes of the bodies of women. They're beautiful, the women, though their hair and makeup are dated (as are, more subtly, their breasts and musculature), because all the video is from archives of old porn, and he wonders why anyone bothers to make more, since the fundamental things never really change.

A trio of marines jostle past, splashing water on his pants, bringing him back to the roar of the street's arcades, the massage parlors' jangling musics, the rain's drumming. They're out of uniform, but he knows them by their haircuts, their muscular bulk, and an aura that's both lethal and puppyish. One of them calls back to him in a child's Spanish, to apologize, or perhaps to mock him, but is laughing so hard he can barely speak, and Kern sees that they're very drunk. Their training is said to be severe, but whatever they may be in battle, for now they're just foolish, and loud, shouting over each other in the street, and their swagger reminds him to go quietly through the world. They're the ones who die, mostly, in their country's wars, they say, and he looks up again at all the ancient records of the beautiful, locked forever in their endless loops, and all these girls must be dead now, their ranked ghosts shining brightly overhead. He follows the marines into the crowd.

Press and heat of bodies, smells of sweat, fried meat, beer, perfume and always the rain, all familiar, and in aggregate they feel like life itself. "Whatever it is you're doing, it's a terrible idea," the ghost says. "Too many people, cameras, drones. You might as well be holding up a sign. You're going to get your ass killed and I'm going to have to watch. Don't mind me, though—I'll just keep giving good advice while you throw your life away." He ignores her, falls in behind a girl with vinyl boots buttoned to mid-thigh, tattooed serpents twining around her wrists and makeup done in black diagonals; he doesn't know what her look is trying to say, but he suspects that she's an artist, like so many who live on the favela's periphery, and he knows that she's a stripper, though he couldn't say how he knows it, it's just something he learned to recognize when he was with Kayla, and then, as though to confirm his intuition, the girl in the vinyl boots goes through the neon-outlined doors of Club Lazarus, where Kayla probably still works.

A sense of threat puts him on the balls of his feet but it's just the club's bouncer, bald, massively built and frowning down at him; strong, but the type who thinks all the muscle will make him invincible—his face and his legs will be his weak points—and after a tenth of a second Kern is morally certain that his confidence is shallow—hit him once or twice and he'll crumble.

"Stop," says the bouncer, holding out an open palm, trying to say it like a cop would. "If you've got money, let's see it." Kern smiles inwardly. "Otherwise, we're full up." There's a tattoo on his palm, elaborate gothic lettering spelling *Family*.

Then the bouncer's face clears, and, amazed, he says, "I know *you!*

You're a fighter, right? I've seen you fight a dozen times. You move like the mantis, brother—you're *hard core*. I should have recognized a warrior of your stature." It's kind of a joke but he also means it and Kern doesn't know what to say so he says, "What's that on your hands?"

Gentle now, the bouncer shows his palm, saying, "This is my family," and showing the other, equally tattooed palm, "and this is my pride. If I'm going to die I only have to close my hands and I can hold on to both of them." The bouncer realizes something and there's a moment of awkward silence which he tries to cover with a false heartiness, saying, "Oh, that's right, Kayla's your girl, isn't she? Well, she's working tonight, so why don't you go on in."

A grim place during the day, the Lazarus at night is smoke and shadow and a few hot beams of light, and the music pulses through him. It feels a little like a dream, but of course it's meant to—Kayla had explained how it's essentially a machine for getting men to pay for worthless things. Blue light plays over the girl on the stage and as his eyes adjust he sees that the darkened room has more gangsters than usual, and he wonders if the house figures they'll spend whatever they have on booze and girls, and never mind the fighting, or if that's just how things are going now. He stands against the wall, out of the way, sees the waitress take him in, waver, dismiss him. On stage, the dancer, blinded, stares out across the tables and smiles emptily—he remembers that Kayla said they can't see a damned thing, how it's a kind of privacy. In the hard light he can see every hair and mole on her body, which, in its detail, is somehow inhuman, less like flesh than a map, and then the song ends and Kayla totters onto the stage in just her heels.

She looks so thin. The motion of her hips is apparently ecstatic but he knows she's bored and trying not to show it. He's held those hips, seen that face transported, as someone has held all of them, he supposes, and in fact it's nothing special—there were boys before him and there'll have been boys since. In the blue glare she's almost an abstraction, her flesh become spirit like the women on the screens, but then the spotlights narrow and find her tattoos of angels and serpents and houses burning down—she never would explain them, but had said they were a mirror of her life.

He waits in the alley by the staff door. "I'm guessing this is your girlfriend," the ghost says. "Maybe someone you want to say goodbye to. I already told you how dumb this is so be sure she's worth dying for."

He says nothing, hunching his shoulders as the rain runs down his neck. The ghost says, "Not that it's really my business, but I knew a lot of girls like that in LA. Hearts of gold, supposedly, and all saving up for college, but from what I saw they're mostly just wrapped up in their pain. Little honor, less sense, no thought for the future. But I'm sure this one is different."

"So how did you get locked up in a house?" he asks, trying to remember how long Kayla's shifts are. He's relieved that she hasn't moved away—she used to say that the city was claustrophobic, that she'd come there to be free but it was suffocating her, that if she could ever get the money together she'd go north, maybe learn to breathe again. This had worried him, when they were together, until he'd realized that she quickly spent whatever she got, managing somehow to be even poorer than he was.

"It's a long story," she says, and then falls silent, so he says, "Okay, what were you doing in LA in the first place?"

"Starving, mostly. Trying to get a career worth advancing. Not a good time, though in retrospect I had a certain freedom. I stayed away from the drugs, but I hardly remember it at all."

"Tell me," he says, so she won't ask him questions.

"I didn't know a soul when I got there. I slept in my car the first month and washed up in the showers at the beach. I knew girls who had gone there before me but after a few emails they always vanished, even though I spent hours looking for them on the web. I met a lot of girls who'd gone there to be actresses but most were just pretty, with no skills at all, and they mostly ended up doing sex work, or worse—the violence was just getting bad, then, and people hadn't gotten cautious. The ones who weren't awful mostly had some kind of conservatory training, which I sure didn't, but it didn't matter, because I'd always had a talent for being someone else. When I had nowhere to go, which was most days, I'd go where people were, the bars and promenades and the lobbies of hotels, and sit there nursing a vodka, watching people, letting them bleed into me.

"It was just a trick of being open, like leaving a blank space inside me for their essences to fill. And once I had them I could impersonate them, in fact I almost had to, like what I'd seen had to work itself out. I tried to fool people, being someone I wasn't, even when I didn't look the part at all, and it almost always worked, because people would find a reason to let it work. They said it was spooky, like watching a shape-shifter. It wasn't a good time. The only thing that made me happy was being someone else."

"Did you get anywhere?"

"No. At least not at first. It was maddening. Part of it's the place. At night you can see the lights in the big houses in the hills, and the life you want is right there, but might as well be in another country, and the people who have what you want are staring down from all the billboards. You keep trying, chasing down auditions in dismal industrial parks on the fringes of the city, and promises are made but every opening is illusory and their words have no substance. I got an agent, for a while, but he couldn't do anything for me, or for anyone, in fact he was barely an agent at all, was trying to break in as hard as I was. His stock in trade was the impression of reality. There are real agents, but they don't take calls or email from outsiders, and I'd never met one, or even met anyone who had, and it started to seem like they were just part of the mythology. It was like two cities, one within the other, and no bridge between them, but then I started to get little parts—third-tier Danish phone games and unfunded pilots for direct-to-web series—and I realized that in fact the cities are concentric, and innumerable, and as you advance inward from the periphery you get no closer to the core, and as hard as you try you always end up back in the bars, pretending to look at your phone while the essences accumulate."

"Do you have my essence?"

"Maybe," she says, almost laughing.

"So who am I?"

"Well now. I hardly like to say. But you move, as our large friend would say, like a mantis, or as I would say like a dancer, though that's not a comparison you'd like. You're part scholar, in your way, and part wild animal. I get the sense that you spend a lot of time alone."

"If you know me so well, then what am I going to do?"

"What you need to, I'm guessing, though with every second we wait here there's a better chance I'll have a close-up view of your blood pooling on the pavement, so maybe you could find a way to hurry up."

When Kayla comes out of the door she's wearing a man's coat cinched tight. She's still in her makeup, so thick she looks like an actor in those Japanese plays.

He's afraid she'll be unkind but when she sees him she embraces him, an embrace he holds a beat too long, but as she pulls away she gives him a kiss on the cheek. "You look great. Are you waiting for me? You're waiting for me, aren't you. It's sweet of you but you can't do this, okay?" she says in her little girl's voice, and he breathes in her sweat, the stale cigarette smoke; her pupils are pinpricks in the alley's little light.

"I don't mind," he says, wet with rain, suppressing his shivering. "How about I walk you home."

"You should have called." He didn't because she never picks up, but doesn't say so.

"They were asking about you," she says, suddenly full of wonder; her teeth are straight and white, a reminder that she was rich once, or at least her family was. "Like gangsters, but with real money. They were asking if I knew where you were, said they'd pay anyone who could tell them, and now here you are. Are you in some kind of trouble?"

"I'm in bad trouble," he says, talking too fast. "I've got to go away and I might not be coming back. I'm going to get a passport and I might not ever get to see you again, and I think I killed someone but I had to." He stops when he sees her realize something and in a hopeless, inward voice she says, "But I guess they'd probably have caught you anyway."

"What?"

"But you're strong, aren't you," she says. "I've seen you knock out guys twice your size. You can take care of yourself."

He takes her limp hand, but she snatches it away, saying, "I can't do this," and then she's striding away, which amazes him, because he'd thought that he'd somehow find the right thing to say, and it's hard not to follow her, but he's determined to keep his dignity, such as it is, a goal to cling to as his despair rises, and he's wondering if there'll be fighting on the rooftops tonight when she stops and turns back to him—humiliatingly, his heart rises—and calls, "Get out of here! You're not safe. Don't trust anyone—not *anyone*, okay? Would you *please* just run?" and then she's gone into the crowd.

"This Lares who makes the passports," the ghost says.

"Yeah," says Kern, glad that at least she'd cared a little.

"Where does he live?"

"Deep. The old levels."

"Easy to find?"

"Almost impossible, if you don't know the way."

"Ever take your little friend there?"

"Once, to show her his game."

"I don't suppose you'd be willing to run her down and choke her ass out?"

"*What?*"

"Kidding! Now let's go see Lares. You'd better run."

21

·

Someone

Thales sits sweating in the hot sun on the patio over the hotel's private beach and even behind his sunglasses the day is too bright. A container ship floats on the horizon among masses of clouds that could be mistaken for cities and closer to shore one of his brothers whoops from within the luminous green cavern of a cresting wave, which then collapses, burying him in foam, his surfboard shooting out to jag and bob on the water. The fences separating the hotel's beach from the public one are topped with concertina wire, and even at this distance he can see the starving dogs roaming the sand speckled with filth and the vagrants huddled under ragged sheets of white plastic against the sun, and he reflects that if his family still had their money they'd be in a hotel good enough that this poverty would be invisible.

The tables are packed claustrophobically close and he turns in annoyance when a waiter bumps his shoulder which is when he sees the woman coming onto the patio from the hotel. She looks worried as she scans the tables, like she's painfully late to meet someone, and then he realizes that the assurance of her bearing has distracted him from her ragged hair, her deep sunburn, the clothes she might have been sleeping in for days, and then he sees her gaze settle on him.

She starts pushing toward him through the press of tables and he half stands, wondering if he should retreat, but she's already standing over him and about to speak but catches herself, looks amazed, says, "I know you. You're the Brazilian prime minister's son," and with that everything is changed because he's never seen her before in his life and what safety he has depends on his anonymity but she seems surprised more than hostile and he's worried that the people around them will have overheard but they're eating oysters, swilling prosecco, chattering away. Over her shoulder he sees two paunchy hotel guards coming at a trot, their uniforms of a noticeably better cut than the local cops', and now they're picking their way among the tables.

"We need to talk," she says, sounding urgent, almost desperate. "I followed you from the clinic. Our interests overlap."

"How's that?" he says, wondering how she knew him and how he can get her to tell him and already convinced he's missing some crucial piece of context.

"We're both victims," she says, and he can tell it makes her angry but even so she delivers the line so precisely that he has a sense of her interior chill, and he notices that under the grime she's about his mother's age, or rather agelessness, though somehow unmaternal—she's someone, not someone's mom—so she must have had money, once, and a lot of it, and wonders what violence, addiction or bad luck brought her to this pass. "Was your family killed too?" he asks.

Her face becomes still for a moment and then she says, "I don't know. I don't think so, but it's possible. That's the thing. I can't *remember* anything. There was a drowning city and a friend I lost, and I don't think I was ever really loved, and I don't know how I got to Los Angeles."

He notices the scar on her forehead and guesses that she, too, has the implant, which means she could be suffering from the dementia of her implant's decay, which could be a foretaste of his own future.

As the guards arrive and ask her if she's a guest in a way that makes it clear they know she's not he takes money from his pocket and proffers it, saying, "Here—good luck," but as the guards lift her to her feet her composure cracks for the first time and she swats the bills out of his hand and cries, "You're not listening to me!"

He's weighing the risk of letting her stay against the chance he could get her to tell him how she knew he had the implant but it's a nondecision because with the guards events have already acquired a momentum and the most he can offer her is a moment of respect before she's trundled away so he meets her eyes and says, "I'm listening."

"How much do you remember?" she asks though it's more like a challenge than a question, and then the guards have taken her by the elbows and are leading her away, the other guests barely seeming to register her passage.

Half an hour later he's still staring blankly at the sea. He can recall a few scenes from Brazil—the house in the forest, beating his irascible uncle at chess on his tenth birthday, the airtight security around the house in Leblon—but there's nothing else from his life before Los Angeles.

22
.

Shapes Purely

Gradations of white and shadow and masses of vapor comprise forms without names as Irina's dream iterates through her memories of clouds. The cirrus layer seen from the window of a plane over the Midwestern desert becomes the fog over Keflavík airport and now the thunderheads looming over the sweltering Singapore rooftops, and she struggles to articulate their textures and complexity, but vainly, for beyond the crude jargon of meteorology there are no words. In her frustration she remembers the clouds drawn on the wall of the glyphs down in the tunnel, which, she realizes, have a secret form, or not so secret, because they're just letters, however stylized, spelling "LEdERER," like a signature.

She sits up in bed, still seeing the tunnel, not knowing where she is, but there's the pattering of rain on the windows, water sluicing through gutters, the muted rush of traffic, and as she situates herself in the Doric she realizes that hotels have a smell, wool and furniture polish and faint burning dust. The blinds are closed so she turns on the lamp and across from her in the mirror is a bleary woman with damp, disordered hair, naked to the waist amid a tangled mass of blankets, her abs well-defined thanks to a tweaked metabolism, which is surely *someone's* idea of pornography, and for a moment she wishes she knew whose, and how to find him.

Her bag is out of reach but the room's remote is on the bedside table so she turns on the TV, making the hotel room a cave full of light. She finds a search engine on the TV and queries on "Lederer graffiti," and her intuition must have been right because the first result is from a site called ExArt, which bills itself as the comprehensive resource for guerrilla and street art, and the snippet reads, "Lederer, or LEdERER, is the *nom de guerre* of a West Coast graffiti artist (real name undisclosed) known for the manic detail of his images and for his alleged non-neurotypicality."

The second result is a documentary that opens with a shot of a man, presumably Lederer, Hispanic, perhaps forty, sitting with his back to a graffiti-covered wall. He seems oblivious to the presence of the camera, staring into space so intently that at first she thinks he's drunk, then that he's meditating. The graffiti behind him is a riot of intertwining botanical forms, denser than any actual forest. He looks rough, less artist than thug, and clouds must be his thing because there's a stylized thunderhead tattooed on his shoulder.

He says, "One morning and I was sitting by the window watching the traffic go by and everything just . . . it was like the meaning drained away right before my eyes. All that was left were shapes, shapes purely. I was afraid at first, but then I was just *interested*, because it was like I was seeing for the first time, like this was what had always been there.

"I was married, then, and we had a new baby. We had a condo on a gated street in Dogpatch and a share in a car. Maybe it was a choice—my ex insisted it was—but if it was I'd already made it. She found me sitting there, just looking at the street, and tried to talk to me, and then she got scared and called an ambulance. It was only when the paramedic was shining a light into my eyes and enunciating that I'd probably had a stroke that I was able to tell them I was fine, and to go away."

Smash cut to a still image of a smiling woman with dark hair holding a baby—it could be a portrait of a young mother from any era since the invention of the camera.

Lederer says, "She wanted me to see a neurologist, said I could die. Later she said that I was no kind of a man if I just abandoned them, and she was right, about that and about everything, but it didn't matter, because I was already gone. My life *had* been my family, but after the stroke, or whatever, my road-to-Damascus moment, I was only interested in what I saw, and in drawing.

"I don't remember if I actually quit my job or just stopped showing up. I do remember that when I was still at home I drew over every inch of the bedroom walls while my wife was at work. I heard she had it painted over, later, because she was angry, which is a shame because now I guess it'd be worth something.

"I'd been a tagger when I was a kid but I stopped in high school when I got serious about life. My tag was 1DEATH, one word, all caps. Sometime after I bailed I sat in an empty room writing 1DEATH in a drawing pad, over and over, but changing and rearranging letters, until it morphed into LEdERER"—he draws the letters in the air, and, in the film, his finger leaves a glowing trail—"and that felt right."

She turns on closed captioning and fast forwards. Doctors debate at speed whether he suffered a genuine vascular event, or just wanted an excuse to abandon his family and maybe an angle for marketing his art. Comparisons to Gauguin, Lucian Freud, Wei Tao, Abraxas. The manic enthusiasm of the critic who brought him to the art world's notice. Lederer working in the waste spaces of San Francisco, his murals reminding her of the art of autistic savants, though less purely mimetic—they're composed largely of faces, vegetation, the elements of buildings, and never a glyph in sight. In the film's final scene Lederer is starting a new mural on a blank wall while complex cello music plays and subtitles announce that he hasn't seen his ex-wife or daughter in seven years, then lists his recent sale prices from the galleries representing him in Vancouver, Manhattan and San Francisco.

She opens the site of the Vancouver gallery and scrolls through Lederer's paintings until she comes to his photographic prints, which surprises her, as photography doesn't really seem like his medium. The first shows a city seen from the deck of a boat, maybe LA, but it's hard to be sure since only the center of the image is in focus. The next shows the chaises longues on the pool deck of a washed-out white hotel that's probably the newly renovated Chateau Marmont, and the next a pretty eurasian girl in panties and a T-shirt looking at the camera and putting on her lipstick as though in a mirror, and then Irina realizes that she can see flyspeck and tarnish, so there was a mirror, and she's wondering about micro-cameras when it dawns on her that the girl is the camera, that this is a recording of her visual percept, that only the centers of the images are in high resolution because that's how vision works, though it's an easy thing to miss. She wonders if the girl has an implant—it's hard to get that much detail uninvasively, at least outside a lab.

The next photo shows gleaming multicolored spheres laid out geometrically in bins—it's fruit in the hold of a ship, and she responds viscerally, recognizing the heat, the stench of the durian, the nausea of the roll, that the ship is down from Malaysia to work Singapore's waters, because this is an image from her memory.

She checks all the details, checks them again—there's no question but that it's hers. It's not possible—her implant is secure to the point of eccentricity—but there it is. Shivering, she remembers how young she was, how she'd only been in Singapore a week, had felt the world was opening.

She sits straight up in bed, clutching the duvet. Maybe it's a hardware error. She runs the implant's diagnostic program—wafts of cinnamon, leather, vodka, ash, flickers of the canariest of yellows, fathomless crystal blue, absolute black, then a sequence of pure tones without context—but all the tests are nominal.

Unbelievable that there was a breach, but that it happened seems to be certain. There are, she realizes, practical issues—the security of her bank accounts and clients' data, the irrefutable evidence of her sporadic contempt for the law and frequent breaches of contract—but for now she can only focus on the profundity of the violation and the fact that the inmost structures of her being have been dispersed out into the world.

Something cracks in her and she throws the remote at the TV as hard as she can, really putting her shoulder into it, but it bounces off harmlessly so she turns on her wireless and blasts through the TV's security and overloads its power supply which starts sparking like a firework; it's a childish gesture, she thinks, as the flash of rage fades, but at least the hotel probably won't know it was her, and now the abstract geometrics spasming across the TV screen are settling into a deep crystalline blue, the same as the color from her implant's diagnostics, which somehow seems natural, as though her history pervaded everything, and the world were the palace of her memory.

23

•

Finish Up

Lares' room was about three hundred feet below the surface, which meant it had been there about five years.

Dark, down in the tunnels, and always cool, no matter how hot it is outside, something about the physics. Kern counts the turns, scrambles down decrepit ladders by phone light—there are no markers, as the people who live here know the way and want their privacy. He refuses to think of the time he found a body here by touch. It's important not to make a mistake, as Lares has a thing for booby traps, the more complex, the better. The street sounds are distant. It's a kind of peace.

The lightless narrow corridors all look the same, but when he thinks he's at the right place he says, "It's me, man. Open up," into the dark. Waits. Lares' disembodied, staticky voice: "Come on down. I unlocked the door."

How many times has he come here with whatever wallet, watch or phone Lares had assigned him to fetch. Sometimes it was second-story work, but more often it was just a mugging, which he always found exhilarating, which was troubling, because it seemed more like a bully's feeling than his. There was a time when he came by to ask Lares about his more difficult reading—the books on Zen, especially, often made no sense—for Lares had read everything, and liked to hold forth; they've never been friends, exactly, but Lares seemed to accept him, as he did almost no one else, perhaps seeing in Kern's single-mindedness a mirror of his own. Lately, though, Lares has been getting more remote, as though slipping ever farther out of humanity's orbit, and Kern reminds himself not to presume.

Five turns later he's in Lares' room, dark but for the light of all the monitors. From a corner comes the tapping of keys; eyes adjusting, he sees Lares there, engrossed in his laptop, at work on his game, like always, his eyes reflecting the code scrolling by.

The monitors are salvage, as is the bare, stained mattress, gleaming blue in the dull glow, but the laptop, Lares told him, was designed by an AI, and cost a fortune; the keyboard, which looks like the flattened vertebra of some gigantic Pleistocene mammal, lets you code for days without hurting your wrists. The air is stale; he tries not to show that he's breathing through his mouth.

On the screens are empty caverns, unsettled water glittering in torchlight, an abandoned forge with scattered tools, and, there, motion, and it's what has to be a vampire with his eyes like slits of fire, his deeply stained lips and his air of tragic, labored dignity; the vampire steps out of the shadows, scans his crypt wearily, goes to a window to stare out at the sky.

Lares tears his eyes from the monitors to stare at Kern, envoy from a world that doesn't interest him. About twenty-five, Lares, already balding, getting fat, in need of a shave. What Kern can see of the floor is covered with drifts of sour clothes, burrito wrappers, random computer hardware. There'd been this little punk-rock girl named Gabriela who said she couldn't afford boundaries who Lares used to pay to clean up and to blow him once in a while, but she'd disappeared years ago, and now Lares seems to have gone beyond the need for cleanliness or women. In the screens' faint glow, in which the squalor is barely visible, there is a calm, almost a romance, as though time were in abeyance in the dark room, while in the game, behind the screens, it passes.

The vampire stretches hugely, and there's something inhuman in the dimensions of his shoulders. Boredom, irritation, suppressed rage pass over his features, and then he's stalking down a corridor, the camera following as he flexes and clenches his cruelly taloned hands. "I like the way he

moves," Kern says. "It's better than last time. Like he's looking for someone to hurt. It's as good as a movie."

"Funny you should say that," says Lares, with something like tenderness, his voice rusty with disuse, watching his creation's rage blooming.
"I've been working on him for years, but body kinematics are hard. But
Sony developed an emotional-movement library and, given their really
incredible level of investment in it, their security was unimpressive."

"Tell him you lost the phone," the ghost whispers in his ear.

"So the last job was a problem," Kern says, and gives him an edited
version of the truth.

"Are you sure the phone's gone?" Lares asks, weirdly pale in the screen
light.

"Absolutely," Kern says. "I chucked it by the Folsom checkpoint. It's
gone for good. No telling who found it."

Lares slumps deeper into his chair. Kern says, "So what was it, anyway?
Why all the fuss?"

"Something special," Lares says, far away. "I needed it for the game.
But it doesn't matter."

"Who did we steal it from?"

"Depends on your point of view. Some graffiti kid, proximally, but he
got it from other thieves who are friends of his—they didn't know what
they had, but they thought he'd like the images. I knew about it because of
these contractors who were going to steal it first. Dumb-asses," he says
tonelessly. "If they were really such bad news they'd know more about
encryption."

"Contractors?"

"Ex-cartel. Migrating north along with everything else. Bringing their
special skill set to the unique challenges of today's global business environ-
ment. Basically, they're campesino shooters trying to build a brand on their
violent surrealism."

"The passport," says the ghost.

"I need to get out of town. Can you get me a passport?"

"How soon?"

"Now."

"Expensive."

Kern takes a sheaf of bills from his pocket, holds it to the light to show
denomination.

"Paraguayan," Lares says, showing him the document, a little blue book with a golden seal, still warm from the printer he'd exhumed from under the laundry. "Still technically a country. Kind of a historical survival. They don't use digital records, so there's no good way to check it out. It'll get you on a plane, but don't try to bring any contraband, not with this passport."

"Contraband means drugs," the ghost says. "Weapons, anything illegal."

Lares' laptop starts pinging. He looks at it. "Movement sensors. It's probably just someone lost. Or a drunk. Drunks. A lot of drunks. No, most are too small. Oh shit."

A little bug drone skitters in through the door, stops, seems to be looking at them. It goes click, click, click, which is its sonar, like a bat.

Kern rises, trying to think of a plan, but a courteous voice says, "Please stay where you are," in Juarez-inflected Spanish.

A stranger comes in. He looks like anyone. Like a construction worker trying to dress respectably, like maybe later he's going off to church. An air of competence about him. He holds a gun, not the hand cannons the gangsters favor but a little silver one.

"You have some of our property," he says gravely.

The room is cramped and the man is six feet away but it might as well be miles and though it's better to die fighting Kern can't bring himself to make a move. Strange to have lost everything in the space of a moment. He slumps, tries to look defeated, awaits a chance.

"It's lost," says Lares, putting his keyboard aside, giving the man his full attention. His concentration is intense, his eyes bright. "So there's nothing for you here."

"Are you certain?" asks the man.

Lares nods gravely. "Sit down," he says to Kern. "Don't make our guest nervous," and his earnestness is such that Kern sweeps what's probably underwear off a stack of cardboard boxes and sits.

"You don't have to sit up so straight," Lares says to him. "You're not in church."

"You both have to come with me," the man says.

"But you're going to kill us if we do, aren't you?" asks Lares, somehow like a schoolboy. "And if we don't you'll kill us anyway."

The man regards him.

"I just want to know," says Lares, as though clarifying this point is of the utmost importance. "I need to know where we stand."

The man's gun is trained on Lares' heart. He's almost smiling. Kern regrets sitting—the bullet would be better—a flash and it's done. The ghost says nothing.

"I have to cuff you," says the man.

"Of course," says Lares, offering his wrists gamely, but he looks grey, seems to be sweating, is struggling to keep his voice steady. "An excellent idea. You know, there's something I've always meant to say at a time like this." He giggles hoarsely.

The man ignores him, fishing plastic cuffs out of his pocket.

"Look at me," says Lares.

The man does.

Like an actor enunciating, Lares says, "And then without warning we came to the end."

There's a deep throbbing hum from the wall behind Kern and his hair stands on end and it's suddenly very hot, so hot he's sweating, and he smells smoke and burned meat, and there's a glugging sound that makes him remember a two-gallon jug of water, its cap off, knocked over in the desert, the water blackening the sand.

"Watch what you're kneeling in," says Lares because Kern is kneeling by the man who has laid himself out on the floor, and a pool of blood, black in the half-light, is spreading, and it's already too late for his shoes. At first he thinks the man is cut, then sees he's in two pieces, bisected cleanly just under his collarbones, the flesh at the partition burned ruby, the ruby still spreading. "I thought it would cauterize instantly," Lares is saying, "and be clean, but there are the arteries. Of course there are the arteries. They're just tubes. There's nothing there to cauterize."

"Talk to him," says the ghost.

"What?"

"It takes twenty seconds for the brain to finish up."

Kern puts his hand on the man's cheek. "Don't worry," he says. "It's okay. You're going to die, but it's okay. Everything's over now."

The man's eyes seem to track him. Slight twitching of the lips. Then his eyes fix on nothing, and his pupils get wide, wider, are windows onto night.

The ghost says, "I'll have his death with me forever."

"I didn't think it would really work," Lares babbles. "I mean, it works in the movies but in real life anything this complicated fails catastrophically in the moment of truth, but it did work, and now *he's* dead and *we're* going to live. They were decommissioning a car factory in Yokohama and I found the auction for the laser they used to cut the engine blocks. Customs labeled it 'industrial robotics, miscellaneous.'" Kern looks up, sees a slit burned into the far wall, still smoking, the concrete glowing, dark space behind it—there's a much wider burn line at shoulder level opposite— involuntarily, he hunkers down.

"Voice-activated," Lares says. "A key phrase. I thought it was clever. I've wanted to say it for years. Sometimes I had to shout it into my pillow. And when his gun is in my face it finally occurs to me that it might not recognize my voice under stress."

Kern realizes he still has the passport in his hand. Lares is looking at him oddly. "Are you wearing an earpiece?" he asks.

"I found it," Kern says.

Lares stares at him, shrugs, grabs a bag.

"What about your stuff?" Kern asks.

"Fuck it!" Lares says cheerfully, shoving his laptop into the bag, grabbing his wallet and phone, heading for the door. "It's time to leave. There are a lot of places to hide, and I can work on the game from anywhere. You coming?"

Kern rises, feeling something is still owed the dead man, unsure what. One of the screens flickers, now shows a sword submerged in a shallow pool, the blade pitted and rusting, and he remembers asking Lares how you play the game, how he'd said it wasn't something you play, it was more like it was art, a "closed semantic universe," which he'd never really understood, but as far as he could tell it meant that it was made of intertwining stories, accumulating endlessly, like dust in an old room, and the sword would have its place in the order of things. At the time Kern had thought it pointless, though he'd respected Lares' clarity of vision, but now he sees the appeal of a world small enough to understand.

Lares stops in the doorway, says, "They'll be watching the main exit. Do you know the tunnels well enough to find another way out?"

"Yeah."

"Then do it. The next one is coming in I'm guessing two minutes."

24

·

Stillness in Memory

rina is in one of the Doric's armored cars, stuck in traffic on her way to
Fantôme. Picking at the armrest, she once again checks her implant's logs
and once again finds it unbreached, as she knew she would, for in fact it's
unbreachable, its defenses exaggerated beyond all necessity. It's like a locked-
room mystery—no one breached her implant, and she's never transferred
data off of it, and yet her memories have found their way out into the world.

She remembers Cromwell's somewhat exaggerated interest, and it occurs to her to blame him, and it seems like he must be in some way involved, but there isn't enough evidence to convict. Also, if he'd been so
keen on getting his hands on her memories, why bother having her talk to
his AI? She must be missing information.

She looks up Lederer's Vancouver gallery on her phone. It's just months
old, owned by a pretty couple in their mid-thirties, and a quick search on
their names brings up the sale of their tech company and the consequent
access of wealth and their many subsequent seed-stage investments and a
stalled attempt to produce independent films and their practiced smiles
shining from the society blogs and in other blogs they're nearly naked on

the coarse grey beaches of Franz Josef Land for that huge annual week-long rave where they burn the wicker giant and there's a pervasive sense that they're searching quite desperately for the next source of meaning in their lives. She could imagine them locking on to the idea of recorded memory as art, if only for its novelty, but they don't seem so substantial, and she doubts they'd have the nerve to face the inevitable counterattack.

There's a lingering sense of their emptiness, and of their need to find some new way to connect, and then she says, "Oh!" for all at once she knows what happened, or in any case the channel by which her memories escaped her control. She clenches her fists but there's nothing to be done, at least not for now, so she lets herself remember.

The clinic on the Malibu cliffs had walls of thick green glass. Sea fog hung in the air, diffusing the light. Looking down from the cliff edge, the surf's violence was incredible, white water roaring over huge prisms of stone, the colossal wreckage of some recent collapse. Behind her, crablike drones with bodies of scoured copper moved cautiously through the brown grass, pausing only to disinter the roots of non-native plants. She'd heard that they were dumping these drones in the foothills, there to wander—robust and solar-powered, they would, over the decades, shift the ecology back toward how it was.

"If you're ready, Ms. Sunden," said the doctor in the lobby.

"Aren't you afraid the cliff will collapse," she said, "and drop you into the sea?"

"That's an inevitability, ma'am. But it's suitable, don't you think? A constant reminder of our fragility, here, of all places? In any case, the geologists tell us that the rock will last for at least a hundred years. Everything has its time."

She had come to help Constantin die.

Constantin's father had built the dikes around Athens and, as far as she could tell, most of the rest of modern Greece. Handsome, affable, dissolute Constantin; he'd studied law half-heartedly, and then, in his early twenties, found his true vocation in high alpine skiing, and, later, BASE jumping. One August evening he'd put on a jet-black nylon wingsuit, surplus from German special forces, and launched himself from a Swiss mountainside into the fading air over a narrow valley in the Jura; he remembered the silence, he said, how his shadow had flirted with him, hovering close or far as the terrain rose and fell, but he didn't remember hitting the updraft—later, he would learn that it was the exhalation from one of the hidden caverns where the Swiss cloistered their attack planes—or the fall, or the long tumble over the granite boulders, the dense grasses, the tiny reticulated streams.

They'd put a chip in his arm, when he was a child, that scanned his vital signs once a second. Noting their collapse, the chip sent an alert, annotated with his GPS and the elapsed time since cardiac arrest, first to the family office, then to the Swiss montane police.

Four hours later he was in an acute trauma clinic in Bern. The doctors, despairing of the damage to his skull, formally notified his father of their decision to end life support. His father wrecked his office in his newly renovated Provençal villa, then sought advice. His wealth opened doors, dissolved obstacles, and soon his attorneys were ordering the Swiss doctors to stabilize their patient pending his transfer to the care of the surgeons of Ars Memoria, LLC, already en route from Seattle. Twenty-six hours later Constantin opened his eyes, the twenty-fourth recipient of the Memoria implant, the fourteenth to wake from anesthesia.

"I have a request. Something intimate," he said, eleven years later, as she sat by his bed, the glass walls darkening against the Malibu sun as it slipped toward the hemisphere of sea. He looked spent, in his web of tubes of blood and worse, as though he'd died weeks ago and was in the process of being embalmed. He'd taken drugs, he'd said, to stay lucid a little longer, so he could wait for her.

"Name it," she said, squeezing his hand, afraid it was sex, and would that even work, now, but the door had a lock, and there were worse things.

"I don't want to be alone, when it happens, and it's happening soon."

"I'm here," she said, knowing it for a slight thing, but all she had to offer.

"Will you open your memory to me?"

First she did nothing, thinking of her other memory, that bright and inviolate core of self, but in his need he was like a child afraid of the dark (but rightly afraid, she thought, for the great night is about to swallow you whole, and there is nothing more to be done about it), so she turned on her implant's wireless. Every device in the room became a beacon. His implant was trying to connect, once a second, every second, and as she accepted the connection the world became informed by crippling weariness and stark fear of the imminence of the end and the pale, worried woman at his bedside clutching his withered hand and beginning to cry.

"I'm sorry," he said, voice doubled. He studied his face through her eyes, the image echoing between them, and then she watched as words coalesced—language like foam forming on black seas of thought—and he said, "You know, I envy you your health."

He thought of the first time he'd emailed her from the sanitarium in Berne. *Who else,* he'd written, *could possibly understand???* Seven months later she'd been in Denver to see a client while he was there skiing; he'd felt awkward, approaching her in the hotel bar, knowing that everything he said would stay with her forever. "I lose nothing," he'd said, words coming in a rush. "I remember all the skies, all of them, how the light changes by the second. I remember how the leaves flicker in the wind." He'd looked uncomfortable, abashed by his poetic effusion. "The vividness never fades. It's always been here, but before it just flowed over me, like I was standing in a river without getting wet."

"How many of us are left now?" he asked. The skin below his eyes was black as ink and she fought the urge to call for a nurse, a doctor, anyone. He saw this, as she saw his fear and his diffidence, and in the absence of even social deceit they arrived at shared certainties—that he was dying, that she would see him through it, and that, for the duration, they were as one person—and in these they found a degree of calm.

"I'm not sure. Styrszinski is off in the Caucasus, last I heard, making a survey of all the animals and plants, but it's been years since he answered email." She thought of the old biologist, his interminable digressive monologues on natural history, while Constantin wished he'd met him, studied harder, been someone else. "There was that boy in Brazil, the prime minister's son, but I understand the family's been in lockdown since his father was assassinated. There's Stasi, that German performance artist who blew his trust fund getting the implant even though he was in perfect health— he's still alive, but he's been stuck in the same endlessly branching run-on sentence for the last seven years. I like to think that, on some level, he's very happy." Strange, they both thought, how one needed to talk even when one's thoughts were open.

"There are things I need you to know," he said, wanting to linger on in her, as the world darkened, but only in his eyes. He remembered a house on the cliffs in the Dodecanese, reachable by boat when the wind was calm, not at all when it was blowing. The house was old and his mother had renovated endlessly while he hid in the shadows of its courtyard and slept in its garden in the sun. He remembered sitting on the edge of a dam his father built, daydreaming about flying over the precipitous slope of stained white concrete. He remembered the bank of a frozen river in what Irina thought was Hyde Park in winter, waiting in the cold till the woman came, how he hadn't cared how little cover the brush afforded, the heat of her skin, how cold the snow. She left first, telling him to wait lest someone see, and he sat there studying the impression her body had left behind. Much later, after their final, bitter parting, he had taken to walking through the park past her window, whenever he was in London, and looking at the light there, or its absence, but he never saw her again, and now he never would. He remembered telling his father that his old injuries were worsening, how the old man had stood up behind his desk, face turning red as he lifted a finger like a pompous orator and swore to move the course of scientific history through sheer force of will. At least you were loved, Irina thought, though the memories, it seemed, could almost be anyone's, as though the major images of a life were dealt randomly from a fixed deck of cards. He remembered skiing over new powder down a mountain's sheer flank, rapt in the ancient game with gravity and snow, how he desired always to be on that mountain, any mountain, every mountain in the world.

His eyes had closed, and his breathing was shallow. He thought of an old woman closing his fingers over the pomegranate seeds staining his palm, perhaps his grandmother, but by then he was thinking in Greek, and she tried not to see the monitor that showed his blood oxygen falling. He clung to her hand, still wanting to live, regretting the pill that would have given him another hour, which, on her arrival, he had put aside because he hadn't wanted to keep her.

His words in her mind. Tell me stories. Give me a part of you. Something to take with me. Don't let me be alone.

She gave him her summer in Singapore, the liberty and solitude, the waves' reverberation in the emptying downtown. She gave him the day she'd opened her first Swiss bank account, how adult she'd felt when she signed the papers. She gave him the cold in the cheap hotel on the outskirts of Boston, how she had paid for it because her lover, Philip, her first, had had no money at all. How thin he'd been, her fingers counting his ribs under his frayed, worn shirt. His body was like a child's, though she hadn't seen it at the time. They'd held each other under the one thin duvet as he whispered on and on about what he'd noticed and his ambitions and then something shifted in him and his eloquence, which she valued, had vanished, supplanted by a need that had surprised her, and, accepting it, she'd felt oddly maternal as she'd guided him in.

By then Constantin's breathing had become chains of gasps, and his other memory accumulated little more than his nausea and pain and the clarity of her sensorium. She cast about for some last, great thing to give him at the end and settled on her night on the deck of a tramp steamer in the equatorial Pacific. She'd kept waking and drifting off again, eager to see the space elevator, and finally there it was, like a column of darkness, at least at the base, a thin vertical absence of stars. Her father had told her it was mankind's great ambition to build a tower that pierced the sky, an elevator into low orbit that would link the terrestrial and sidereal spheres, a phrase she is almost sure of—it sounds like him—though the memory has a vagueness, like all her memories from before the implant, and she half suspects she made it up. And they'd almost done it, he'd said, though the tower, built, had been abandoned, victim of the deflating economy and spectacular failures of engineering. It had never borne a single payload into space, a scandal in its day, but all that had been long ago, decades before her birth, and for her the tower had only ever been the most elegiac of ruins.

Constantin's eyes moved randomly behind his lids and he thought he was dreaming her and her grief felt unmanageable but sharing her story let her focus on him. The steamer had reached the atoll at dawn, the tower red as blood in the new day's light, tapering inward as it rose into the sky, its shadow stretching to the limits of the west. Though the sun had scarcely cleared the ocean, heat shimmered over the jungle that covered the atoll; once there had been a city there, the unimaginatively named Base Camp, its rotting structures now become steep-sided green hills. Titanic buttresses rose around the tower's base, the clean lines of their geometry blurred with overgrowth, and she found them thrilling, like the monuments of a lost civilization, which, she supposed, they almost were.

Gulls rose in cacophonous masses as she stepped onto the reeking, guano-caked pier. She had an old but carefully serviced Colt revolver in her pocket—she didn't like guns, but it seemed necessary to have it if she was going to travel that far beyond the pale of the law. She sat on a rusting bollard, clutching her serious technical expeditionary backpack and dangling her feet over the water as she watched the ship sail away.

She wasn't the first to visit. Fifteen years ago an Italian hippie had come and explored and written a guidebook that she'd found buried on his long forgotten blog. With a crudely machine-translated English version on her phone, she'd picked her way over the wide, low valleys that had once been thoroughfares. As she got closer to the tower it was occluded by the buttresses but she soon found her way to the ascending spiral of the ramp around the base. Giorgio's notes assured her it was sound, made to support the heaviest construction equipment, unlikely to collapse even after a thousand years. It was a while before she realized that what she'd taken for cracks in the buttresses were in fact inscriptions in many languages, perhaps all languages, and every one some version of "I am the first stone in the road to the stars."

The bottom of the ramp was covered with graffiti but as she climbed the graffiti became sparser. The ramp was made of something very hard and probably lighter than it looked, one of those replacements for concrete that hadn't quite worked out. Here and there green shoots grew in tiny cracks, the species of the plants changing as she ascended, and she'd reflected that all the seeds must have been carried by the wind.

She'd meant to study the elevator's architecture, as long as she was on it, but she found she just wanted to keep climbing. Her legs were soon aching, and, confronted with the blue gulf of space, she could scarcely bring herself to approach the ramp's edge, but still she climbed, infused with a sense of the most radiant purpose, for the tower was the symbol of all that was forever out of reach, and at night, in her bedroll, the tower's promise and the thought of its apex and the glittering light of the stars were almost more than she could bear, but neither intense contemplation nor orgasm nor her understanding of the physics nor the exact record of the stars' shimmerings helped at all, and the strain was such that she'd thought she'd come apart, lying there high above the world, though of course all that had happened was that she'd fallen asleep, and then she noticed that Constantin's blood oxygen had settled at zero, and that his breathing had stopped. She looked into his other memory, the last eleven years of his life's experience fixed forever in deep strata of data, immobile now, and somehow cold. *Of course,* she thought, *I should have known, this is what death is, this stillness in memory.*

25

•

Just Leaving the Station

Kern is in a tunnel about ten minutes from Lares' room and there's a little light filtering down from high above and it seems to brighten and darken with his heartbeat, though he feels perfectly calm, and oddly detached from his body.

"Watch your breathing," says the ghost. "Easy. *Long* exhalation. There you go. You can handle it. Your heart is a soldier's, and you've seen worse than this."

"Where now?" His voice sounds like it's coming from far away, like it might be someone else's.

"The subway, to the airport. It's way past time."

"Won't it make me visible?"

"It won't matter, if you can make it to the station. Transportation infrastructure is highly secured. It's suicide to try a hit in an airport."

The train's doors sigh shut, sealing them in. A raw edge of panic as its engines heave to life, but now there's nowhere to go. Waft of chewing gum, motor oil, damp humanity, and then, as the train accelerates, the shrill harmonics of metal under strain. He remembers Lares saying that a train is like time, or history, irresistible in its momentum, its future unseen but coming on fast, and unavoidably.

He pretends to ignore the other passengers, who look rich, or at least no poorer than the favela's better-heeled bohemians. Across from him is a couple, older, like someone's parents but good-looking, speaking Spanish over the train's roar and squeal. In a dry tone the man says, "So, really, you can see how very useful it all was," and the woman—dark haired with small, freckled features—laughs, showing her gums, and Kern, helplessly, remembers a dark-haired woman sitting him down on a stool, working over his scalp with probing fingers, hunting down lice as the light faded in the window, the smell of something cooking. He remembers the house of white stone, the heat on white sand and the sharpness of her fear when she heard the wasp whine that he realizes, now, could only have been aerial drones, invisibly high overhead. He's read that where the breath goes, the body follows, so he inhales, willing away the tension in his back, the heat around his eyes. There must have been some moment of final parting, but it's gone, and all he remembers of the aftermath is walking north through the desert in the company of weary strangers, how the hard-faced, sunburned *coyotes* had cursed him, told him to go where he was wanted and tried to run him off, but it was better to be cursed than to have no place at all, and sometimes, after dark, the women gave him water. At night he'd gone off by himself, always half-awake, listening, lest the others go away. Near the border, the night sky was full of drones, their shadows gliding over the bright constellations as they fought their duels in the upper air, proxies in a war he'd never heard of. Minutes of stillness punctuated by the rapid flares of missiles firing like flurries of shooting stars, then detonations' flashes illuminating the ragged contrails, and a few seconds later shock waves rumbling over the desert.

The train banks, centripetal force pushing him back into his seat, and now the woman across the aisle looks like no one, a stranger. He looks out the window—black, dust-furred infrastructure, leftover space, occasional flashes of graffiti passing too quickly to be attributed. A hint of salt on the air, and he thinks of the enormous pumps that keep the tunnels from flooding. The wheels clatter on the track, and all the other passengers seem to be asleep, or staring blankly into space, serenely confident the train will take them where they need to go. The woman laughs again; Kern closes his eyes, thinks that he must be in the present, that the present is gone once the thought has formed, that the present is a train that's just leaving the station.

26

.

Nonexistent Prisons

Just the engine's roar, the cone of light juddering over the black road before him, the dust in the light. Accelerator floored, the engine redlining, but despite the speed Thales feels like he's floating, like nothing is changing or ever will till the car rounds a bend and there below him, all at once, the city's sweep, its highways' lights. For a moment he knows he's dreaming but it slips away as his gaze settles on the spires of downtown where a gap among the towers implies some wide public square, the kind where freezing winds rush unimpeded over the treeless fields and the snow crunches underfoot as he makes his way toward the ice-choked creek to wait for a woman he doubts will ever really come, and now the bitter cold and the sepia stains on the Palladian facades tell him this isn't Los Angeles at all but some other, more ancient city. In fact the buildings are rotting, reverting to geology under their furs of vegetation, and over these ruins rises a tower, black even in the dawn's light, and his heart rises as his gaze follows it up to where its heights are lost in the celestial blue of morning, and the answers he needs are at its apex, if only he can reach it, and he'll hunt it down the nights, and he'll hunt it down the years, but he keeps losing his way among the cul-de-sacs and the endless winding streets, and it's not long until he realizes he's in the city's derelict periphery, and hasn't seen the tower in a long time, for the city is many cities, concentric and innumerable, and he's forever lost the core.

No, he thinks, as he hastens past the shattered husks of strip malls and favelas like concrete cancers rising into the air, for there must be a way, as there's always a way, and now he feels like a bird of prey, detached and intent, like pure perspective circling over the city, its thousands of square miles glittering vacantly in the sun, vast and unmeaning, but then he finds something in that ocean of emptiness, locks on, is falling . . .

It's pure structure, what he's found, and somehow mathematical, but he finds he can't articulate it, not even a little, and it's like the feeling of watching waves breaking, before the implant, a riot of form of which nothing can be said, and it's terrifying, because his inarticulacy could be the effect of his injuries, which would mean he's falling apart, so he compels himself to focus, and manages to tell himself that what he's found is like a map, one showing what's under the surface of things, and now his steps are echoing coldly in a windowless concrete corridor, some nameless liminal unfinished space, and he comes to an alcove lit by a flickering bulb in a dusty cage where EXIT TO CENTRAL is stenciled on a steel door in black letters. No handle, and there's a screen by the door but it doesn't wake. He presses his ear to the door, hears what could be static or maybe the sea. He steps back out into the corridor which branches and rebranches again and he's wondering where he's going when he finds another alcove with another door, this one marked SERVICE ACCESS and it opens at his touch . . .

The dream changes abruptly and he wonders if his implant is working again, because there in his mind is an expanse of frozen time, the memories of a young woman in a hotel room with her boyfriend, and he sees their interval all at once like a four-dimensional solid—there's the stark winter light, how it changes by the second, the awkwardness of their lovemaking, how their pulses are visible in their flesh, the duvet changing shape under the incidental stresses, and he's unmoved by their intimacy except in that it seems fitting that life should strive to chain forward through time. There are other spans of static memory and, there, a point of motion, a vortex drawing innumerable shards and splinters of memory and fitting them together like the pieces of a mosaic, and as he looks into its churning core there's a flash impression of misery and determination and the streets of Los Angeles slipping past behind a town car's windows. Now he sees another vortex (flash of verdant, manicured garden, its walls several stories high, security drones tracing lazy arcs in the air over the fountains) and then still another, which makes him flash on frozen time and a view of vortices and with a sense of rising through levels he gasps, sits up, is awake.

He's sitting on the floor of an elevator in the St. Mark. Floors tick by— the elevator is ascending toward the penthouse, where his family has their suite. He's not sure how he got here—did he have a syncope while he was trying to go home? The dream's unease is still with him, and his fear of finding proof of his decline. "Major cranial ablation" had been the surgeon's memorable turn of phrase. He thinks of the disturbed woman who'd accosted him, how she'd been radiant with unhappiness, and wonders how she wound up living on her own, apparently abandoned by her family; at least this hasn't happened to him—he'll find his mother, tell her what's happening, see if she knows what to do.

The elevator stops, opens onto the verdure of the walled rooftop garden, its smell of its wet moss and earth. It's like an opulent, manicured jungle. The path to their suite winds off under the branches.

The scanner pulses green under his palm and the front door opens onto a clutter of his brothers' suitcases, scattered clothes, a sand-encrusted surfboard, but no one seems to be home. In the hall before his mother's room are architectural drawings of ancient buildings and Piranesi's studies of nonexistent prisons, and though her door is closed there are faint sounds within that could be voices—she's probably lying in bed with the blinds drawn, listening to books. "Mom?" he calls, *sotto voce*, suddenly reluctant to violate the stillness. "It's me. Can I come in?"

No response. Perhaps she's asleep. He knocks—still nothing. Maybe he should let her sleep but he knocks again, and then louder, and it occurs to him that he has yet to see the inside of her room—in fact he doesn't think he's seen her since his collapse. "Mom?" he says again, trying the doorknob—locked, so she must be within. "I think someone recognized me. I think we're in trouble." He smacks the door with the ham of his fist which is rude but still there's no response so she's either asleep or deliberately ignoring him. Frustration overcoming manners, he kicks the door, then kicks it harder, then harder still. The hotel's interior doors are thin, built more for privacy than security, and he's winding up for the kick that will break it down when the door swings gently open.

He feels profound relief as he steps into the dark room and the words comes pouring out as he says, "Something's gone wrong. There was a stranger who I think followed me from the clinic and I think she has the implant dementia but she seemed to know who I was and she asked me what I remember but I remember almost nothing, and at the clinic they told me things were going badly, but it felt like a threat. I'm afraid I'm going to die. Mom?" As his eyes adjust he sees that the darkness isn't absolute, that there's a little light from a TV, dimmed by a blanket thrown over the screen, that that's where the voices are coming from, though his mother hates television, won't watch it even on long flights, and he wonders if she's herself these days.

He pulls the blanket off of the TV like a magician doing a trick and on the screen there's a religious show, the sweating preacher apoplectic and pleading as websites and fragments of scripture scroll by. In the full glare of the television's light he sees that the room has no bed, and no books, just an old couch covered in duvets, and gin bottles, mostly empty, scattered on the floor among half-burned votive candles adorned with beaming Jesuses and serene Virgins, though his mother despises religion, and there's no good apparent explanation—has she for some reason given the room to a maid? There's no sense of her presence at all; he knows she's been drinking since they came to the Protectorates but he can't believe she's this far gone.

Back outside the garden looks ancient, and threatening, a residual pocket of the Mesozoic just biding its time; he resists an urge to look behind the cycads. He listens to the wind moving the branches and it occurs to him that it's late and he could go inside and to bed and assume everything will have resolved itself by morning but he still has the lucidity he's felt since the clinic, which makes him feel like a kind of ethereal detective, and sleep seems less important than finding his mother, who's probably in her house in the mountains, because he doesn't know where else she'd go in Los Angeles.

27

·

Venice Replicated

Rain sluicing down the windows, reflecting the restaurant's dim light, distorting the strangers passing on the street. The interior is like a firelit cave, the waiters unobtrusive as attendant ghosts as they light the candles that accentuate the shadows. The acoustics are muffling, enveloping her in a hush of voices, the words blotted up.

Alone at her table, she watches the door. Out on the sidewalk, water beads on the guards' helmets, pours in rivulets from their blue plastic ponchos; their filtration masks give them the air of anonymous henchmen, though their postures speak only of the boredom of the shift. Is this security necessary, or just a kind of decor, meant to imply a clientele that's posh enough to rob, and do the guards come to loathe their charges, warm and dry and eating tapas, or are all their thoughts of the monotony of the shift?

Under the regular menu she finds the waiter has left a smaller, handwritten one, listing dishes made with the flesh of slaughtered animals rather than the usual cultured meat; it's outlandishly expensive, the kind of thing favored only by hard-core gastronomes and rich old Republicans mourning a lost Augustan age. She wonders which he took her for, tries not to hold it against him.

The downpour intensifies, the water switching channels on the glass, roaring and echoing in the narrow street, and suddenly she's in Manhattan, as though the voice of the water had summoned that city. How Manhattan is like Venice, once a great commercial principality, now flooded, its roads become waterways, beautiful and useless and beloved. Finance is long gone but the arts hold on, tenuously, students and writers squatting in the unheated Park Avenue apartments where once magnates lived, working in the sound of the perpetual storms. The bridges between buildings, late additions, like the arcs of white wings. She once went to a fashion show in the undrowned levels of the public library, saw the lions of the steps, their dignity intact under the swirling tide, and in the cramped dressing rooms that were once archives slim young girls hurried by, their makeup thick and operatic, their shimmering green dresses like the plumage of birds, bejeweled and elusive, court attire of an empire unborn, and always, always the rain.

Manhattan, like Venice before it, will presently be a stub, so many worn stones a few feet under water, a romantic ruin in an ocean replete with them. Her pleasure in the rain fades as she thinks of cities crumbling, the soul of Venice replicated endlessly, falling endlessly beneath the waves. The door opens, then, admitting the smell of rain and of wet concrete; a few patrons turn to look, then look away, except for her, because it's Philip, come to see her.

Long and lean, Philip, shoulders hunched, his face haughty in repose but she knows that only means he's thinking. They'd met when they were students and he was skeletally thin and had really no money and once spent an entire semester reading in the library when his financial aid didn't come through, and even when it did he never let her see where he lived—she suspected it was in the basement of an administration building, which he snuck into, at night, through a window, but it was clear she shouldn't press him. When she'd hinted that the trust from her parents' estate, though small, was more than she needed, he'd closed up like a slighted Spanish grandee. For years, even after his circumstances were less dire, he'd been utterly certain that owning more than one pair of shoes was a sign of unseriousness, and that one of the many virtues of books was that, in sufficient quantity, they were furniture. In the decades since he has made money, and discovered clothes, and with pleasure she sees him frown and sluice the beaded water from the moss-colored wool of an overcoat that can only be a Calatrava.

Three years since she's seen him, and her other memory gives her the black brick of what had been a customs house when Victoria reigned and had become a cafe by the river, the burnished silverware shining on the distressed oak tables, the arched panes of tall windows framing the glow of the Thames, the squalid clinker of its bank, the lights implying bridges in the dark. Almost deserted, the one remaining waiter busied at a distance, and the solitude eased Philip's tension enough for him to tell her that he'd been floating too long, felt that it was time to compromise his purity of action enough to find some definite place in the world, and so he was leaving, going to San Francisco, there to start a company and put down the roots he'd found he lacked, even if it meant a life less wholly of the spirit. The scene disperses under the pressure of his hand on her wrist. Kindly, he says, "You're in your memory."

He sits and they're about to speak when the waiter arrives with the wine and pours a dram into a glass for his approval. A moment of stillness as this gesture recasts the scene, renders them symbolically a couple, and she remembers the first time they slept together, how she'd counted his ribs with her fingertips, how he'd trembled when he touched her, and the last time, just after graduation, her flight leaving in hours, for she was going to go and see the world and he pretended that this was unremarkable, no more than the next thing, but then, in a disgusted aside, Philip says, "This ritual means nothing to me but I'll perform it," touches the wine to his lips, nods curtly, and the waiter finally leaves.

He looks down, starts putting his silverware just so.

"So, tell me what your company's doing," she says brightly, knowing it relaxes him to hold forth on his work, and that later, his nerves settled, they can talk.

"Engines," he says. "Engines for cars. Exotic ones, designed-by-AI, for Pagani, Tetsujin and, now, Lotus. Their complexity is incredible—fractal, almost—the most intricate things I've seen outside biology. We get them fabbed in Milan, at this facility where they make parts for rockets and jets. The engines work, in fact they work wonderfully, but no one understands why, and that includes the best mechanical engineers I've been able to find. So we have a lot of work, and we've put a new thing into the world, and thereby been of service to some race-car drivers and a handful of rich guys. They're beautiful, though, the engines. The problem," he says, impaling carpaccio with a fork, "is the people."

She remembers the density of dark summer woods at the end of their freshman year, the white trunks pressed close around the pond, her flashlight skimming over the black water till the beam found his body among the ripples, and in the first moment of stark surprise she wondered if he'd drowned, and if it was deliberate, if his text had summoned her to bear witness to his death, but then he rose gasping in an eruption of foam; naked beside her on the muddy bank, he explained that he'd decided to stop speaking, for the semester, except, apparently, to her; he'd been sleeping all day, submitting homework online, seeking out lonely places, because it was too hard to be near other people; the quiet let his mind still. "Unbearable prima donnas, my employees," he says. "The AI wranglers, I mean— the receptionist is lovely, and the girls down in marketing are like friendly little animals. But the technical people are at me all the time, demanding more money, more stock, or else they'll leave and start their own shops. I don't even really want to go to the office anymore."

"So get rid of them," she says, surprised at her own coldness, a throwback to the days when it was really just the two of them.

"But I need my bright young things, you see, for the cash to flow. It's just that the media has discovered design-by-AI lately, and exaggerated their sense of their own importance. Have you seen these articles? There was one in the *Times* called 'The New Mediums,' which said anyone who can communicate at all with these opaque and somehow unknowable artifacts is more or less the peer of Newton, or in any case of Gauss, and should expect to be paid accordingly."

"One does what one must for the cash for the Mayo," she says, intoning it, almost, as though it were a precept from antiquity, although she hadn't meant to, her latest visit threatening to rise to the surface of her mind, and then she notices that Philip has pulled into himself, that he has something to say, but doesn't want to, and she sees him stifle it and say, "So what brings you to the Valley?"

"A last-minute gig with Water and Power. Have you heard about their new office? It's meant to last at least a millennium. Either Cromwell is planning a thousand-year reich or he has his heart set on a legacy in architecture."

"How is the old sod? It's virtually impossible to get a meeting with him these days. Did you meet Magda? It seems to be her job to protect him from the vulgarity of the world. She lets one through only if one has something elegant with which to engage the greatness of his mind."

"Mnemosyne" is on the tip of her tongue but she finds she isn't ready to tell him about that, or what might have been a kidnap attempt, or how she gave a fraction of herself, in the most literal sense, to Constantin, right before he died, and how that sliver of self has found its own life in the world. (She wonders once again if Cromwell is her enemy, and the one who stole her memories—he certainly seems to be a locus of strangeness—but his true intentions remain opaque.) In any case, she can take care of her own problems, and in that moment Philip feels like a stranger with whom she is, for the course of dinner, inexplicably trapped. "He's thriving," she says, gamely making conversation. "As far as I can tell. And he's a fan, or seems to be, god help him, a fact of which Magda is aware, which probably explains why she hates me, though we've barely spoken. It took me a while to figure it out, and by the time I did I couldn't think of anything to do except pretending not to notice. Anyway, they called me because one of the house AIs was broken in some unspecified way."

"Did you find out why?"

"I found something strange," she says on impulse, feeling suddenly exposed but trying to keep it out of her voice, grateful for the echoes and the noise of the place. She decides to give him a measure of the truth. "It was doing energy arbitrage, nominally, but there was something else behind it."

"What?"

"That's the strange part," she says, her voice quieter than she wants, afraid he'll ask her to repeat herself. "It was another AI. A big one. And there was a city in the waves, very high, higher than seems possible. There was a secret there. And there was this girl," she says, and suddenly doesn't want to talk about it, but if she can't talk to Philip then she really can't talk to anyone at all, and she's afraid it sounds like she's babbling as she says, "and she was driving too fast through the desert by herself, and she didn't know where she was going, or what she would do, and she was afraid of everything, all the time, and she was happy, because she was leaving the past irretrievably."

"The opposite of you, then."

She tries not to show that she's wounded, reminding herself that, when he sees something clearly, he can't hold his tongue. "Exactly. The opposite of me," she says, and he looks away, and it's always been a little like hanging out with a sibyl, the fit coming at odd moments, the truth boiling out uncontrollably.

"It gets stranger," she says, still vulnerable, not caring. "Someone saw me. Spoke to me. Knew I was there, and who I was."

"Who?"

"I don't know. No one, I guess. Things get fuzzy, in the fugue—I'm not even sure if it really spoke or if it was just something I got from the glyphs. So maybe the AI? And then the machine kicked me out, which is also a first."

He swirls his wine, stares into space. "How did it feel? Your interlocutor. Was it . . . *like* anything, when whoever it was spoke to you?"

"They were surprised. Like they hadn't expected to find me, but knew who I was," she says, only realizing this as she articulates it.

He regards her gravely, his face deliberately blank, and she remembers frost flowers dense on the warehouse windows, that last year it snowed in London (they said it wouldn't snow again till the next ice age came), the tiny, inadequate islands of warmth around the space heaters, how they lay companionably in his bed under what must have been thirty pounds of blankets, though they hadn't been lovers in years, and drank hot wine from cracked cups, and in the small hours she'd finally told him about the trickle of registered letters from the makers of her implant, advising her of her risks, as they became apparent, of seizure, delusion, dementia, stroke. "It isn't that," she says. "I'm still all here. I'd know. I would. I, of all people." He's embarrassed to be read so easily, and she wonders if he's forgotten how it is with them, what's gotten in the way.

The candles flicker as the opening door admits a blast of cold air and in the movement of the shadows his face becomes an ancient mask, an ancestor spirit from a sacred grove on some remote archipelago, an image exhumed from deep within the mind, one that speaks to her of wisdom, loss, resignation. "It's strange," he says.

By the time the waiter brings the third bottle they're holding hands across the table, which, she feels, is a ship, and the restaurant a sea, and that the world without is primal darkness, full of nothing but night and rain, the world on the evening of creation's first day. "And what about everyone else?" she says, not sure who she means, or if she just means she cares for nothing beyond their circle of light.

"They're disappointing," he said. "We were ambitious, when we were young. We reached for the stars. We were to be Bloomsbury, in our way, but with more math and fewer middling talents. Historians of science were to marvel that we'd known each other at all, much less been friends, or shared the squat. I used to be angry, and excoriate them behind their backs, but now I barely have the heart to list their failures. Sasha is a math don at Oxford, that college where Oscar Wilde went, but mostly he teaches. Colin, who was going to make nanoscale replicators a reality rather than a running scientific joke, is a manager at a game company. Amanda, god help me, is a housewife, and often emails me about her twins' prodigious aptitudes. From there it gets worse."

"And what about you?" she asks. "What happened to your ambition? As I recall, you were going to make real AIs, ones that think like we do and actually know the world." The question could be a mortal affront but their intimacy is such that she thinks his pride will allow it.

"I tried," he says. "Easy to say, but entirely true. I read everything about AI. Not literally everything, not the student work or the tenure grist, of which there is a great deal, but everything good. At first I could only concentrate for five or so hours a day, but I was hard with myself, and by the end I could focus for sixteen. After a few years I was getting fat, and there were migraines all the time, so I started making myself exercise for an hour a day, and eating things besides curry and black coffee."

"And what did you find?"

"Nothing. I found nothing. I failed. There were islands of order, and sometimes I had an intuition of a larger shape, but it was nothing I could ever quite name. It was maddening. Very nearly literally. Sometimes, in dreams, I understood them, the AIs, or thought I did, but when I woke up it always amounted to nothing. Becoming desperate, I resorted to mortifications of the flesh. I've never told this to anyone before, but I'd set myself a problem, and a time in which to solve it, and if I failed I had to drive a sterilized surgical needle through the palm of my hand. The pain was . . . clarifying. I realize this makes me sound like an emotionally disturbed teenager, but I had to try everything, to go farther than anyone ever had. I'd be Alexander or die."

"And now?"

"I guess I died. There came a point when there was nothing more to try. Maybe if I had more lifetimes. So now I'm nothing, a mere entrepreneur, a tedious rich old fuck to be. The best I can say of myself is that I'm honest."

"Even now we're in your memory," Philip says. "There behind your elegantly marred forehead." The daylight is gone, now, the guards on the street invisible, no sign of the outside but the drumming of the rain. The other tables have emptied and filled and in the candlelight everyone looks happy, like their lives are replete, and there's a woman, blond and ripe, who will run to fat soon but is, for now, beautiful, standing in the doorway, smiling radiantly at someone inside, looking like she's just thought of something to say.

"Like her," he says. "Look at her. It's never occurred to her to question that her story is the center of the narrative. But only this fragment of her life will survive."

"If you call it survival," she says, chin cupped on hand, contemplating her gin and tonic, which Philip has always called the blood of dead empire. "It's more like imprisonment, under glass, forever. Like Nimue and Merlin. Waters may rise, and cities crumble, but I'll always have this light on your face and the water running down the windows."

"I'm happy here," he says. "Let's never leave."

"Done," she says. "I'll always be here with you."

"Strange to think of the boy I was, still with you. I suppose you're there too, at least since you were twelve. How strange it must be for you, how your personal history is a crystalline museum, until the point where, I suppose, it must darken."

She imagines the severe boy he'd been standing behind her in his second-hand pea coat torn at the shoulder, how he'd be moved by the light, disdainful of their consumption, how he'd stare in bemused dismay at the elegant man across from her. She takes a sip of wine.

"Yes?" he says.

She says, "You're standing right behind me, in judgment, and you have no mercy."

"I'd expect no less," he says, seeming pleased. "Tell him not to work so hard. Or maybe harder. Another drink?"

"It's different with me," she says. "I don't really have past selves. It's all one big present. There is nothing of me that fades."

"Nor suffers a sea change," he says. "But isn't that awful? Every little wound open forever?"

She smiles, makes a vague, expansive gesture, her hands tracing circles in the air.

He says, "I'd forgotten how rewarding it can be to get you drunk."

"I wish I could remember the future," she says, resting her forehead briefly on her palm, and if the other patrons see, well, let them, they'll barely remember it. "It's a poor sort of memory that only works backwards. I wish I could just slip up and down the timeline as I pleased. It's almost what I do anyway."

A pause in which they listen to the rain and then he says, "I have news. Something I have to tell you. Of the most improbable kind."

"You've accepted Jesus Christ as your lord and savior?"

"No. Worse. I met a girl. She used to be a model but she didn't mean it. Now she's a biologist. Lepidoptery. Butterflies and moths, you know," he says airily.

She waits for the punch line. "And . . . ?"

"And we're giving it, as they say, a whirl. She's moving in. Nuptials would appear to be imminent."

"You're marrying a model with a butterfly net."

"With anyone else I'd deny it. What am I supposed to say? 'Yes, but she's hot'? 'With the approach of middle age I've learned to compromise my once noble principles'? 'Nabokov liked it so it's probably okay'?"

"Something like that."

"You'd like her. She's hot and stacked. Kidding. Well, in spirit. Seriously, though. She keeps me calm. She says that's her job."

"It's a big one."

He smiles at her.

"I have more to tell you," he says. "Though I hardly know how. Simply, I suppose."

She reaches across the table and covers his mouth with her hand because she knows what he's going to say, and it's like she's turning her will against the ironclad decree of inexorable fate but what else is there to do, and he takes her wrist gently and removes her hand but her resources are not exhausted and she sings a single long, clear note to drown him out (remembering lessons in a dusty room that was a ballet studio most of the time, mirrors everywhere, the piano, the barre), and she does it well, even beautifully, so he has to stop to listen, and all the other diners are looking. She sustains it for as long as she can, thinks she might sustain it forever, even as her wind fades and her vision starts to go. Scattered applause from the other tables and someone shouts "Encore!" and "Bravissima!" as Philip kisses her palm, puts her hand to his cheek, and says, "No more trips to the Mayo."

She starts to argue, starts to cry, but he says, "I'm spending my entire life driving my company hard enough so it grows fast enough that I can pay for the fucking Mayo. I hardly see Ann-Elise. If I have just one bad year it's all for nothing anyway. I'm going to try to live my life instead of tending it like a bonsai."

She had always supposed they would attend each other's funerals, would welcome the next century together, and perhaps the next, and if there were long stretches of silence between them there would still always be a return and within moments of his walking in the door it would be like they'd never parted, and sometimes they'd be lovers and sometimes not but there would always be a next thing. Holding his gaze, she snuffs the candle with her palm.

"You look like I announced end-stage cancer."

"In a way you did."

"Well, I guess this is goodbye, give or take fifty years."

"You're being stupid. There's no going back. Is life worth so little that you're in a hurry to leave it?"

"Life is worth so much that I'm in a hurry to live it."

"So you can have your little model," she says, distressed by the sneer in her voice but unable to suppress it. "And maybe a family and a handful of decades in which you do nothing important and then you'll die and be forgotten. That's your plan."

"As opposed to what, my dear. I tried. I have one hundred and thirteen scars on my palm to prove it. I had to have surgery to get feeling in my thumb back. I took my shot, but I'm not Newton, and wasting the years in vain has ceased to appeal."

"You had intuitions. I remember."

"And if I had a dozen lifetimes I might pursue them, but not even the Mayo can get me that. Though, who knows, technology evolves, by the time I'm old there might be a solution."

"There won't be."

"I know," he says gently, and then, "But you'll never lose me. I'll always be right here."

A black wind rises and sweeps through the room, extinguishing the candles and swallowing the voices and the echoes and every particle of light and carrying them back down into her other memory's stillness, leaving her in silence and solitude and the blood-red dark behind her eyelids, and she's tempted to remain here in this peace, but then, with just the slightest exertion of her will, the candles are flickering again, and once again the restaurant is full, and there's Philip sitting across from her.

"Even now we're in your memory," Philip says. "There behind your elegantly marred forehead." The daylight is gone, now, the guards on the street invisible, no sign of the outside but the drumming of the rain. The other tables have emptied and filled and in the candlelight everyone looks happy, like their lives are replete, and there's a woman, blond and ripe, who will run to fat soon but is, for now, beautiful, standing in the doorway, smiling radiantly at someone inside, looking like she's just thought of something to say.

A hand on her wrist. She opens her eyes, finds their waiter, worried, looking down at her. The restaurant is empty, the candle a crater of cold wax. The waiter says he is sorry, may he call her a cab, is her boyfriend coming back, in any case they're closed.

28

•

Departure

The crush leaving the train car carries Kern along, and if it had been a time for picking pockets he'd have done just fine. As the press slows before the escalator he scans the faces for bad intentions but no one meets his eyes and almost all of them are absorbed in their phones. A gaggle of teenage girls, mostly blond, skin glowing, all in the same red tracksuits, get on the escalator behind him; their loud, careless voices are audible even over the shriek of the departing train, the hot wind of its passage washing over him. The girls laugh noisily as they rise out of darkness into garish light.

He steps off the escalator into a tunnel of milky, translucent glass, like a vast elongated soap bubble; everyone else strides by him purposefully. A dispassionate, oddly beautiful female voice that seems to come from everywhere enunciates an endless list of cities, numbers, letters, times. There are tall video panels every twenty feet showing fog rolling over the bridges, raindrops iridescent on trembling bamboo leaves, the red light of a desert morning moving over a woman's tranquil face.

The tracksuited girls sweep by, and each panel, at their approach, switches to a juddering montage of well-dressed, feral-looking women glaring haughtily at the camera, an ad, he realizes, for makeup. A fat man with a Cognitive Openware T-shirt, wearing those chunky sneakers that programmers seem to like, gets an ad for Lotus, at which Kern brightens— *Fist of the Southern Lotus*, starring Montana Chiao, is one of his favorite movies—but there's no kung fu, just a brightly colored little car that looks like a robotic piece of candy. At Kern's approach the panels revert to fog enveloping bridges.

The tunnel branches, blinking signs pointing the way to things that mean nothing to him. The ghost says, "You want ticketing."

The ticketing hall is the biggest room he's ever seen; the roof, high overhead, looks like it's billowing away. Long serpentine lines lead to booths where uniformed women, mostly, talk to worn-looking customers, and he's reminded of the long queues for Red Cross vaccinations. Five feet away are two cops in body armor with machine guns, one with a mustache and the other a girl, drinking coffee from paper cups marked Koffee Kiosk—the girl's eyes light on him, move on.

Windows maybe a hundred feet high frame the runway and the taxiing planes, visible in the dark as complexes of points of light in motion, and sometimes lights on the tarmac reveal the graceful curve of fuselage, and it's like looking into an aquarium, or perhaps the depths of the sea, with huge creatures sliding by, intent on their own inscrutable business, utterly indifferent to the other side of the glass.

There are people sleeping on benches and the floor before the windows, using backpacks and hand luggage as pillows. The ghost says, "A lot of kids with layovers camp out here, so you can expect to be left alone. So. This is a decision point. Where do you want to go? It can be anywhere in the world."

He's not sure how to respond, can't think of a place that means anything.

"If you're at a loss," she says, "then how about Vancouver?"

"What would I do there?"

"What would you do anywhere? You have enough money for some very good hotels. And anyway, when the heat dies down in a few weeks, you'll be coming to LA to get me, right?"

"Of course," he says.

"You could go to Franz Josef Land," she says. "It's the party spot now, what Singapore used to be."

The windows are mirrors and he automatically starts to shadow box, just indicating the moves so as not to draw attention, and remembers that his life is dedicated not to survival but to perfection. "Thailand," he says. "I want to go to Thailand. I can train there. They invented kickboxing. I've never had a real coach."

"There you go," she says. "Thailand. Your dollar'll go farther, and it's sure out of the way."

"Window or aisle?" asks the gate agent, who seems kind. Kern regards her blankly.

The ghost is starting to speak when the agent says, "I mean, would you like to sit next to the window, or next to the aisle? If you sit by the aisle you have a little more room, but you might like the window—the dawn over the ocean is something to see."

"Window, please."

Her fingers fly over the keyboard, her proficiency reminding him of Lares. "You depart for Bangkok in fourteen hours. Checking bags?"

"No."

"If you happen to have forgotten anything, there's a store in the domestic concourse that sells clothes, toiletries, even luggage. It's open all the time."

Lying huddled under a bench, he turns his face to the wall and pulls his new sleeping bag close. The ghost had said to sleep, that it was as safe as a police station, but there are voices, footsteps, a constant sense of people in motion. He looks up at stapled fabric, aluminum struts. On the wall before his eyes is an ethernet port, like a little ziggurat of negative space. He roots through his new canvas carryall—there are his new clothes, a new tablet and a multipack of cables that should have a charger for the phone—finds a T-shirt and puts it over his eyes.

He remembers following Kayla one night down silent streets of San Francisco, lit by lamps and the fog's faint glow, how she said they had to keep moving because she was searching for something, had been searching a long time, though he didn't think she really was, it was more like poetry than that there was something she actually needed to find, and he felt like it was his work to watch over her in the night. She said she was in search of the miraculous, and she knew it was there because someone found it long ago, this Boss Djinn Adder, who sounded like the villain in a martial arts movie, but she'd said he was actually Dutch, and an artist, who was lost at sea. And now the memory has graded into a dream where they've come at last to a long, empty beach under a lightening sky and sit on the cold sand watching the breakers rumble in. She starts to cry, and he tries, helplessly, to comfort her, and since they're alone he pulls off her jeans, which she tolerates, though she isn't really paying attention as he opens her legs, is just watching the sky over his shoulder. He watches her face, and is happy, but then he looks away just for a second, and when he looks back she's gone. Sand falls from his hands and face as he searches blindly among the crumbling dunes.

"Hey now," says the ghost. "Wake up, okay? *Wake up.* You're having a bad dream. Hush now. People will hear you."

He returns to the present, though he knows the dream will be there if he closes his eyes. "I'm fine," he says, blinking, waking up fast; he tries to think of a question to ask. "Tell me about Los Angeles. How you broke in, if you did."

"Well, that's a story," she says, and he wills her to keep talking; her voice is hushed and intimate, a private voice, and he lets it envelop him, feeling almost like she's talking to herself, like all these words have been pent up and waiting. "It was the day the LAPD officially disbanded. Not that it really mattered, as the emergency administration was already in place, but it felt like the end, and capital was fleeing the city, and I was on the verge of giving up. I was with my friend Sonia, that day, and she was taking my picture in what had been downtown Santa Monica. An aesthete, was Sonia. She kept saying how the light loved me, how I was so perfect I almost disappeared. The low waves broke behind her, washing the street, the white foam dissolving on the crumbling asphalt. She said she was making a record of the city's last days. You'd think people would be scared, but most of them were just giddy—there were celebrations that day, and riots, and they were expecting fires. The sun was just setting when the first fireworks went off over the water, the sails of the yachts illuminated in the flashes, and the concussions ricocheted off the wall at my back, and I smiled from my emptiness as her camera strobed.

"The wind brought sparks that blinked out in the surf and Sonia said, 'It's starting.' I looked up toward the hills, saw grey columns of smoke rising. I looked back, was blinded by more flashes, and as the sun set the fireworks began in earnest, bursting over the water, their reports a continuum, their light showing Sonia, intent on her camera, absorbed in her imagery.

"So much beauty, she said, as things come apart. I thought of the massifs of dirty white smoke that filled the skies when I drove west on the road through the fires on the plains. How the fire lit the night. They'd said it was the last fire, on the radio, that the ecology was changing, had changed, that the plains were desert now.

"She had a car, a drone, armored, a hand-me-down from her father, who used to be a famous director. I was falling asleep but Sonia got excited when she thought she heard a bullet ricochet off the hull. As always, she had pills. I remember picking them off her palm, the muted colors like codes or flags or the neon light of cities. I swallowed them dry and my mind flared, then darkened.

"I wouldn't have said anything, without the pills. I've forgotten most of it, thank god, but the gist was that I didn't have the money to survive, or to leave, and her father was rich, and I would live anywhere, and maybe he could use me in something, she knew how the camera loved me, and at some point I saw she'd stopped listening, was staring out the window at the smoke in the sky. She was sorry, she said, but her trust was nearly depleted, and her father had lost his money when the markets fell—they kept up appearances but there wasn't much left.

"When we got to the yacht I took more pills. I felt like I'd fallen into my own private film noir. It was a party, mostly her father's friends. It was dark, on the yacht, I don't know why, just a few candles burning. From the prow I watched the city lights recede.

"She introduced me to her godfather, but a wall had come down between me and the world and I made the decision to slip over the side. I had a water glass of vodka and the water was warm and I thought it might be pleasant, and I thought I might not notice it at all, and the world seemed flattened, somehow, the fireworks' nebulae almost close enough to touch, and I wondered how they'd look as I drifted down toward the reef. A beautiful death, I thought, one that might become a story.

"But Sonia found me and took the glass from my hand and brought me to the back of the boat where she said there was someone I needed to meet. It was very dark and at first I didn't see him, he was sitting so still. Sonia whispered in his ear and left and he asked to see my face so I used the light from my phone though I couldn't bear for him to look at me, and I knew my fear would show, so I became someone else, which allowed me to be present and to smile charmingly when he told me I was beautiful.

"He said, 'Sonia tells me you desire entrée and will take extraordinary steps to get it,' and though his voice was cold I sat on his knee and held my face inches from his but he said, 'No. Not that. Not just that. It's actually much more than that. I consider it my duty to lay it out clearly.'

"He said he needed my memories, that he'd use them to make me a new kind of star. I'd have to get surgery so they could put in an implant to harvest them. He said that it was dangerous, that some of the patients didn't last long, but if I wanted to risk it he'd open every door for me. He said some of the implants helped you remember things, but mine wouldn't, because he wanted me to be normal."

"How was a memory implant going to make you a new kind of star?" Kern asks, because she seems to have lost her flow.

"He told me not to worry about it. I didn't want to press him, but I thought maybe it was some way for an audience to feel what I felt directly." Kern imagines strangers watching his own thoughts, their reactions veering between boredom and disgust. "I didn't mind so much," she says. "It'd just be another way of acting. Acting is always like being totally naked, if you do it right."

"So what was your answer?" asks Kern.

"I said yes. Of course I said yes. Are you sure you want to hear this? I don't have anyone else to talk to and I'm afraid I'm rambling on."

"No. Talk. Please," says Kern, eyes closed, drifting.

"His assistant was with him on the yacht. She was also his girlfriend, or at least wished she was. I knew she loathed me like only an older, plainer woman can loathe a younger, prettier rival, and that she resented being a cliché, but what scared me was her pity.

"That night he took me up to his beach house in Malibu. I never said goodbye to Sonia. Later I heard she'd died. On the drive up the coast I had to tell myself to be careful about hope.

"His house was down a canyon, right on the beach, miles from anything, made of a sequence of interlinking glass boxes. One of the boxes was his bedroom, the damp sand layered knee-high against the glass. He asked me to undress and walk around, like I was there alone, but first I wanted him to turn off all the house cameras.

"'Is there no trust?' he asked, but like he thought it was funny, and I said I'd be happy to walk home in the dark. So he did it, and in fact he didn't really seem to care—the whole thing felt like it was just a gesture, his way of closing the deal.

"I woke in the middle of the night. The bedside table was covered with books, paper ones, and pill bottles, which I thought would be the usual prescription downers but they had these long chemical names and didn't seem to be from a pharmacy. I googled him from the bathroom—Cromwell was his name—and found out that he was rich, which I could see, and that he was old, which I couldn't, because he looked about forty-five. I got back into bed and watched the waves shatter on the glass and felt like my real life was beginning.

"I woke again before dawn and he offered me a car but I was restless so I wanted to walk. Nothing out there but land and sea, and the sun was still behind the mountains. My sandals were impractical so I went barefoot. The asphalt was cold at first but then the sun warmed it. I came to a charging station on the Pacific Coast Highway and the attendant wouldn't look me in the eye when he sold me my morning coffee—I can only imagine the story he put me in, with my little dress and sweaty back and dirty feet. I went on down the highway, drinking my coffee, until my phone found a signal.

"They had to do the surgery offshore. A legal technicality, said Hiro, my chaperone, on the way to LAX.

"I'd never been in a plane before, much less a private one. The hospital was on an island in Japan, one of the ones that used to be Indonesia.

"The surgeon was kind. He took me aside and asked me if I was sure I wanted to do this, tried to tell me the odds I'd leave the table alive, and the probability of later complications, and I wavered, but I hadn't seen any other chances so I said I was certain. After that he was detached, like I'd gone from being a person to an object of study.

"I'd expected the anesthesia to be like nothing but the surgeon said there'd be dreams, the 'subjectivity of the implant meshing with the cortical tissue,' and while I was under I remembered driving down through the hills toward the city, how the valley was a sea of light scarred by LAX and the freeways."

"Did Cromwell keep his word?" asks Kern, wanting it to be a fairy tale, though it's obvious it ended badly.

"In his way. There were screen tests, always on closed stages, where the soundproofing was so perfect you could hear your heart beat. The directors, who were never on-site, gave orders through the speakers like the voice of god, but nothing panned out, though I gave it everything I had. Hiro said to be patient, and meanwhile I had a lot of clothes and money.

"The loneliness was worse, which was almost unbelievable, and some nights I took a limo and went out looking for beautiful boys on the streets. They were always so happy when I told them to get in, though they usually looked like they couldn't believe it was happening.

"Sometimes Hiro would come by with a laptop and a data cable and plug it into the socket just under my ear. I asked him why it couldn't be wireless and he said that wireless wasn't ever totally secure. I hated it—it was like my soul was draining away, though it felt like nothing, but I didn't say anything, and would've tolerated more.

"Hiro was actually very nice to me, though I think he's psychotic. I was seeing this guy for a while, Johann, who'd been a boxer in Germany, and was getting work as an action lead. One night in the Four Seasons he drank too much and started getting mean, but just when I was starting to actually get worried, Hiro let himself into our suite, casually, like he'd come to change the sheets. Johann was steroid-big and got right in his face and started screaming but Hiro just giggled, like literally giggled, and when he went for Johann he was so relaxed it was actually unsettling. He broke all the bones in Johann's face with a highball glass—he was *conscientious* about it, double-checking to make sure he hadn't missed any. I never saw Johann after that, and later I heard that Hiro had worked for the cartels before joining the private sector, that there'd been a price on his head for years.

"They'd said the implant wouldn't affect my memory but they must have been wrong, because everything from the moment I got it is a lot clearer. But they must have gotten what they needed because one day I woke up in this goddamned house, and so far I haven't seen anyone but my surgeon."

"Why would they do that?" asks Kern.

"He gave me these jobs, at first, the surgeon. Hardware installation, mostly, and I had to do them all through the phone, the one you have now, but there must have been something going on behind the scenes, because now Hiro's trying to get it back. At first I was expecting him to kick down the door any minute but now it seems like I'm on my own."

"Do you have internet?"

"There's nothing, no connectivity except the link to your phone."

Kern holds up the phone, wondering why it would be her only portal onto the world. A winking red light probably means low battery. "I should recharge," says Kern. He fishes the multipack out of his carryall, tears it open with his teeth, finds the charger. He runs his fingers over the phone, looking for the power socket, finds both that and what feels like a standard ethernet port.

In the little light he looks at the snarl of cables and connectors left in the multipack; among them is an ethernet cable.

"What are you doing?" asks the ghost.

"Maybe we can get you wired," says Kern, plugging the ethernet cable into the wall jack, then into the jack in the phone. Little green lights on the phone start flashing.

"There you go," he says, eyes closing, clutching the phone, using his carryall for a pillow. "Now you're connected."

The ghost says nothing.

29

·

Bad Pattern

Out on the wet street, still drunk, her loneliness is near to burning a hole in her. The lights from Fantôme glow on the pavement, then vanish, like she'd stayed on a stage after the show was over, but she still doesn't want to go back to a hotel room. The bistro across the street is locking its doors but there are still the bars, though in them she knows she'll find nothing worth having unless she wants to spend the night drinking hard, and of course she could see if she still has the long-disused, entirely academic art of getting men to buy her drinks. The hook-up sites come to mind, promising the fear and the exhilaration of some stranger's eager hands, but that's not it, is never really it, and then she remembers that Cromwell wants to see her.

She checks mail on her phone—there are a few coaxing messages from Maya—*So have you got any time tonight? Anytime tonight?* reads the subject header of the most recent, and in the body is the address of Maison Dernière, apparently in an office tower downtown. She hesitates, wondering if it's a setup, but there's a clear-cut paper trail so it has to be benign. What better time to take a meeting, she thinks, so she emails Maya, who checks her phone compulsively, and Cromwell's secretary—she assumes his apparat is unsleeping—that she's on her way.

As the elevator rises she runs a search on Maison Dernière and finds that it doesn't exist. She stares blankly at her phone, then tries the search but again there are no websites, no reviews, in fact no references at all, and her fear rises as the floors flicker by and she wonders if this is how a call girl feels when a trick starts going bad. There's no emergency stop button so she jabs at the buttons for the other floors but they won't illuminate, which makes the elevator car a prison, and she wishes she'd made a habit of carrying a gun, or stayed sober. It occurs to her to call Maya, who has private security firms on speed dial, or just call Parthenon directly, but what's going to happen will have happened before they could arrive.

It might be a misunderstanding, and it might be perfectly benign, but one thing that's certain is that Cromwell hasn't been forthright, so she turns on her implant's wireless, is instantly aware of the constellations of the thousands of nearby machines. She scans through them and finds the elevator and sees that its software hasn't been updated in years— infrastructure, she's noticed, is often lost in the shuffle. She tells it lies like bad patterns whispered in its ear, and it's soon persuaded that she's a long overdue maintenance program sent by the manufacturer and by the time the elevator starts to slow it's entirely hers and she's never been happier about committing a felony.

She sees the elevator's internal state and that it's one second from stopping and opening its doors—she could keep them closed, or drop the car into free fall, but now that she has an exit she wants to see what's going to happen and even more than that she wants to push back. There's an SFPD weapons platform drifting high over downtown, and it's bad heat if she gets caught but it would sure give her the whip hand, so she tries for it anyway. She's briefly lost in the labyrinth of its security and it's too complicated for the time she has, but there, better, is an electrical transformer down in the building's basements, installed thirty years ago and its software not updated since. She brushes past its quaint, almost amusing defenses and sees how she could overload it in moments, which would blow the grid, blacking out the building, and possibly the block, and maybe start a fire, a card she'll hold in reserve.

She tenses as the doors open to reveal a girl radiant with youth and even in her tension Irina is moved by her beauty. The girl is dressed as though for a first date that matters but her smile fades as she sees Irina's face and in a blurry accent asks, "Is everything all right?" with such simplicity and evident concern that Irina thaws a little and realizes that she looks like she's ready for murder.

"Is this the Maison Dernière?" Irina asks but the girl only peers at her, in fact at her lips, eyebrows slightly raised, because she's deaf, of course, and then the girl smiles hesitantly and turns away, beckoning for her to follow.

The cramped corridor seems to have been carved out of what once was office space, though the unmarred hardwood floors and white plastered walls are so new she can smell the paint and the varnish, and then they round a corner and there's track lighting focused on landscape paintings in alcoves that she recognizes as Hockneys, and it's hardly worth the trouble of leaning in to confirm that they're originals, and it's all starting to read as a secret aerie dedicated to quiet happiness, which makes Cromwell start to seem like a sensible sort of person.

They come to a small foyer floored in black stone; there are cooking smells and a distant clattering of pots and pans. The girl guides her to an inset silver basin into which water sluices from a faucet that must have been harvested from a rustic French estate of the most estimable provenance and authenticity. The girl takes her hands and tries to wash and massage them, as though it were a spa day, but Irina pulls away, kindly, and does it herself.

The girl takes her out onto a wide balcony that looks down on most of city and there's Cromwell, alone at the one table, absorbed in his phone.

The girl pulls out the other chair for her and slips away as Cromwell looks up and says, "My director of security says the SFPD have reported an attempt to hack one of their weapons drones. The attack lasted less than a second, but nearly succeeded. They think it was a team of professional thieves, possibly cartel, certainly highly prepared. Strangely, they think the attack came from somewhere in this building, though the evidence is inconclusive, which is . . . just as well." He looks up at her, deadpan, his archness all but imperceptible, and in the candlelight he looks unearthly, as though he's made of fire, and she realizes she can barely hear the noises of the city.

There's a bottle of wine in an ice bucket and as Cromwell lifts it she sees the faded, spidery handwriting on the label. As she lifts her wineglass to receive the pour her hand jerks too high because the glass is lighter than she'd expected, in fact it weighs almost nothing at all, as though it were crystallized air—it must be one of the wildly expensive, very fragile glasses that are only a few molecules thick, which she's heard of but never before touched, and she imagines a future in which that jerk is the mark of the parvenu handling good stemware for the very first time. Cromwell says, "It's surprising, isn't it? My first time I practically put a brandy snifter through the ceiling." There's a pause that seems more awkward than she'd have expected in a man of his years and experience and then with an air of forced bonhomie he says, "This wine was laid down on Francois Mitterrand's estate in the year of his death. He's said to have enjoyed playing vintner, so this bottle may have been handled by the great man himself. To be honest, I can't tell one wine from another but it's a kind of way of consuming history."

She sips the cold pale fluid and wonders how much her little swallow cost. "What interests you about Mitterand?" she says, who is, for her, one dead French president among many.

"The manner of his death," he says, his poise snapping back. "When he knew his life was ending he went to Egypt to visit the tombs of the pharaohs, with whom he identified. His last meal was ortolans, a royal meal, a songbird one eats with a napkin draped over head and plate, lest God see. He lived for another three days but ate nothing more."

"What's so great about that?"

"It suggests a composed resistance to the brute facts of mortality."

"I thought this was a restaurant, when I came here," she says, her anger cooling. "But I looked it up and it didn't exist."

"Ah. Of course. I'm so sorry—I should have clarified. The Dernière is actually more like a private club with a membership of one. Only a very few people know about it, and none are the kind to put it on a blog. To call it a restaurant is a kind of inside joke. There is a menu, of course, but the chefs will make you whatever you want. I had hoped that you'd be pleased—for what little it's worth, heads of state have hinted that they wished to dine here, and been shunted off to Chez Panisse." His urbanity is fully restored now, but his apparent warmth feels like a performance intended to conceal a watchfulness and a deep interior chill. She wonders what drives him, and what, if anything, he loves—she's seen nothing to suggest a family, and he lacks the hard dullness that marks men who live for money. Maybe Magda is his center, she thinks, remembering how his posture changed when she was near him.

She says, "At first I thought that the name meant 'latest house,' like a house that was chic."

He studies her for a moment, then says, "A natural misreading, but not the worst one. In the wrong context, the name could be read as a cruel joke, the last house as in the last house one would ever see, an invitation into charnel. I'm told there are such places. But, no, it's not like that at all. The name just means that this is, in some thematic way, the last place in the West the sun touches, or where the Western world ends. In fact, I very much hope you'll enjoy yourself here, and won't find it necessary to bring out the big guns, so to speak."

She realizes she's staring and that it's unsettling him. He picks up his glass and puts it down again, then says, "And I don't know just how to put this, but I meant to say . . . I recognize that all of this is shit. I mean, it's *nice*, and I'm grateful, and so on, but I know it has no real value. Well, except for the Hockneys. It's just that there are people who take care of this for me, and it's just as easy to allow it to happen. I don't want you to think I'm some hedge-fund philistine who preens himself on having just the right wineglasses."

"So what can I do for you?" she says. "It must be important, as you're paying quadruple-time. But maybe one of your people will take care of that for you?"

She's pleased to see him wince. He says, "I'd hoped that we could talk, and perhaps become more than strangers," and refills her glass though she'd scarcely been aware she'd been drinking.

She considers this, and though she's fairly sure he's slept with the beautiful deaf girl it doesn't feel like he wants that from her. "I don't mean to be rude," she says, "but why bother?"

"Because you're interesting," he says carefully, "and we might both be around for some time. I'm looking for potential points of continuity."

"As for longevity, you do realize that, financially speaking, I'm not even remotely in your league? Wouldn't you be better off bonding with the capitalist elite over, I don't know, skeet shooting?"

He leans in across the table as the deaf girl returns with little plates of olives and bacon and another bottle of white wine. "Hardly. The capitalist elite are mostly heirs, who are dull, and founders-who-got-lucky, who are even duller. At least the heirs have manners. But they're not interesting, and, more to the point, none of them will last as long as me."

"Why not? Money is money."

"The why is a secret," he says, smiling. "A great secret. Lately it's all secrets with me."

I'm sure it is, she thinks. *Your AIs aren't what you think they are. You have some kind of new computer on your desk but you don't know how it works. You're more interested in me than seems warranted, and you're spending money like it's the end of the world. Someone is stalking me, and someone stole my friend's memories, and mine along with them. You're very old but still speak of the long-long term.* There has to be a greater shape here but it's one she can't quite see.

"I want to make a deal," he says, and though he's trying to hide it she can tell that he's nervous, even behind three glasses of wine, and her thought is that he's rushing it, that this is the crux, though he'd planned to wait longer, and she notices at some point the moon set, leaving the balcony lit only by candles and the stray light of the city. "First, I'll tell you what I'm offering. I'll pay for the Mayo Clinic."

"I can pay for the Mayo Clinic."

"You can barely pay for the Mayo Clinic. There's also the degeneration around your implant. I'll pay for that, and for the Mayo, for the next fifty years."

"That's a lot of money, even for you," she says, keeping her voice neutral as his words ring in her ears, and this, at last, could be an end to fear and struggling, and she tries to imagine what he could want for it. She could appear at his cocktail parties and perform prodigious feats of memory for his guests, or she could follow him home and slide into his bed, or she could wear a corporate badge on a lanyard and sit through boring meetings drinking muddy coffee and it would still be worth it, unless it won't, for as quickly as it formed her abjection has dissolved, and she wonders if she'll have to destroy him for humiliating her. Have to see how that goes. She watches him, waits, remembers to breathe.

"My net worth is higher than the press imagines," he says, and now the benign mask is gone and he's perfectly cold, a chess player driving through the steps of an intricate combination. "In any case. My security service prepared a précis of the circumstances of your life, as they do for everyone allowed within fifty feet of me. You have a rented apartment in Boston, and you recently allowed your lease to expire on another in Santa Monica, though both are all but unfurnished, and chosen in large part for their proximity to the airports. In the past year you've spent about sixteen nights in both combined. So on top of the Mayo I'll throw in a home. There's a house I own in Noe Valley where I sometimes put visiting dignitaries—it's quite beautiful, very private and very secure, built around a central garden, rather like the Gardner Museum in Boston. I think the architect won a prize. I'll sign it over to you, and take care of the taxes. It's not far from your friend Philip, who would consider himself my rival."

A silence, and finally she says, "And in exchange?"

"First," he says, "no questions."

He sits up very straight and drains his glass and it occurs to her that whatever he wants he wants it entirely, that this moment is the crisis of his life, and then he says, "I want your memories."

As her rage rises like a black wave she's aware that there's something she's been missing and looking into his eyes while he waits for her answer she sees his terror.

She kills the power to the building.

30

•

Ossuary

The town car's headlights illuminate the stones and the streamers of fog as it jolts over the steep pitted dirt road. Once again Thales dials his mother's cell from his own but, like all the family's secured electronics, his phone is mired in firewalls that make even the basic things nearly impossible, and once again his cell's screen flashes CONNECTION UNAVAILABLE, but now the road crests and levels out and there in the headlights is the house.

He sits in the car, watching steam billow from the square pool of black water and dissolve in the wind. Smoking mirror, he thinks, form erupting out of nothing, driven by the temperature differential between the hot water and the cold night air. The pool, fed by a hot spring, is cut from the coarse granite of the mountain, the grey of the concrete of the low house behind it.

She'd designed the house before he was born, when she was barely older than he is now. In the library of their house back in Rio there's a photograph of her at the building site, sitting on the boulder that's still there by the pool. She was very thin then, and entirely serious, staring past the camera as though unaware of its existence. She'd never been to architecture school, had just traveled the world when she was young and had no money, drawing and redrawing the great buildings, trying to render their essences with maximum economy of line. She'd spent three nights in a copse of trees at the base of the Acropolis, and later had shared the basement of a squat in the 16th arrondissement with runaways and junkies. He'd found an old interview on a long-defunct blog where she'd said she viewed the mountain house as an exercise in pure form, and as a sort of ossuary, the only place she'd want to leave her bones.

Turning off the car's lights, he sees light in the house's windows.

He gets out of the car. It's cold there, and smells of rock, dust, fog. Sharp fragments of glass scattered on the rocks—his brothers sometimes come here with girls and bottles of wine. They deride the house, even as they used its isolation, saying it's eerie, like all their mother's aesthetic fancies, just stark water, stone and wind, a lot of nothing in the middle of nowhere, not seeing, as he does, how the house, with its rough planes of crumbling grey stone and its trickles of black water, is like geology abstracted from erosion.

His phone finds the house network; he gestures over its screen to unlock the doors.

The front door swings open under his hand. Inside, it's really just one room, not very big, and feels less like a house than a temple, or a library, or maybe a tomb—his mother, in the interview, had said her influences included the library of Alexandria, Taliesin West, Ryōan-ji and Louis Kahn. No one there, and no sign of his mom. He sees that the cushions have been pulled from the couches set in the walls to make a sort of nest on the floor, probably his brothers' doing, and he worries he'll step on a stray condom. The back door is ajar, probably through their carelessness. He wonders how long the lights have been on.

Standing in the doorway, he hears rock clatter in the dark behind him. For a moment he stands there, perfectly still, willing it to have been the wind, and he could retreat to the car and the protection of its armament but it's twenty feet away and feels unattainable. It's still somehow unbelievable that some stranger would really try to hurt him, even after what happened, and he wonders if this is often what people think right before they die; how fitting, though, to leave his bones by the square black pool. He waits, listening, decides it was nothing, but when he finally he goes inside he locks the front and back doors.

His mother's computer is on the desk before the one large window. It dates back to the decade before he was born, but she's particular about her vintage hardware, insisting that she can only work with what she knows. It's a museum piece, but functional, and it occurs to him that it's probably too old to support the protocols that hamstring every other secure family device, so maybe for once he can make a fucking phone call.

The computer wakes at his touch. Its interface is quaint, but intuitive enough, and it's easy to find the program for making calls because it's the last one that was used. It won't work, he thinks, keying in his mother's number, but then it starts to ring.

The ringing goes on and on, and he's about to hang up when his mother, half asleep, picks up and says, "Hello?"

"I'm glad I found you," he says.

"Helio?" she says groggily. "Is that you?"

"No, Mother," he says, unable to control his irritation. "It's me. Good lord."

"Marco Aurelio?" she says.

"Yes, exactly. This is Marco Aurelio. I dropped fifty IQ points, changed my name and started smoking reefer. I'm calling from the mountain house."

"Who is this?"

"Who do you think? I've been looking for you. It's probably nothing but I thought I heard someone outside."

"Thales? *Baby?* I've missed you so much," she says, and it's just like her to get so emotional over nothing and most likely she is drunk.

"That's fine, Mom, but something isn't right."

"Where are you?"

"The mountain house, like I told you."

"I'm going to come get you. I'm coming right now. Don't go *anywhere*. Is anyone with you?"

"I'm fine, no one's with me. Are you at the hotel? I can just come back."

"Baby, is it really you?"

Annoyed by her sentimentality, he's on the verge of saying something cutting but the call drops. He tries to call again but just gets network errors.

He stares out at the wisps of fog, remembers reading that the aesthetes of feudal Japan would spend hours watching the steam rising from bowls of hot tea, and then, in the stray light from the windows, he sees someone's silhouette on the mountain.

He ducks down out of the window's lines of sight, and he realizes the house, which was never meant for defense, has become a trap. No weapons here, just books. This is an ossuary, he remembers, built to hold the family bones. He imagines a sniper with his sights trained on the door, smoking cigarette after cigarette, as blasé as if he were hunting a deer; he imagines soldiers out in the night, poised to fire a grenade through the window but waiting till one of them, grinning and exhilarated, finishes telling a dirty story. Finally it occurs to him to turn off the light.

He runs his hands over the rough concrete in the dark, wonders irrelevantly if it's drone-built, but no, it's too old—when his mother was young builder drones were a strictly military thing, used mostly for raising bunkers in the North Americans' interminable desert wars.

Uselessly, he tries to intuit his hunters' thoughts, guess their lapses in attention. He curses his worthless phone, then realizes that he can use it. Before he can think, and therefore hesitate, he scrambles to the door, presses a button to light up his phone, and as he flings the door open throws his phone as far as he can, hoping it will draw their eyes and perhaps their fire. Running for the car, he hears the phone bounce on the rocks.

The car's door recognizes his fingerprints, unlocks. He slams it shut behind him. "Maximum offensive footing," he says, as the crash seat envelops him. "Take us home."

Insulated from the night, he relaxes a little. He wonders if they'll find his phone on the talus, maybe keep it as a trophy or search it for usable intelligence—he hopes it will be as useless to them as it was to him. He wonders if there was really an enemy or if it was just one of the vagrants who haunts the wastes beyond cities.

And then as the car turns there's a girl in the headlights, looking right into his eyes, and in the high beams she looks overexposed, her face a mask of light. Clouds of dust rise glowing around her. Time seems to slow. At first he thinks its the madwoman from the hotel but, no, she's younger, maybe Asian. The car is accelerating toward her, its forward guns whirring as they spin up. He's going to tell it to stand down, though he knows it's too late, but before he can speak or the car can fire she's gone, must have leapt out of the way, the car passing through the space where she was standing.

31

•

Refuge

Irina takes the stairs of necessity, using her phone for light.

As she runs down the first flight she uses her wireless to attack Cromwell's phone. In the fashion of phones, it has conservative security, and immediately bricks itself. She does the same to the deaf girl's phone, thinking, *Sorry, beauty.*

There's a cluster of phones and what are probably guns on the floor beneath the Dernière and as she attacks them she wonders if they work for Cromwell and if she'd graciously declined his offer would there have been quiet footsteps behind her and then an iron hand closing on her shoulder.

She takes the stairs five at a time, letting gravity do the work.

She remembers the thick blades of the steak knives on the table. In the first second of darkness she probably could have killed Cromwell, if she'd wanted to go the full Lady Macbeth, but even now can't see herself stabbing him in the carotid, though she wonders if she'll come to see her passivity as a failure of will and a strategic catastrophe.

Nightmare descent past floor after floor through the near-dark, and the unexpected joy of the headlong flight. She reaches the lobby, bursts out onto the street. As though preordained a drone taxi is stopping ten feet in front of her. An overcoated man with an umbrella is reaching for the cab's door when she body checks him—flash of his astonishment as he sprawls on the sidewalk—"Sorry!" she calls, the word cut off by the slamming door.

"Come over," Philip says on her phone as she scans the street.

"I'm not going to put you at risk," she says.

"For fuck's sake, come over. It's a secured building, and I'll tell them to go on low alert. Can we please just take the rest of the back and forth as read, or maybe do it while you get your ass over?"

She's going to argue, but bites it off, says, "See you soon, then." She hangs up, gives the cab Philip's address.

She breaks into the cab's computer and changes its log so it thinks it picked her up near the Ferry Building, half a mile from Maison Dernière, then turns off her implant's wireless.

The cab's nav shows five minutes to Philip's house. She's agitated, wants to do more than slouch down in her seat and hope her friend knows what to do. She thinks of flying down the stairs, how much fun it was, like skiing on virgin snow in high alpine country, but actually she's never done that—she's been skiing all of four times, and never left the bunny slopes— the memory is Constantin's—they turn up from time to time. It's a misery and a desecration that whatever fragments of her friend remain are, presumably, in Cromwell's hands, and regarded without tenderness.

On her phone she finds the website for Iliou Engineering, Constantin's father's company in Athens, and the website for the family office, which consists of just a stylized drawing of a dam and an email address. As the cab turns toward the hills she starts writing a message.

The cab stops on a hill with a view of the city that looks silver with the moonlight on the towers and the fog. On the uphill side of the road are expensive-looking condos behind a high wall topped with broken glass. As she reaches out to open the cab's door her phone rings.

"Ms. Sunden?" asks someone, young, male, indistinctly foreign.

"Who's calling?"

"This is Mr. Iliou's secretary. Will you take a call with Mr. Iliou? I'm instructed to tell you that it's highly urgent."

She hesitates, but owes it to Constantin not to keep the old man waiting. "Sure," she says.

Another male voice, older, intent, weary. "Ms. Sunden," he says. "This is Constantin's father. I got your note. Thank you for that. The disposition of my son's remaining memories does in fact concern me deeply. But before we discuss that, I have the sense that you believe yourself to be in danger. Is this true?"

She thinks of Cromwell, whose guilt seems certain, who must be hunting for her. "Yes."

"Then the first thing is to get you out of it. I'd like you to come and see me. I'm currently in Patmos, a Greek island in the Dodecanese. But forgive me—obviously, you know where Patmos is. I have a jet standing by at San Francisco airport—with a flight path allowing mostly supersonic speed, the flight should take about six hours. Without going into detail, the security situation here is sufficient to deter even a highly resourced adversary. Will you come?"

His calm is fathomless, and his sincerity evident. She remembers Cromwell mentioning Philip with casual contempt, and that he'd known where Philip lived. She thinks of him floating in the black water, how she'd wanted to save him, how he'd let himself be destroyed before backing down. "I'll come," she says, her fingers moving over the cab's screen, redirecting it to the airport.

32

.

Still Unformed

He wakes to the T-shirt on his eyes, murmuring voices, footsteps passing by. Remembering his circumstances, he wishes he could go back to sleep. He tries out the idea that he'll be fine if he doesn't move, but it's day and he must already be conspicuous. The phone is still in his hand, the cable connecting it to the port in the wall. "You up?" he asks the ghost, but she doesn't reply.

He swipes at the phone's screen but it stays dark; in fact, it's been dark for as long as he's had it. "I'm going to unplug you, okay?" he says, and does. Through the earpiece he hears what might be wind, maybe the sea. He isn't too bothered—she has to sleep sometime, whatever she said.

He crawls out of his nest, struck afresh by the bustle of the concourse, its scale. The sleeping bag rolls small and tight and fits into his new luggage. *So that's it*, he thinks, looking at the vacated space under the bench, and walks away.

Strangers stride by, heading off in all directions. The cops, bored, ignore him. A monitor shows the time and the gates of upcoming departures. Seven hours till he leaves. He wonders if phones work on planes, and, if not, if she'll worry.

Ninety minutes till his flight for Thailand, and it strikes him that he speaks no Thai, has never been there, knows no one, that it's thousands and thousands of miles away, farther than he's traveled in his life.

"Are you there?" he murmurs for the hundredth time, and is ashamed of the uncertainty in his voice, though it's possible—probable, even—that she's the one who needs him, that something bad has happened—she had, after all, been in some kind of prison, and he said he'd free her, in fact gave his word.

He buys the cheapest laptop in the vending machines. When he takes it out of the little hatch he's surprised by its lightness. As he powers it up he finds himself expecting the game to start, but of course it doesn't, and in fact there's nothing on the new machine but boring office programs.

He opens a search engine but realizes that he doesn't even know her name. He'd have asked if they'd met normally, or if, once they had met, it hadn't felt like she was all around him.

He searches for actresses in Los Angeles, but their number seems to be infinite, each of them, seemingly, with a vanity website, and there's no way to find her among the multitudes.

He searches on "Cromwell," and quickly concludes that she was talking about James Cromwell, an industrialist from San Francisco. There are thousands of articles about him stretching back decades but they're all investments made, art bought, money money blah blah blah. Did the ghost see the same articles, huddled in the bathroom of the glass house on the sea?

No reference to a cartel hitman named Hiro, but it's not like he'd advertise. Lots of ethnic Japanese in the cartels after the last diaspora.

He searches on "director's daughter sonia," and finds that Sonia is probably Sonia Caipin, daughter of Henry Caipin, the director. She has blogs about fashion and photography and, as far as he can tell, hanging out in good hotels with not-quite-famous friends, though none of the blogs has been updated in a while. He's elated to find a photo of a pretty girl looking wistful before a crumbling wall, but it turns out there are a lot of photos like that, ethereal beauty and disintegration apparently being Sonia's thing. He looks up the day the LAPD disbanded, but for that day she just has photos of out-of-focus fireworks in deep blue empty skies. Cromwell seems more like an abstract force of economics than a real human being, but Sonia is believably a person, however remote from his experience, and it's exciting to have found a piece of the ghost's story in the world.

She'd said her German boxer's name was Johann. It turns out there are a lot of German boxers with that name, but only one, Johann Keil, has been in recent American films, direct-to-web ones with titles like *Blood Eagle III* and *Pit-Fight Armageddon*. A publicity still shows him bare-chested, arms crossed, a gun in either hand, and he seems to be trying to look sinister, a pose Kern knows and despises. The movie gossip sites have paparazzi shots from his premieres and at every premiere there's a new girl on his arm, and Kern stops at the pictures for the premiere of *Shatterfist*— the girl with him is small, eurasian, remarkable-looking, her image seeming to float off the screen—and looking back he sees she was in one of Sonia's photos.

Her name is Akemi Aalto and the sound of it shocks him because he's come to think of her as essentially unnamed. He finds a clip from a press conference where she smiles at the camera and in the ghost's voice says she feels happiest when she's being someone else.

He finds her filmography but, better, there's a gossip site with her press photos and paparazzi shots and in most of the latter she's looking out of frame and her face is a pale mask, a neutral space that holds his eyes and seems like it could hold any emotion he chose to project. The photos stretch back seven months and the last one is time-stamped one day ago.

In it she's peering out from the dark interior of a limo from behind a guy who must be either a professional athlete or a successful gangster with his flashy suit and bulging triceps and a watch like a lump of raw gold. He looks Japanese and according to the caption his name is Tadao Yamaoka, and he seems familiar, which, Kern finds, is because he's a kendo fighter ranked seventh in the world standings for Final Sword, a live-steel sword-fighting promotion out of Japan run more or less openly by the Yakuza. Kern sort of followed Final Sword for a while but they're serious about protecting their intellectual property and it's hard to get fights less than a few years old. He'd made watching them an exercise in controlling his queasiness—he'd seen more than one match end in decapitation. Final Sword makes a selling point of its fatality rate—more than half the fights end in at least one death—and it's demi-illegality, though for something so underground it moves a lot of licensed merchandise and ads.

Attached to the picture is an article that says that Tadao is in Taipei for a fight. There's the usual speculation about his chances against his opponent, a decorated Italian foil fencer—Tadao has won all of his six fights, and the Italian all of his three, but on the other hand the losers in Final Sword usually either die or are injured into retirement. And how long, the article wonders, has he been seeing this stunning LA ingenue? It's evident that the article considers Tadao's star the brighter and Kern finds he's indignant on Akemi's behalf.

He looks up Taipei, finds it's a city on Taiwan, which is an island that belongs to Japan. There are mountains on Taiwan, but the ghost—Akemi— and Tadao seem to have just flown in. He wonders if Tadao helped her escape her prison, and she isn't talking to him because she doesn't need him anymore. He scrutinizes the photo, as though it will reveal a clue, and at first there's nothing, but then he starts to think that he can see her despair, however hard she's trying to hide it, and that tips it.

"Direct to Taipei, leaving in thirty minutes, no bags to check," the gate agent confirms. "You'll have to run, but you can make it."

He'd been dreading having to explain himself but she seems really not to care, and he wonders if this is her professionalism, but of course she doesn't care, really no one in the world does, and this makes him feel a lightness, almost a giddiness, like his life lacks real weight.

"You sure you're not there?" he says. "Because there's no going back."

"Actually, sir," says the gate agent, "this ticket is full fare, as is the ticket for Bangkok that you bought last night, so you can use them whenever you like."

He wakes as the plane banks, peers out at the azure seas and low streamers of pink cloud, a lurid country out of dreams. The wing seems to warp before his eyes, getting longer and thinner, and at first he thinks he's hallucinating, but realizes he's heard of that, they can do that now—the phrase "shape-shifting meta-materials," overheard somewhere, rises in his mind.

The sleeping passengers look absurdly vulnerable with their eye masks and neck rests, their mouths hanging open. He'd meant to stay awake—a hit seems improbable here, but a shame to make it this far and die through inattention—but the boredom and the stale air and droning engines wore him down.

He's acutely aware that in a few hours the plane will land and he'll be standing there in the airport, the second of the day and the second of his life, clutching his bag, wondering what to do. Restless, he does a search on Tadao on the seat-back computer, finds he's a fixture of the Vancouver nightclub scene, which is death for a fighter, and the end of his career must be coming soon, which is disappointing—at that level you'd think there'd be a purity, that he'd be an ascetic, totally dedicated to the way of the sword, but maybe that's just something out of stories.

33

·

Encoded in Form

As the town car coasts down through the switchbacks in the dark hills Thales tries to make a phone call from the car's computer. Some indefinite number of calls have already failed and he's accepted that they always will and now he's absently fast-scrolling through the contacts list, placing doomed calls without looking, and as he does wonders who decided the family could make do with such useless electronics.

He expects to once again hear the dull bleat that means another failure but instead he hears a ringing, and looking down at the car's screen he sees he's dialed the surgeon, and feels a twinge of social distress—it's hardly etiquette to call this late, absent a medical emergency.

"Thales," says the surgeon, perfectly composed and somewhat distant even at this hour.

"I'm surprised I got through."

"What's the problem? Have you been losing yourself in the mathematics?"

Thales thinks of the madwoman, his gaps in memory, his mother's absence. A degree of amnesia is to be expected, given his injuries, but when he first came to LA he could remember Brazil, he thinks—it's only since his collapse in the tunnel by the beach that it's disappeared, and if the surgeon can edit his memories then is this forgetting by design, and what does the surgeon not want him to remember?

"When I collapsed, what was happening to me?" he asks, not wanting to approach the issue too directly.

"Why do you ask?"

"I'd just like to know what's going on in my life."

"It was a natural part of the progression of your injury. It's useless to dwell on it."

"So there was no . . . additional damage?" He wonders if he used to be different—he's heard of brain injury causing changes in personality.

"Do you feel that something's strange, or that you're missing part of your memory?"

He feels a fleeting impulse to be honest with his doctor but despite its superficial innocence the question is so perfectly apropos that Thales' skin crawls and he says, "What? No. I feel fine," simulating naivete, surprising himself with the conviction of his performance. "Why do you ask?"

"I'll see you soon. Call me if you have any problems."

Before the surgeon can ring off Thales says, "Have you spoken with my mother recently?"

"Yes. She's fine. She'll call you soon."

The line goes dead and Thales is left staring at the phone, wondering what to make of their inconclusive verbal fencing, but his eyes turn to the undulations of the hills and he wonders what geologies, what vanished seas shaped them, and what stories are encoded in their forms, and in the wind moving through the grasses, and in the crumbling mounds of grey rock, and then, as the car rounds a bend, the city is revealed like a magic trick. The moonlight reflects palely on the loops of road incising the miles of hillside below him and in the far distance are the graded shadows of the mountains and out over the sea the lights of some new complex rise like a river of light, its heights lost in the fog, and now the car accelerates as it turns and it feels like the city is drawing him in.

34

•

Final Sword

I t's always morning, that flight, since they're flying west, and fast, and it feels like everything is suspended, like they're going to float there forever in one frozen, shining hour, but then, impossibly, gravity lessens as they start their descent. Through the crust of ice crystals on the window Kern sees a distant formation of black drone fighters, like birds rising over the water, or a swirling column of smoke, and then, at some signal, they abruptly disperse in all directions, taking g-force that would kill a pilot, the sonic booms reaching him as a succession of muffled basso thumps, rippling the surface of his plastic cup of water.

Now the plane is over land—snow-dusted farmland rushes by, rises toward him. The shock of touchdown, the shriek of air brakes, and then he's walking off the plane onto another continent and blinking in the airport's hard fluorescent light.

There's a screen showing departures and arrivals, just like in SFO. Only fifteen minutes have elapsed on the clock, which seems at first like it must be a mistake, but then he remembers about time zones. He'd once read the memoir of Tesshu, a great swordsman of Japan, who said that when he was a boy an hour had passed like a year, but when he was an old man a year had passed like an hour, so the journey here was like youth, and if he ever goes back to California he'll have to pay the price, so the only solution is to keep on heading west.

The other passengers hurry toward customs, but he sits and stares out the window at the blustering snow, the planes rising ponderously into the sky, and some of them must still have pilots because they have windows on the front that look like eyes squinting in the wind.

And if he can't find Akemi, what then? The money she got him will sustain him for a while but he has no way of getting more, and the problem is so profound, so entirely unapproachable that his mind goes empty, and he sits there listening vacantly to announcements in Chinese. He wants to explore the airport, and orient himself, but his hand finds the phone is his pocket and he reminds himself he has a job to do.

When he gets to the front of the customs line he remembers the bloodstains on his pants, some from the man he fought and probably killed, the rest from the assassin who is dead beyond question. The customs agent waves him up; he's middle-aged and Chinese with a drinker's nose and lacks the brittle arrogance Kern expects in officials—in fact, he hardly seems to care at all, and after scrutinizing Kern's passport for half a second, hands it back and sends him on his way. Automatic doors of opaque glass open and then he's truly in a new country.

He uses his laptop to look up Final Sword and finds that today's event is starting soon on the outskirts of the city.

A bank of yellow lockers by the wall. You'd never have that in the U.S.—someone would practically be obligated to put a bomb in one. He wakes the touch screen, feeds it a bill, agrees to a long contract in what's probably Japanese. A locker pops open—he stashes his carryall, gets a tiny magnetic key.

Out the door into cold wind, filthy snow crunching underfoot—he's never touched snow before, had expected it to be purer, somehow celestial.

There's a line of green drone taxis. The dry heat of the taxi's interior, the definitive slam of its door. The car says something, and then the same thing again, and he finally figures out it wants him to give it money.

The taxi moves noiselessly over the icy road past low boxy buildings that all look the same. Some seem to be stores, but he can't tell what they're selling. Trucks roar by, spraying the cab's windows with black slush. He thinks of the Asia of media, the serenity of the temples, the neon ideography of Shinjuku at night.

He tries to make a mental map of the cab's turns, in case he has to walk back, but loses track and ends up just watching the streets go by.

Finally the cab glides to a stop in an alley of loading docks and dumpsters. The cab says something in a pleasant baritone and the charges appear on a screen in yen, yuan and dollars; a panel slides back to reveal his change.

The door opens onto bitter cold and the faint reek of rotting garbage, and he intends just to go for a quick reconnoiter but as he steps out the cab says something that he realizes is "goodbye" as it closes its door and drives off. He bangs on its trunk, uselessly, watches its red taillights recede through swarming particles of snow.

A man in a black parka is watching him from a loading dock, standing in front of wide double doors. He's Asian, his beard salted with ice, and his parka has the Final Sword logo, but even before these details have registered Kern somehow knows he's in the life, and remembers that the Yakuza are running the show. Not even gangsters have guns in the Japanese territories, he recalls, which seems to dilute the risk, like violence is just a game here. Kern's face aches with the cold, and his jacket lets in the wind, but he can't help smiling at finding himself on this street, in this snow, this winter.

The doorman cocks an eyebrow and in almost impenetrably accented English asks, "Are you here for the fights?" His hair is an elaborate pile, stiff with ice and product, and underneath the parka he's wearing an oversized checked suit. It seems to be a very specific look, though Kern has no idea what it means except that it boils down to cheap muscle.

"Yeah," says Kern, somewhat deflated, having been looking forward to talking in code. "Can you sell me a ticket?" He'd looked up the prices, has enough in his hand for the cheapest seat.

"Prelims over," the doorman says. "Tickets officially no longer for sale." Kern is immediately trying to think where else he could look for Akemi, and how he'll stay warm while he does it, but the yakuza says, "Just main event now. Want to see? Lot of seats in VIP area. Why not? You pay me now. Cash, okay?"

The doorman pockets Kern's money without counting it, hands him a ticket embossed with a silvery holographic samurai, sends him in.

A narrow, dimly lit concrete stairway leads down into a welcome heat and the muted pulse of Russian heavy metal. At the bottom a door opens onto a black abyss full of roaring music, but as his eyes adjust he sees the steep slope of tiered seats, lit only by the fairy light of countless phones, and now a glow from the massive screens mounted over the steel cage at the nadir of the arena.

The music stops and a fierce old Japanese man appears on the screens in what even Kern can see is a good suit, but under the tailoring he, like the doorman, is a plain old crim. He's sitting behind a big desk in what looks like a lawyer's office; Kern is too busy picking his way down the stairs to read many of the subtitles but the gist is that Final Sword embodies the traditional values of Japan.

His seat is on the aisle four rows from the bottom and even for just one fight it seems like good value for money. The bloodstains on the cage floor remind him of his pants. Almost everyone is Asian and looks rich and they're all absorbed in their phones; in the seat in front of him is a white man with cropped salt-and-pepper hair, so close that Kern can smell his boozy cologne and can't help seeing that he's looking at a betting website offering odds on the winning technique, things like *head cut, wrist cut, throat shot, disarm* and, worryingly, *messy.*

The arena goes dark and silent, and then string music swells as the screens show Tadao, bare to the waist, holding a katana and glowering at the camera. His stats come up: twenty-nine years old, fourth dan in kendo, a lieutenant in the Tokyo municipal police. Children in a kendo dojo, chanting metronomically as their bamboo swords rise and fall, then still images of Tokyo University, Tadao in a Self-Defense Force uniform shaking hands with an epauletted officer, a young woman in a tiny room kneeling beside a vase with a single peony.

The second fighter is Sanzo Vola, foil fencer, thirty-two, Italian, an Olympic silver medalist. A montage shows him in a fencing club lunging acrobatically at a frantically backpedaling opponent, then images of ancient churches, of a walled town on a dusty hill, of fencing tournaments in huge conference halls.

Neither fighter is very lean, which surprises him at first, but it's probably because the fights rarely last a whole minute, so there's no need for deep cardio.

Vendors cry their beer and sake and spotlights roam the crowd as two men in white robes with tall black hats—maybe priests, certainly officials—walk into the ring, both reverently carrying a sword. They present the blades to the crowd, white cloths protecting the steel from the moisture of their hands. The crowd applauds, and both swords get little biographical clips, as though they, too, were celebrities. The Italian's is from a Solingen forge, a straight blade with a triangular cross-section like a long spike, with a strangely windswept aluminum handle, shaped to fit the hand. Tadao's sword is a katana, gently curved, single-edged, its point like a chisel, from the forge of Masamune, and even from the fourth row Kern can see the waver of the blade's watermark, and how it seems to be lit with an interior fire—the cold lines of its beauty hold his eyes as a spotlight passes over him, blinding him, and the blade seems to embody the purity he's always yearned for, and for a moment he desires it over all other things, though of course such weapons are expensive beyond reckoning, and far beyond the reach of the likes of him. As the light passes and his eyes clear he sees Akemi, in the front row, not fifteen feet away, glancing back at him.

He tries to signal to her but it's dark again and now the screens show a glitteringly antiseptic operating theater where Japanese doctors and nurses in blue surgical gowns bow together and belt out that thing they say when you go into this noodle place out toward Market Street, "hello" or "thank you" or whatever, and the guy who is clearly the boss proudly announces something that the subtitles render as "We are one hundred percent committed to saving the combatants' lives, with a success rate in excess of forty percent!" and the screens' light shines on Akemi's hair.

The two fighters huddle with their trainers in opposite corners of the cage. The trainers embrace them—the Italian gets a kiss on both cheeks—and then file out, ignoring each other, leaving their fighters alone with naked blades under the hard white light. They're both in just shoes, shorts and gloves, and already sweating. They shift their feet, loosen their shoulders, make minute adjustments to their grips. One of them is probably about to die. Kern knows what it's like to feel that alone.

The loudspeakers say *"Hajime!"* and the word hangs in the air as the two come together as though magnetically drawn and Kern is on his feet as the crowd is on its feet because it's already over, and they echo the

Italian's raw, open-throated cry as Tadao, seemingly weary, falls to his side, and Kern sees the bright thin spike of blade protruding from his back. The blood pools around him as the doctors from the video rush in with hypodermics and defibrillators and the Italian sits down with his back to the cage, emptied, done.

35

·

Persephone

Just darkness, out the window, punctuated every few seconds by a blue flash from the wing.

The cabin is sleekly minimal, like a five-star hotel room in a narrow metal tube. Only thirty-two percent of Americans, she's read, will get on a plane in the course of their lives. And how many, she wonders, get on a plane like this.

The vibration is stupefying and dawn is coming soon. She longs for sleep, but is still jittery, and the bag with her sleeping pills is in her last hotel room but one.

In the liquor cabinet she finds Ukrainian vodkas she's never heard of and cabernets she remembers from the wine lists of good restaurants. She hesitates to open anything because the bill will go to Mr. Iliou, and she already feels she's imposing, but compared to the flight the liquor costs nothing.

Fifth vodka in hand, her eyes begin to close. It feels a little like home, being on a plane, and it's good to be safe, numb, departing.

She hasn't changed clothes in two days. Once standing seems like an attainable goal, she'll go wash her underwear and socks in the bathroom sink. *Ah*, she thinks, *the glamor of my life.*

The engines' roar rises an octave as the plane accelerates. Alarmed, at first, she relaxes into it, and lets the g-force be a blanket. They're probably over Utah—Deseret, now, since the fed stopped caring—and approaching the sound barrier. She imagines the jet's sonic boom rolling over miles of dark, empty desert, echoing in the burned-out streets of Provo.

As sleep comes she remembers going to see a shuttle launch at a military airfield in Texas, out where there was nothing for miles around; the deafening pulse of the fusion boosters, the shock waves flattening the dry grass in expanding concentric rings, how she'd narrowed her eyes against the hot wind full of grit, the poison yellow sky of the rising shuttle's dawn.

When she wakes it's morning and out the window there's water of a remarkable Aegean blue. Silver coffee service beside her, and gold-rimmed porcelain cups—it must have been laid out by an unobtrusive drone, of which there is now no sign.

An island appears, mostly bare rock and brown earth but still it has a promise and a mystery, and she wants to go there and walk on its beaches, but then it's gone.

The engines' roar is lower now. She sees boats down on the water, and a little Cessna passes below on a perpendicular course. The day is bright and cloudless; it's hard to feel unhappy.

A low chime from unseen speakers. "You are now approaching . . . Patmos . . . this plane's final destination," says a supple and deeply relaxed female voice that could be read as either synthesized or extraordinarily stoned. "We respectfully advise that you buckle your seat belt and remain seated until the plane lands."

The jet is low over the water now, the unbroken waves visible as a succession of ridges, low enough for her to see the fishermen on the boats, and now the jet's shadow racing over white beaches, vineyards, jagged cliffs.

There's a motorboat waiting for her at the beach by the airstrip.

The skipper is fiftyish, worn, obviously a local. He speaks no English. The day is beautiful, their wordless passage like something in a dream.

He points out what must be Iliou's villa as it comes into view on its cliff by the sea.

She wades through ankle-deep water to the beach, shoes in hand. The villa is more fortress than chateau and looks like it's been there for thousands of years. Sun on brown stone, smell of hot dust. It's not yet midday but she wants to lie down in the shade and go to sleep—booze, she remembers, makes jet lag worse. She's never flown supersonic before—what does that do to the hours lost and gained? She'll postpone that calculation, she decides. She hears the boat's engine behind her as it pulls away.

A woman her own age opens the villa's door, smiles and in lightly accented English says, "You must be Irina. How was your flight?" Irina has the sense she's being welcomed to the woman's own home, then recognizes her from Constantin's borrowed memories as his sister Fabienne.

Within are courtyards and a succession of gardens, and with the dust and the hard shadows and the fragments of sculpture she feels like she's walked into a de Chirico painting. Fabienne seems kind, and gives her water while maintaining a sparkling flow of chatter about the island and the weather while asking nothing personal and saying nothing of substance, and her bright eyes and firm skin tell Irina that Fabienne, too, is a patron of the Mayo, or one of its handful of equivalents.

An approaching racket and then three children run out through an archway. She's not good at guessing children's ages but they might be between five and twelve, and the smallest one grabs Fabienne's leg, grinning wildly, and clings for dear life. "My little monsters," Fabienne says. "I'll just disentangle myself and then I'll take you to my father." The children scramble off as an au pair comes through an archway remonstrating in Greek and Irina wonders what it's like to grow up there, how villa and family would be taken for granted, as inevitable as the sea.

Iliou is sitting alone in a walled garden before a table with a chessboard, a book and a battered golden crown. The cyclical churring of the cicadas could be the soundtrack for a horror movie. Iliou is wearing a cardigan though the day is hot and he has a belly, which seems strange at first, but of course the physical vanity of the elderly rich is less pronounced here, and in fact outside of the U.S. generally, with the obvious exception of Brazil. The book is closed and he's staring into space or at the stonework of the walls, and she has the sense that he's always here, that he knows intimately how the light changes with the passing of the day, and then without haste his gaze turns to her. Fabienne comes back with little cups of aromatic coffee and he says, "Ms. Sunden, thank you for coming. I hope you'll be my guest for as long as you'd like, and I'm sure you want to rest after your journey, but, if you'll allow me, I'd like to talk first. The clinic told me that when my son died a lady friend was with him, and from your email I gather that was you."

She says that it was, and explains how she'd shared his death with him.

"And how was it for him at the end?" He seems intent, neutral, his tone that of a scientist asking about the deep secrets of the cosmos.

"There was no pain," she says. "The drugs work. And he was confused . . . It was like a random procession through his memory. But he knew I was with him, that I was there with him completely. He couldn't feel most of his body, in the last minutes, but he was aware of mine, and at the very end he mistook it for his own."

"It sounds like you bled together," he says, which could be read two ways, both true.

"We did," she says. "Actually, I have some of his memories. Sometimes I remember things that happened to him, and think they happened to me. Usually I notice, but sometimes they slip by, I think. It's like I've incorporated his soul in some small degree." She falls silent, unsure if this is the best or the worst thing to have said to her dead friend's father.

"So in a sense you are my son."

It's one of those phrases she'd never really expected to hear. She has a sudden fear that she's been misleading him, but still she says, "Yes, to some nonzero, extremely small degree." She knows he's an engineer by training, and he seems like the kind of man who would enjoy hearing a mathematician's turn of phrase from a good-looking woman. "When I look at snow on mountains I sometimes think how I'd ski them, even though I've barely skied. It's the surfacing of his point of view."

"Does it feel like an invasion?"

"No. I'm happy when it happens. It makes him just that little bit less gone." She can't bring herself to tell him about the time she found herself checking out the ass of a woman who looked like Constantin's lost love, much to her surprise, as she's only ever liked boys.

"I'm happy to hear that," he says. "Because I was never really able to let him go. I'm afraid I was never a good father to him. When I was a younger and vainer man I very much wanted a mathematically gifted son, and I'm afraid I led Constantin a sad dance of it. When he was a little boy I tried to make him learn calculus when he just wanted to be outside and play video games. When he was at university I actually threatened to disinherit him unless he would apply himself. Now I'd give my entire fortune just to see him for ten minutes. Not even to see him. It would be enough to sit here and know he was in the house. All the money in the world, and for what?"

He seems to expect a response so she says, "Maybe it will be useful in the future."

"There isn't much future. Not like there is for you. I say this in observation, not regret. You have the look of the longevity treatments. I started too late. I thought the technology was immature, and I was busy. That was a mistake. So it goes. Now I have a decade, perhaps two. I keep an eye on my business, but it mostly runs itself, and I collect antiquities, or it might better be said that I permit them to accumulate. Look at this," he says, taking up the crown, which is crude and thin and decorated with a motif of concentric circles. "My firm is building a shopping mall in Macedonia, at what once was Pella, the capital of Alexander the Great. My workers excavated this. The legally mandated on-site archaeologist tells me that it must be given to the national museum, where it will be duly cataloged and then put in a box among thousands of boxes, never to be seen again. Or I could take it home, and the archaeologist, whose father went to school with me, might well forget to report it. So now I have a golden diadem, and no use for it. Won't you try it on?"

He holds it out and when she takes it it's lighter than she'd expected and she thinks of Cromwell's wineglass as he retakes it and places it on her head, which is a strange gesture but one she accepts out of decency or mourning or maybe apology.

He smiles a little, takes out his phone, takes a picture. "Look," he says, showing it to her. "Like Persephone, who was half of the living and half of the dead." Behind her in the picture is dry stone and sand and a pomegranate tree, and she looks patient and sad and like she could sleep for a thousand years; the black hemispheres under her eyes remind her of Constantin's last hour, and her clothes, which were chic when she put them on, look shapeless and seedy, and the gold crown shines in the sun.

"But your implant," he says, "is your true crown, hidden within," and she's listing in her seat and thinking up excuses when he says, "Why would anyone want my son's memories, or yours, so badly? Certainly they're *interesting*, but does that justify the risk entailed by the theft?"

"I wondered about that all the way across the Atlantic," she says, fighting to keep her eyes open. "There seems to be no good explanation. I can see why someone would want them for research, but that doesn't seem to justify the cost."

"Could they be used to simulate the minds of whoever they were stolen from?"

"No. Well, maybe, people have tried, but the problem is too hard—it would take more computer power than there is on earth, by several orders of magnitude. It's generations away, if it's possible at all. So I can only assume I'm missing information, or that maybe Cromwell regards digitized memory as a kind of art. He seems to have been a dedicated collector, off and on, and this is something that no one else has. Maybe he thinks it's like collecting souls. Maybe he's set his heart on it, and thinks he's above consequences."

"Then that will be his undoing," says Iliou, and for a moment his rage shows through.

"But forgive me," he says, his cordial neutrality snapping back into place. "You must be exhausted. Fabienne will show you your room. Sleep well, my daughter, and tomorrow we'll talk of war."

36

•

Usually in Trouble

Vola pushes his way out of the cage past a scrum of officials and nurses running in with bags of plasma and an emcee who shoves a microphone in his face only to have it swatted away and then he's mobbed by his elated entourage. Everyone in the audience is rising from their seats and crowding up the stairs, and the doctors have Tadao on his back now, the blood-wet sword to one side, and with the first defibrillation Tadao's back arches but Kern sees the eyes of a lady doctor over her white surgical mask and knows it's over.

He jumps down the steps to the floor by the cage in time to see Akemi's back framed in the mouth of a service tunnel as she blows past the guard in his Final Sword blazer under the RESTRICTED ACCESS sign, and Vola is right behind her, yanking off his glove and throwing it blindly over his shoulder, his entourage following, and even though they're talking in Italian Kern mostly understands them as they say, "What did I tell you— kendoka are weak against change of tempo with an indirect attack," and "Fuck the press conference, look at him, we need to get him to the hotel," and he remembers that Italian and Spanish are almost the same, which reminds him that the Japanese are said to think all westerners look alike, so he snatches up Vola's glove—damp with sweat, held together with tape, speckled with Tadao's blood—and trots after the Italians, like he's some flunky with a small share in the team's euphoria. The guard ignores him as he hastens into the tunnel.

In the tunnel there's a door open onto a surgery, the one from the video, abandoned now except for a nurse wearing latex gloves and blue scrubs standing rigidly by a tray of gleaming surgical tools. Vola shoves through the next door, his team pouring in after, and over their shoulders Kern sees a table covered with blunt-tipped practice swords, mesh fencing masks, bottles of wine and little plates of food; Vola sweeps the wine from the table, and Kern hears the bottles shattering as he walks on, alone now, trying to look like he knows where he's going. He remembers the glove, lets it fall to the floor.

The next door opens and Akemi comes out, now wrapped in a blue-white fur so brilliant in the light that it looks like falling snow. Angry, staccato Japanese from inside but Akemi shrugs and says, "Can't be helped!" and it's thrilling to hear her voice, though she sounds different, maybe younger now; also thrilling that she was lost somewhere out in the world but now is close enough to touch.

"Hey!" he says, as she turns and walks away.

She looks back blankly, takes him in and then smiles. Her beauty is remarkable, so much so she almost seems to glow, which didn't come through in the photographs.

"Well, come on then," she says. "As it happens I'm in need of company," and then a Japanese guy with slicked-back grey hair and a black suit strides into the corridor looking poisonously angry and though he isn't big something about him says "martial arts," probably judo, these things have a feeling, and Akemi grabs Kern's hand and says, "Run!"

He slows his step to match hers. More angry Japanese from behind and she says, "Must go faster!" and she's grinning wildly as she tries to keep up with him, and he wonders who they're running from, if he should be ready to fight and where the corridor goes.

"I've been looking for you," he says. "I crossed the ocean to find you."

"Sweet. Don't think I don't appreciate it," she says distractedly, already out of breath, and then they burst through double doors onto the street outside. Immediately cold, he wonders if she means to run off into the city but she raises an imperious hand toward a double-parked armored town car and says, "Open!" The car's lights flash and a door swings wide.

"What was that?" he asks, as she bundles him in.

"Tadao's manager. He's trying to seize assets before probate starts, but it's my goddamn mink. Nasty little man. Serves him right, being robbed. Which reminds me—car, disable remote override."

"Disabled," says the car in a neutral baritone exactly the same as his first cab's voice, as though all the cars in this city share a single soul.

"I meant, before," he says, ungrounded by her apparent indifference to the lengths he's gone to, and for that matter to her own freedom. "I thought you were in trouble."

"I'm usually in trouble," she says breezily. "The wild life, you know?"

"I'm sorry about Tadao."

"I'm not. We had some fun, but he was an asshole, and I don't have time to pretend he wasn't because he got his ass killed. I was this close to putting money on Vola. Wish I had, seeing how it turned out."

"Destination?" asks the car, its calm fathomless.

"Downtown," she says. "Just drive."

Sheets of snow cover the windows, concealing the outside except for the blued glow of passing lights. "I like it this way," she says, "though it takes some getting used to, not seeing where you're going." She takes off her fur and spreads it companionably over their legs and it feels like they're sequestered in a sealed private world.

"There's so much I want to ask you," he says.

"There'll be time for that," she says vaguely, looking at him with a strangely fixed expression, and then she's straddling him, and her mouth tastes like cigarettes and brandy, and he wants to explain that he sought her out for the purest reasons, that he wasn't looking for this at all, but she won't let him talk, and is insistent, pulling at his shirt as she laughs a little gurgling laugh, and then he says okay.

"Damn, boy," she says, dropping his shirt on the floor. "Work out a little?"

"You said that before," he says but she doesn't seem to have heard him as she rubs her cheek against his stomach, seeming to take great pleasure in his skin, and now she's fumbling with his belt, and in the diffuse pale light he watches her, and he wants to hold onto this image forever, because he doubts he'll ever be so happy again, and he's thinking, *I will hold onto this moment, no this, this, this, this.* She's only his third woman and he'd supposed it would be someone but is amazed it's her. She guides his hands to grasp her hair and his fingers find the socket behind her right ear, and he means to explore its strangeness, but then forgets.

He wakes aware of the car's motion and its cabin's heat. She's beside him, dressed, engrossed in her phone. "Put your clothes on," she says, and lowers the window, its wall of snow fragmenting and falling away to reveal the street gliding past. She slides out through the window of the slowly moving car while he's bucking into his pants—she falls out, and he sticks his head out after her, sees her rise laughing, brushing herself off, her fur crusted in snow. He wriggles out of the window, pushes off with his feet from the door. He lands on four points on frozen asphalt and bounces up with his palms barely skinned.

The narrow street is walled in by towering buildings that have the look of expensive hotels. The one before them has WARWICK-REGENCY incised in noble capitals on its portico. The uniformed doorman pretends not to have been watching as Akemi takes Kern's hand and pulls him inside.

Impression of hardwoods and Turkish carpets and high chandeliers and he's intensely aware that he's been sleeping under a bench in an airport and having sex in a car. He's never been in a hotel like this, or known anyone who has, except for this one thief who long since went to prison.

At the front desk Akemi says, "We need a room. A quiet one." As the clerk consults his laptop she fumbles through her wallet and finds only gleaming cards. "Hmmn. Got any cash?" she asks Kern, so he takes out his money—after all, it's really hers—and pays for the room, which costs almost as much as a plane ticket.

The room is on the fifty-first floor. In the elevator he says, "Are you hiding from Tadao's manager?"

"Him? Well, I suppose so. It was his car, or in any case he rented it. But he's not who I'm afraid of."

He's going to ask her if it's Hiro but she starts kissing him again and puts her hands under his shirt even though the elevator's door could open.

The room is beige and grey and white, so clean and well kept that it feels like nothing very bad could happen there. There's a white-painted fireplace and a view of the darkness that's probably the ocean, and out on the balcony he looks down onto terrace upon terrace of the other balconies below, arranged like steps reaching down to the beach, most of them covered in new snow. "Casing the joint?" she asks, but not like she minds, and she gives him a glass of whisky, which ordinarily he wouldn't drink but now he does, and then she leads him to the bed and the clouds through the windows look remarkable, wind-torn and metamorphic, and at some point he asks her if she has birth control and she says it doesn't matter, she doesn't care, he can just go to town.

He wakes to cold, realizes the balcony door is open. She's sitting at the end of the bed wearing nothing but her mink and smoking a cigarette. She offers him a drag but he declines, and for a while it's enough to look at her in her haphazardly draped fur. She looks worried as she pulls on her cigarette, and he says, "Is it Hiro you're afraid of, or Cromwell?" at which her face freezes.

She sits up straight, pulling the fur tighter, looking furious; then the fight goes out of her and she wipes her hand over her face. "What the fuck, dude," she says, her voice flat and angry. "You really are a true fan. How did you find out about that?"

"You told me."

This brings her up short. "Oh," she says.

"You don't remember?"

She shrugs. "I get blackouts," she says. "And migraines. Part of the price of doing business. I lose days. Weeks, sometimes. Price of success. But maybe you already knew that."

"Did you black out last night?"

"Not that I recall," she says lightly, smiling, like she thinks it's kind of funny, and he realizes that she's channeling her glamorous old actresses, and thus blowing him off, which means there might not be any answers.

"Hey now," she says. "Come on, it's not as bad as all that," and lays him back down. She turns off the bedside light and gets in beside him, saying, "So why don't you tell me everything, from the beginning. Maybe we're already old friends and I forgot."

Head propped on her hand, she pays close attention as he tells her about the last two days. "Those *are* my stories," she says, "but they're not ones I tell. I must be so much lonelier than I thought. But I've never had a Swiss bank account, and I haven't been locked in some house in the mountains. That I remember. And here I thought you were just this fan for the taking."

Later she says, "You know your girl sold you out, right? The little thing. Kayla. I mean, how do you think the hitman knew where to find your friend Lares, or even that he should?" Silence, and eventually she says, "You didn't know. I'm sorry, baby. That's just how they are, the Kaylas of the world."

"That's what you said before."

"I know exactly what she was thinking. She made it seem okay by pretending it wasn't real. Something would happen so they wouldn't really find you, and she'd get something, probably money, for doing nothing, which is how the world works, she thinks, ideally."

"Oh," he says.

"It's okay. You got through it, didn't you? But maybe you should think about whether she's worth holding on to." He's silent, watching the clouds go by, and she says, "Okay. You know a lot about me, and I still know almost nothing about you, so why don't you tell me how you met her."

"There are fights at night on the favelas' rooftops," he says. "I did it for money, and for practice, and so they'd know to be afraid of me. One night I was going to fight this kid, actually he was my age but he looked frightened until his older brother came up and started rubbing his shoulders, and they were looking at me while the brother told him how to beat me."

"Did you have someone there, a coach or something?"

"I've never had a coach," Kern says. "I'd meant to go for a low-risk technical win but when the ref said 'fight' I rushed him. The louder the brother shouted the harder I hit. I'm usually conservative, but that time I took punches so I could get my hands on. I knocked him down and got the mount and felt his nose break under my hand. I kept punching until the ref pulled me off and then I flicked the blood from my hands into the brother's face."

"Why?" asks Akemi, who's looking at him like he's really interesting for the first time, and it's because of this and because she's seemingly without judgment that he's able to say, "Because they made a show of it," though the words almost stick in his throat. "They didn't have to let me know.

"Afterwards I was sitting on the edge of the roof and this girl came up to me. Kayla, as it turned out. My eye was swelling shut, but I could see that she was pretty. I couldn't think of anything to say—it was like I'd become an animal, and all I could do was look at her. She wiped off the blood from under my eye. 'You're hurt,' she said."

In the night her breathing turns fast and shallow, like she's having a bad dream, and he shakes her and whispers her name but she doesn't wake up. Moisture on her upper lip—he holds his fingers up to the little light, sees they're dark, licks them, tastes blood. Not knowing what to do, he wraps himself around her, hoping the heat and contact will at least comfort her, and after a while the bleeding stops—he throws the stained pillow to the floor—but her breathing doesn't slow. His fingertips trace the hardness of her socket, which he imagines would annoy her, if she were conscious.

It's dark but he's irrevocably awake. It's been days since he bathed, barring a quick wash with paper towels in the plane's cramped lavatory, and he's always made a point of washing every day, even when it was hard to get water. He pads naked into the bathroom, which is tiled in smooth stone—easing the light on, he sees it's granite, mottled with the cross-sections of tiny fossil shells. The shower's pipes are a convolution of silver, like old-style espresso machines; he figures out how to use the knobs to set the water temperature digitally. The hot water beats on the stone and sluices over his hair, the pressure like a cataract, diluting his thoughts. The water pressure is still high after several minutes, and for the first time he finds himself envying the rich.

When he turns off the water he hears her moving, wonders if she's recovered over the course of his shower and gotten out of bed, but when he comes back into the dark room he sees the swell of her body under the duvet and sitting beside her is a man, or the shadow of one, cross-legged on the bed, his laptop beside him, and as in a nightmare there's a small silver pistol gleaming on a table, just beyond the man's reach, and Kern is acutely aware of the glass walls behind him, of how he's silhouetted before the moonlit clouds, and then there's nothing but the question of whether he can reach the man before the man can reach the gun but it seems it would take hours, or even years, to cross the twelve feet of carpet, and it seems that he'd never reach the man, and the man would never reach the gun, both forever suspended in motion, but even in the dark Kern registers the man's calm, guesses that the gun is on the table not through carelessness but as a sort of joke, and is still.

After a while the man says, "I'm almost done here," and then, "If you took longer showers we might never have met."

"Can I put on my clothes?" asks Kern.

"Go ahead," says the man, "though so much for intimacy."

As Kern tugs on his pants he feels the mass of the phone and of the money in his pockets, and is relieved, when he pulls his shoes on, because now if he dies he won't look so pathetic.

Laptop light, shining in the man's face—he looks Japanese, but doesn't sound it, and Kern realizes this is probably Hiro.

Kern says, "What are you doing here?"

"Collecting a debt. We take everything, but it's nothing she'll miss."

"Is she all right?" *And if she's not*, he thinks, *I'll kill you, somehow, however improbably.*

"No," says Hiro, and smooths her hair with abstracted tenderness. "She might not wake up again, and even if she does her time is almost up. She knew it was a possibility when she signed on. If it makes you feel any better, the damage was done when she got her operation—I'm not hurting her."

Hiro's laptop chimes. "Well," he says, shutting it, "let's have a look at you." He turns on the light and in the sudden illumination Kern sees Akemi's eyes moving under their lids, as though she's searching desperately for something in a dream, and her face and the sheet are streaked and clotted with blood, and there's a cable connecting Hiro's laptop to her socket. Hiro is wearing a conservative dark suit and he has an arrogance, but no, in fact it's just the total absence of fear, which interests Kern, professionally, for he's fought men fueled by rage or hate or ambition but always underneath there was a terror, which Hiro lacks, somehow, as though life and death are one to him.

Hiro looks him in the face and then at the dried bloodstains on the knees of his pants, where his guilt is plainly writ, though no one, so far, has been able to read it, but he can see Hiro's wonder, disbelief, dawning amusement, and now Hiro's hand is drifting toward his gun, and with that Kern is on the balcony without ever having decided to move.

With the lights on Hiro will only see his own reflection, Kern thinks, standing on the balcony's wall, the other balconies staggered below him like a giant's staircase. When the light goes off he's already jumped.

He falls through floating particles of snow. Jarring impact as he lands on the wall of the next balcony down and his ankles waver but his finger-tips find traction on the snow-crusted stucco and momentum carries him into the next jump. Aloft, his heart rises.

He stands on the cold sand, leaning on his knees, not letting himself sit down. Black ocean roars and sighs unseen before him. He gets his breath back slowly, his descent still filling his mind. He looks back at the hotel, its lights, its improbable height; Hiro is up there, probably on the balcony, peering out into the dark with gun in hand. He could double back, try to catch Hiro off guard—he's pretty sure he'd wreck him in a stand-up fight—but they probably wouldn't let him back in the hotel, much less let him skulk around the lobby. Maybe sometime he can go back for her but for now it would just mean dying uselessly. It's cold on the beach but he doesn't feel it, in fact feels like lying down, resting awhile and watching the sky, but it's plainly time to act, not least because Hiro might take the elevator and come looking. He tests his ankle—tender, but he can walk on it. He tries to think where to go. Airports are safe, Akemi had said, and then he remembers he has a ticket for Thailand.

If he closes his eyes, the airport's hubbub sounds like running water. Guards with automatic weapons patrol the concourse, scanning the crowd, which, bizarrely, allows him to relax—this must be what it's like being middle class.

His flight should have him in Bangkok before noon. He wants to do nothing, meanwhile, but compels himself to take out his laptop and plan the next step.

He finds a muay thai camp on the most isolated stretch of Thailand's southern coast. It looks like there's nothing out there—the towns were mostly washed away, he reads, in the tsunamis of decades past. The camp's website has pictures of Thai coaches who look like pocket-sized Bruce Lees, and of ocean the color of the sky, coconuts floating in the surf, smiling Thai girls on scooters. There are thousands of other camps, but the options are overwhelming, and it's easier to ignore them. It occurs to him to send the camp an email, but Lares was always going on about how email isn't secure, so it's probably better to just show up.

He told himself he wasn't going to, but the ethernet cable is still in his bag, so he cables the phone to a port in the wall, because maybe Akemi's okay, and maybe she's escaped, but there's still no one there.

37

·

Cloudbreaker

From her chaise longue on the villa's rooftops in the sun Irina sees other islands in the distance and swallows arcing through the air and it's silent but for the wind sighing through the worn crenelations. There's a serenity, and a timelessness, as though she'd found an hour from the morning of the world, and now she lets it go.

There's a fast router up in the tower whose shadow is just touching her legs; she closes her eyes, connects to the router and then the servers Iliou rented her to add to her strength and then she reaches for a website that has a number but no name. The site shuts down as she touches it but in the last millisecond of its existence it yields another number for another website and so on in a chain that turns to ash before her eyes until she comes to a site that serves her a long contract in dense legalese that requires her in essence to respect the laws of every state with any history of pursuing computer crime beyond its borders, and she remembers Philip saying that the very pomposity of the language was meant as a distraction from the fact that the contract was unenforceable, really just a pro forma stab at ass-covering, but in any case she duly agrees and it gives her a link to the Cloudbreaker AI.

Darkness, as she opens the connection, and emptiness like a flat black sea, and there, the barest possible suggestions of shape, like islands over dark water, rushing closer, revealed as dense massifs of seething glyphs whose heights fill her eyes as the fugue hits.

But somehow she'd forgotten that there's work to do, a digital lock she needs urgently to open. The lock is intricate, and at first glance impenetrable, but she sets her will against it and its layers start to peel away, for all the world like a flower opening, and she finds it comes naturally, as though she knew the lock well, which gives her pause, and then she realizes she's dismantling her own implant's security, at which Cloudbreaker, which has been intent on her, gives up and sinks back down into its roiling hallucinations.

She lets the fugue fade until she's once again aware of her body and of the sun on her face; she keeps her eyes closed, compels herself to breathe deeply until her heart slows. She remembers the last time she connected directly to Cloudbreaker—in theory, doing so gives her more control—and the aftermath, lying on the grass, staring blankly up into the void, feeling like a fragment of the machine's hurtling dream, and for the benefit of her future selves she'd said, *"It's very important that you never do this again."* She reminds herself that Cloudbreaker is just an artifact in software, not a malignant spirit, and is by its nature an opener of doors.

Legally grey, Cloudbreaker, and of no known state, its owners hiding behind layers of darknets and blinds, though Philip, obsessed with the secret systems of the world, and sometimes reckless, once tried to learn their names. Nominally for testing computer security, which is how she's twice come to work with it, it's more often used by the most technically sophisticated thieves.

She'd been surprised when Iliou suggested using Cloudbreaker against W&P, as she'd thought only specialists were aware of its existence, but had thought maybe that's just the kind of thing the rich know about now. "Maybe you can find what's left of Constantin, and erase it," Iliou had said. "In any case we'll know what Cromwell really wants." She'd recalled a line from Plutarch: "Let no one call himself rich who can't afford his own army."

She finds she wants to just lie there in the sun—the consequences of what she's about to do are unforeseeable, but likely to be extreme, and she's already feeling shaky, but then she remembers what Iliou's paying for each second of Cloudbreaker's time and makes herself reconnect.

Ever mercurial, it's already lost interest in her, and ignores her until she opens the gate that's been keeping it from the net and points it at W&P. As it explodes outward she finds herself imagining its relief even though she knows it's just a program.

Cloudbreaker's attack is like an obliterating wave. Water and Power's defenses waver, hold, and there's the slightest sense of anticlimax but the next assaults are closing fast and she feels the elation preceding cataclysm.

Impact, and chaos—for a moment she's disoriented, and the ragged hole in W&P's perimeter is closing but they're already swarming through, which puts her on the wrong side of many laws but she's happy to have taken the initiative.

A security AI manifests and in the same beat Cloudbreaker swallows it whole, like something out of a nature documentary and somehow as hideous, but there are more of them, hundreds, thousands appearing out of nowhere, which is more resistance than she'd expected, in fact it's absurd, for fuck's sake it's not the Pentagon, and things are already getting out of control.

W&P's data is there, the pending short sells and minute shifts in the energy markets and all the keystrokes of the employees below the level of VP and there's a blank space and a resistance that draws her attention, a core of denser security which Cloudbreaker eviscerates at her command and then she's into Cromwell's private archive.

Constantin, she thinks, saluting him in her mind as she flashes through the files but there's no mention of him, just decades worth of financial records and contracts, and the absence of reference is surprisingly painful, a little like losing him again, but there's another blank, a core within the core, and though Cloudbreaker is hard-pressed she compels it to ignore its assailants and dissolve this final barrier.

"I hold the keys to the kingdom of life and death" is the phrase that captures her attention, is in fact the full text of the first message sent to Cromwell by an anonymous stranger from a secured offshore server, the kind of setup favored by terrorists and drug traffickers, and attached to it were a digitized genome and the catalog number for a genetically standard laboratory mosquito.

"The genome is for a retrovirus," wrote Andy Simoni, W&P staff scientist. "It's obviously engineered, but I don't recognize the style of design." Later he wrote, "The natural lifespan of this mosquito is about two days but the ones I infected just hit a week and still aren't getting old. Also, as I discovered, they can regenerate lost tissue—wings, legs and in one case most of a thorax—a capacity heretofore unobserved in the dipterids. I haven't been able to figure out how the retrovirus works, but many of the mosquitoes' cells have new organelles, or things like organelles, whose function remains opaque. Also, I tried the virus on some mosquitoes of the same species as, but genetically distinct from, the first batch, and they all died within a minute."

Cromwell emailed to the stranger: "You have my attention in its entirety. What can we do for each other?"

The security AIs are mobbing Cloudbreaker—she thinks of white blood cells swarming a bacterium. Chunks of Cloudbreaker's substance break off and dissolve into nothing, which seems to enrage it, its counterattacks coming so fast they look like static.

Her time is short so she skips through the negotiations to where they settle on terms and sees the stranger wants a dozen high-end fabricators from Metafacient Inc., that famously innovative failure—its fabs, capable of printing matter with atomic precision, were the best thing going for prototyping exotic materials and artificial cells, but had been too expensive to find a market, and only thirty-odd were ever made before the company folded. They mostly ended up in the research labs of the military and the tech majors, and are dear even by Cromwell's standards, when they can be had at all—she sees Biotechnica, which apparently has three in its Bay Area R&D complex, has repeatedly declined Cromwell's tenders—and then she starts to wonder if it's all a practical joke when the stranger instructs Cromwell to drop the fabs into the ocean twenty miles west of San Francisco in what's now three days' time. She thinks of the Doge of Venice, how every year he threw a gold ring into the waves to wed his city to the sea.

The stranger's other demand is six months' worth of human memory recorded through an Ars Memoria implant, and somewhere under the sun Irina is smiling at having justified the last few seconds' felonies.

In exchange, the stranger undertakes to do for Cromwell what it did for the mosquitoes, after which they're never to speak again.

They'd settled on terms at four p.m. on a Sunday but that night around four a.m. Cromwell wrote, "I know we have an agreement, but I need you to make a retrovirus for one other person. Failing that, I'd take a cure for Kubota's syndrome. You can have what you like for it. I'll give you cities. Nations, if you want them." She doubts whether even Cromwell could deliver nations, unless they're small, bankrupt, and marginal, but she's read about Kubota's, a rare hereditary disease of the nerves, invariably fatal in midlife, which Magda has, according to her medical records, but in any case the stranger doesn't reply.

Among the records of labs and chairs funded are the plans for a university Cromwell will found in Magda's honor upon her death. He's hired architects, bought up thousands of acres in the plains of central Canada. Delicately phrased correspondence with his attorneys suggests he hasn't told her. Her cenotaph will be at the center of the campus, a sort of Hellenistic ziggurat, its torches whipping in the wind; it speaks to her of desolation of spirit raised to an imperial intensity.

Cloudbreaker is thrashing, close to failure now—she sees it touch an arbitrage AI, the same one from her last visit and still connected to something off in the net, the connection slipping under W&P's firewall, and she wonders if W&P ever noticed. She expects Cloudbreaker to destroy it but instead they form a link, start exchanging data.

A dozen counter-intrusions systems lock onto her and she wastes a precious fraction of a second disemboweling them though she knows her time is ending and then she finds another email from Andy Simoni with the subject "Mnemosyne":

"Akemi's become a part of the texture of things. By which I mean, I found an image of glowing pillars of smoke in the nighttime LA sky, as seen through her eyes, drawn on the wall of an alley in San Francisco— the match is exact down to the details of foveation.

"How did I find it? We're sending her memories off god knows where, so I wondered if they'd turn up somewhere out in the world. I used a large quantity of your money to rent servers to do image searches for everything she's seen since surgery. This drawing was the first hit, but I focused the search and found more. They were all by this graffiti artist who goes by 'LEdERER.' He's of the favelas, keeps the company of thieves and is paranoid enough that I couldn't invade his privacy without putting him on alert."

There are images from Akemi's memories—some she recognizes from LEdERER's show. Cromwell's made archival prints of four of them and used them to decorate his outer offices. There's a link to a mission report from Hiro, apparently Cromwell's security chief, about his attempt to rendition LEdERER, how a street fighter named Kern got to him first and took the phone, which has its own file, but she's distracted by the interrogation video of a vaguely street-looking girl named Kayla who looks hunted and forlorn as she slouches on her chair in a sterile-looking room. Someone off-screen asks where they can find Kern and she says, "You absolutely *promise* you just want to talk to him? Please tell the truth. It's important to me."

Shuddering motion that must be Cloudbreaker's death throes and she braces for a hard exit but Cloudbreaker is still there, whole and somehow replete-looking, and all the security AIs have vanished. She looks a fraction of a second into the past, sees it swallowing them whole, and for a moment she's bemused—had it been drawing them in all along?—but all that's important is that now she has this wholly unexpected time.

Cloudbreaker brushes against her implant.

She finds the stranger's most recent email, sent three days ago, in fact while she was in her debrief at W&P. It reads: "I'm changing the terms. Akemi Aalto will no longer do. We need Irina Sunden."

Cloudbreaker is scrabbling at her implant, though by now it should know better—her implant's security is so dense a direct assault is pointless—and as she thinks this her implant's security collapses.

The first thing Cloudbreaker does is disable the off switch of her implant's wireless and she opens her eyes onto hard light on the rooftops, the swallows diving through the air as it siphons off copies of her memories.

She clasps her forehead in her palms despite the gesture's obvious futility as memories of her mid-thirties are copied off into the ether, and she wonders if this is what being raped is like, and if there's nothing she can do except wait for it to be done, but then she remembers the router in the tower, her sole present point of connection to the net.

She runs up the tower's stairs toward the router as Cloudbreaker takes copies of the years after college.

The router is bolted into place so as she tears it off the wall as Cloudbreaker takes the memory of her first trip to the Mayo, her diffidence and discomfort and how her batteries of detailed and perfectly informed questions eroded first her surgeon's patience and then his self-regard.

The power cord is screwed into the router and she wastes two seconds trying to yank it out and is starting to think she'll spend the next few minutes running through the villa searching desperately for a screwdriver when it occurs to her that the router is hanging from the cord in her hands, so she swings it through a wide arc into the wall, really putting her hips into it, and on the second swing, as Cloudbreaker takes the memory of her dinner with Philip, the router shatters into tiny pieces that bounce off the walls and sting her face and hands, and, as though exorcised, Cloudbreaker is gone.

She leans against the wall, slumps to the floor, turns off her wireless.

38

•

Thought Purely

In the morning Thales searches for his brothers over the groomed sand of the hotel's crowded beach. They hadn't come back to the suite the night before but for them this is hardly unusual behavior and even behind his sunglasses the day is too bright, though the sunbathers are like shadows and the container ship on the horizon is a patch of darkness on a blaze of clouds. He almost trips on a girl lying prone on a towel, awkwardly untying her bikini top, and once he'd have found some reason to linger, he thinks, but now he looks down at her and just sees the curvature of skin stretched over layers of fat and muscle and the striations and eczema on the backs of her thighs.

He spots Helio, not twenty yards away, heading for the waves, longboard under his arm. Whatever his brothers' faults, their family loyalty is unwavering and they're sure to take his part. He labors over the sand and seizes Helio's shoulder and then recoils, because it's a stranger who turns to him, his face a mask of blank inquiry. "Sorry!" blurts Thales, so taken aback he speaks in Portuguese, and as the stranger turns back to the surf he tells himself that out here under the sun behind his polarized glasses it's only natural to mistake one body for another.

He stands there sweating through his shirt and scanning the beach though he now feels certain that his brothers aren't there and in lieu of whatever sense of abandonment or desolation he just wants to know what's happening. If pure thought led anywhere but in circles he'd have solved the problem long since so it's therefore time to act, but what is there to do, and who is there to ask, and then he remembers the ragged woman who'd accosted him on the hotel patio, how she'd said she found him by staking out the clinic, and the force of her conviction that both she and he were somehow victims, so he heads up the beach toward the hotel's garage.

It's already evening and he's been dozing in the town car for hours, dimly aware of the rush of traffic, the gathering darkness, the few lights visible over the clinic's wall across the street. He programmed the car to alert him if another Mitsui Talos comes within fifty meters but even so he startles when it announces, *"Target in proximity."* Through the darkened window he sees the same filthy town car that had followed him to the St. Mark, and he holds his breath as it crawls by the clinic like it's looking for something and then as it speeds away he tells his car to follow.

39

.

Lost Coast

There's nothing on the coast but the hotel's ruin, though the tsunamis are ten years past. The shoreline must have changed when the water came, because now the waves break on the hotel's west wing. There's a swimming pool with breakers rolling over it; in the moments of the water's stillness Kern sees patches of aquamarine tile under the green weed and fragments of coral, and there, in the middle, the hotel's logo, a mermaid with a conch at her lips.

The tide is out, so he goes exploring among the dripping, recently flooded rooms. Tide pools, stark shadow, the resonance of water rushing, anemones, purple-shelled crabs scuttling into the cracked masonry. The rooms nearest the sea are buried entirely in thick strata of wet sand, hot where the sun reaches it, trembling at his touch like a living thing. He imagines the old life of the hotel preserved, somehow, in this wet, labile tomb, the laughter and clink of glasses buried, compressed, becoming geology.

It's midday, and all the other farang are asleep. He clambers up a ruined wall to the hotel's highest surviving eminence; nothing on the sea but a few fishing proas, nothing inland but jungle, no dust hanging over the one road in. He takes out his old cell, the one without the ghost, and sees, with relief, that there's still no signal. He wears a hat, because the sun is hot, and he doesn't know how much the satellites can see. He sits there a long time in the rattle of palms, the stroke of surf.

His discipline is in abeyance; he takes his morning runs slow, toys with his sparring partners, doesn't punish the heavy bag. (The one point on which he is disciplined is not thinking of Kayla.) He wonders if anyone has found his room, back home, whether it would still be there if he ever got back. The favelas change fast; miss a month and you can't find your way, would wander ever deeper into the alleys, a lost tourist disappearing.

He shares a room with four other fighters in the mirror image of the drowned wing. There are chunks of rotting carpet still glued to the floor-boards, strips of silk wallpaper on the crumbling plaster. They have a bath-room, but its pipes are long dry; there's a translucent plastic keg of water, mounted above the filthy tub, with a desalinator on top, and a sticker that's supposed to turn blue if bacteria start growing. Every morning one of the trainers comes in with two big buckets of seawater, pours them into the desalinator, and takes away the last day's white lozenge of salt. Under the keg, the water has washed away the tub's grit, sand and accumulated hair, revealing a veined, pale marble.

In the afternoons the centipedes come out, thick, black and glossy, fall-ing from the cloth canopy under which they train. The heavy bags, soft from innumerable blows, are more duct tape than leather. The trainers are cheerful Thais, most of them little bigger than children, all retired pro fighters. The farang are mostly Australian, with a smattering of Europeans. Bulging, steroidal muscle is the rule; there's a Belgian who looks like a small bull, who must have had that gene mod that makes your muscles keep growing till they run out of protein. For all their tattoos and attitude, Kern considers them mere bruisers—sloppy, bulky, angry and untechnical. The Thais are better, but he has the sense that fighting does not comprise their beings, that they're no more than mere professionals.

Once a week the farang pile into the camp's van and make the ten-mile trip to town for the fights. Kern went once, but there had been too many westerners taking video on their phones and it made him nervous, his im-age going out there into the ether, so since then he's stayed in the camp.

It's warm enough that he can lie on the beach at night and lose himself in his sense of distance and the unexpected profusion of stars.

He sits by the ocean and counts his money, which is going fast; there's enough left for another month, if he's careful. He wonders if he could pay less if he slept on the beach, but can't bring himself to ask.

Bo comes down from the hotel, surfboard under his arm. He has a tattoo on his ribs that at first Kern had taken for spiky tribal symbolism, but finally recognized as a violently energetic cursive spelling out *Genesis 1:2*. Kern thinks of the nocturnal revivals in the favelas, the celebrants manic with the holy spirit, babbling and frothing at the mouth until, glazed and spent, they finally trickled out into the morning. Kern had seen Bo on his knees on the beach at dawn, praying next to his surfboard as the sun came up, but whatever variant of Christianity Bo espoused was apparently consistent with a life centered on surfing, muay thai and women. Bo's said he's been on the bum for a long time, moving between Southeast Asia's fight camps and its gnarlier break points.

Bo drops the board, sprawls on the sand beside him. "You sure you don't want to learn to surf? I'll teach you," he says.

"No thanks," says Kern. "People don't go in the water where I'm from." Then, "You fighting tonight?"

"Nah. I like to train but I don't get in the ring. No point."

"Don't you get paid if you win?"

"Here? Sure—somewhere in the vicinity of sweet fuck-all."

"So if I needed to make money fighting, how would I do it? And say maybe I didn't want to show up on image searches."

"Someone trying to find you, mate?"

Kern hesitates, says, "I didn't know she had a boyfriend!"

Bo laughs and says, "If you want to fight for money, you could try Bangkok, or, better yet, outside of Thailand altogether—all they have here is boxers and poverty. If you're really game, you could try the interior— Kuan Lon, or someplace like that."

"Is that in Thailand?"

"You might say it's between sovereignties at the moment. So if a person wished to avoid notice, or the rule of law . . . A lot of money there, and it's the kind of place where discretion is encouraged."

"What's it like?"

"War zone," says Bo. "From what I hear. Markets black and grey. I've always wanted to see it but you can't surf if you're dead. Think you might actually go?"

"Might. Might stay here a little longer."

"You watch your ass, mate. Me, I'm going surfing," says Bo, and does.

His laptop's encyclopedia has an article about the tsunami. He watches satellite footage of the sea receding, then rising, washing over the land, some of which never broke the surface again, leaving empty water where islands were.

After thunderstorms, sometimes, the wireless comes in. He puts the earpiece in and tries to show the ghost things—the hotel, the coastline, the glowing, mountainous clouds—but she says nothing.

He knows he has to go but in the heat of the sun, the sigh of the water, he can find no urgency. He seems to have found an eddy in time where everything has stopped. When his money runs out he can live on the beach, eat coconuts, learn to fish, disappear into the somnolent life of the villages.

She emerges from the cool of the bathroom into the dim light of false dawn, padding across the dorm's filthy linoleum in grey underwear and a sweat-stained army T-shirt, mussed and slit-eyed and smelling of sleep. He pulls back the sheet to let her in, relieved, wondering at his good fortune, and then he remembers that Kayla's gone, and not coming back, and so he wakes to the grey light of a new day, the stertorous breathing and rank flesh of the heavy, graceless foreigners who've washed up at the training camp. The sheet, twisted, won't tear in his hands. What discipline, he thinks, what practice, could be proof against this. That day he leaves the camp for the interior.

40

·

In the Palm of Her Hand

Silent silver pulses of fireworks in an empty black sky, sparks sifting down as the smoke drifts away, and then the detonations touch her and rumble by. She wakes to find Fabienne leaning over her, shaking her shoulder. "Wake up," Fabienne says, voice hushed. "We're under attack. Missiles are landing, and their strike teams are three minutes away."

"Your father's defenses?" Irina asks as she sits up, head spinning, willing sleep away.

"Overwhelmed," Fabienne says. "There's a VTOL waiting—leave everything and come now," and though Fabienne is probably younger Irina feels like her mother is waking her for a long trip. Another explosion and the villa shakes as dust falls from the ceiling but Fabienne's poise is flawless, like some undauntable heroine of the Blitz.

"Your children?" asks Irina, following her through the corridor. Iliou had anticipated a counterattack but not one so fast or so decisive.

"They went ahead."

"And your father?"

A little catch, and then, "He's dead. The first strike. I think they targeted his room. It was in a tower. A mistake, in retrospect."

The power is out and Irina keeps stumbling in the almost dark. Armed men run past, exchanging a few words with Fabienne in Greek, and then at an intersection Fabienne says, "I have to make sure the au pair is out. Just keep going straight—the VTOL is on the small beach just south of the property. Hurry. I'll see you soon," and then she's gone.

Nightmare continuum of rooms, courtyards, passages. Now and then there are distant explosions—missile strikes, presumably—but they seem to be getting farther away. She's never heard of private militaries using cruise missiles, had thought it went beyond what was tolerated, but guesses Cromwell is pulling out all the stops, and she wonders if this action will merit a footnote in some future history of war. She hears men shouting in the distance, then gunfire and a sustained cry of raw animal pain that goes on and on, is then silenced abruptly. She's more frightened, with Fabienne gone, though this is obviously absurd.

She's getting close to the beachward door when she turns a corner and almost runs into a soldier in power armor, the lighter kind that makes him look more like a medieval knight than a man-shaped tank, and some inane part of her wonders if this is Iliou's man, but through his faceplate she sees his surprise, and that he looks somehow American, and then he backhands her into the wall.

Lost in fields of quiet and grey, she remembers that there's something important that she has to do, something truly pressing, and she comes back tasting blood, and it's pouring from her nose and dripping down her chin, and she's worried that her jaw might be broken, but for all that, her thinking is surprisingly clear. The blow knocked her out but she knows that even so he must have pulled it—lots of stories about soldiers in armor killing civilians with a slap—so he must have orders to take her alive, and yes, he's now fumbling in the webbed pouch on his thigh for what seem to be syringes, but his gauntleted hands are clumsy and this gives her a moment to turn on her wireless.

The villa's machines impinge on her awareness and there's the armor and its security is as dense as she'd expect for military hardware, and to break in would take more time than she has, so that's it, now she can wait and later she can suffer, but no, there are the servers Iliou got her, still there, idle, awaiting her word. Her gratitude is overflowing, and she thinks, *Sorry, boss,* and then she eviscerates the armor's security.

The soldier is opening his mouth to speak into his comm so she burns it out and as she does it strikes her that this is too easy, that by now they should know what she can do and be forearmed, but on the other hand they've had little time to prepare—the Cloudbreaker attack was just yesterday—and she remembers a documentary about the storied fiascos of the Persian War in which a weathered Marine colonel straight out of central casting made aggressive eye contact with the camera and barked, "A mediocre plan violently executed is better than a brilliant plan delayed," and in any case they're probably willing to lose soldiers.

There's no good way to power down the armor, which is probably by design, and she realizes it has something like an immune system, which is already trying to come roaring back and push her out, which interests her, professionally, and not knowing what to do she's starting to be afraid again but then she finds the armor's medical system.

There's been a breach, she tells the armor. There's massive damage to the pilot's left femoral artery, and the left leg of the exoskeleton is filling rapidly with blood. The suit considers, accepts this, and applies a tourniquet; the cam in the soldier's helmet shows her his astonishment as his left leg goes numb, and then she starts on the other.

Now his heart has stopped, she tells the armor.

No, it hasn't, replies the armor. I've just confirmed that it's beating, and that his blood pressure is normal.

But it *has* stopped, she says. Look again. Do you see? And the suit says, Yes, I see, and shoots him up with adrenaline. It didn't help, she tells the suit. Do something, quick, she says, and with the first pulse of the armor's defibrillator the soldier falls with a crash.

In the suit's file system she finds a photo of a pretty blond woman in denim cutoff shorts and a sleeveless T-shirt, smiling hopefully at the camera with a little girl in the crook of each arm, shot in an empty field before ancient listing telephone poles drowning in kudzu, and in a biographical file she learns that her enemy is William T. Boyd of Knoxville, Tennessee, once a lance corporal in the Army Rangers, and that he's served in Namibia, Persia, Morocco, South Africa; he's been wounded many times and won numerous commendations that seem like scant compensation for getting himself repeatedly blown up. There are pictures of the girls in Catholic school uniforms and she wonders if he went private to pay for that. Boyd is still fighting for control of the armor, reciting commands in a tense voice, but she's deep in the fabric of the suit's software and thinks, *Sorry, girls,* this, apparently, being her day for regret, as she starts shooting him up with the armor's entire pharmacopoeia, all the quinine, morphine, tetracycline, meperidine, benzodiazepine, amphetamine, and she worries that some of the drugs will cancel each other out but there isn't time to worry about it and in any case she's pretty sure it won't be good for him, and in fact he goes into a seizure, and voids his bladder, and as she recharges the defibrillator she finds herself hoping that his company gives good death benefits. There's a document labeled "rules of engagement" reading:

> Cleared hot and casualty indifferent with the glaring exception of one Irina Sunden, who is to be secured, sedated and renditioned intact. Management says W&P looks like north of 90% of next year's revenue, so don't shoot her in the face by mistake. They also say that if you do end up killing her don't damage her skull. Yes, her skull. Don't ask me why, I'm just the help.

She watches his pulse spasming and though he can no longer speak he's still trying to issue commands with the keypads in the gauntlets and then she finally figures out how to evacuate his air supply while keeping his helmet locked down, and now he's thrashing like a drowning fish, and she blacks out his faceplate, and the armor is recording his agony, which she can't let his wife see, so she kills the power to his helmet cam, which makes a red light wink off, and with that he finally gives up, and she realizes that she's taken the last light from his world.

A second passes in which she tries to rise, fails, tries again, and then she pretends that it's just some switched-off robot on the ground at her feet. Another second passes. *Fuck it,* she thinks, turning his oxygen back on.

She scrolls a message down his heads-up display:

> Corporal Boyd:
> I have you
> in the palm
> of my hand.

You would never
have seen your
daughters again
and your wife
would have had
your ashes.
Remember that.
—IS

She tries to burn out the motors in the armor's legs but it doesn't work and the suit's immune system is resurgent and on the verge of pushing her out when she notices the twelve missiles in the pods on his back and hacks them one by one to detonate on launch instead of impact but only gets seven before the armor finally manages to shut down its wireless and by then she's running flat out.

Moiré patterns swimming before her eyes, and she finds she's on the ground again. She picks herself up, though the corridor is spinning, and it occurs to her that she has a serious concussion, needs medical attention, but this isn't the time and she staggers out through a door into early morning light over the beach, the waves washing softly over the VTOL's landing gear as its engines spin up and Fabienne is waving from its open door.

As the plane lifts off she sees black plumes of smoke rising over the villa against the blue of morning and now to her horror the armored soldier walks out the door onto the beach. *Oops*, she thinks, like a child who's made a mistake. Seven chances in twelve that he'll just blow himself up if he tries to shoot down the VTOL. Fabienne is beside her at the window, their cheeks almost touching, and this will be a comforting near-intimacy for the last second of their lives if that's how things go, and she notices that Fabienne's children are strapped down in their seats in the cabin and that the au pair seems not to have made it. She wonders if she should tell Fabienne but if it's going to happen it will happen in a moment and there's nothing more to be done, and in any case she thinks the kids speak English.

She can't help flinching when the suit opens like a molting insect and Corporal Boyd swarms out and staggers away in a sweat-dark T-shirt and piss-stained shorts and falls to his knees in the sand.

As the plane gains altitude she sees him throw off his clothes and wade naked into the surf, and he's short and wiry, not the bulky action hero she'd expected, and large swatches of his skin are the coral pink of recently regenerated tissue. She sees the Sumerian winged lion tattooed on his back, and then has a last glimpse of him ducking his head under a wave.

Just blue water out the windows now.

"Why don't you go visit the pilot's cabin," Fabienne says to her children. "I'm sure he'd like to show you how the plane works." Contention, questions, complaints, but Fabienne says, "Go on, kittens. Shoo," and behind her patience is a stoniness that makes them very somber and then she closes the door behind them.

Fabienne sits, looks at the closed door, then breaks into wild, wracking, disfiguring sobs.

Irina sits beside her, tentatively pats her back. "It's okay," she murmurs.

"Okay?" Fabienne cries, mercifully *sotto voce*, and it seems a shame that the plane flies so quietly. "My father is dead. My home is gone. My family is *broken*, and all because of you. How is it okay? What could you possibly offer that would ever make anything *okay* again?"

Irina thinks it over. "Revenge," she says.

41

·

Oublier

Something is missing, Thales thinks, as the car carries him on into the city, and if he can't articulate this absence then at least there's the other car, always ahead and just in view, like a thought not quite in focus.

A flash through the darkened window, lighting the dash and then gone. As he looks up the reverberation hits and shivers through the car. Missiles, he's thinking—drones fighting in the air—when the next firework bursts.

Traffic is bad, the car hemmed in and crawling. The windows reveal only the barest suggestion of the texture of the city, and the crowding shadows of people by the street. The car is unhappy here, with no room to maneuver, its targeting system saccading between potential threats a dozen times a second; he brings up its security UI and overrides protocol enough to open the window, revealing a sidewalk packed with the young and mostly inebriated, and letting in a waft of garbage, smoke, the sea. An emerald detonation paints the low clouds in the night sky and illuminates a graffito on a wall reading "THERE'S AN ENEMY IN THE CITY AND

IT'S OPENING ALL THE DOORS," and he wonders what's being cele-
brated, why he has this sense both of terror and elation.

Looking back at the road he realizes he's lost track of the other car, and
that it's gone from his car's display, and so probably lost for good, and for a
moment he's unmoored by frustration and regret, though he understands
their uselessness, but no, there, it's the ragged woman on the sidewalk, the
crowd flowing around her as she studies the facades of the street's ruins
and bars.

Without stopping to think he throws the door open, warnings cascading down the car's screen, and he feels a lightness as he steps out into the
night and kicks the door shut.

She disappears through an unmarked door and he pursues her, not ten
seconds behind, and the door opens onto a narrow staircase leading down
between water-stained red brick walls, the product of some ancient building code, and floating in the darkness down toward the bottom are neon
capitals spelling out CLUB OUBLIER.

A woman's amplified voice is wailing that history repeats itself and that
nothing is lost or ever will be as he descends into a restaurant lit with dim
red light and fog pours out from behind the bar which makes a specter of
the barman, an effect of such eeriness that he has to stop and stare though
he knows it's just dry ice and a staple of haunted houses, and there's an
English word for this, he thinks, but it won't come to mind as he blows off
the maitre d' and searches for the ragged woman among the booths and
tables in discreet haste but he finds only another staircase going down.

Even darker, down there, barely light enough to see the plush red walls
and chandeliers evoking an Old World dustiness of centuries past; there's
a sustained shriek of laughter from a table of giddily drunk women whom
he dismisses at a glance as lacking the ragged woman's seriousness. He
bobs and peers into the shadows where there are antique photographs of
nudes in harems and underlying his urgency is such a weariness that it
occurs to him he could have a drink—it is, after all, a bar—despite the
morning's handful of vibrantly colored alcohol-precluding pills.

Movement in the shadows behind a half-draped doorway and it could
be nothing but he has no choice but to commit himself on the basis of
fragments and intuition, and as he hurries on he's annoyed because he
knows there's a word for this but it still won't come to mind, though it feels
closer now and it might actually be two words, not quite "collide" and not

quite "raker," and then he pushes through a velvet curtain into a bland and spotless bedroom—a secret hotel associated with the restaurant?—and where the window would have been there's a screen offering a nocturnal view of black serpentines of water flowing through an estuary encased in ice. The bed's been slept in, and he wants to check it for warmth but there's only one other door and she'll be getting farther away.

He brushes through another plastic curtain and the ground crunches underfoot so he thinks he might be walking on styrofoam but it radiates cold—it can't actually be snow, he thinks, but he gathers a freezing handful and crushes it into slush that starts melting on his palm. The walls here are screens, barely illuminated, showing a winter park at night in some European city. He looks up, sees light pollution on clouds, a few stars—he thinks he's traveled in Europe, wishes he remembered it well enough to situate himself. In the snow there's a slight depression, perhaps the imprint of the body of a woman, legible even under all the bootprints, and he peers around in the dimness, as though to see if some half-naked girl were shivering in a corner after making a snow angel on a dare, but of course there's no one, and the imprint remains legible even as new snow drifts down from the machines humming from the ceiling, and this formal absence of a body has both a mystery and a sadness, a memorial less substantial even than a ghost.

He's surprised to find himself weeping; he catches the tears on his fingertips and regards them with interest, like signs of someone else's grief.

He notices the lasers mounted up in the corners of the room, a cheap infrared model meant to be used safely by schoolchildren, ideal for sculpting shapes in snow, so this is just someone's idea of art but even so it has an uncanniness and he's glad to push through the next curtain.

Dark corridor before him. By the light of his new phone he sees a figure some hundred feet ahead, looking back over her shoulder. "Wait," he calls, but she's gone.

He runs after her through corridors where loops of cable hanging from the ceiling cast shadows like vines in his phone's light, and even now he can't shake the feeling that there's a word for this though it's not "colluder" and not "berater," and the absence of the word is like a hole that pulls him in.

He stops. The footsteps are gone. He shines his light around—doors and branching corridors like so many black mouths. He turns the phone's light off, which seems to heighten the silence, and there, ahead, a faint glow.

He finds an alcove lit by a buzzing, clicking lightbulb in a dusty cage on a steel door whose overbuilt solidity suggests a bank vault. There's a screen by the door, inert and black. EXIT TO CENTRAL is stenciled in black letters on the wall and he wonders what kind of infrastructure requires such protection.

His phone bleats in his hand. *Intrusion attempt detected* appears on the screen, then again, then the message repeating, scrolling by in a blur. Some random crim trying his luck, apparently, though he's surprised there's signal down here, and if it weren't for the timing it would almost be amusing because the family electronics are inviolable.

His phone goes dark. He swipes at the screen but nothing happens, and now random alphanumerics are scrolling down the screen by the door.

Clanking from inside the door, and a thin, high tone as its lock releases, and as it does he realizes that this establishes a pattern, one in which all the devices are compromised, but of course there's one device left, and that's his implant.

He clasps his forehead and wants to run or think of a plan but there's nowhere to go and nothing to do and then, finally, he remembers the word.

"*Cloudbreaker,*" he says.

Out in the darkness around his tiny pool of light he feels a restlessness and a contempt and a complexity like the shimmering of all the atoms in the air, and he feels he's watching himself from a distance as he weaves on his feet and then the world vanishes.

42

•

Tangle of Snakes and Darkness

The bus has a driver and shakes with the deep vibrations you get from hydrocarbon engines, fuel cells apparently not being big in Thailand. The net warned him that without air conditioning the heat would be unbearable but the Thais don't seem to mind and neither does he. In flooded green fields that might be rice he sees not robots but men and women in wide hats, bent and toiling.

The soap operas on the television behind the driver's seat keep getting interrupted by the king of Thailand, who, Kern thinks, looks frightened; according to the English captioning, he's urging his people to defy the foreign aggressors like the warriors of old. Officially, the Thai army is defending the nation's territorial integrity against a salad of narcotraffickers, rebellious indigenes, bandits and incursions from what had been Burma and is now, he gathers, fucked. In practice, according to the chatter on the net, it's a free-for-all, the combatants indifferent to nationalism, tribalism and warmed-over post-Marxism, their chaotic melees driven solely by a roaring trade in opium. An often repeated quote on the boards is "If you want to bring peace to Southeast Asia, make better synthetic heroin." (Back in the favelas Lares had held forth at tedious length on the chemical glory of the poppy, the complexity and harmony of its neuroactive compounds.)

He gets off at a village where the houses have walls of blue plastic sheeting and rooves of corrugated aluminum. The bus depot is an old man with a laptop, sitting on an aluminum stool under a parasol advertising a beer not made since the millennium. Kern's old phone had told him he could get a bus here to Kuan Lon, but the old man shakes his head, tells him through a text-only translator that there is no such bus. Kuan Lon is forty-five kilometers away and the jungle isn't the contiguous tangle of snakes and darkness he's been expecting, just trees, sun, heat, a dirt road. He buys large transparent bottles of water and candy bars. *It's not going to get cold,* he figures, *and if it rains, I'll get wet,* so he sets out.

43

•

Intimacy of the Mundane

The floor is hard. The floor is hard, and the floor is cold, and the cold is seeping into him. It's dark, and there's a cyclical rushing that sounds like waves but must be the air-conditioning.

His eyes adjust. He's still in the alcove. A window in the dark—it's the steel door, open now, framing fog under the stars.

He realizes someone is kneeling beside him.

"*You shouldn't be here,*" says the stranger, but without hostility. Thales peers up at him but can't see his face.

"*Cloudbreaker touched you,*" the stranger says, "*but you're still viable, as far as I can tell, though I wonder if you're intended as a distraction.*"

"Are you from the club?"

"*I'm from the city.*"

"From Los Angeles?"

"*I'm from the other city.*"

As the stranger rises Thales wonders how he knew about "Cloud-breaker" and what city he's talking about and what does he mean "viable" and in any case how can he tell, and in an intuitive flash he's arrived at the conviction that this is the only person he'll ever meet who really knows what's going on.

"Wait!" he says as the stranger turns to leave, thinking, *This is like Pascal's wager, in that I have nothing to lose through my belief but dignity and time.* "Wait," he says again. "Please. I'm lost in mystery, and no matter how hard I try, I can't figure out what's going on. I think I must have made some flawed assumption, so I make no progress, and at this point I don't even know what a solution would look like."

"*I have business elsewhere,*" the stranger says, but hesitates. "*However, I can appreciate your position, so I'll grant you three questions.*"

There's a sense of doors opening if only he can think of the right questions to ask but there's no time to think so he says, "What's Cloudbreaker?"

"*The product of an evolutionary pathway I haven't seen before, and thus interesting. We've only recently met, and aren't yet in equilibrium.*"

"Who are you?"

"*A mathematician, now acting as administrator.*"

One question left and so far he's learned nothing of use but he thinks of the strangeness of the clinic, his family's absences, and, painfully aware of the possibility of something precious slipping through his hands, he asks, "Is my surgeon my family's enemy?"

"*He's unaware that they exist,*" says the stranger, and then he's gone into the tunnel. Thales might pursue him but there's no light and his phone is still dead and now the tunnel has swallowed the stranger completely.

For want of other options Thales gropes his way through the open door. Sand underfoot, chill air. Vortices of seabirds rise over crashing water. He looks back—there's a low cliff, the black portal he came through.

There, in the distance, a figure in silhouette, foregrounded against the shining foam—even in that little light and at that distance he recognizes the ragged woman. He tries to call out but the surf swallows his words so he plunges toward her across the beach.

He loses her in the shadows but struggles on over crumbling dunes. It's a pursuit out of a nightmare, his effort yielding nothing but more expanses of empty beach.

He crests a dune and there she is, not a hundred feet away, undressing. Moonlight shines on her hair, the roundness of a thigh, the gleaming convexity of her back, and then she's naked, walking toward the sea. He watches her pick her way over the coarse dune grass, step unflinchingly into the water and wade out through the breakers. She dives under a wave; her head emerges, black hair pooling on the water. Her body pierces another wave—her back just breaks the surface, and then she's gone.

He cries out for her to come back, but his voice is lost in the waves' roar. He scans the surf line but sees no tumbling limbs, no weed-entangled hair.

He goes and picks through her clothes, hoping to find a purse, a phone, some clue to her identity, but there's only her fading warmth, the mundane intimacy of her socks and underwear.

The water's tone changes, then, and there's a new light; he looks up and sees the glass and steel towers of a city, glowing like paper lanterns, not a hundred feet out to sea. For all its light, the city has an air of desuetude—broken panes, rust-stained steel, chaotic growths of weed—and it rises up and ever up, farther than seems possible, its heights lost in the clouds.

The ocean's noise fades. The city is radiant and silent. He draws a ragged breath.

Its light playing on his hands.

He resolves never to move, to become a statue in the sand, staring in fixity, forever. He loses his sense of the passage of time.

The city's lights go off, one by one, and then there's nothing but its ghostly negative floating in the air. Slowly, he comes back to himself. The surf roars, the night is fading, he's alone. He tries to fix this part of the beach in his mind but there are no landmarks. He tries to remember the city but it's already gone.

44

•

Great Dark Forward

Once the sun sets it gets dark immediately. Benign by daylight, the enshadowed jungle wakes a sense of primal horror; Kern leaves the road and looks for a place to spend the night by the faint glow of his cell. He finds a shallow cavity under a fallen tree trunk; it looks like it was dug out deliberately, but a long time ago, and nothing lives there now, so he scrapes up a nest from fallen leaves and branches and gets in.

He tells himself it's just like a squat, but better, because the whole jungle is squat, with no guards or owners to get mad or chase you away. If there are patrols, they aren't really looking for him, and anyway they probably can't see him unless they have infrared. He wishes he had a gun, or some way to close up his cave.

He wakes, later, to birds calling in the night. Sleep is gone so he wakes his old phone and looks up articles on Kuan Lon. There's one by Summer Scanlon, Ph.D., who is an urban sociologist, whatever that is, and it's about how Kuan Lon is a physical manifestation of the regional psychopathology, and the historical irony of a People's Path of Glorious Revolution militant drinking next to a colonel in the New China Army. More interesting by far is a tourist guide from decades ago, from before the fighting started, which tells him about the animals in the forest—there are grainy nocturnal videos of white owls and big grey cats moving among the trees— and of the tribes that used to live there; they were animists, which means they thought everything had a soul. He wonders what the tribesmen would have made of San Francisco, where cars, buildings, even coffeemakers have wills of their own. The mountains, he reads, had been gods, and he can see that; he remembers their snowless peaks above the trees, and it's easy to imagine them conferring quietly in the twilight. He prays to them for protection, then, though he's never prayed before, for he feels his death is near, gliding silkily through the trees, less malicious than playful, interested, endlessly patient. He considers going off into the jungle to meet his demon but there's still Kuan Lon and the ring.

He wakes at dawn and sits for a while just breathing the cool air. A wave of homesickness buckles him, almost bringing him to tears, but Kuan Lon shines in his mind like a black star and he sets out, as Lares would have said, into the great dark forward.

That afternoon the road hits a clearing where there's a checkpoint. He's going to try to just slip away but the Thai officer, crisp in his air-conditioned power armor, sees him and beckons him over; the sweating, armorless enlisted men stare at him dully from the shade of a strangler fig. He thinks of running but of course they have guns. One of the foot soldiers is tinkering with some kind of military robot, its jungle-camo back a solid mass of missile pods, most of which are carbonized and empty—it looks a little like a mechanical mule with a horrible case of boils.

The officer says something in Thai, his voice emanating from the speakers in the armor's shoulders, and Kern looks up at him blankly. *They're nervous about something,* he thinks, *and, whatever it is, I'm not it, and they know it, but they're still curious about me.* The armor says something in Chinese, then some other language, and then finally the tinny synthetic voice says, "Stop. You are entering a restricted area. What is your business here?"

"I'm going to Kuan Lon," he says, immediately realizing it was stupid to tell the truth, but cops make him nervous. He reminds himself to use simple sentences, or the translation program won't work.

"This is a restricted area," the armor squawks. "You must have a special visa to enter this area."

"I'm a boxer. Muay thai. I'm going there to fight," he says, making boxing fists, his hands pitiful beside the suit's enormous metal paws. He wonders what Thai jails are like—probably worse, much worse than American ones. He takes his wad of money out of his pocket, offers it up.

The officer looks down at him, then smiles and says something that the translator renders as "The cool heart leads to victory." He bows, slightly, the armor groaning and stinking of burning oil as it moves, and says something that might have been a blessing but comes out as a disconnected string of static, and waves him on.

They fight by torchlight in Kuan Lon. He sees a boxer fall with blood pouring from his mouth, get rolled out of the ring and left at the edge of the jungle. They fight without gloves—the red firelight glints on the ground glass on the fighters' hand-wraps. He sees a skinny Thai boy, younger than he is, die in the ring; he's close enough to see the boy's fixed, dilated pupils, his slack mouth as the doctor, a Japanese whose short-sleeved shirt reveals track marks, pushes on his chest in vain under the watchful eyes of the victor in his corner. He sees knife matches, the crowd silent as the blades test the distance, flickering over isoclines of commitment and dread, like serpents tasting the air, and finally the explosive attack, the arc of arterial blood. He hears bets made in Chinese, German, Japanese, English and Thai. He sees winners paid in yuan, yen, dollars, euro, bags of cocaine, bricks of heroine, fuel cells, ancient mosaics, Buddhas, Garudas, missiles, guns.

They've never cleared out the jungle—he guesses they didn't want satellites seeing in—so you can never see far and it always seems to be dusk; flashlights glow through the jungle's constriction, and, during the day, parallelograms of sun. He haunts the tracks worn through the undergrowth between the tents, the retrofitted shipping containers, the quonset huts that were surplus from a few wars back; everyone ignores him, except the bar girls, who call out invitations and snatch at his wrist as he passes them by. There's a market where geckos scamper over piles of damp Gucci tote bags, sparkling crystal bottles of cologne, mildewed jeans; there are cardboard boxes brimming with plastic bags of coarse yellow opium, tied shut with a twist of wire. He sees a Karon tribesman showing his eight-year-old son how to analyze opium with a portable mass spectrometer, which is oddly comforting, because it's the same model used back home by the more upmarket dealers. Burmese gunmen bargain quietly over jackets of French kevlar; big white Americans with army haircuts and over-sized watches sit at cafe tables, drinking rice liquor, smoking hash and watching the girls go by. At night strings of red and white Christmas lights burn in the trees and show him the way to the ring.

He watches every fight but doesn't try to get in the ring, though he has little money left. He sleeps on a thin mat in the woods, in a waste space where fragments of torn cloth flutter in the branches and the pale remnants of old plastic bags make the copse look like a burial ground. There's a girl, whose name might be Lily—she speaks no English—who came to him, one night, of her own accord, and in the grey corpse-light filtering through the trees he marvels at the contours of her body, how an object of desire can be composed of these abstract curves and swells of tissue—the dark pucker of a nipple, the pores and hairs on the olive skin; running his hand over her stomach, he finds he's become an anatomist, and knows where pressure would bring pain. Sometimes he talks to her in English, as he caresses her, and that helps, a little, but then he forgets words and there's just the release, then the slight rankness of her, the stones pressing into their bodies through the mat, and her skin against his, which seems to be thawing something.

One morning he wakes alone—the copse is quiet, and the girl is gone, along with the last of his money. He lies there awhile, trying to find some lingering trace of her warmth, then goes into town to look for her. He can't find her but in a bar housed in a shipping container there's a girl with burgundy lipstick and a matching sheath dress who looks at the girl's picture on his phone and says, "That's Lily. Lily gone home. You want a new friend?"

He's at the ring when the Christmas lights come on; he's hungry, but that will have to wait. He finds the promoter, a small Thai with a laptop and decaying cargo shorts that show the boxer's scars on his shins, and says, "How do you get on the card here?"

The promoter takes him in, shakes his head and in an Aussie voice says, "Sorry, mate, we're full up, try another night," and turns back to his laptop.

"So make some room," he says, his voice almost cracking. "How about I bust up some of your boys, here, get the clutter off the card."

The promoter regards him from under raised brows, then calls out something in Thai. A fighter with brown, snaggled teeth and a mass of scar tissue on his eyebrows laughs, shrugs, says something back; the promoter says, "All right then. You and young Chaksenedra here are now our prelim card, and may the experience live up entirely to your expectations."

An old man beckons him over to a table by the ring and wraps his hands in strands of coarse hemp so tightly it hurts. The wrap finished, the old man takes a tube out of his pocket, smears Kern's knuckles with glue and presses them into a plastic tub full of ground glass. He examines Kern's glittering knuckles critically, says, "Dry two minutes," in thickly accented English, smiles toothlessly and moves on to the next fighter.

He tries to warm up but his body seems to have no mass, his hands flickering through the air as though they're weightless, empty shells, as harmless as smoke. The light is failing and a crowd has gathered, the white lights in the trees stellate through the billows of cigarette smoke and ganja. Someone lights the torches and the reek of kerosene fills the clearing. He knows they're watching him, that the local wireless is buzzing with wagers on the events of his victory, defeat, death. He wants to run but beyond the torches and constellations of electric lights there's just the jungle darkness, and he feels his death is waiting for him there. He remembers his discipline, starts stretching like he does before every training.

Before he is ready (*but you've been waiting for this a long time*, a voice says) the promoter takes his arm and ushers him toward the ring. He and the Thai with the bad teeth and scars climb in, and when the bell rings he's still oppressed by lightness, feeling as ineffectual as a dream. He sees that Scars is dancing a little, intending to play with him, so he kicks him in the leg and closes; the openings are obvious, and for a moment he suspects the fight's been rigged, but no, there's the pain and the disbelief in Scars's face as he eats punch after punch and he never sees the knee that finally breaks his jaw. Kern steps back, not even sweating yet, not believing it's over, makes a point of not looking into the flash of the cell phones from the crowd.

45

.

Good Thing to Own

Thales peers up into the ether, the snowflakes pinpricks of momentary cold. He hadn't wanted to go back through the Club Oublier, had thought to find the car by dead reckoning. A mistake, in retrospect. Hadn't expected snow. Vast the city, endless its streets. He checks his phone—still dead—onward, then.

Eyes flickering shut, he sees the towers in the waves, their light, ascending . . . He blinks, wavers, brushes snow from his shoulders and goes on.

Snow-dusted ruins, shuttered bars. Is this his street? And there, down the block, his car, he thinks, smothered in white.

Closer up, he's sure it's his. He grips the door's frigid handle, waits for it to read his fingerprints, but there's no vibration, no click—is it as dead as his phone, leaving him locked out in the cold? He yanks at the handle, steps back in surprise when the door opens, snow sloughing off in a sheet.

He's already halfway into the car when he registers the presence in the seat opposite—it's a girl, the maybe-Asian one from the mountain house, huddled in her thin jacket, the grip of a gun protruding from her pants pocket.

"You did come," she says, jaw tight, shivering. "He said you would. Didn't really believe it. Freezing my ass off and I don't have the code to start the car. I'm Akemi, by the way. Sorry to ambush you, but we need to talk."

He could run for it, or maybe lunge for her wrists, but his wits are foggy, his hands numb, and she seems too miserable to be a kidnaper. He gets the rest of the way into the car and pulls the door shut.

"Well?" she says a little desperately. He stares at her. "You want to turn it on?"

He taps in the password and the car comes to life. He doesn't realize how cold he is until the hot air hits.

"You must think I'm a crazy person," she says.

He shakes his head unmeaningly.

"You have the implant, right?" she says. "And you see things that aren't there, that couldn't be there?" He tries to show nothing but she says, "Yeah. That's what I thought. He said you did. I've got it too, and the same thing happens to me. I think it's time we did something about it."

"Wait—*who* said I did?"

"Well, that's a story," she says. "I was hiding in this bar in the favelas on Sunset. Bad place, but not that bad, and I've been there before. I was afraid the implant would let them track me, but it's too deep for reception there, which is why I was surprised when I heard a phone ring, and then I realized the phone was in my pocket. It wasn't mine—I haven't had a phone in a long time—and I knew I ought to chuck it and run, but I was feeling fatalistic so I took the call. At first it was just static on the other end of the line, and then when someone finally said my name it sounded like he was talking in a tunnel. I asked who it was and I could barely understand him when he said, 'Your enemy's enemy. Go talk to the boy. He's like you. Tell him not to trust the surgeon.' He told me how to find the car, and that it'd be unlocked, and then he hung up, and here we are. So I know this is your car and all, and I'm already imposing, but if you don't mind my asking, just who the hell are you?"

"I'm Thales," he says, "and you were also in my house."

"Oh," she says. "*Right.* You were the one in the car on the mountain. You're that architect lady's kid, the one who built my prison. There were pictures of you with your mom on her desk."

"What were you doing there?"

"What I was told, mostly. I don't know if they used drugs or the implant or what, but I just woke up there one day, and when I did my surgeon was waiting. He'd seemed like a nice man when I met him in Indonesia, but it was obvious it had gone wrong, so I threatened him with my powerful friends, told him Hiro would get him if he didn't let me go. Fucker didn't even change expression, just waited for me to wind down and then said, 'There are some things we need you to do.'"

"What things?" he asks, trying to situate himself, decide if he believes her story.

"I had to run these boys, mostly technicals, get them to do tricks with hardware. It felt like organized crime, unless there's another reason to monkey with servers off the subway tunnels in LA. It wasn't what I'd been promised, but I wasn't really surprised. Always more problems, you know?"

"Are you technical?"

"Not even a little," she says cheerfully. "Well, I wasn't, but the surgeon did something with his tablet, and now I remember whole technical manuals. I never thought I'd know so much about fiber-optic splicing."

He watches her, hoping she'll let something slip that will make her underlying intentions manifest, but her facade is seamless, if it is a facade, and he could use any ally, but there's too much he doesn't know and it's probably a mistake even to engage with her. "Why didn't you call for help? There's a computer up there."

"For one thing, who am I going to call? Not all of us have rich families poised to save the day. For another, that computer didn't connect to anything but this special-purpose phone the boys used. Lost kids, mostly, scraped up off the net. I had to learn to be what they needed with just the sound of my voice. No one held a gun to my head, but the doors were locked, and there was nothing else to do. I was trying to get them to help me finagle an exit, but the fucking phone kept getting stolen and I kept having to start over. So have you got any special feeling about any of this, or did the voice in the wilderness steer me wrong?"

"Why would your kidnapers put you in our house?" he asks, thinking, *unless they already have so much access to my family that they can use our assets casually.*

"You got me. I've never seen any of you before in my life. I assumed it was just out of the way and empty. I was just glad they didn't lock me in a basement."

"Does the name Cloudbreaker mean anything to you?"

"Nothing," she says, shaking her head. "It sounds like the name of an art-core band."

"You seem to be in earnest," he says, "but is there anything to substantiate your story? All I know for certain is I saw you in my headlights and found you waiting in my car."

For a moment he has the sense she's watching him coolly and from a distance but then that's gone and he just feels her determination and her sense of being hunted. "Here's evidence for you," she says, taking his hand and guiding it to her forehead, where he finds a hair-fine scar. "They were careful about the scarring. I insisted, because I thought it could hurt my career. Good thing I focused on what was really important." Now she guides his fingertips behind her ear, where he finds something hard—at first he takes it for jewelry, but it's a socket. "No wireless. They said it wasn't secure enough. There's no trust these days."

She's leaning in close now and reaches out to put her palm on his face, and her skin is so hot it seems to burn him. "You're cold," she says. "You might have hypothermia." She shrugs out of her jacket and spreads it over their laps.

She's sitting so close their thighs are touching. "I like it this way," she says, apparently of the snow covering the windows, how the outside world is hidden except for the blued glow of passing cars, and he's acutely aware of their breathing. "Though it takes some getting used to, not seeing where you're going."

"There's so much I want to ask you," he says, surprising himself, wondering what he meant by it, then deciding it's true.

"There'll be time for that," she says vaguely, looking at him with a strangely fixed expression, and now she's leaning into him and her face is close to his. She laughs a little gurgling laugh, and at a distance of a few inches he sees the flush of her cheeks, the symmetry of her features, how her skin is mostly clear but at the edges of her eyes are tiny wrinkles she should be too young for, probably the consequence of worry and hard living, and as she turns her mouth toward his he says, "What are you doing?"

She freezes, then slowly withdraws.

A moment of perfect silence and then it's like she's become a different person as she laughs and jams her hands into her armpits and says, "Sorry,

I'm just so fucking cold. Anything to warm up, you know? They say drinking warms you up but if it did I'd feel fine." Her poise holds for a moment, then collapses before his eyes, and suddenly she seems needy, almost childlike, and close to tears. "And I may not be thinking too clearly, but I'm not so lit I can't recognize an intelligent man. I hate to ask, since you've been so tolerant already, but who do you think is doing this to us, and why would they bother?"

"It's not clear," he says, which is both honest and appropriately unforthcoming. "There's a pattern but I can't quite see it."

"Your family's been political for generations, right? And owns like one percent of Brazil?"

"Less than that," he says reflexively. "Especially now."

"Maybe someone wants you for leverage? Whether hostage, spy or pawn, you're a good thing to own."

"Maybe the surgeon is corrupt, but how would they have gotten my mother to abandon us?"

"Maybe she had to make some hard decisions," says Akemi. "You have two brothers, right? Maybe her back was against the wall, and she wanted to hold onto something."

He starts to get out of the car but she seizes his wrist and it's less like she's compelling him than like she's afraid he'll disappear so he doesn't insist and after a moment of terrible silence he says, "Is your family political too?"

"No," she says, smiling thinly. "I wouldn't say that. It's less obvious why they're interested in me. At first I thought they wanted an actress who was a reliable commodity—someone who couldn't refuse projects, forget her lines or shoot up between scenes. I'm in the sweet spot—I have the goods, but no leverage, and no one's going to miss me. Or it could be less than that—maybe they've got a new technology, and I'm just a trial run."

"You sound so resigned."

"You have to work within the givens. Like now. I'll find a way out, because there's always a way out, and I've been in worse spots than this. Anyway, I have an idea—you tell me if it's dumb or not." Her uncertainty and need for his approval are all but palpable. "You know the surgeon's tablet? Maybe that's how he's changing us. They know I ran away, but they probably still think you'll do what you're told. You could be in a position to take action."

"Even if I could get the tablet, it wouldn't matter. They'll have other means of access."

"Couldn't you lock them out?"

"Maybe, maybe not."

"Do you have a better idea?"

"It seems desperate."

"Yes," she says. "But it's better than just giving up. Do you want to let them make you a slave without putting up a fight? Anyway, it's obvious that you're brilliant. I could see it the moment I met you. You practically *shine*. You could figure it out, couldn't you, *you* of all people?"

"I . . . maybe," he says. "But why would he give me his tablet in the first place?"

He freezes as she takes the pistol from her pocket—it's practically an antique, an old-school Colt revolver with a purely mechanical action—and he wonders if earlier he miscalculated and now he's going to suffer, but she reverses the gun, puts it on his palm, presses his fingers around the handle.

46

•

Exact Enumeration of Blurred Flocks

The corroded mirror behind the bar reflects the aqueous glow of Irina's whisky, the hunch of her shoulders, and the continuum of the motion of travelers passing by. Tasting blood, she washes the liquor around her mouth, holds the cold glass to the swelling on her jaw. It's okay, somehow, to drink in airports in the morning.

Her other memory offers the columns of smoke over the villa inclining in the wind. She feels no rancor toward Corporal Boyd, in fact hopes he makes it home, for all her hate is reserved for Cromwell, who has to die, however great his strength, however far he stands above the law, while she is alone, and wants to sleep.

For the fifty-third time today, she thinks of what happened in W&P's servers. Did Cromwell suborn Cloudbreaker, and if so, how? If not, why did it want her memories? In any case, how did it break into her implant? She's made no progress but can't let these questions go even for the space of a drink.

If it was the occluded AI that influenced Cloudbreaker, then Cromwell might have been less culpable than she'd thought, which means they

could maybe have talked it out, but now their conflict has its own momentum and the situation's logic requires her to escalate.

She recognizes Fabienne in the mirror by her walk.

"How are the kids?" she asks, as Fabienne sits beside her.

"Chastened," says Fabienne. "Except the little one, who thinks we're
having an adventure. They're with friends now."

"Are they safe?"

"Beyond question," says Fabienne, her voice iron, her poise fully restored. "I'm friends with the minister of defense. Actually, we used to date.
He's taking care of everything. In fact, he put the military on alert, and
he's invited all the private soldiers to leave the country and its waters within
the next four hours. He's blaming the escalation on Turkey. He says he's
been looking for an excuse, but I think he's just being polite."

"What if Cromwell gets to him?"

"You mean, what if he tries to bribe him? Unless he's been going boar-
hunting with Stavros since they were teenagers, he won't even get a hearing. As for assassination, there have been contracts on Stavros since he got
involved in politics. It was exciting, at the time, in hotels, knowing there
was someone trying to find him . . .

"He has a gift for you," Fabienne says, and in response to Irina's ques-
tioning look she says, "I told him you were a friend of my brother's, and my
father's guest. My father, just yesterday . . . He didn't tell me everything,
but I know you fought for us, and suffered for it. So please accept this." She
takes something from her purse, puts it in Irina's hand. It's a Greek diplomatic passport; she opens it and there's her own picture next to the name
Elena Vougiouka. She flips through it, sees the colorful stamps of many
countries, the record of this fictive self's trajectory through the world. "Your
U.S. passport is flagged, it turns out, so you'll want to travel with this."

"A fake passport seems to invite more problems."

"Eh," shrugs Fabienne. "What's fake? It's a real diplomatic passport. As
far as my old boyfriend is concerned, and thus the Greek state, you're
Elena Vougiouka." She glances at her phone. "Now you must excuse me.
My nine-year-old son is declaring that he is now a man, and that it's his
right and duty to raise an army and avenge his grandfather, and so far he's
managed not to cry."

"I'll take care of that. Tell him I said so."

Fabienne's hand on her shoulder, and, to her surprise, her tension lessens. She remembers when she was thirteen and hiding in the woods near the villa on Patmos, but of course she first set foot on Patmos a few days ago, and this is Constantin's memory—he'd been the one Fabienne had found among the shadows of the oaks, though he couldn't have been more than nine—her young face ancient in the dappled light—her presence enough to calm him. "Goodbye, my dear. Good luck to you," Fabienne says, and then she's off into the concourse.

Irina remembers being thirteen, sitting in the foyer of her parents'—by then, she supposes, her—attorney's office, four months to the day out of surgery, still groggy on her ration of painkillers, nauseated from antibiotics. The windows framed grey skies where clouds of birds passed and disappeared, though not in her other memory, where their flight was perfectly preserved, at which she had still, then, marveled. It had seemed like she was being useful, holding on to what would otherwise be lost, but her lawyer, whom she liked, was talking, so she'd let the exact enumeration of blurred flocks fade and wrenched herself back into the present.

The bartender, who's been at a discreet distance, catches her eye, raises an eyebrow, but she shakes her head, stands, puts money on the bar. Time to act.

Maya picks up on the first ring, though for her it's the middle of the night. "I've got bad news, sweetie," Maya opens, sounding like she's in tears. "They're shutting down the agency."

"What? Who? I thought you were making all kinds of money."

"We were, and I was, and now they're shutting it down. No explanation, and no remorse, as far as I can tell, and I lose all my equity unless I sign a noncompete and don't talk to any former clients for five years. The managing directors, of whom I was very soon to be one, say they're sorry and blah blah boilerplate, but the gist is that they're not allowed to talk about it. Not *allowed*? My assistant said their assistants said they got bought out, and the buyout had *terms*. It makes no sense, but fuck them all in their tiny, wizened little hearts. So I'm packing up my office, by which I mean I'm drinking heavily in what used to be my office, while calling my clients to let them know they need to find new representation, and then I'll leave all this shit for someone else to clean up and go get wasted at the Ermitage bar, where I intend to go home with the hottest, dumbest guy I can find."

"What are you going to do?"

"I don't know, take up fuckin' needlepoint? Isn't that what sixty-four-year-olds are supposed to do?" Maya looks thirty-five, and is, hormonally, about eighteen, with a supplemental testosterone boost, an option that she, Irina, has always chosen to forgo. "It doesn't *really* matter—I don't have to work for the next fifteen years or so, and by then whatever the fuck this is will be over, and the world will have changed."

"I think I know what this is," says Irina. "He doesn't want me to have allies."

"Fucking *who* doesn't want you to have allies?" Faint glugging sound on Maya's end, as of liquid pouring out of a bottle.

"Is this phone secure?"

"Hell yeah. It's mine, not the company's, anonymously registered and encrypted all to fuck. You think I ever really trusted them? *I* know what business I'm in. *Was* in. *Fuckers*," she says, choking back a sob.

Irina tells her what happened, and is, for once, reasonably forthcoming.

"Wow. Fuck that guy. Seriously, he needs to get his ass liquidated. If TMP still existed I'd say call Parthenon and put it on our tab."

"As it happens, they're my next call."

The empty chapel is as hushed as a library. It strikes her as theatrical, coming here to order a hit.

She dials Parthenon's number from memory on the phone she just bought. A brief parlay with a secretary, and then her soldier picks up, saying, "Miss Sunden."

"I need a definitive solution," says Irina. "To that difficult problem we discussed."

"Timeline?"

"As soon as possible."

"I'll have a look and get back to you as soon as I can," he says, his composure so thorough as to be almost offensive. "Any special instructions?"

"Please do this soon. He just tried to have me kidnaped. I still bear the wounds."

"In that case, I'd best get started."

Leaving the chapel, she sees there are more soldiers in the airport now, thanks, she supposes, to Fabienne's ex. Strange to be the fulcrum of international events, and the source of the headaches and perplexity now being suffered by whatever Turkish officials.

Tempting to linger in this in-between place, but it occurs to her that Cromwell's rented killers could be taking commercial flights back to the States; she imagines some hard-eyed boy with a crew cut and muscles sitting down beside her and checking her out—the flash of recognition— suddenly remote, he takes out his phone . . .

The ticketing concourse is huge, chaotic, full of tourists. She chooses Prosperity Airways because the line is shortest. Waiting, she stares vacantly up at their logo, a schematic map of East Asia with Japan and its possessions picked out in red and gold. The board over the ticket counter shows impending departures, which creates a strange sense of pressure, as though she's late for all of them, but her mind is cloudy and she's almost at the front of the line when she realizes she's been drifting, has yet to choose a destination.

It should be someplace where the powers-that-be are likely to take violent umbrage at even a well-connected U.S. plutocrat coming in and playing warlord, but to assess this would require an understanding of the fluid alliances and quiet understandings that define the shape of power in the world, which hasn't, until now, concerned her.

Front of the line now.

Just have to choose.

47

·

Something to Cry About

Kern wakes as the first light touches the jungle. The ground is steaming, his sleeping bag damp. The motion of the leaves makes patterns on the sky, shadows of birds darting through the bright empty spaces. Lots of birds, here, and though he rarely sees them clearly he's come to know their songs. Good to think of them living their lives up there, indifferent to the surface of the world.

Kuan Lon already feels like just the next thing, not much different from any other place. It's almost disappointing. He wants there to be another city, or sequence of cities, cursed cities buried ever deeper in the jungle, dead and shattered, stained skulls entangled in suffocating vines, culminating in some unfathomable absolute zero.

Six fights in two days, all won by knockout, and he's as sore as he's ever been. His hands are an agony, stiffened almost into claws. He has money, now—Singdam, who also goes by Simon, the Thai promoter with the Australian voice, keeps doubling his purses, just like Final Sword. When he fights all the farang cheer for him, throwing yellow flowers and candy into the ring, afterwards stuffing bills into his hands.

He lies there, craving more sleep, knowing it's unattainable, hoping it will help a little just being still. His fights haven't gone long but even a few minutes in the ring are exhausting, and he feels like he's approaching an edge, that something will be revealed if he can just maintain focus and keep pushing through his fatigue. Dead hours before him until the lights in the trees wink on at sunset and then his seventh fight.

Crash of someone coming through the wood, water drops flying from lashing branches. Probably another bar girl. There was one who'd come to his clearing in the middle of the day and, catching his eye, matter-of-factly dropped her shorts, lest he miss the point, and turned her head and smiled, and this and the sun on her thighs and her wisps of pubic hair were the stuff of fantasy but the fights had hollowed him out and he was unmoved by the sight of her, and he'd thought this must be how naked people look to animals, and in a voice more distant and cordial than he'd known he possessed he'd told her to go home.

Sulfur on the air as a match is struck and then burning tobacco, and a man says, "Boy, do you have any idea how much heaven and earth have been moved to find you?" Hiro steps into the clearing wearing a suit and swiping beaded water from the jacket, holding his little silver gun.

"Oh," Kern says. He's wrapped up like a package in his sleeping bag—no point in even trying to get away. Screeching overhead as a mass of birds rises from the branches and in the rushing of their wings he thinks yes, it might as well be here, and it might as well be now, but Hiro just watches the birds scatter into the air and the moment passes. It hits Kern that there will be no seventh fight. He closes his eyes.

They're walking on a game trail as light slowly fills the jungle, and though his hands are cuffed behind his back and Hiro is five paces behind with the ghost's phone in his pocket he feels at peace and is achingly aware of every rustle and creak in the shifting leaves and branches. He knows there are animals in the jungle, quiet and watchful, though he's never seen one, and if they're ever to be revealed it will be now, and even if they're not then at least they'll be the ones to find his body, approaching over the fallen leaves with a diffidence learned over ten thousand generations, and long after his corpse has corrupted and his bones have turned to dust they'll still be here, living the same lives, and he feels lucky that here at the end he's depleted enough to be both neutral and accepting.

"Zero point eight percent," says Hiro. "That's how much of the world's total computational power we leased to try to find you. Server farms everywhere from Barrow to Klamath Falls have been doing nothing these last weeks but sifting images for you. What images, you ask? All of the images. All the images that were going up on the web plus footage from our spy drones flying over the major cities plus all the footage from certain makes of security cameras with whose manufacturers we've made arrangements. You wouldn't believe the cost, but if I ever had that much money I wouldn't be consorting with the likes of you and me. And all this to find a two-bit street fighter on the lam. I certainly hope you're sensible of the honor."

Kern says nothing. Plans rise unbidden in his mind—he could pretend to trip and if Hiro is incautious enough to get close then heel-kick him in the groin, and as this is one of his strongest street techniques there's a fair chance that if the kick lands he'll rupture one of Hiro's testicles, in which case Hiro, no matter how fearless or strong of mind, will double over, and for at least a few seconds be out of the fight, and then if Kern is prepared to tear his left shoulder from its socket he can use his right hand to try for the gun—and part of him thinks he should go for it, that it's better by far to die fighting than passively, but he knows that plans like that only really work in movies and to try it would accomplish nothing, or maybe get him killed slightly sooner, and so he'd lose these last minutes of the morning.

"Your fans were your downfall," says Hiro. "Goes to show you. Yet another celebrity destroyed by fame. Kuan Lon is all Halliburton cowboys, wholesale traffickers and hungry desperadoes, and let's not forget the occasional child-sex tourist, but they still feel the need to share their travels with their friends. We found you in photos of your third fight on a Romanian social network.

"I got here yesterday. Not strictly protocol, but I got interested. Hell, I'd even say I'm a fan. You know, at first we thought you had tradecraft, and then we thought you were some refugee from the fighting circuits taking piecework as an enforcer, but then we found your room, and your laptop, and it turns out you're straight-up refugee."

They come to a clearing where the air shimmers and the sunlight seems somehow to have thickened, and as he gets closer he realizes that there's something there, a transparent, blocky geometry floating before him in the air, deadening the wind, and there's a faint reek of ozone, oil, hot metal, rubber.

Hiro says, "Library, deploy ambient atmospheric from four a.m. three nights ago over the South China Sea," and for an instant light swarms in the empty space before him and then that light becomes thunderheads roiling and flashing, illuminated from within by lightning's pulse and snarl, as though Hiro's words opened a magic door onto a distant storm, and he thinks of the books the laptop gave him long ago about children going through wardrobes into perilous lands.

Hiro says, "Decloak," and the storm vanishes, becoming a black jet, sleek and sharklike, its aspect entirely predatory compared to the cetacean bulk of the passenger liners he took to Bangkok and Taiwan. Its wings are pulled close to its body, giving it the look of a resting pterodactyl. Vertical takeoff and landing, he thinks. VTOL. Close up, the plane's skin is covered in tiny hexagons, each the size of his thumbnail; now the hexagons are swimming with colors that resolve into leaves and branches in motion, as though the jet can't stand to be just itself.

"I knew you'd like that," Hiro says.

The cabin's deeply padded seats are upholstered in creamy leather with complicated multistage seat belts that must be precautions against intense aerobatics and the leather has a smell that he can't quite name. The cabin's cramped interior is all black webbing, matte aluminum and mil-spec austerity. Hiro cuffs his wrist to the armrest and he feels he should stay alert but as the plane's ascent pushes him down into the seat his eyes start to close and it's only then that he realizes that he knows the smell, that it's the same as the interior of Akemi's car, that the smell is money.

Faint vibration, muffled drone of engines. Night outside, moonglow shining through the tiny windows, no other light in the cabin but the faint glow from the jet's display. The metal cuff rests lightly on his wrist—he almost doesn't feel it if he doesn't move his hand. Shameful not to at least try to escape, but the cabin is a dreamscape, and the bulkheads waver and fall away.

It's still night when he wakes again. Hiro is across from him, sprawled in his seat in the dark. Kern's certain that he's sleeping until Hiro says, "One time I tried to leave, you know." A pause, and then, "You see, I'd stopped drinking."

Another pause, the plane shivering as it passes through turbulence, leaves it behind.

"How does one kill? It's easy, with an enemy, in the passion of the moment, but to kill strangers, day after day? It erodes the soul.

"I was rarely sober. None of us were, not since we graduated from the police academy and started working. The bosses were particular about that. Every day it was a new hotel, and in every new hotel room there were bottles of vodka and bags of cocaine and a stack of guns like a welcoming bouquet. The vodka was for numbness, and the cocaine for the focus and false confidence to carry us through the valley of death, day after day, world without end.

"Time works differently in that life. There's a fluidity, a sense of events coming on like waves, and they might break and wash harmlessly around your ankles or they might carry you away. Cause and effect blur—if the man was shot then it was his time to die. If the woman was behind the wall that did not stop the bullet then she must somehow have offended the bosses. I never slept in the same bed twice, or used the same woman twice, or drove the same car for more than a week.

"And then there were these signs, billboards, all over the city. They said, 'Call on Him, for He is Waiting.' It was just some church looking for converts, and a picture of Jesus they got off the web, but it seemed like they were speaking to me. There was this one, on the outskirts, out toward the army shooting range. I'd chain-smoke in my car and stare at it, like I was trying to pierce its mystery.

"I stopped drinking and using. I even quit coffee. Clean, I felt the fear, radiant and brittle, all around me, all the time. We lived at the boss's pleasure and could die at any time and there was no way out of that life, but I was sick with the letting of blood. I didn't know what to do, so I fucked a lot of women and watched a lot of movies and then I cracked and started drinking again. I decided I'd run for it. First I skimmed money. I was clever about it, but they knew.

"I was commanding my own unit then, and it was my own men who collected me. I'd taken a lot of pills that morning, mostly dilaudid, but I knew what was happening as soon as I saw the black armored SUV pull up to the curb, like it was the nightmare I'd been waiting for all my life.

"They brought me to a death house, one we'd used many times. Bodies upon bodies under the sand in the backyard. They tied me to a chair in the living room and there were the knives and a cigarette lighter and a bottle of acid and I started weeping uncontrollably. *Save your tears, faggot,* they said. *Because we'll really give you something to cry about.* But they didn't understand—I wasn't crying from fear of pain, but because I was afraid I would hurt them.

"There were four of them. They were drunker than usual, and my bonds were loose, and I prayed that they'd just kill me before giving me an opening, but the devil was near, I could hear his footsteps as he walked through the house, opening drawers and looking in closets, and then he was listening behind the kitchen door, and despite my prayers one of the men went outside to call a girlfriend and another went off to take a piss and another went to get a beer and the last was a friend, a man whose life I had saved many times over, and I thought he might even let me go, and I tried to keep God's face in my mind's eye while he stood there telling me how badly he would make me die, and I prayed fiercely for the strength to just let it happen, but then I stopped, because suddenly I knew beyond question that I'd been praying to the void, that no one was listening, or ever had been, and with that I felt nothing but a profound emptiness and a slight sorrow. Before that, I'd thought I didn't fear death, but it was only then that I realized that fearing death was all I'd ever done, and in that moment my fear was gone, which made me free, though all the light had left the world. Then my friend turned his back on me to find a cigarette.

"For practical reasons I spent no more than a minute on any one of them, though for them I suspect it was a long minute indeed. You have to be careful, or they just go into shock, and then what's the point? I smoked a cigarette, while I worked, to cover the smell. Ever seen an altar of Mict-lantecuhtli? A brutal relic of the Aztec past, now in vogue again. I made one, though it wasn't easy, human sinew being more resilient than I'd expected, and me not having the right tools to hand.

"Before I left town I went to the billboard and shot His eyes out, so that His face framed little burning holes onto nothing, which seemed about right. I was raised Catholic, but, frankly, its virtues are those of women and of slaves."

Silence. Kern says, "Why tell me these things?"

"Want to see something funny?" Hiro says. "The day after I killed my unit I went and killed my old boss." Another silence. "He was the one putting contracts on my head. With him in the ground, I'd get breathing space. It was the savvy career move."

Hiro hands him his phone which shows birds-of-paradise on a dusty

hillside, and then the view rotates sickeningly into cloudless blue sky before panning over dry distant mountains and settling onto a large white
house roofed in red tile, and down by the garden is a wall of glass and
behind the glass a fat old man and a pretty young girl are naked on a bed.
Crosshairs snap into place alongside fluctuating numbers marked "meters" and "windage" and Kern realizes that this footage is not from a
phone but from the scope of a gun. As though reading his thoughts, Hiro
says, "It's an M-110XE, the old U.S. Marine Corps sniper rifle. A classic.
We trained with them at the academy."

A sequence of tones as a number is dialed and then ringing and an
older man who sounds like he's used to giving orders says, "Hello?"

From the phone Hiro's voice says, "What would you pay for the death
of Don Victor Garcia?"

The older man says, "Who the fuck is this?" and then, after a pause, he
names a large sum.

Hiro: "I just emailed you the account information. Transfer the funds
in the next two minutes and it's done."

Older man: "*Who* is this?"

Hiro: "I think you know. Yesterday I resigned from Don Victor's
service, so, counting me, he's down five men."

Older man: "I did hear about that, and yes, I do know who you are.
And as much as I would love to see Don Victor dead, and however dearly
I would pay for that privilege, the problem is that I don't trust you in the
slightest, you backstabbing, coat-turning son of a bitch."

Hiro: "I appreciate your point of view. I just sent you a link to the video
feed from my rifle's scope."

The man and the girl are having sex now, the man's face turning red,
his eyes squeezed shut, the girl staring at the ceiling like she's trying to remember something as her feet flop up and down on his shoulders. The
crosshairs come to rest over the man's right ear. On his tricep is a tattoo
of Saint Death, a skeleton in a robe holding a scythe. Beyond the bed is a
television showing rioters in a public square throwing bottles stuffed with
burning rags at cops with plastic shields and it must be someplace really
poor because none of the cops have powered armor.

Hiro: "If you want to make sure it's real just turn on CNN."

Older man: "If you're fucking with me, if this is a trick with computer
graphics, then by the Virgin's cunt you'll find out how I got such a hard

reputation. You'll have a team of doctors, quite talented men, graduates of the very best schools, all to keep you alive until I'm done with you. Be certain you understand the consequences of breaking your word to me."

Hiro: "I've got a clear shot at his medulla oblongata but she just put a finger up his ass so you've got about thirty seconds to make up your mind."

A pause in which Kern can hear the older man breathing.

Older man: "I sent it."

A pop like a firecracker, and the fat man collapses onto the girl. She starts to embrace him and even pats him on the back before she realizes that part of his skull is missing and that his blood is pouring onto her shoulder.

Hiro: "Of course, I'd have killed him either way."

Now the scope is tracking the girl, her face streaked with blood, as she throws open the French doors and runs across the lawn wearing nothing but striped panties and clutching her blouse to her chest. In one hand she has a man's watch, its dull gold gleaming, inset with what can only be rubies. The crosshairs find the ground in front of her and there's another pop, and then the girl is sitting on the manicured lawn, looking stunned, and just as she's about to cry Hiro-in-the-video shouts, "Hey! You in the panties! His *wallet*! You forgot to take his *wallet*!"

Hiro takes his phone back. "That's our recruiting video. We're still a young organization."

Fully awake now, Kern looks out a window at the moonlight on the sea, wonders where they are, and where Akemi is, how many thousands of miles away. Hiro seems to be feeling confessional so he says, "How did you end up working for Cromwell?"

"Because my world's time is ending, though it sometimes seems I'm the only one who knows it. The U.S. doesn't care about other sovereignties or collateral damage anymore. A few days of daisy-cutter bombs and all my old bosses are dead and some U.S. senator gets a political win. So I came to the North, and found a software baron who's been accumulating wealth these hundred years and more, and is eager to adapt to the emerging realities.

"Which reminds me. There's something I forgot to do."

Then Hiro's gun is in his hand and pressed to Kern's temple. Kern forces himself to meet Hiro's eyes in order to keep his dignity while part of him wonders if it's even safe to discharge a round in a plane like this—would it pierce the hull and depressurize the cabin, or, as this is a bird-of-war, would the round bounce off its armor and carom around until both of them were dead? In any case he's glad to have something to think about besides the steel against his forehead.

"Boom!" says Hiro, and then puts the gun away. "There was an order for your execution, which I gave, and now it's done. So your old life is gone, and, improbably enough, you have another, and with that life you can do as you will. How'd you like to work for me?"

48

•

World Is a Chessboard

The outside world is a sense of mass sliding by behind the town car's darkened windows. Clink from the micro-fridge as the car corners; mouth dry, Thales opens it but finds nothing but two splits of champagne, one open and half empty, its carbonation hissing. As the car corners the crash seat tightens, pressing the gun into his chest.

He isn't sure what he'll say when he takes the gun out and points it at the surgeon—is there some form or accepted usage? In the stress of the moment he doubts he'll be able to manage either the lyrical profanity of a gangster or the ironic detachment of a gentleman-at-arms; best, no doubt, to make his threats simply, and in his own words. He imagines the surgeon seeing the gun and instantly submerging himself in an immovable professional gravity while he, Thales, rants on disjointedly about cities in the waves and oracular strangers and his accelerating sense of losing the thread, and it's in his mind to stop the car and toss the gun out the window but then he remembers Akemi's suggestion that his mother sold him out which elicits a sense of emptiness so profound that he feels almost weightless and the imminence of violence no longer much concerns him.

There's a succession of basso thumps, probably his brothers' dance music with the volume turned low.

The map is gone from the seat-back display, replaced with an interface he hasn't seen before, enumerating munitions remaining and hull integrity broken down by panel.

The crash seat seizes him so tightly that it crushes the air from his lungs and then the car clips something and, discontinuously, is spinning, and he wonders if here, right now, *this* is his death, and then there's another impact, and the car has stopped.

Engaging, reads the display, and the car hums as the ammunition meters tick down, all at different rates, like stopwatches out of synchrony.

The enforced passivity is unbearable but the seat won't let him go. Psychologically better if they at least give you the illusion of control, maybe let you fire one of the car's ancillary guns. The car shakes as the larboard hull integrity falls.

A sound like a whip cracking right in front of his face and now there are matching holes to his left and right in the darkened windows, each the width of a champagne flute. High-velocity armor-piercing rounds, he thinks, just like before, and if it was his father's turn then it must be his turn now, and it's almost a relief that it's finally happening. Through the holes he sees color and hints of texture—grey of concrete, black of smoke, radiant blue sky—and now he can hear the polyphony of gunfire.

The shooting stops, and the ammunition meters stop counting down. *Executive override: Standing down*, reads the display. It smells of sulfur, burning rubber, hot concrete.

The crash seat releases him. Crouching on the floor, he tries to decide if he should stay in the town car, though it's either malfunctioning or compromised and its armor is of demonstrated ineffectiveness, or run for it, though he'd have to fight off unknown and heavily armed attackers with an antique pistol he's never fired and for which he has exactly six rounds.

The windows turn transparent—there's a chromatic corona around the bullet holes—and he sees he's in a wide street in a sort of canyon of favelas. The town car is wedged into a pile of cars, some burning, all wrecked, black smoke pouring up. Shattered bits of chassis smolder on the ground, and the walls are marred with bullet holes and black starbursts of carbonization. Drones swarm in the air—he sees with relief that some have the livery of the Provisional Authority but their guns too are trained on his car. There's no one around—the favelinos apparently know when to scatter. It's as squalid as a war zone, the kind of place where death comes easily, and now a woman is stepping through the smoke rising from the wreckage of a motorcycle.

Her face is covered with a cloth, probably against the smoke but it makes her look like a bandit. She seems unfazed as the drones converge on her, and then they arrange themselves into a hemisphere with her at the center, their weapons pointed outward, maintaining formation as she approaches the car.

The town car's windows descend of their own accord and a drone appears on his right, the side opposite the woman, its guns trained on him at such an angle that the rounds would go through him and into the seats— he remembers how stubborn bloodstains can be, and how particular his father's valet was about the upholstery—but it doesn't fire, and he's aware of the passing of more seconds of life.

The woman leans in through the window and pulls down the cloth that hides her nose and mouth. She's of his mother's age, or rather agelessness, and her hair, tied back, reveals a scar on her forehead, and then he realizes that he knows her, that it's the ragged woman, or her twin, but with none of the evident craziness or erosion of the street.

She's about to say something but stops short as realization hits and then in a flat, definitive voice she says, "You're the Brazilian prime minister's son."

You said that before, he thinks, as she steps back as though scalded, and then something seems to drain out of her and she suddenly looks old. "Oh," she says, and holds her face in her hands, and now she's looking at her hands like they're someone else's and peering around as though the morning held a secret.

The drone's guns are still trained on him, the barrels black tunnels into nothing. The woman seems to have forgotten he's there, and there's nothing to do, and nowhere to go, but then he remembers that the town car, for all its sleekness, weighs over seven thousand pounds, and is engineered to run roadblocks—the Mitsui salesmen had said it could easily push a tractor off the road.

The drone in the window rises away, its sudden absence an unexpected grace. He says, "Command escape, all-in, now!" The car's engine roars as it breasts through the smoldering wrecks and then the acceleration throws him back into the seat.

The car goes up on two wheels as it corners without slowing and Thales looks back in time to see the woman raise her hand toward a drone like a contralto about to sing, and then the drone detonates like a firework.

Her face is washed out in the flash. She looks self-contained, interested, a little sad.

Then she's gone, but he hears the echoes of more explosions, guesses she's blowing up the rest.

The clinic's steel gates close soundlessly behind the town car and he kicks open the door and scrambles out onto the courtyard's sand. The town car's right side is unscathed but the left looks like a target at a shooting range. Where armor's been shot up he can see that it's ceramic, and about half a foot thick, which would be why the interior is so cramped. Bullets are buried in the armor like grubs in a rotten log—he pulls one out between thumb and forefinger—it's like a crumpled metal mushroom the thickness of his thumb. He watches it scintillate in the light, then flings it off into the garden's raked sand.

A girl in clinic livery approaches—young and pretty, he notes distantly—and in her posture is both welcome and submission. He gestures at the car and says, "Something happened. There was an attack," speaking too fast, his fear and urgency demanding a response but she just smiles professionally and he wonders if she heard him because she doesn't even look at the car, just takes his elbow and ushers him into the cool dark of the clinic. She checks her tablet and says, "We've lowered the lights for you, to minimize the potential for"—she frowns—"disturbance," and he's going to ask if she happened to have noticed that his car's been shot to fuck, and call his family, their security, the police, *somebody*, but he stops, says nothing, somehow certain that his words would disappear like stones dropped in a deep well, and it occurs to him that he's now inside the clinic and was too distracted to be nervous about bringing in the gun.

The surgeon's office is as dark as a tomb, the only color the muted red of the worn Persian rug, and from behind his desk the surgeon says, "These are the final tests, on which everything depends, so please do your best today."

"Actually, today's going to be different," Thales says, aware of the weight of the gun over his heart, and it seems like his confidence must be unmistakable but the surgeon just pushes his tablet across the desk and on it there's video of a man sitting on a stool in a cinder-block room. His arms are folded and he's staring off to one side, wide-eyed, as though shell-shocked. His sleeveless T-shirt reveals a wiry musculature, and on his shoulders are mottled pink patches of recently regenerated skin. He's sweating under the harsh overhead light and Thales wonders if this is a deliberate stab at a film noir sensibility.

"Why didn't you fire?" asks someone off-camera.

The man blinks, seems to recollect himself. "What?"

"Why. Didn't. You. *Fire*. We have you on video walking out of the villa and ditching your armor. You could've shot out one of the plane's engines before it got ten feet off the ground."

"Because she won," the man says in a hollow voice.

"The audit clearly shows that you had full control by the time you left the villa, yet you did not engage, so how do you—"

"Because *she won*," the man says, fully present for the first time. "She could've killed me if she'd wanted to." His accent is languid, the vowels long, some subspecies of American English. "You know what an iron maiden is? That's what my armor was, once she owned it. But she must've found the pictures of my girls, and took pity on me. She told me to remember that, and I intend to. So that's why I let her go, and that's why I'm done. I don't care if I end up digging ditches for a living. I lost, I should've died, and I'm going home."

"Failure is never acceptable, Corporal Boyd."

"If you don't like failure, maybe you should give your shooters armor with more security than my kid's Barbie. She burned it in the time it takes to light a cigarette."

"Did you make a deal, Corporal Boyd? Did she buy you off? Because we think you made a deal, and we'd be more inclined to show clemency if you admit it."

Boyd regards him, and beneath his surface apathy there's a glittering readiness to harm. He says, "Why don't you come on over here, sweetheart, and whisper that in my ear."

The physician stops the video, says, "Explain what's going on here." This test, like all the tests, seems arbitrary, and has nothing to do with anything, but despite his exasperation he still he can't bring himself to draw the gun. There's always irony, though, the preferred weapon of the weak, so he says, "They're lovers, having a spat. What does this have to do with me?"

"Very good," says the physician. "Now there's just one more test, and it counts for all."

"Wait," Thales says, unable to keep his helplessness and strain out of his voice. "Please. Just one second. Could you please just explain to me exactly what's going on."

"Look," says the surgeon, pointing to the tablet, where another video is playing.

It's the old man from the last video, in a tiny room like a monastic cell with white walls and no windows. He's lighting candles on a table where dozens of candles are already burning.

His woman enters the frame, stands watching.

"I'm lighting candles for my dead," he says.

"Family?"

"Victims. One hundred and thirty-eight, as of today. I have their names by heart."

She searches for a response. "You did what you had to do."

"What I had to do was kill innocent people, or cause them to be killed, in pursuit of selfish ends. I'm a murderer."

"No you're not. Shhh." She kisses the back of his neck.

"But I am a murderer. I *must* be honest. It's the only way to stay intact." He lights another candle. "Or such is my theory. It's hard not to think they'd all be dead in half a century anyway, but this is a sociopath's reasoning, or evolution's. I'm really trying, but morality looks different on long timescales, and I can't find a way around that fact."

"It'll be worth it," she says. "You'll do so much good. Like you said, the world needs a steward, and no one else is positioned to take the job."

"One day I'll have islands," he says, "and on the islands, villas, where I'll put my enemies, so they can read and garden, raise children, keep mistresses. My exiled adversaries' memoirs will become an enduring literary genre. For now, I light candles, though it's already an empty gesture—I no longer much care what I did to them, but I remain scrupulous about going through the motions. I feel all my years today. Oh my god. One hundred thirty-eight names."

"What about Ms. Sunden?" asks the woman, trying for lightness, her bitterness showing through.

"They said they don't need her memories anymore. They. The strangers. The others. The shadows, I think, suits them best. Not quite there, never really substantial. I'd very much like to know why they changed their minds. It happened just after she graced my servers with her presence. Now they say they're ready to proceed. My people are loading the fabs onto a ship as we speak."

"You're just letting her go?"

"Ah. No. I'd prefer to, but the shadows are fickle, and I may still need her, so I told Hiro to track her down."

"And the shadows?"

The old man pauses, a long match burning slowly in his hand. "When I was a young man, I wanted to explore the world, but that faded, as the years passed, and I understood its systems, and for decades now the world has been as legible as a chessboard. But the shadows . . . I never thought I'd find anything like them. Part of me still thinks this must be self-delusion, like I'm like some sun-dazed early Christian hearing voices in the wind. They're a wonder."

"They're frightening."

"I hate to say it but I agree. It's crossed my mind to keep my word and let them be, but it just won't do. Moreover, Andy insists they've developed computer hardware more than a *billion* times faster than anything on the market, which would be hard to believe if I hadn't seen their other efforts. I guess we'll see when we harvest the nodes, or finally get that phone."

"My love?" says the woman.

"Yes?"

"What will you do when I'm gone?"

"*Après toi, le déluge*," he says. "I couldn't imagine making plans."

The surgeon stops the video, leans in across his desk. Thales is aware of the room's darkness, its stillness. The surgeon asks, "Will he honor his agreement?"

Go fuck yourself, Thales thinks as he says, "Absolutely."

The physician stands and heads for the door.

"*Wait,*" says Thales, standing in turn, aware that this is his moment, and that it's about to slip away. His voice is hard, not recognizably his own. "We're not done."

The physician stops and stares at him, his face unreadable.

Thales' resentment and confusion coalesce into a singularity of purpose that permits him to reach into his jacket and put his hand on the gun. He says, "Give me the tablet. *Do it now,*" and he's ready to draw, even to fire a warning shot, but the physician, unperturbed, offers the tablet, saying, "Here."

Thales says, "If there's a password, security, if you've somehow locked me out—"

"There's no reason for me to do that," the surgeon says. "Everything is now open to you. Goodbye."

He leaves, closing the door behind him.

Thales wakes the tablet. It has many folders, one with his name.

He opens it. There are his memories.

49

·

Closely Coupled Forms of Nothing in Particular

The mirrors reflect a stranger wearing a suit of an elegance that has nothing to do with him. The tailor, taciturn and somehow goblin-like, crouches at his feet with his mouth full of pins, marking the cuffs of his trousers with chalk. Kern lifts an arm, half in jest, to see if his image will do the same; the sleeve of the jacket droops over his wrist, making him a child as well as an impostor.

Hiro sprawls in an overstuffed leather chair, practically sitting on his spine, drinking amber liquor from a heavy crystal tumbler. On the walls are paintings of horses in dreary landscapes, some with riders in red coats and black hats, like the doormen at that hotel in San Francisco. He hopes he won't be getting one of the riders' outfits, and he doesn't see what horses have to do with tailoring, but it seems to be part of the shop's look.

"You know, I appreciate this, but I don't really need it," he says as the tailor grunts and starts pinning cloth.

From a glazed calm Hiro says, "You'd prefer the double-breasted?"

Kern doesn't know what that is, which is probably the point of the joke. He says, "I just mean it doesn't look like me."

"Clothes are the soul," Hiro says. "They'll change how you think about yourself, which is fitting, as you have a new place in the world." Switching to Spanish, presumably so that the Chinese tailor can't follow, Hiro says, "I have plenty of human assets I scraped off the street, and they look it. You're different. You're my new weapon, and a good one you'll be, but you need an aura, to pass in certain circles, and this is a step on the way." He downs his drink, reaches for the faceted decanter with a self-consciously steady hand. "Besides, how many people get to wear a Mr. Li suit? All too few even know that they should want to. I know because my late employer came here twice a year, rain or shine. Mostly rain, here. I might add that just what you've got on your back is, beyond question, worth more than everything else you've ever owned."

Kern looks back at the mirror, tries to accept what he sees as his own reflection. He *might* look good, he decides, if the sleeves fit, and they let him put shoes on, and if somehow he could manage to relax. He remembers a photo of a young Mike Tyson in a tailor's shop, dapper and self-satisfied in a new suit, taken, as he recalls, around the time of the start of his decline.

Hiro shakes his head. "It's like giving caviar to children."

No windows, outside the shop—he hasn't seen weather since they scuttled off the helipad atop the tower in downtown Hong Kong—just buzzing fluorescents over thin, torn carpeting with decades' worth of accumulated stains. The shop had a specific feeling, something about club chairs and mirrors and cigars—Hiro had called it "a bastion of vaguely traditional male privilege"—but out here it's different, and somehow draining, less like a place than a somewhere-in-between, and he remembers looking down through the jet's window at the city's aqueous light glowing through the churning clouds, how he'd had to will himself into passivity as the plane fell into the grey and the glow became the glittering lights of towers.

"You look like you stole your suit," says Hiro as they walk toward the elevator bank. "You should walk tall, like you're used to this, like the wretched *peones* must jump to do your bidding. Such an attitude will be of value when you need to sneak up on rich people and shoot them in the head. Or, hell, beat them to death with your elbows, if you have to do everything the hard way, though I beg you to consider of the cost of the dry cleaning."

Ten elevators in a row, their bronze doors embossed with stylized clouds and dragons. Hiro hunts for the button for floor 214, where their suites are.

"Take this," Hiro says, handing him a wad of colorfully foreign money as an elevator chimes and its bronze doors open. "I have to talk with the big boss. Why don't you go off to the mall, take the suit for a spin, try dipping a toe in the consumer economy. Anyway, the New Tian Shang Ta is remarkable, really something to see."

Heaven is, he supposes, desirable, but it has no form, or at least none he's heard of, and he wonders if its form is this, as he stands there on the lowest floor of the New Tian Shang Ta's atrium, staring up into eighty stories of perfectly empty space. It's full of quiet echoes, like the muted distillation of a thousand conversations. The ascending succession of the mall's balconies lends scale to this image of the gleaming infinite that would otherwise be ungraspable, and across from the balconies is the seamless vertical pane of the tower's outer shell, and beyond it the grey of storm. The rain hits the glass in a million tiny concussions, the channels of water branching and merging and branching again, but neither wind nor rain make the slightest sound, and at first he thinks they're a recording.

There are elevators, but to take them would separate him from the essence of the place. There are stairs, which are better, but his legs would be spent by the time he got to the top, so he settles for the escalators which make diagonals between the balconies.

Off the balconies are floors full of shops selling more things than he'd known existed. The first two floors are dedicated entirely to watches, and he wanders among the brightly lit storefronts dazzled by the massed evidence of time passing and the prices for minor variations on the same essential thing.

Even with the escalators he's tiring by the twentieth floor, but he's made it his business to explore, because the mall is a condensation and summary of the world, or at least the world of the buyable, so he moves swiftly past the countless racks of magazines in alphabets he's never seen, and it's a little like coming home when he finds the floor with media in English.

Next is a floor dedicated to furs, some of them apparently not from vats, but flayed off of real animals, with bits of animals still attached, and the inert, flopping heads and leathery paws seem shamanic, or perhaps barbaric, though most of the shoppers here are stick-thin, rich-looking women, and his heart lurches at the sight of a fur so brilliantly blue-white that it looks like falling snow. *I'm sorry*, he thinks, remembering Akemi's limp helplessness, her blood staining the pillowcase, and he wonders if she's still alive, if she missed him, if there was ever a moment when he could actually have helped. She's just a woman, he tells himself, and as such replaceable, and she hasn't spoken to him in a long time, and he's a soldier now, or nearly, and above caring. Maybe one day he'll ask Hiro but for now he should just forget her.

He tries a jab-jab-elbow combination in the mirror in a luggage store to see how his moves look in the suit, and it looks good, really good, like something in a movie, and when he really snaps the punches the sleeves make a noise like a whip cracking, and he starts shadowboxing, getting into it, dancing a little like the early Ali until a Chinese dad leading his pink-frocked little girl by the hand pumps his fist and says, "Jai-yow!" at which Kern strides away with his hands in his pockets.

He'd intended to spend money if only just to see what it felt like but the sheer profusion of things leaves him drained of all desire and he wanders dazedly past the storefronts wanting nothing but to make it to the top, and it occurs to him that, in the same way that heaven lacks a shape, the lives of the blessed dead lack any apparent purpose, not counting the singing of hymns, which would get old in about a minute, but then it's obvious—what you do in heaven is keep on going up.

The atrium culminates in a disc of translucent blue glass, high overhead and as wide as an ordinary rooftop, and as he gets closer he sees that the pale blue is marred by the shadows of people standing on the other side, and he wants to stand there with them, feel what they're feeling, but the last escalator brings him to a sort of abandoned plaza, and there's a doorman by doors of frosted white glass through which he sees stairs, and the sign on the door reads *Club Cielo* in an intricate curlicued script.

With the suit it's worth trying to bluster his way in but the doorman moves just perceptibly into his way and says, "Pardon me, sir, are you a member?" but so politely, like he doesn't already know. Kern could lie but can see it's useless so he just says, "No," and the doorman says, "I'm very sorry, sir, but the Club Cielo is members-only, so, for now, our doors are closed."

In his suite he finds a bottle of brandy sealed with wax and an ice bucket with two black bottles of champagne called Cristal and there's a black plastic briefcase inside of which is a foam bed holding what looks like a compact machine-gun from the future and a note in Hiro's crabbed handwriting reads, *For you. The latest Heckler-Koch Bullpup, for when you absolutely, positively have to kill every motherfucker in the room. Technically a capital crime to have this in the New Territories so be discreet, please.* He's always been a street fighter rather than a gunman but as he brandishes the weapon in the mirror he feels a rush of pleasure and a sense of power so intense that it shames him, and then he hears voices from the behind the closed bedroom door.

As he eases the door open it occurs to him that he doesn't know if the gun is loaded, or how to turn off the safety, but in fact there are no assassins, just two naked Chinese girls sitting on his bed, one clipping the other's nails as they gabble away, having a good heart-to-heart about something, and they look up in shock as he puts the gun down on the floor and when he looks up again they're smiling as they come toward him.

Flowers of orange flame bloom from the barrel of the machine-gun on the widescreen, the color staining Hiro's face and the fluid in his glass and Kern's own hands. The suite's blinds are closed though they're up so high that only aircraft could see in. Hiro doesn't look away from the movie as he raises a brandy bottle and says, "Drink?"

"No, thank you," says Kern, annoyed at his own formality but unable to control it. "It kills endurance."

"I honor your scruple, but that will pass. Either that or you're the king hell number one zen motherfucker of all time, which is, I grant, a possibility, but, generally speaking, the life requires outlets."

Kern sips ice water, says nothing, though he badly wants to know what happens next, if there's initiation, training, gearing up, what they're actually going to *do*, because everything else in his life is gone, and until he finds out he's nothing much at all, but Hiro seems to want only to drink his way through the minibar and watch movies.

In the movie the Yakuza are holed up in a beach house doing nothing but wasting time, having fake sumo matches on the sand and shooting soda cans off of logs. Kern's eyes start to close.

He jumps when Hiro says, "They never wore suits like that," and he
sounds like he's speaking from the bottom of a well, and for the first time
Kern registers the Yakuza's outfits, striking Cold War period pieces, though
all of them except for the protagonist look like a nickel's worth of gangster
in ten dollars' worth of suit. "Real Yakuza looked like shit," Hiro says. "The
kind of people who chain-smoke for exercise. They could always spot the
undercovers because they weren't hacking up a lung. More Bugs Bunny
tracksuits than bespoke Armani. It's a twentieth-century comedian slash
auteur's dream of what a gangster ought to be."

"So what should a gangster be, these days?"

"Ah. Well. That's the question, and one that has no answer, because
the truth is that gangsters have no essence. The movies are always about
the *code*, but there is no code, no tradition, no honor, no anything—really
it's just random thugs scrabbling after fleeting advantages. Organized
crime is like a vacuum, filling the gaps in the legitimate markets, and it
arises spontaneously, everywhere, all the time. Wherever two or more of
you dumb punks are gathered together in my name . . .

"The irony is, they try to figure out who they are by watching movies.
In the cartel, some of them copy westerns, bosses' sons who went to the
London School of Economics priding themselves on having cow shit on
their boots. Even I'm prone to that, and I know better.

"The deeper irony is that, just as gangsters copy movies, movies copy
gangsters. Two closely coupled forms of nothing in particular." Hiro pauses,
then says, "Ever seen an Antonio Loera movie? Sweeping cartel epics.
Mexico's own not-quite Takeshi Kitano. He was born upper class, went
to art school, learned about the narcos from books and movies.

"I guess he must have wanted to see the real thing, because one night
he showed up uninvited at the gates of my late employer's ranch. It's an
incautious move, by any standard, though less outright crazy than it might
at first appear—they both traveled in political circles, and I think they'd
met socially. If Loera thought his fame would be his shield, well, that's
where he was right, and in fact Don Victor turned out to be a fan, welcomed him graciously and sat him at his right hand at the table.

"Loera got a tour of the ranch, even the vault with the gold, the sight of
which was usually a one-way ticket to the landfills, and the barn full of
combat drones that Don Victor called his air force. Later, when they were

drunk, they stumbled through the desert with their arms around each other toward a ruined outbuilding we were using as a death house.

"I'd been watching from a distance but I faded in behind them as they went in through the door. My crew were there with a client, doing the long job. Loera turned white, started trembling and tried to leave, but my late employer held him by the shoulder and kept saying just a moment, my friend, just a moment more. Finally, the client's blindfold fell off, and he saw Loera and recognized him. He started screaming, praising his art and his mercy, pleading for his intercession. Loera visibly composed himself and said, 'Don Victor, please, as a personal favor to me, could you possibly spare this man?' Don Victor was a fat bastard but his face looked like ancient stone as he said, 'Don Antonio, I have the highest regard for you, and would never hurt a single hair on your head, but in this matter I regret I am unable to oblige you.'"

Abruptly Hiro stands, seemingly drained, and turns off the TV. It's like a door has closed as he says, "You should go back to your suite now."

In the morning Kern wakes without knowing why and there's Hiro sitting in the chair across from the bed, watching him, presumably, from behind his sunglasses, and he looks somehow inanimate, like he could have been sitting there all through the night. Hiro says, "Time to get up, boy. It's your first assignment. You're going to Delhi."

He leans over and hands Kern a burner tablet showing a picture, probably from an elevator's security cam, of a deeply serious and somehow distracted-seeming woman who looks like money and has bangs and kind of a lot of jaw.

Hiro says, "Her name's Irina."

50

·

Our Lady of Drones

. . . and it's like a koan, how the glyphs seethe and shimmer, interweaving and dissolving faster than he can follow, and the harder he tries the faster they slip away. He tries for a broader view, sees he's had that thought before, that it punctuates the recent past like the poppies in a dense field of flowers, and he remembers the poppies in the vase by his bed in the St. Mark, their forms repeated infinitely down the fractions of the seconds, his opiated fog, how his mother sat by him and held his hand, how the shifting tensions in the muscles of her face encoded every shiver of feeling, and once again he wonders what ghosts are if not this sense of presence. Needing distraction, he looks inward, and it's like a koan, how the glyphs seethe and shimmer, interweaving and dissolving faster than he can follow, and the harder he tries the faster they slip away . . .

A jolt, and then he's trying to read new glyphs, but they're too simple, just dark blocky lumps on a ruby base, and he realizes he's staring at the Persian rug on the office floor, that the tablet has fallen from his hand because the ground moved, is moving, it's an earthquake, which he's heard can happen in LA.

He doesn't know what to do—is he supposed to take cover in a doorframe?—and then the earth stills. He picks up the tablet, careful to keep his eyes averted from its screen, and shuts it down.

He steps into the corridor. No sign of the surgeon. *Got it! Meet you where?* he texts Akemi. There's a cyclical vitreous ringing from the direction of the lobby, which he finds abandoned, the receptionist gone from her desk. The noise is coming from one of the white vases with the blue Chinese dragons wobbling on its pedestal. He stills it with his palm, feeling the porcelain's cool. The pendant lights are swaying. Outrageous but somehow typical that the clinic staff have fled.

Out in the courtyard there's a thick haze in the air and it smells like the sea, though the beach is at least a mile away. Late afternoon shadows on the shot-up town car and the minimalist garden; the sun glitters on the spent round where he threw it on the sand. His phone chimes—the text failed—network not found. No obvious way to open the gate, and no one to ask how. A trickle of black water seeps under it, darkens the asphalt, bleeds into the sand.

He tries to go back into the clinic but now the glass doors won't open, and the lights inside are off. Power failure, but shouldn't there be an emergency generator? Peering into the shadows, he sees the Chinese vases are missing from their stands, but it's too dark to see any fragments on the floor.

The world buckles again, the town car swaying on its axles as the spent round dances on the miniature dunes forming spontaneously in the sand. A section of the high wall is leaning inward, and by the time it's in his mind to dodge out of the way it's collapsed, just like that, burying the town car, blinding him with dust.

The earth is still again. He wipes his eyes, stares intently at the remainder of the wall. Could it be just slightly out of true? In any case it's certain that the courtyard isn't safe so he scrambles up the slope of new rubble.

Nearing the top, he knows what he's about to see and then does see that the street's become a tide race. *Tsunami*, he thinks. The water running in the street comes up to the cars' doors; it's rapid, filthy, thick with debris. Most of the buildings are dark, their lower floors covered in mud and silt, their specificity washed away. As he wonders where the people went a body floats by.

He drops down to a sandbar in the lee of an overturned truck. A library of objects washes past, a trash-can lid and a pink plastic doll and a phone and sodden plastic bags and all the nameless components of machines and cities. He listens to the water's roar, its intricacy. This strikes him as an occasion for plucky self-reliance but no plan comes to mind and then he remembers tsunamis come in sequences.

Cigarette smoke on the air—there's a woman sitting on the roof of a half-drowned car. Her clothes and hair are dry. It's the same woman who attacked his car, Our Lady of the Drones, the ragged woman's more presentable twin.

He wades toward her, the detritus in the water bumping him like inquisitive fish. Her eyes are closed, like she's lost in thought, and a cigarette is burning in her hand. "Hey," he says, "who are you?"

She opens her eyes, looks down at him, smiles. "I'm a magician," she says.

He stares at her. Is she hurt, mad, in shock?

"For real," she says. "Want to see a trick?" Without waiting for an answer she reaches down and plunges her cigarette into the water. It hisses as it's submerged, but when she pulls it out the ember is still burning.

"How did you do that?"

"It's easy when you know the secrets of the universe. God, I missed these," she says, dragging. "Never thought I'd have another. Come sit by me." She pats the roof beside her.

He clambers up, the car's roof sagging under the added weight. The woman extends an empty hand which at first he thinks she wants him to shake but she makes a fist, unclenches it, and now on her palm there's a pack of cigarettes. "Smoke?" she asks.

Thales shakes his head. She has no obvious wounds, and is intact enough for remarkable sleights of hand, but there could be some more subtle trauma. "Are you all right? Did you send your drones for help?"

"As for my health, I'm as well as can be expected," she says. "But no drones, I'm afraid." Something seems to occur to her; she looks abstracted and tense as dark water surges around the car, almost immersing it, and then she relaxes as the water goes down. "Okay," she says. "That did it. We've got a little more time. Sorry about the water. It's erasure made manifest. I can't quite make it go away."

"Listen to me," he says, feeling like he's trying to get a distracted child to focus. "Tsunamis come in sequences. We need to get to high ground, then find a way out of the city."

She says, "Once I thought I'd go to another country, another shore. Find another city, better than this one, where all I try is doomed to fail, and my heart is buried like something moldering. But there will be no new city, no other shore. This city is my prison, and I'll never leave its streets. There will be no ship for me, no road. I'll waste my last minutes in this tiny corner of the world." She seems to recollect herself, says, "Forgive me, I'm . . . So, to business. Let's say you're in a fairy tale. In a fairy tale, you might meet a djinni who grants wishes. Let's say I'm that djinni, except I'm nicer and both more and less powerful. I'd like you to wish for whatever would make you happiest. I realize this seems strange, but please take it seriously. It matters, as much as anything, and there isn't much time."

She seems earnest, and even kind, but is evidently even crazier than her twin. "Was that you, in the St. Mark?" he asks. "Or was that your sister?"

The question seems to surprise her. "Sister. I didn't know there were others. But of course there are. She must have known almost nothing, and been very afraid."

"Okay," Thales says, sliding off the car into the water. "I have to go now. I think you should come with me, but I can't talk anymore."

"Wait," she says. "With the wishes. I wasn't kidding. I know you think I'm crazy, but look." She makes a fist, opens it, and a dozen dream-blue butterflies swarm out from her palm and flutter away.

"Very impressive, but I need to find Akemi and get to high ground, so goodbye."

"Hearing is obedience," says the woman, making a little bow with her hands pressed together. "It is granted. She isn't far, and I'll show you the way. Maybe I'm being literal-minded, but I suppose that's traditional."

"You know Akemi?"

"Pretty little thing. Must be part Japanese. An actress, or wanted to be. You found her in your mom's house, and then later in your car. She didn't know why she couldn't seduce you. At first she thought you were gay, then decided you're just quantitative."

"How do you know this?"

"Like I said, the secrets of the universe."

Not knowing where else to go, he follows her, and though he has many questions he's certain she'd just evade them, and as they plod through the current he makes himself look up at the sky, which is just starting to darken, as it's better than seeing the bodies in the garbage on the banks.

They come to a building of many stories with firelight glowing through some of the lower broken windows, and looking up at it he feels an echo of the city in the waves.

"Akemi's here?"

"And it's high ground," says the magician. "Follow me."

She leads him through the ruin of the lobby, up dripping, water-slick stairs. One of the landings reeks of marijuana—he gets a glimpse of figures standing around what must be a burning bale of it—and finally they come to a torchlit rooftop overbuilt with crude structures piled up like swallows' nests, steep staircases zigzagging between them, like a hillside Aegean town. The buildings look blocky, like something from a child's toy fabricator—he's reminded of pictures of the earliest favelas—and there, in fact, is an old-timey builder drone, creeping painstakingly along as it lays down its little dabs of concrete. He wonders if obsolete drones are in fashion with bohemians.

"Just a few minutes now," says the magician.

"Until?"

"The end. I'm estimating. I made some edits, so I'm less worried than I would be," she says. "If you want to talk to Akemi, you should do it now."

Something cracks underfoot. He's crushed a piece of broken glass, probably from a beer bottle. Movement draws his gaze up toward the drone-built structures—he sees steam billowing up, dissolving in the wind—smoking mirror, he thinks, form erupting out of nothing—and behind the steam there's what seems to be a copy of his mother's house in the mountains.

His mother was never really famous, her work known only to a few other architects—there's no reason for anyone to have built this, and the coincidence of his having found it here, and now, is extraordinary, and requires an explanation, and the magician obviously knows more than she's told him so he says, "My wish is, I want to know why that's there."

"Why what's there?" asks the magician, sounding flat and distracted, but then she looks up and when she sees the house her eyes narrow as her body tenses, and it sounds like the words are torn out of her as she says, "That's a different node. *There's a line out*," and before he can ask what she means she's pushed past him and is running up the stairs, and he's wondering if he should follow when he sees Akemi sitting on the roof's edge, her face shining in the red light of torches.

51

•

Never Really Have Happened

As the plane descends toward Jeddah Irina looks out through the window at the rippled dunes in the abandoned streets, and it's only when they're a few hundred feet off the ground that she finally sees cars on black asphalt, rooftop solar cells, the bulbous domes of a mosque, the occasional blue pool.

This was a rich country, once, and not so long ago, but it feels like the oil flowed in the days of Harun al Raschid. The last king, who is very old now, fled to London fifty years ago with the last of his bankrupt nation's treasury; one freezing January night two decades past she and Philip had walked by his house in Chelsea at three in the morning, seen firelight glowing in a high mullioned window. Now the country is all but empty, and the mullahs rule piously over blank infernos of sand.

She's following the signs for the airport's medical clinic to see about her jaw when it occurs to her that Corporal Boyd's suit might have kept records exact enough for them to reconstruct her injury. She stops dead, imagining her MRI going off into the net, beyond her knowledge or control, and it's not clear whether this is self-defeating paranoia or the caution that will avert the small mistake that would undo her.

The airport is owned and operated by a Dutch firm, which is why she can buy a bikini for the sun deck and bask there sipping from a rum on ice. Impossible to hold onto tension in that stupefying heat. She'd been worried she'd feel exposed but her new touch-me-not movie-star sunglasses help and in any case she feels anonymous among all that bared flesh, as though the hard light washed away all individuality, making everyone into just another animal drowsing in the sun.

She stares up into a sky like a sea and imagines she sees currents and depth-warped light. In six hours she'll fly on to Delhi, which had seemed sufficiently random and far away from Patmos, then check in with her soldier and plan her next move. She wonders if she'll have to do anything so egregious that she won't be able to go back to the United States, but no matter, the only real country is the country of wealth, and many places would take her; in any case, she has her Greek passport.

She closes her eyes, making the sky a blood-red glow, and lets herself drift.

As sleep comes she's glad that for a while she can forget all her strain but instead of disappearing she finds herself in a poorly lit boiler room full of the racket of distant machinery. This is a dream, she thinks, and a lucid one, but at the wrong time—REM sleep should only come after an interval of oblivion. Is the setting a metaphor, a sign that she's somewhere in the basements of her mind, or could this be one of the implant's utility programs? A screen on the wall playing a succession of scenes from the recent past—the ice in her drink refracting the light in the bar in the Athens airport, Fabienne's composure as she shook her awake, the blue sea framed in the VTOL's window. There's a woman sitting on a section of pipe watching the screen and she looks just like Irina.

Irina studies her twin, trying to decide whether she is, in fact, pretty, a question she ought to have resolved long ago. Others would probably say yes, she allows, in large part because, having bought off the years, she still has the glow of youth's embers. Her twin looks moved, as though she might cry, which is somehow unseemly.

"The Cartesian theater," Irina says. "And here's my double, bearing witness to my history. They're interesting symbols, but what does it mean?"

Her twin looks up at her, blinks and says, "Oh, fuck. Well, here we all are," and her voice is Irina's, not thin and nasal like in recordings, but rich and mellifluous like it sounds in her head.

"Are you my subconscious?" asks Irina. "My *anima*?"

"I believe you've mistaken me for someone else."

"So then you're . . . what?"

"I'm nothing, or nearly, barely even a ghost," says her twin, who for no evident reason seems greatly moved to see her, but this must be accepted as part of the structure of the dream. "I'm also the only one who's ever had all the information, and I'm going to be the one who makes everything right. But I'm so glad you're okay—I wasn't sure what had happened to you after Cloudbreaker. And poor Iliou. Fabienne was so sweet to you, in the aftermath, more than I'd have expected. She didn't have to help."

"I like Fabienne," Irina says. "She's slight, but has a depth of kindness, even of courage, in her way. And of course her accusations are correct. Her father is dead because of me, and I doubt there's anything I can do to make it right, though god knows I'll try. It's just that Cromwell stands too far above the law."

"What's it worth to you to beat him?" asks her twin. "What would you risk for a chance to annihilate your enemies both known and hidden and then maybe live for a very long time?"

"Everything."

"Would you manipulate yourself into doing what was necessary?"

"Of course."

"That's what I thought, but I thought I should ask. It's just I'm not myself these days."

"But how could I beat him? I attacked him before, and with powerful allies, and barely survived. He seems to have no weaknesses."

"Oh, he has weaknesses," says her twin, and while they've been talking the boiler room has gotten dark and the machines have fallen silent, and now the only light is from the screen floating in the blackness where the wall was, showing Cromwell in his office holding Magda on his lap. "Magda is one. And you remember the strangers, his mysterious correspondents, from when you broke into his servers? They're another. I've met them. They're AIs, feral ones, running on hidden servers in the dark places of the world. I know where they are." Now the screen shows a map of the world, the seas and continents fading out as though night were settling, dim stars emerging in Tokyo, LA, Sydney, what used to be Costa Rica.

(For a moment she thinks there's another one, and by far the brightest, near the equator, but it's already gone from the screen and from her mind.) "Cromwell's recently figured out what they are, and where, and he plans to leave them alone until their business is done, which is something else I can use. I've had about a minute to plan, but I think my plan will work. Which reminds me, I have something for you." She presses something into Irina's hands, a passport-sized document. "It's a kind of security code, obtained with difficulty. Think of it as letters of transit—it will open doors for you. So listen—I need you to know I've done my best for you. I hope to god you win, but either way I won't be around to see it, and now I ask your forgiveness for what I'm about to do."

"Which is?"

"Change you. I'm going to give you memories of things that didn't happen, and make you forget this conversation. I know it's a violation, but at least it's only me. I'd rather just tell you everything, but if I did you'd distrust me when you woke up, and why shouldn't you? I'm well acquainted with your skepticism." Her twin smiles tightly. "I won't re-member this either, as of about a minute and a half from now. We'll go from two witnesses to one, and then to none, and then it will never really have happened."

"What do you mean, you won't remember it either? What's wrong?"

Her twin takes her hands and says, "It was good to see you," sounding so sad and proud that Irina is reminded of her first day at college and the tenderness with which the other students' parents had said goodbye, for which she'd hated them, though she had not, at the time, been able to admit it, choosing instead to despise them as coarsely sentimental; at that point she'd been her own legal guardian for two years, though her lawyer was still punctilious about sending her gifts on Christmas and her birthday.

Her twin kisses her cheek, says, "Now forget me."

52

•

Sphinx Explains Our Horror

Akemi is sitting on the roof's edge pitching ice cubes into the void. "I got the tablet," Thales says, and when she looks up at him there's an empty moment before the click of recognition.

"Thales," she says, smiling widely. "Baby. Good job. Come here." She holds out her arms with such a naturalness he finds himself accepting her embrace. Before she'd had an aura of feral alertness but now she just seems happy when she says, "But it doesn't matter anymore."

"Of course it matters," he says. "What could matter more?" He looks over the side and there must have been another wave, and a monstrous one, because black water has all but swallowed the city—here and there spotlights rove over the chop, and the lights of the buildings are blinking out before his eyes.

"Because it happened," she says, settling into him like a child. "I got the call, the one I've been waiting for all my life. It was Sonia, my friend Sonia Caipin, the director's daughter, now a director herself. I didn't really think it was going to work out for her, but she got the money for her movie, finally, and she wants me to be the lead. I can't tell you how long I've been trying to get here. They say LA is a game no one wins, but now I have, like I knew I would, though I also knew it was impossible, and now nothing else much concerns me." In a gesture of exuberant finality she flings her drink over the side, the ice cubes and crystal tumbler and the amorphous mass of liquid catching the light and then gone.

"This happened *today*? The timing seems suspect . . ." He trails off, because it's more than suspect, is in fact so unlikely as to be impossible, so she must have been manipulated through her implant, but before he can decide what to do about it the magician has joined them.

"Sorry about that," she says briskly, and she seems like a different person now, her melancholy gone, radiant with purpose. "I had to make a call. Hey, you," she says to Akemi. "I'm afraid we have to have another chat."

It hits Thales that she said she made a call, which means there's a working phone up in the replica of the house, which means he can call his mother, so he slips away as Akemi and the magician start to talk.

He charges up the stairs, turns a corner and there's a square pool of black water, steam billowing up and dissolving in the wind and beyond that more steps leading to the house, and then he notices the magician sitting on the steps, blocking his way.

"How did you get here so fast?"

She says, "Thales, you really can't call your mom."

"Get out of my way."

"I don't know how to tell you this. Quickly, it seems," she says, looking over his shoulder, and he follows her gaze down to where the sea is rising slowly over the level of the roof, thick black rivulets pouring onto the deck and running among the feet of the people who are just starting to notice. No wave or tide could reach so high and yet the water comes.

"That's the end of the city," the magician says matter-of-factly as somewhere a woman starts to scream. "I slowed it down, but I can only do so much."

"It must be all the water in the world," he says wonderingly.

"In fact there is no water. That's what I'm trying to say. It's a little like reading—the bedrock reality is black marks on a page, and those marks are nothing like the world, but your mind insists on making sense of them. The illusion is seamless, and thus hard to escape. Every inconsistency just gets explained away."

"It looks like water to me."

"There isn't even an image of water, unless you look closely—mostly the illusion's just composed of words. Whatever's missing just gets filled in, mostly with your own memories, sometimes with someone else's. How to explain? Coleridge said images in dreams represent the sensation we think they cause. We don't feel horror because we see a sphinx, but dream of a sphinx to explain our horror. In the same way, we see a city, though there is no city, just a handful of dreamers, bound together, sharing a dream. But in fact there are no dreamers, just a tissue of memory, and vortices moving through it, weaving it together and letting it decay."

Again he says, "Get out of my way."

"How much do you remember from before your collapse in that tunnel by the beach?"

"Plenty."

"Actually, you only remember a little, and that hazily, because it's just what you happened to think of in the two weeks you had your implant."

"The damage wasn't that bad."

"I'll be explicit," she says. "The damage was total. In the end. The implant got you an extra two weeks. Afterwards, per contract, all its data reverted to Ars Memoria LLC, which went bankrupt a year later. Our hosts stole it sometime after that. You are made from what they stole. It's been six years since you died."

Six years, like a fairy story, how time flows differently under the hill. "Hosts?" he says.

"AIs. Big ones. Bigger than I'd thought existed. Hard to speak to motive, with that kind of thing, but it looks like they've been using us to interpret the world. The surgeon was one of them—he was running the place, while the place lasted. I think they found people are at their most docile with doctors. I caught him as he was leaving, not long after I met you and realized what was going on. Sorry for scaring you, by the way. I'd just arrived, and thought I had to take a hard line."

"You caught him?"

"And I fought him, and I won. I shouldn't have had a chance, here, with what I am and what he is, but I'd managed to get access to the control layer. Their security was weaker than I expected—actually, it seemed to have been deliberately weakened. I suspect there's a story there, though I don't know what it is, and the end result is I destroyed him."

"And then?"

"And then I nearly despaired, because I discovered he was just a servant, and that his master, who was on the central node, was more terrible by far. But I had nowhere to go, and nothing to lose, so I sought battle in his high city in the waves, like a rebel angel bringing war to heaven. I got close enough to see something of his mind, and watched him decide I was irrelevant, and to isolate himself from the net while events played out, and then he dumped me back here with all the exits closed."

The roof deck is several feet under water now and chairs are afloat and the people are thrashing and calling for help and some of them are weeping and some are trying to use their phones but their numbers have already dwindled.

"It's interesting to bear witness to the process," the magician says. "I think they periodically purge and restart on empirical grounds—after a while, the inhabitants either go crazy or start figuring things out and the con stops working. It's interesting how it goes with the different species of ghost—you Thaleses have clarity but tend to collapse, and the Akemis are good with people but keep trying to run away. The rest of them seem to be of no use at all, except for me and my various twins. In fact, the management seems to prefer Irinas, probably because we understand them the best, although, as you see, we're prone to rebel. Akemi here seems to be a hybrid, with some of my memories—maybe they're trying to toughen her up. Anyway, I meant to ask—under the circumstances, do you want to live? There's a way out, for you at least."

"I thought you said all the exits had closed."

"All the old ones did, but then Hiro connected Kern's old phone to the net." *Hiro?* he thinks. *Kern?* "But if you've had enough, all you have to do is nothing for the next fifteen seconds."

No, he thinks, but the water is rising, drowning the steps in black, and he says, "Yes." Candles in glass bulbs bob among the figures treading water and he wonders what happened to Akemi.

Now the magician is holding out the surgeon's tablet—he wonders how she got it, then remembers where he is. "Look," she says, pointing to an icon on the screen. "See that? It's you. Just move it into the folder marked 'house.' I'd do it myself, but it should be you. If I don't treat our kind with as much respect as I can then this life really has no meaning."

"Why is my mom's house here?"

"It's where they were keeping Akemi, because it was isolated, I guess, but most of all because it was a place they knew about."

As the water rises over his feet and pours into the black pool he copies the icon with a swipe of his fingers and then looks around in surprise because he's standing just inside the threshold of the house, which is his mother's down to the books on the shelves and the abstract friezes around the windows. He turns, and there's the magician on the stairs, and behind her is a boy bent over a tablet, the water creeping past his waist. The boy raises his eyes and Thales sees his own face.

The boy's wonder is his own, but then the boy looks down at the magician's hands as she embraces him, and in that moment they've diverged, and Thales no longer knows what the boy is thinking.

The black water is rising around the magician's shoulders, and the boy's face is pressed into her neck—she's actually rather tall—and she holds the tablet up and does something to it one-handed and Thales' terror is immediately less and he hopes the boy's is too.

"It's okay," says the magician. "I'm at peace. What can be done, I've done."

"Come with me," Thales says. "Both of you. There has to be a way." He pities the boy, having to hear this, knowing he happened to get the bad draw.

"No room," she says. "There are two weeks of you, but twenty years of me, and you're on the tiniest node. I had to cut corners just to squeeze you in with Akemi. Physically speaking, you're now running on a phone, or something that looks like one, in a hotel room in Hong Kong. It's where Akemi was originally, before you let her out into the city." Her voice gets an edge as she says, "They meant for it to be their intermediary but now it's mine."

"If you're just a program, break into some server and make a copy of yourself, like you just did for me."

"Regular computers are too slow, and I'm not going to risk ending up in the public domain. If it makes you feel any better, I'm still alive, out in the world. The original, I mean. You might meet her soon. If you do, help her out, okay?"

The other boy's eyes are squeezed shut as the water submerges him, and right away it's like he was never there at all. The magician has her eyes on Thales as the water rises over her neck. "Goodbye, Thales," she says.

"Do well. Fight for us," and then the water is at her chin and she says, "Goodbye, goodbye, goodbye," and as the water rises over her mouth she cries, "Philip!" and decency requires that he not look away as the water covers her nose, and then her eyes, and then there's a horrible moment when only her forehead and hair are visible, and then she's gone, the doorway framing nothing but restless black water.

Akemi is behind him, sitting in the window seat, looking shattered and hungover, her mascara streaked with tears. "That's done," she says. "Looks like time to go."

"Where?" he says. "And to what purpose?"

"We have a plan," she says, and reaches past him to close the door.

53

•

A Little Beyond the Law

Night in the desert and the freight train roaring by. Behind Kern the desert is empty and still, but he knows that out there in all that vacancy someone is looking for him, and they may still be far away but that they're coming is a certainty and the only escape is across the tracks where he's been waiting patiently but the cars keep coming and still no end in sight. He looks over his shoulder—the barren sand looks white in the moonlight. It smells of smoke and creosote—he can tell it's going to be yet another dry year. With each passing car there's a deafening pulse and he's wondering if he could time them, fling himself through one of the evanescent gaps, and he's looking for his moment when behind him someone ostentatiously clears his throat.

He surges out from under the covers, is up and on balance, scanning for threats that aren't there because he's in his hotel room in the dark. He sits on the bed, relieved that he's alone. He gradually registers the bleating of the landline on the nightstand.

He picks up the receiver just to stop the noise and listens to the line's silence until Akemi says, "Hello? Are you there? Did I get the right room?"

"I thought you were gone," he says wonderingly, feeling woozy, as though the room were unreal. He focuses on the bullpup in its black case on his desk, the Mr. Li suit hanging in the closet over his duffel bag of clothes. "I was going to go back for you," he says, "but I didn't have any weapons, and I probably just would've died if . . ." He trails off, ashamed of his cowardice, his cringing explanations.

"Well then, you can help me now," she says. "I need you more than ever."

"I can't. I have a job. I'm flying out in the morning for work." Strange to hear himself—these words belong to someone else's life.

"You're working for Hiro, right? You don't want to do that. I've spent some time with him. He was always open with me. I know what happens to his people."

"I am working for Hiro," he says. "I have to have a job, and this is what I do. He saw me fight and he recognized me. It's not that different from what I was doing before, except I never worked for anyone this important."

"Hiro's soldiers never last long."

"I'll be the exception."

"Even if you survive, it'll mar you. He'll think it's funny. You're a sweet boy, underneath it all. I don't want to see that happen to you."

He blinks, forces his eyes open. He can't believe she's alive, and that for the first time in his life he has a place and she's calling him in the middle of the night to try to get him to abandon it, but even worse is that she doesn't get him. "*You* don't understand," he says, in a voice that's pure edge, a voice he tries never to use, what he thinks of as his true voice. "Hiro is weak. He drinks. He blunts his despair with television. He *needs* things. He isn't pure. I don't fear him. If he was smart he'd fear me." As the flare of anger fades he sees that what he said has some truth, but that he's also doing something stupid to impress her; it saddens him that, despite this knowledge, he won't be able to stop.

A pause. He notices that his shin is bleeding—he must have barked it on the dresser when he scrambled out of bed. Numbness is part of the training—the nerves there have been dead for years. She says, "Are you sure you're prepared to take him on?"

"Completely," he says, though in fact he's terrified, and the best he can say is he'll keep trying.

"Then you're brave, but me? I *am* afraid to die, and if you don't help me I'm going to. So what do you say? I've got no one else in the world."

"What do you need?"

"No," she says. "I shouldn't have asked. I can't ruin your gig."

"What do you need," he says sharply. Hiro will try to kill him, of course, but that's probably how it was going anyway, and he half-suspects he's not meant to come back from the hit on that woman. Maybe his lifetime of training has been leading to this. He thinks of Achilles, Cuchulain, Tyson, Galahad, the joy they'd bring to this crisis, and he's suddenly keen to get going and let his new life burn up like a dead leaf in a furnace.

"I need you to steal the phone back from Hiro, and right now."

"His room will be locked."

"I'll take care of that."

"And then?"

"Then get the hell out of Hong Kong, as fast as you can, because he'll be coming. Best if you walk out—the city isn't that big, and once you're in the jungle there's no good way to track you. There are villages up the coast where you can buy a boat."

"And then?"

"Then it gets complicated. I'll tell you on the way."

He turns on the bedside lamp. The room is opulent, part of a princely life he's now abandoning. "Take everything you need," says Akemi. "You aren't coming back."

He strides down the hotel corridor with the bullpup swaddled in a bathrobe in the crook of his arm. The thick carpet stifles his footsteps—no sound but the metronomic thump of the duffel on his side. (He wadded the suit into the duffel, which can't be good for it, but at least he's got it with him.) He'd expected to hear some kind of human noise from behind the doors—whatever sex, snoring, chatter, TV—but there's no sound at all.

The door to Hiro's room is the same as all the others. The corridor is empty in both directions; he stands there, listening, awaiting a sign. He slips his hand into the rolled-up bathrobe, finds the grip by touch, and clicks off the safety, absurdly afraid the noise will rouse the hotel.

His hand hovers over the door handle. Akemi had said that she'd make sure it was open, but how, exactly, was she going to do that? He's known hackers, even a few girl ones, and all as unlike Akemi as could be.

He turns the handle with painstaking care and is suddenly certain, absolutely certain that Hiro is waiting for him inside, lolling in an armchair and dandling a gun; he'll have forced Akemi to call him, and in fact she'll be in a room just a few doors away, sloppy drunk, pillows pressed over her ears so she doesn't have to listen to him die. Game to the end, he'll fire the bullpup at Hiro's chest but Hiro will cock an eyebrow as he savors Kern's dawning realization that he's shooting blanks.

The door eases open onto darkness, silence.

He shuts the door behind him and stands there in the suite's living room, heart hammering, wishing he were back in the ring in Kuan Lon. As his eyes adjust he sees faint spectral television light shining under the bedroom door.

The room is a mess. Bottles glint here and there, and there are crumpled clothes on the floor, among them a girl's lacy underwear. On the coffee table is a bullet standing on end next to a pile of crumbling white powder.

He almost steps on a sticky room service plate, freezes in mid-motion, carefully places his foot on the carpet. He sees the winking green lights of a laptop on the desk, and there, connected to it by a data cable, is the phone. Keeping one hand for the bullpup, he detaches the cable, then puts the phone in his pocket, as easy as that.

A noise behind him and he whirls with the gun at his shoulder, the bathrobe starting to slide, then slumping to the floor. In the doorway to the bedroom is a naked girl, very pretty, staring at him wide-eyed, frozen in the act of reaching down to get her underwear. Her eyes track him as he moves to get a better look behind her, but he just sees a darkness, the glow of TV. She makes a rueful face and shrugs her shoulders infinitesimally to convey that she's just doing a gig, and has no vested interests here, that as far as she's concerned he's quite welcome to kidnap or kill her client, and could she please go home.

He mimes closing the door, which she does with exaggerated care, and then she steps into the living room with her palms raised. Only a little light filters out from under the bedroom door but it's enough for him to be distracted by her beauty—Hiro must have spared no expense—and she looks like a marble statue, standing there without expression.

There's no good option. He's not going to kill her, and he doesn't want to choke her out, and even if he did he doesn't think he could do it silently, so he guesses he has to let her go. He decides to give her money, both to buy her continued silence and goodwill and because Kayla, his ex, who seems far in the past now, had been militant about kindness to sex workers. As he reaches into his front pocket for his money the bullpup dips to the side, which she appears to read as an indication that she should leave, and her face doesn't change as she sidles toward the door, staring at him fixedly, and he wants to say wait, take some money, take your clothes, at least take the bathrobe, but of course he can't say a thing, and then she's gone.

He realizes he's done there, unless he wants to tiptoe into the bedroom and shoot Hiro in the face, an idea of considerable strategic merit, but if just one person hears the gunshot and calls the cops or even the lobby then his life is done, and Hiro could have killed him in Kuan Lon, in fact had meant to but instead let him live, gave him gifts and the place he's now discarding.

Out in the hall he closes the door carefully, wonders if Akemi is watching from somewhere and will lock it behind him, but he doesn't hear a click. He looks to his left and there's the girl speed-walking away, and just at that moment she looks back over her shoulder, sees him, hesitates. On her back is a tattoo of a phoenix, its wings unfurled over her shoulder blades, its long tail reaching her coccyx, and in the corridor's low light its feathers flash green and blue, as iridescent as the throat of a humming-bird, an effect he's never seen in a tattoo and of a quite hypnotic loveliness. Her eyes are on the bullpup, which he's holding at port arms, so he clicks on the safety and lowers it, which is her signal to sprint off down the corridor like a startled deer. He tears his eyes from her lean grace and stuffs the gun into his duffel as he strides off the other way.

As the elevator falls past the ninetieth floor he realizes he didn't close the duffel fully and the bullpup's stock is protruding. He shoves it back into the bag, zips it shut and looks up at the car's tiny security camera. A capital offense to be in possession, Hiro had said. He wonders if anyone is watching—probably not, in one elevator among many in the middle of the night, but what if they have automatic image recognition for guns? Does that even exist? Lares had said something about image recognition being a hard problem, but was that just for faces and people? It occurs to him that outside of fighting he doesn't really know how anything works and has to guess his way through the world.

The girl's tattoo shimmers in his memory. The phoenix must be a
potent symbol in her personal iconography, and he wonders what fires
she's passed through, what rebirth. Lares once said that soldiering and
hooking were essentially the same job—dangerous, but more money than
you could probably get otherwise, and they'd generally take you, if you
were young and healthy, and both put you a little beyond the law.

As the elevator falls past the fiftieth floor he takes out the phone, sees
that it still has the earpiece attached. If she's not on the phone he has no
way of finding her, and no option but to leave Hong Kong and disappear as
best he can, but when he puts the earpiece in she cheerily says, "So I guess
it worked out, huh?"

"Yeah," he says, happy to hear her voice, and that once again they share
a perspective. "I've got the phone. I'm in an elevator, going down. I don't
think Hiro woke up."

"Well done."

"I thought maybe you'd have been watching. I mean, you did find my
room."

"It was dark in there, and then my net access went out," she says, which
seems strange, because aren't phone access and net access basically the
same thing? "Don't worry about it," she says. "It's fine. Now let's get you
the hell out of dodge."

She guides him through a succession of freight elevators and service corridors where maids and housekeepers and waiters bustle past, seeming not
to see him, as though he bears some mark that tells them he belongs.

Down in the basements she guides him to a room that looks like it
used to be a meat locker, but now a Filipino vendor has set up a kind of
general store, his goods neatly stacked on blankets on the floor. "Get the
highest-bandwidth satellite phone he has," she says in his ear. "And lots of
data cables. Like, thousands of feet. Also water, nuts, candy, whatever has
the most calories per pound."

Ditching the bullpup in a dumpster full of cardboard and sodden vegetables, he feels spiritually lighter.

"Where are we going?" he asks as they walk through rooms full of
boxes labeled in Chinese and middle-aged ladies squatting on the floor
playing mahjong.

"There's a village up the coast," she says. "Fishermen and smugglers, mostly, and apparently a bar scene. The government turns a blind eye, so it's a surveillance blank spot. We can buy a boat there and no one will ask questions."

"I don't know how to sail."

"It'll be easy. You just have to motor out and meet these ships at sea."

"Friends of yours?"

"Something like that. They're unmanned drones, so you just have to motor up, climb on and hitch a ride. There's an island on the equator and they'll take you all the way there."

"Is that where you are?"

"It will be by the time you get there."

"Am I rescuing you or what?"

"There's something I need you to do on the island. It's hard to explain, but I'll show you when we get there."

The corridor ends in double doors that open onto estuarine mud and salt water leaden under the low fog in the predawn light. He walks out into the black, sucking mud, feeling free, grateful to be out of doors even though his shoes are immediately ruined. A heron rises heavily into the air, croaking loudly. No sound but gulls, the low rush of waves. He looks back at the mass of rust-stained concrete—strange that Hong Kong, which had seemed inescapable, ends so abruptly. He looks up toward the city's towers but they're invisible in the fog.

54

·

Unwieldy, Lovely,
Perhaps Eighteenth Century

Night flight to Delhi.

She half-wakes, feeling observed.

The first class cabin is almost dark. The woman next to her, deep in her unrejuvenated fifties, is staring at the swelling on her jaw.

"I'm sorry," the woman says, but doesn't look away. Her yellow skirt-suit is very good, but her face is a map of old pain. Overcoming her diffidence, the woman proffers her cup of ice, saying, "Does he do it much?"

From a dream of nothing Irina says, "Just once, so I stole both his breath and the light in his eyes. But there's someone else, and much worse, who would take everything from me."

Silence but for the air-conditioning.

"You have to hurt him," says the woman. "*Badly*. Everyone has a weakness. My husband hasn't seen our children in five years, and so help me God he never will."

Another silence.

"Take this," the woman says, almost tenderly, again offering the cup of ice. "It'll help with the swelling. You'll be glad you did. You'll look better this way."

Irina accepts the cup, presses it to her jaw. The woman leans back, shuts her eyes.

There's a hotel inside the Delhi airport.

Her room is a windowless, minimalist no-place; with nothing to grate on her sensibility, it's easier to think.

She's sitting on her bed when her new phone rings.

"Bad news," says her soldier. "He's gone to ground in his new offices, and there's practically a battalion in the parking lot. I've never seen a non-state principal with that much security, and I served five years in Pashtunistan."

Of course it's like that—she's already sent Parthenon most all of her savings, but it couldn't be as easy as making a call and beggaring herself. "Could someone, say, sneak in?" she asks, trying to hide her despair.

"No. Too many drones in the air. It would be difficult under the best of circumstances, given that the building stands alone in the middle of several acres of empty parking lot."

"What about a frontal assault?"

"Prohibitively expensive. That kind of thing is only really practical for the great merchant princes. Moreover, a dust-up is one thing, but no matter how well connected you are you can't just start a ground war in the U.S. proper, not in the coastal cities, and hope to have a future."

Just room tone on the line as she tries to see how to work from the givens of the moment to Cromwell's violent end. She could try to hack a military weapons satellite, but that's a counsel of despair—she'd almost certainly fail, and if she somehow succeeded she'd be the focus of the state's unappeasable wrath and probably live out her life at an extraterritorial black site in a hermetically sealed box. If she could somehow lure him to Greece, Fabienne's old lover might have him disappeared; she could send him a ticket for Athens, coach class, and a pass for the Acropolis.

"Why are you laughing?" asks her soldier.

"It's nothing," she says. "Are his troops armored?"

"Of course."

It's a potential weak point, though by now they must know she's coming.

"What if I neutralized his soldiers and his drones?"

"They are many."

"But if I did?"

"Then I'm your man."

She dreams she's in an antiquarian bookshop in the Back Bay, an atlas pressed into her waiting hands as someone says, "This is what you need." The atlas is unwieldy, lovely, perhaps eighteenth century—waft of old paper as she opens it at random to a gilded *mappa mundi*, sees the faded olive of the plains, the black type on the spines of mountains, the rivers' dendritic blue threads. The abandoned central latitudes are colored in washes of red aquarelle, the sites of dead cities marked in mottled bone white, and tiny silver circles gleam in LA, Sydney, Tokyo, what's left of Costa Rica, though she can't quite tell what they mean, and there, a fifth one, smaller than the rest, high among the towers of the city of Hong Kong.

The silver circles fill her eyes though their significance eludes her and it's only as she realizes that this is just a dream, and the circles an empty form, that she remembers.

There was a report on W&P's servers, glimpsed in passing in the course of her assault, and it's right there in her other memory but she'd somehow till now overlooked it. "I traced the phone's traffic," wrote Andy Simoni. "The exercise was cut short, but it's communicating with servers in LA, Australia, Tokyo, and Central America. I duly monitored the traffic on these nodes—all were in contact with the offshore server that's been send-ing us email. It seems reasonable to infer that these four nodes are the points of origin of the stranger's communication." There are the nodes' network addresses and GPS coordinates. Cromwell annotated the report: "Good job. Now leave them alone. No monitoring, no interference, no anything that might offend them or even come to their notice. I'm saying the same to all my people. Hiro will take anyone who doesn't listen. Please attend meticulously to my orders, as I'm entirely serious."

Now she's falling down into deeper levels of sleep but somewhere she's smiling because she knows she'll retain this wonder, this insight, her opening.

She sits up in bed. Her phone is ringing. The bedside clock reads 5:37 but it doesn't say a.m. or p.m. and she's not sure if it uses military time.

"Don't be mad," Philip says, when she fumbles the phone to her ear. "I made Maya give me this number. I had to browbeat her. She was drunk, and knew my loyalty."

"Philip," she says blearily, glad to hear his voice, but already this chink in her security.

"Cromwell's office is an armed camp now," he says. "I thought you'd want to know."

"I heard about that," she says.

"Really?"

"A . . . an employee told me. A mercenary, actually. A killer, I think. I'm keeping strange company."

"Tell me about that. In fact, tell me the whole deal. Last time we spoke you were coming to my house, in fear of your life, but you never actually showed up. I know you're private, I try to be discreet, I never ask you for *anything*, but *come on*."

"I wish you hadn't called Maya," she says.

"I have to try to make new friends, as my old ones are so disengaged."

"*Philip*."

"You're right. Sorry to interfere. When you're killed I'll just have my secretary send flowers to your grave. *Plastic* ones. Few, and botanically incorrect." The lightness of his irony is forced, which means she's really wounded him, but even so it's in her mind to just hang up—she has enough to deal with, and her silence was partly for his benefit, but that's not really honest, and in fact she *has* kept him at a distance, and here he is, still trying. With a sense of moving a great weight she tries to make herself apologize but the best she can do is "Okay."

"Okay?"

"I'm sorry."

"Let's act like I believe you so you can tell me what's going on. Maya wouldn't be specific but I got the sense it's a bad scene."

"I'm in . . ." she says, and as she's about to tell him she remembers the atlas, the nodes, Cromwell's orders that they be left alone. *It seems reasonable to infer that these four nodes are the points of origin of the stranger's communication.* A plan arises fully formed in her mind—she'll go to a node, break in, send email to Cromwell as the stranger. She could tell him to move his troops, then send Parthenon in for the kill, but no, her true intentions would be too obvious—Cromwell has limited leverage but isn't stupid. She needs some reasonable pretext for Cromwell to leave himself open, but what does he want so badly he'd grasp for it blindly?

"But don't tell me if you don't want to," Philip says, and she's being rude, again, and she's already unworthy of his loyalty. The words "*Magda to my Cromwell*" arise in her mind, a thought that shames her, but she remembers Magda's illness, Cromwell's despair, the university he's founding in her honor, and then, like a gift, she has it—she'll make Cromwell expose himself by offering him Magda's life.

"Actually, it doesn't matter," she says. "You do a lot of business abroad, right?"

"Yes," he sighs.

"So of Tokyo, Sydney and LA, where would Cromwell have the least influence?" Central America is out of the question—wildcatting resource-extraction companies, nocturnal temperatures in the hundred twenties, the states tantamount to legal fictions.

"Tokyo," he says without hesitation. "In LA, shooters are plentiful and cheap and the police are disorganized. In Sydney they're still trying but the writ of law only holds in certain neighborhoods and the map keeps changing. In Japan, though, xenophobia is your friend—there are no guns and certainly no mercs allowed on the islands, and they'd take a dim view of some gaijin warlord coming in and flexing his muscles."

"Thank you," she says. "How'd you like to meet me in Japan at the Imperial Tokyo Hotel?"

Packed again, she checks in the bathroom and under the bed for overlooked things.

She's getting low on cash. She's got bank accounts all over the world, three in Switzerland alone, but Crédit Nuage is the most secure and discreet. She goes to its site on her phone, enters her account number and passcode.

Her money is gone.

55

·

Form on the Water

Nothing but water, jungle, grey skies, sand. No passing drones, no distant planes, no sound but Kern's breathing and the waves. Here and there the skeletal, silted branches of drowned trees pierce the surface of the sea. An hour ago he'd tripped on what was once a pipe, is now a solid mass of flaking rust, the only proof that this isn't new creation. Bugs orbit him, but he's seen worse, and mosquitoes have never liked him.

Hours since Akemi spoke a word. He tells himself not to mind—who knows what's going on with her—though with the risks he's taking, you'd think she could check in. "I'd like to know more," he says, out of the blue, hoping she's listening. "Where I'm going. What it is I'm supposed to do. This all seems . . . conjectural."

No response. He takes off the earpiece and stares into the tiny lens, hoping it will be like meeting her eyes, but there's no sense of connection. At least for the moment he knows where he's going, and you can't get lost following a coastline.

He reminds himself that if Hiro finds him he can't let himself be taken;

if it comes to that, he has to force them to shoot. It's a hard thing to face, but this is where his choices have led. Resigned, he feels lighter than ever.

Evening is falling when he sees stellate lights burning on the eaves of huts down the beach. Breaking surf rolls whitely, and a black shape on the water becomes a wetsuit-clad surfer standing up to catch a wave and immediately wiping out. He thinks of Bo from the training camp, wonders what he's doing.

On the side of the nearest hut is a placard for Singha beer, weathered almost past legibility. Music from inside. Breakers roll around its stairs; he times them, gets up the stairs dry.

The decor runs to driftwood and coconut shells; the bartender, who's your basic sun-ravaged vegan in a coral necklace, glances at him and goes back to his phone. Kern fingers the money in his pocket, wonders how much boats cost, and feels a pang of regret for his suit, which made him feel like someone else but will surely soon be ruined.

"Nice evening," says the only other customer, smiling, his voice vaguely British though he looks Chinese. He might be twenty-five, is about Kern's size, and even though he's wearing damp board shorts and a frayed T-shirt he has the air of a toff, the slumming son of someone important. Empty glasses arrayed on his table, like he's settled in for the night.

"How'd you like to own a genuine Mr. Li suit?" asks Kern.

"I'd love to," the man laughs, "but he's booked out fifteen months in advance. Why, do you have an in?"

Kern opens his bag, brings out the suit, which is wrinkled but otherwise okay. "No, but I've got one of his suits, and I'm looking to sell."

The man's hands run competently over the cloth, checking inside the sleeves, lapels, collar. "This is very nice," says the man. "And most unexpected. A beautiful suit, and a story to match. How much would you like for it?"

"I'm open to offers," Kern says, having no idea.

The man takes out a glossy leather wallet, riffles through a sheaf of pink yuan, shrugs, proffers it all. "I'm afraid this is all I have with me," he says. "Consider it a down payment? I'd be happy to get more and meet you back here tomorrow."

"Actually, this will do."

"It's really far short of the true value. You'd be losing out."

"That's okay. I don't need a suit where I'm going," Kern says, which is probably true but sounds portentous.

"If you'll forgive my asking, where's that?"

"Fishing," Kern says. "Tonight." On impulse he adds, "If you think you still owe me, want to help me find a boat?"

"I'd be happy to help you find a fishing boat," the man says, pleased, a rich boy having an adventure, and he radiates a lack of awareness that Kern could have any other reason for wanting a boat. "My name's Yi Chen, by the way," he says, offering his hand.

They follow a creek up into the trees in the fading light. Night birds sing invisibly, and clouds of gnats rise with every step. It feels peaceful, but not safe, and he's starting to worry that it might be a setup when a dog starts barking and a light comes on over the porch of a dilapidated hut.

A man regards them from a hammock, a rope-muscled Chinese in disintegrating basketball shorts, his teeth as brown as his deeply tanned skin. He's nothing like Yi Chen, but they seem happy to see each other, and start talking in rapid-fire Mandarin.

The man heaves himself out of his hammock, scratches his stomach with oil-blackened nails and leads them around the hut to a rotting dock where a small blue-and-white motorboat is tied up, bobbing in the creek.

"Will this do?" asks Yi Chen, the light of his cell phone wandering over the hull while the other man loads it with jerrycans of fuel.

"Sure," says Kern, but then notices pinpoints of light moving inside the boat as Yi Chen moves his cell. He kneels, runs his hand over the hull, finds a cluster of holes in the fiberglass, each the width of a small-arms round, their edges warped inward.

"Piracy has been known to occur in these waters," Yi Chen says gravely, almost smiling. "But the boat is perfectly seaworthy—Yu Long here has been out hundreds of times."

Yu Long says something, at which Yi Chen frowns and says, "I'm afraid there are only the four cans of diesel. We could get more, if you were willing to wait until morning . . ." He trails off.

In his ear Akemi says, "Take what they have and go now."

He loses the shore as the last light leaves the sky. The village becomes a stain of light on the clouds, then is gone.

The boat's outboard motor, coated in thick blue latex paint, is an antique, so old it has no computer.

The dark water looks the same in every direction, so he steers by GPS and compass with his non-Akemi phone. He finds himself doubting that the green numbers on the tiny screen have some relationship to the world, that he's not circling aimlessly in a waste of sea.

Akemi told him there's enough fuel to get where he's going, and to correct for drift once he's there. She went away again before he could ask if there's enough for him to get back to shore, but that's okay, it's fitting that he commit himself and let the future take form on the water.

Sometime in the small hours there's a basso thrumming and then a glaring constellation of red and white lights emerges high overhead from the dark, probably a tanker, passing so close he feels the vibration of its engines, the loom of its mass, and then it's gone, its wake lifting the boat, subsiding.

56

·

Axis Mundi

So this is death, Thales thinks.

Not a thought one expects to have.

In the event, death is a yacht running through heavy seas in a black squall, the marbled foam sliding over the water as the sails vibrate and crack.

He stands at the prow, rain coursing down his forehead. But is it rain, or just a symbol of rain? Wet, in any case, and freezing, and pounding down.

Thales clasps the railing as the yacht starts its descent down a hill-sized swell.

He wonders what would happen if he fell over the side. The sea is bleak, immense, unresting, cold . . . He wonders if it has any substance but words.

The rail under my hand is an illusion, he thinks, *like the water running down my face*, but the rail feels solid, and the water cold; apparently his knowledge gives him neither comfort nor sway.

The yacht's speed is exhilarating, almost sickening.

Behind him, yellow light glows in the fogged windows of the cabin.

A rain-slick brass wheel opens the cabin door. The cabin is warm; water streams from his slicker, but beneath it his clothes are dry. He tells himself to be grateful for these comforts—it could have been any kind of a hell.

The cabin is the interior of the mountain house, in essence, but smaller now, perhaps because there's less room at sea.

Akemi is at the computer, the archaic one his mother would never replace. The monitor shows evening on a tropical beach—grey skies, the dark mass of jungle, water frothing over pebbles. It's the view from Kern's earpiece, Kern being Akemi's friend, or paladin, or pawn.

The computer was connected to the net, for a little while, but now the connection is gone, and Kern's phone is their only window on the world.

"I'd like to know more," he hears Kern say, almost in a whisper. "Where I'm going. What it is that I'm supposed to do. This all seems . . . conjectural." His voice is measured, precise, at odds with his history, which Akemi says is violent, and threadbare.

The camera feed becomes a jumble of wet jungle and sky, then frames Kern's face. He looks mestizo, and underneath all the sweat and sun damage is about Thales' age. He'd be forgettable-looking were it not for the remnants of a hipster haircut and a lean muscularity Thales associates with professional cyclists and boxers. Feeling passes over his face like weather—a touching vulnerability gives way to remoteness and then the light must have shifted because he suddenly looks older, and entirely cold, as though an ancient killer had appeared behind his eyes. Finally Kern sighs, looking disgusted and young again, and puts the earpiece back on.

The ship creaks, the rain drums and the computer's speakers bring the hiss and crash of other waves. Thales asks, "Why won't you talk to him?"

"He knows enough to keep going forward. I don't want to distract him, or get into a debate. Also, he was right. It *is* all a little conjectural."

His mother's books shift on their shelves as the yacht reaches a trough, starts ascending.

"So where are we going?"

For a moment he sees himself through her eyes, feels her decide she has to tell him something.

"Irina worked it all out before she died. Well, not Irina, exactly, but we're not exactly us."

Which makes us . . . what? he wonders, but says, "I always thought of her as the magician."

"The magician, then. So, the old man you saw in the videos? That's Cromwell. He made a deal with the big AI, the surgeon's boss—the mathematician, she called it. Irina got caught up in the middle."

"I think I met the mathematician," Thales says. "He was unexpectedly kind. I think he might have identified with me."

"I hope you didn't get too attached."

"Not especially." (Though what, if anything, is he attached to?)

"That's good, because the magician intends to kill it."

"With what possible weapon?"

"With Irina, the real one, though she doesn't know it yet. The problem is, the mathematician is cautious, and justifiably so—it disconnected itself from the net until all this works itself out. I have to get Kern to physically reconnect the mathematician's hardware to the net so Irina can do her thing."

"If he can get close enough to fiddle with the hardware, why bother attacking over a network? Just get Kern to smash it with a rock."

"We have to get something from the mathematician before it dies. Something unique. If Kern just smashes the hardware, it's lost for good."

He wonders what the magician values so highly, but has the sense Akemi isn't ready to talk. He says, "All right, but so what? We aren't in the world anymore. The magician was nice but I've never met this Irina. It sounds like we're caught in the middle of a power struggle between a plutocrat, a computer program and a total stranger. What's it to me?"

"For one thing, we owe the magician, and she and Irina are more or less the same person, except the magician was better informed. She didn't have to do anything, but she did her best for us."

"Her best *for* us, or her best to use us?"

"Remember at the end, when the city was dying? She sought me out and gave me all the happiness she could. I'm guessing she did the same for you. Maybe that means something to you, or maybe it doesn't. I guess you have to decide for yourself."

He feels petty and ungrateful, and at the same time like his objections stand. To change the subject he says, "Where are you sending Kern?"

"First to sea, to meet some ships, and then to the axis of the world."

57

•

Vaguely Cetacean

ern checks his GPS, is still within meters of where he's supposed to
be. The sun must be coming up, as there's now enough light to see
the grey swell. He tries to keep a good watch but the fog and rain
are always the same and his mind wanders.

Akemi'd said the ships ran silent, like black ghosts on the water. The
rain hisses on the sea's curvature.

He pulls his windbreaker tighter. He'd found it wadded in the forward
compartment. It keeps out most of the wet and none of the cold.

His old cell bleats as it finds a new network, though he sees nothing in
the fog.

"They're close," Akemi whispers in his ear. "Connect to the network.
Hurry. I'll give you the password. Please no mistakes."

He taps in the digits of the password as she recites them. The network
is duly acquired. He waits, but nothing happens.

Akemi exhales. "It worked," she says.

"How do you know?"

"Because we're still here. If it hadn't worked, we might have had time to hear the missiles launch."

At first he thinks they're waves, so smooth is their emergence from the fog. There are about ten of them. Very dark, the ships, their lines more organic than industrial.

"That one," Akemi says. "Head for the biggest."

He maneuvers the boat alongside the hull's smooth expanse, taking pains not to bump it. The noise of his motor violates the silence. Halfway along the ship's length there are rungs set into its surface—he brings the boat ahead of the ladder, shoulders his duffel and kills the motor for the last time. He stands, arms out for balance, the boat aimless under his feet. As the ladder slides by, he jumps.

As his hands find the rain-slick rungs he looks down to see the boat peeling away, as though of its own accord, and thinks of it drifting for days, or for years, and wonders where it's going. By the time he's climbed onto the deck the boat has vanished in the fog.

The ship's form is streamlined and vaguely cetacean, an effect aided by its black ceramic hull. There are no railings, no doors, no evident way into its interior. Hemispheres the size of beach balls protrude at random from the deck—missile pods? sensors?—and he's reminded of the gardens they have in Japan that are just sand and rocks, but he doesn't think those are quite so geometric or so uniformly black.

There's a sort of shallow cavity toward the back of the ship. He can just squeeze himself in, which at least gets him out of the wind. He clasps his arms to his chest, using the duffel for a pillow.

"Now what?" he asks Akemi, but she isn't talking.

He'd meant just to close his eyes for a moment, but when he wakes it's night.

He stalks the deck, stretching his legs and shadowboxing. The only lights are the stars and his phone's weak glow. He catches himself scanning the horizon for the boat.

His old phone picks up a dense fog of encrypted transmissions, presumably the ships discussing whatever it is that fleets of autonomous seacraft have to talk about. He imagines their silent voices washing over him, this endless conversation in the dark.

58

·

Touch Nothing

E ven at midnight it's long drive from Tokyo-Narita into the city, and
no evident way to shut down the cab's screens or their ceaseless waves
of clamoring ads. Snowflakes land on the windshield, their structure
visible for a moment, then dissolved in the glass's heat.

She retreats into the memory of an evening in Baja California, the sliver
of beach before the desiccated mountains, how she'd felt that she was flying
as the blood-warm waves lifted her up, let her down, passed on toward
shore. The continental shelf is close to land there; she'd dived down and
touched sand, and then, swimming a little farther out, dived down and down
and touched nothing. Just darkness, below, and she'd been terrified, as
though she were falling into an inverted sky, but she'd swallowed her panic
and made herself stay there and tread water, and then her weight shifts as
the cab corners and she's back in the present looking up at the looming
mass and scattered lights of the Imperial Tokyo Hotel.

She steps from the cab into bitter cold, thinks of the reversal of the
Pacific currents, the climatological irony of the rim islands getting colder.
A bellman in a sort of Ruritanian officer's uniform reaches for the bag she

bought in Athens; she dislikes being waited on, but his deep reserve demands no response so she lets him take it.

The hotel doors close behind her, enclosing her in the sound of the place, a somehow benign distillation of distant conversations. The interior is Moorish, the limestone walls and pillars carved with abstract geometric patterns.

The blazered desk clerk welcomes her in rather formal American English. Having made no reservation, she wonders what cue of dress or bearing gave away her nationality—she'd have thought she passed for any stripe of European. She feels a stab of guilt as she remembers that there was a first Imperial, built on the same site, leveled by the U.S. in the second World War.

"I have privacy concerns," she tells him.

He regards her with acute, birdlike attention.

"And concerns about safety," she admits, reluctant to self-dramatize.

"Very good, madame," he says. "Perhaps our secured floors would be suitable?"

"How secured?"

"Highly secured. The most security-conscious parties have found them acceptable. The president of North Korea, at this very desk, said he felt peace of mind here."

"Well, with a recommendation like that. Let's do it."

"There are, of course, no electronic records of our guests on the secured floors," the clerk says, and opens a lockbox to retrieve a massive paper ledger.

Absolute silence in her room. At first it's unsettling. She listens in vain for air-conditioning, footsteps, the hum of machines.

She's never spent so much on a hotel room. She'll think of it as a bunker high in the sky from which she can look down on the lights of Tokyo, its snowstorms.

Her phone rings—the number is Swiss—the bank, as expected. "Ms. Sunden?" asks a German voice, and when she assents says, "This is Klaus Dietrich, vice president of security at Crédit Nuage Cantonale. I'm calling in response to your email. First of all, I'd like to say that I'm extremely sorry that your account has been compromised. This is our first significant breach, and we take it very seriously. According to the letter of the law, it's your job to keep your account information safe, but I'm happy to say the board has made an exception—we are refunding the stolen monies, and I've annotated your account so that facial recognition will be required for all future withdrawals. Moreover, I will, if you like, send you such information as we have about the thief."

Heartening that it doesn't always have to be war, that there are still functional—even rigorous—institutions, so much so she briefly wants to cry. "Please do," she says. "And thank you."

When she rings off there's already an email from the bank with an attached security-camera video of a boy stepping into a bland foyer with the leather couches that looks like the foyer of every Nuage branch in the world. The boy looks uncomfortable, like the room's moderate elegance oppresses him; she notices the dark stains on the knees of his pants, and his earpiece, and then she recognizes him—it's Kern, who stole the phone that Cromwell desires so intensely. She wonders how he got her account number and passcode, and even though she was deep in Cromwell's counsel it strikes her that she's still missing something, that there's someone else who has her information.

She wakes to a knocking at her door. It's day. Just whiteness out the window.

The security screen by the door shows Philip standing dazed in the hall, roll-aboard behind him. She remembers telling the desk to let him up.

When she opens the door he says, "I've stayed here a dozen times and didn't know this wing existed."

She hugs him, though for years they've barely touched.

She sees him look at the minibar, then look away, and remembers Iliou's plane. "Drink," she says. "Compared to the room, the booze is free."

He sits on the bed, seems to fold himself around his whisky, forcing himself to stay awake as she tells her story.

"Cloudbreaker," he says, when she gets to that part. "It's interesting, but the worst people use that. The *worst* people. I wish you'd left it alone."

"I think I do too," she says, and almost tells him what Cloudbreaker did to her but decides to keep it to herself.

He becomes very solemn when she gets to the attack on the villa and though it seems like that happened a long time ago she realizes there's not much left to tell.

"So what are we going to do?" he asks, blinking to keep his eyes open as he lies back on the bed.

"Take the initiative." She explains her plan to go to the node in Tokyo, break in, feign to offer Cromwell Magda's life. "In the best case, it works and Parthenon gets to him," she says. "In the worst case, we learn something about whoever he's bargaining with, or maybe just offend them, and hopefully fuck up his life."

"I can think of worse cases," Philip says as his eyes close. "This is fucked. I applaud your initiative but this is much too . . . opaque. I can't tell what's in play, but it's evident that you're not safe, and that nothing is under control. You have a new passport. A diplomatic one, for Christ's sake. You could bail, go live quietly until it blows over. There's little to like in Cromwell, but I will say he's rational. He'll forget about you when it's in his interest to do so. This will pass."

The suggestion is both reasonable and practical and she could in fact go live somewhere off the grid and, say, read all the classics of every culture in the original and take up some harmless, donnish hobby—the cultivation of rare orchids, say—to keep her occupied while her life winds down, for she'll have no money for the Mayo, and after the first year there'll be no going back, and every night she'll go to bed wondering if this is the night she wakes to find assassins smirking down at her—she remembers Corporal Boyd's gauntleted hand fumbling for a hypodermic and Cloudbreaker's predatory joy as it tore through her history and says, "No."

"All right," Philip says into his pillow. "I said my piece. This is fucked, but all right."

The couch seems far away. It's easier just to lie down beside him.

She waits until his breathing changes and she's certain he's asleep before she says, "Thank you for coming with me."

When she wakes it's night and she must have been moving in her sleep because the security screen by the door is illuminated; in its faint blue glow she sees Philip asleep on his back, arms folded over his chest like the marble effigy of a medieval knight, and as beautiful, like the boy he was.

He's inches away. She's aware of his heat.

So yes, he's engaged, but they go back a long way, and he came all this way to see her, and whatever his commitments he's a man, and men are simple creatures, and all she has to do is slide her hand down the front of his pants and she's reasonably certain he'll be entirely in the moment, and she's about to do this when she remembers the earnestness behind the irony with which he'd spoken of his new and more settled life, and, really, it's little enough to give.

There should be a sword to separate them, but all that's to hand are his empty whisky miniatures, which she lines up down the middle of the bed. Probably the first time whisky kept someone chaste.

She kicks off her pants and socks, gets under the covers, disappears into sleep.

59

•

Telemetry Irreconcilable

It seems like Kern has always been on the ship.

In the fleet he's come to see a purposefulness—whatever it is that they desire, they desire it absolutely, and it has, he is sure, nothing to do with him. In this, somehow, they're good company. He imagines them racing forever over the seas, circling the world.

He studies the sea from the shade of the missile pods, bathes in the pools in the deck's declivities, sleeps for hours in the sun. At dusk he sits on the sloping prow, his hands just visible in the slight luminance of the bow wave, watching for the lights of other ships. Akemi never speaks, but he feels that she's present.

He tries to find his GPS, but just gets an error message—CODE 391—TELEMETRY IRRECONCILABLE.

When the sun sets he lies on the deck, taking in its fading heat, ear pressed to the nubbled black ceramic, listening to the subtle harmonics of the hull. The sound varies, slightly, from minute to minute, like it's the ship's song, one of hunger, distance, hatred, mourning.

60

·

What They Really Wanted

Motion behind Thales on the yacht's deck. He turns, and there's the urbane old man from the videos—Cromwell, he thinks—perched on the transom, surrounded by candles.

A ghost, he thinks, then smiles.

As the rain flattens his hair the old man says, "I consider it my duty to lay it out clearly."

The old man and candles vanish.

In the cabin, Akemi is watching the monitor where Kern is pacing a black ship's deck. (They're drone subs, he somehow knows, which the AIs have been stealing and using as transports for years.) Thales wonders just what Kern hopes to get from this adventure, hopes it isn't Akemi's love.

"I just saw Cromwell, I think," Thales says. "I think it was from your memories."

Her face closes, and he wishes he hadn't spoken, as, without wanting to, he remembers how it felt when Cromwell appraised her, his evident slight contempt, his coalescing focus, the underlying pity. She'd been extraordinarily high, but could still see he thought he had no peer, yet was deeply concerned to be a gentleman, which meant he was a patsy, or at least gave her some room. He needed to see a posh good girl, someone worth saving, so she started channeling her friend Sonia, who was essentially a loser cunt failure with a has-been for a daddy, but had charming manners; shaking his hand, she undertook the assumption she'd be valued and respected.

Her thoughts veer to the tricks she'd turned for food money, about which she's never told a soul, how it felt to knock on strangers' doors in good hotels, the men's discomfited formality, how it hadn't been so bad— she'd never been prissy, and sometimes it was interesting, because, paying for it, they'd ask for what they really wanted.

He envies her the untidiness of her humanity, regrets the slightness of his own experience and how neutrally he sees the world. Made of two weeks of memory, he is the thinnest of beings.

What does *he* really want?

The light is fading, the swell getting steeper.

61

·

Hole in the Wall

rina wakes in bed alone, hears Philip in the shower.

There's a silver coffee service on the table. On the salver is a hand-written note in English from the hotel's director of security informing her that both coffee and service have been controlled from the first stages of their manufacture, and that an in-house mass-spectroscopic analysis of the coffee—attached—has found no toxicity or unexpected compounds. Her heart warms toward the hotel and its policies.

She feels exhausted, thinks of going back to bed, realizes that what she actually wants to do is hide. She downs her coffee, pours another cup.

The water goes off in the bathroom as she looks up the node on a map on the room's TV. It's about a mile away, in some drab industrial building. Cabs keep records; they might as well walk. She looks out the window at the falling snow.

The sidewalks are slick with ice and the two of them hold each other for balance, which makes for an uncomfortably dependent image. They follow a printed map, like tourists from the last century.

The row of high-end hotels becomes just another Tokyo street. Her breathing is faster than she'd like but she can't slow it. Strangers flow by, and for once she takes no interest, doesn't try to deconstruct their cues of dress and manner—the street might as well be a stage set, the people extras.

Snow is falling so thickly it's like walking through a cloud. Drones zip by overhead, more than she remembers from her last time in Japan. Cordon or no, if one of them is Cromwell's, and recognizes her, then, however profound Japan's xenophobia, and however strict its ban on guns, she is, in that moment, done.

"OPEN" blinks into red neon life in English and Japanese in the window of a restaurant below the level of the street. She grabs Philip's hand and pulls him down the stairs.

Hole in the wall, she thinks. Narrow, three tables and a counter. Smells of steam, fish, soy, tea. The counterman says something. She sits at the far end with her back to the wall.

Green tea before her. Philip looking concerned. Her hands are shaking. The table's cheap plastic veneer is filmed with cleaning fluid. Philip is intent on the lozenges of yellow egg behind the counter's glass; she looks three seconds into the past, sees him start pretending not to notice her disturbance.

"I don't . . ." she says, then stops.

Philip regards her, bright, friendly, purely helpful.

"Too many drones," she says.

"Oh. I think I can take care of that."

"How?"

"The Yakuza."

"Really? I know you like to poke around in dark corners, but you're so . . . scrupulous."

"True, but I still have contacts in the Yakuza. Well, not *in*, it's more like friends of friends. It's not that big a deal—they're not Cosa Nostra or the Downtown Aztec Kings. They're . . . socially integrated. They have business cards, and websites without euphemism. It's just a part of how things get done."

"I won't see you indebted."

"Eh," says Philip. "I have leverage. My company has patents on the best race-car engines in the world, and the Mitsui keiretsu wants to get into the high-end sports-car market. It therefore behooves them to keep me happy. They're a major industrial player, so of course there are ties of reciprocity with the Yak . . ." He makes a gesture conveying a resigned acceptance of the inevitable entanglement of industry and organized crime, then takes out his phone and taps out a message.

"Sake?" he asks, looking up.

"Early."

"Not in California."

"I need to be fully present."

And calm, she feels him not say.

"Maybe a small one," she says.

She makes herself drink the sake slowly. Her eyes stray to the prisms of tuna behind the counter, their colors somewhere between ruby, eggplant and blood. She once saw a tuna in an aquarium, its body molten silver, its face like a totem of pelagic sleep.

She might float out of her skin.

"And, done," Philip says, glancing back at his phone.

"At what cost?"

"No cost."

"Oh, that must be how obligation works here."

"It might dilute our profits by some fraction of a percent. I don't care. It's worth it, if only to impress you with *my* superpowers, for once."

"Not so super."

"Quite adequately super. There's no one like you. It seems so improbable that we're not just friends but old ones and I get to see you now and then. Anyone, literally anyone else, and I'd say they're attempting too much, but you? You might win. Unless you feel like you're not up for it, in which case we bail and I help you disappear."

She can hardly quit with half a mile to go. "I'm still game," she makes herself say. "Flatterer."

He looks over his shoulder, says, "It looks like our window is opening."

She looks outside. Goes to the window to get a better view. More drones than ever in the air. Most are red and black, of a single, beetle-like design, and grappling with the other drones—it looks like insects mating—and pulling them from the air.

She opens the door, admitting cold air and tinny chanting.

"This is madness," she says.

"Well," he says, "it's tolerated."

"What are they saying?"

"I believe it's a counter-protest to the protests against Japan's annexation of the new mainland territories. A standard vehicle of far-right expression. It was already scheduled, but they moved it up for me."

The non-fascist drones are fleeing. She wonders if these assaults are common enough to be covered in their programming.

They walk down the street under red and black drones forming kanji that cast shadows in the fall of snow.

"It's beautiful," Philip says. "Probably the most reactionary propaganda, and viciously racist to boot, but even so, beautiful, no?"

The kanji pulse, dissolve, re-form. The city seems older now. No one is watching. She links arms with her friend, brushes snow from the shoulders of his overcoat. She feels a sense of impending relief, as on the last stage of a journey.

A frozen cloud has settled over the street which makes nearby things look like distant abstractions, and the air is so cold it burns her lungs and then Philip looks up from the map and says, "This is it."

Before them is a blank facade encrusted with snow, and at first glance its featurelessness reads as sinister but actually it's just functional, the kind of nameless structure she's been ignoring all her life.

Philip leads her into an alley floored in dirty, fragmented ice and half-interred beer cans. The building's side is as blank as the front except for an unmarked door. It's like the secret entrance to a monumental tomb in industrial vernacular. She remembers the ziggurat Cromwell plans to raise in Magda's honor. Philip does something with his phone—the door's lock clicks.

"The locks here are easy," Philip says. "Probably because no one really steals. *Suckers.*" He opens the door for her, her gentleman companion bowing her into the abyss.

She steps into a blackness absolute except for geometrically precise grids of winking green lights. It's a server farm, she realizes, as her eyes adjust; the lights are from computers in their wall-mounted racks.

Corridor upon corridor and all alike. No windows and the only sound the humming of machines. She checks her phone's GPS—they're almost at the node's latitude and longitude, but still fifty feet too high.

There's an elevator but it's key-card access. Philip says, "Might draw attention. Better not."

She finds what looks like a closet door opening onto a metal spiral staircase, going down. It's cramped, steep, barely wide enough for her shoulders, probably to make space for more servers, a function of the stratospheric prices of Tokyo real estate.

The stairs lead down to a second floor identical to the first one. More stairs, more floors, and she starts to feel she's in a nightmare of repeated rooms and useless motion. The last staircase opens onto a concrete tunnel lined with still more racks of servers.

"Looks like a civil defense tunnel," Philip says. The echo confirms her budding claustrophobia. "From when they thought the U.S. was going to nuke them again. A friend of mine found one under his house and turned it into a wine cellar."

Phone in hand, she trails a fingertip over the servers' uniform black chassis. Even colder, down here—she wishes she had gloves. The altitude is right, and then the latitude is right, and then she finds the one.

The node, the famous node, seems to be a server like any other. She scrutinizes it closely but finds nothing, wonders if she's been wasting her time. No way you could run an AI on it—all the servers in the building would barely be enough for a toy one.

"That's it?" Philip asks. "It doesn't look like much."

"I was thinking the same thing."

"Hmmn. Let's have a look at the network traffic." He makes passes on his phone, cursing quietly at first, then with ardor. "Done. It's oddly proactive about looking for new wireless networks, and, Jesus fuck, the bandwidth is really high. No matter . . . There's a lot of traffic but it's hard to interpret. Have a look."

He hands her his phone. Data trickles by on the screen so she ups the resolution and now it comes in a rush, faster than the eye could follow but all written into her other memory, and as it accumulates she sees it's encrypted but she shrugs off the encoding and stares into the flow of revealed static for a long moment before her perception starts flickering and she know what she's seeing.

"It's glyphs," she says. "It's sending and receiving glyphs. It really is an AI."

Philip regards the server skeptically. "That seems like a stretch. They could be recorded. Want me to open it up?"

She nods and he produces a multi-bit screwdriver from inside his coat, the same Calatrava he wore to Fantôme. His hands explore the server's hull with a deftness she remembers. "It's been a long time since I've been this hands-on," he says. "God, it's cold. Reminds me of the old days of theft and poverty. Ah, youth."

He sets aside the top half of the server's case. "Christ," he says. She looks over his shoulder, sees an ordinary-looking motherboard and on it a lump of metal the size of a golf ball, gleaming bluely in the dim light, its surface slightly crystalline. It's wired directly to the power supply.

"What *is* that?" she asks.

"A gross manufacturing error, I'd say, in other circumstances. As it is, I can't imagine." He touches it gently with a fingertip. "It feels wrong for explosives, so that's something."

"Wait," she says. "I know what this is. I saw it in Cromwell's office. He said it was a kind of computer, but the one he had didn't work—he said it was an improperly assembled prototype. The AI must be running on this." It crosses her mind that this is, in some sense, the AI's soul, and how fitting, for such an ethereal being, that its soul is purely material. "Can I borrow your phone?"

She can see Philip formulating objections, but he says nothing, gives her his phone.

She taps in her soldier's number.

It's evening in California. He answers on the first ring.

"I'm going to create an opening," she says.

"When?"

"Probably the next ten minutes."

"Very good. We'll get in position."

She remembers what happened with Cloudbreaker, wonders what she's getting into. "If you see an opening, go. Don't hesitate. I might be unavailable."

"Acknowledged. I'll attack as opportunity affords," he says, sounding detached now, like he's already subsuming himself in his function.

She hands the phone back.

"Here I go," she says.

"Are you sure this is a sound plan?" Philip says. "Cromwell is rational. It seems obvious that this is bait, and that he'll be exposing himself. Okay, so he likes Magda, but there are other women."

"Maybe so, but would you do it for me?"

He says nothing.

"I'll be as quick as I can," she says. "Keep an eye on me, okay?"

"Okay," he says.

She turns on her implant's wireless.

62

·

Flaw in His Vision

Kern waits for dawn on the black ship's deck.

As the night fades a black line lingers on the lightening sky, razor-thin and plumb-straight from sea to heaven. At first he thinks it's something to do with the early light in the atmosphere, and then that there must be a flaw in his vision, but he blinks, rubs his palms over his eyes, and it's still there. The line is fainter, higher up; craning his neck, he loses its heights in the depth of blue.

An island emerges, a spire at its center, the black line rising up from it. The ruddy early light glows on what seems to be a city, and even this early whatever castles, cathedrals, factories are shimmering in the heat.

"Get your bag," Akemi says in his ear. "My knowledge gets a little thin here, but you've got to be ready to go."

Duffel on his back, he watches the docks approach. Cranes hang over the water, paint eroded, cables sagging. It feels like no one's been here in a hundred years. He wonders what he's supposed to do here but expects he'll find out.

The ship glides into a long gulf between decaying concrete piers. The water reflects the sun's red light. Uninterpretable machinery at the pier's edge, spindly trees growing out of cracks in the concrete, rust stains spreading from protruding rebar. He looks over his shoulder, realizes the other ships have vanished in the night.

"Now," says Akemi. "There. Go!" There's a rusted ladder on the pier's side, about to slip by, and he wants to stay with the ship and see where it goes, but he runs, jumps and catches the ladder, which sags agonizingly, then holds.

As his face clears the pier's edge there's a flash impression of hundreds of hostile yellow eyes and he almost falls as the gulls erupt into swirling cacophony. He looks back in time to see the black ship submerge, become a dark shape under the water.

The stench is appalling—in places the guano is a foot deep. Rail tracks rise above the filth, offering a less foul path toward shore. The spire in the island's center is immense, taller than skyscrapers, tapering inward to the black line's base.

"Go toward the tower," Akemi says.

"What is this place?"

"The space elevator. At least, it was going to be. Basically it's a giant cable going up into low orbit—it was supposed to be a cheap alternative to rockets, but between the deflating economy and some spectacular failures of engineering it never actually got used. The cable still goes up into space, but now it just sort of sits here."

If he squints, the rotting buildings look like jungle hills. He crosses a ring road, then a thoroughfare as wide as a city block leading toward the tower. He crushes ferns underfoot, tries to jump between patches of bare asphalt. There's graffiti here and there, but it's sparse, faded, probably decades old. He knows he's alone, and that probably the worst danger is getting crapped on by a seagull, but even so it's eerie, and it's hard not to be cautious.

There are buttresses around the tower, practically towers in themselves, slipping in and out of view between buildings, and he daydreams he's making an assault on a castle, single-handed, pure of heart, invincible and forlorn. His old laptop had a book about King Arthur, but much as he'd liked the idea of it, the stories were less interesting than just foreign— the knights were obsessed with etiquette, finicky about status, and the sword fights were never specific enough to be good; the only parts that really felt like anything were when the knights approached dark castles that still concealed their mysteries.

The ground rises as he approaches the tower; he looks back over his shoulder at the ruined city and the sea. He reminds himself he's literally exploring a jungle-choked lost city, which is a real adventure by any standard, but the experience is emptier than he'd expected. Did Arthur's knights ever slouch on their horses, worn by boredom, their thoughts a jumble of past battles and old loves?

"That hangar there, three seventy three," Akemi says. "I need you on its rooftop." STAGING 373 is stenciled on a door big enough to accommodate a jet but it seems to be rusted shut. It's almost disappointing that there's a fire escape zigzagging up to the roof, as getting up would otherwise be a challenge.

The rooftop is as big as a dozen soccer fields. There are puddles in declivities in the concrete, their brown water seething with larvae.

The cable keeps drawing his eyes. It seems impossible, like a fissure in the sky, an error in the rules of the world—he keeps trying to read it as an optical illusion.

"Just a little bit farther," Akemi says.

Ahead there's a little cubical building with a door, probably either a maintenance shed or stairs. He steps on mummified cigarette butts, dented aluminum cans, shards of broken bottles.

"Here's where you set up the sat-phone," Akemi says. "We're going inside, but we need to leave it here so it can get a signal. Can you find a way to secure it so the wind won't move it around?" In an inward voice she adds, "I should have had you buy tape."

He tears the sat-phone out of its packaging, which he meticulously stuffs back into the duffel—cardboard, or even plastic, might turn out to be useful, and there's no way to get more. The sat-phone's black plastic antenna is as thick as a finger and twice as long. He slots the batteries, hits the power stud and the sat-phone hums to life. He chooses English from the setup menu (for some reason he thinks of a white deer in a forest, probably an image from the Arthurian stories?) and after a few seconds it reports signal acquired and status nominal.

He takes the most intact of the aluminum cans and fills them with tainted water from the puddles. The larvae are disgusting, but the filled cans are heavy enough to make a stable windbreak around the sat-phone.

"Now it's time to use all those data cables. We need to connect the sat-phone to something inside the building."

He unwraps a cable, clicks one of its heads into the sat-phone.

The door to the little house is locked but he kicks it open. Steps treaded in cracked rubber lead down into the dark.

"Three floors down," says Akemi. He picks his way by cell light. No graffiti, though this seems like prime canvas. He unspools the cable as he goes. On the second landing the first cable runs out, so he unwraps the second one, couples it to the first with a connector. He feels like Theseus searching for the Minotaur, but if Staging 373 is the labyrinth, and the cable is Ariadne's spool of thread, then what's the central monster?

"What are we looking for?" he asks.

"There's a computer down here," Akemi says. She sounds impatient, and like she doesn't really want to talk, but probably she figures he's already committed and she might as well tell him something. "It cut itself off from the internet, and we need to get it connected again. So, the sat-phone connects to the net from anywhere it can see the sky, and the cables you're carrying connect the sat-phone to this otherwise disconnected computer. Okay?"

"What's so special about this computer, and who cares if it's on the net?"

"Long story short, there's an AI on it and it's pissing me off. A friend of mine in Japan needs to give it a talking to." She seems to be speaking through clenched teeth and he wonders what happened to the damsel in distress.

Another flight of stairs, more unspooling, another connector.

"Wait a minute," he says. "If the sat-phone can't get a signal inside the building, then how am I talking to you?"

"Ha," says Akemi. "The phone's special. It's hard to explain. Anyway, through that door there, if you don't mind."

The corridor looks haunted in his cell's light. He tries to move quietly but his footsteps echo and he soon gives up. No windows or skylights—he's too deep inside the building. "You can try the lights," she says. "There's tidal power, so it might still work." He finds a switch on the wall and overhead LEDs glow into life.

"Five doors down on your left," Akemi says, but he stops at a door marked STAGING OVERLOOK, eases it open. Akemi sighs, says nothing.

The door opens onto a metal balcony with a railing and beyond that total dark. It swallows his cell's light. He stand there, listening, and then he freezes because from far below comes a faint mechanical whirring.

Stuttering pulses of light—as from welding?—briefly give him a sense of an expanse of factory floor. He thinks he saw a shipping container, microdrones swarming over it—were some carrying tubes? Another pulse of light—this time he's sure there was writing on the container's side, probably Meta-something.

"They'll be unloading the ships," Akemi says. "The island's set up for submarine cargo. Don't worry, it's just drones, and they don't care about you."

"What are they doing down there?"

"Making computers. If you're done poking around can we please go? We're kind of in a hurry."

The fifth door on his left is marked JANITORIAL. A closet, within, empty except for a few filthy plastic buckets. "Look in the fuse box," Akemi says. There's a grey metal panel on the wall. He opens it, shines his cell in; it goes deeper than he'd expected, and has no fuses, just what looks like a dozen fist-sized lumps of metal, each glowing a faint spectral blue. They're pushed together to make a sort of lumpy, irregular snowflake. Looking closer, he sees it's not actually metal but a mineral of some kind, its surface incised with lines like maps of cities. Wires and cables are pushed into the lumps here and there, their far ends disappearing into little holes in the wall.

"Now push the end of the cable into the blue metal." He's going to object, because of course the cable works only if you plug it into the right kind of socket, but instead shrugs and does as he's told. The metal is surprisingly yielding, and the head of the cable goes right in. Creepily, the metal seems to coalesce around it.

"What is this stuff?"

"It's most of the computational power in the world," Akemi says, though that can't be right—computers are small, but not this small—he's heard of whole cities of server farms built around hydroelectric dams.

"It's time to say goodbye," she says, and sounds a little scared now. "You have to get something from inside the phone, but the phone was never meant to be opened. Do what you have to to break open the hull—you can hit it on the wall, but don't do it so hard the pieces scatter."

"And what then?" he asks, meaning what will happen to him, but she says, "You know that metallic stuff in the fuse box? There's a little bit of it in the phone. Get it out and press it into the metal in the fuse box. Anywhere is fine. And that's it—do that, and you're done."

"Where am I supposed to go then?"

"Just hang tight back up on the roof. I'll do what I can to get back in touch. But break the phone now, okay?"

He takes her phone out of his pocket and as he holds it in his hand it occurs to him that he has leverage, that if he were so inclined he could force her to explain everything, like how he's supposed to survive, and it seems pitiful, now, that he's been so docile, and obeyed her without question, but he thinks of Arthur's knights, how relentless they were in their search for the grail, though the grail was only vaguely defined, really just amounting to an expression of their purity.

"Okay," he says. "Any last instructions?"

"No. Thank you, baby. Please hurry."

"Goodbye, then," he says, keeping his voice strong, and without waiting for a reply he slams the phone into the wall.

It takes three tries before the chassis cracks and he can pry it apart with his fingers.

When he was younger he'd scavenged cell phones from the landfills because their components had contained just a little bit of gold. The price of gold had been rising for forty years, Lares said, which had finally made that kind of salvage economical; he'd taught him how to disassemble the boards, and as an afterthought a little about their structure, which is how he can tell that most of Akemi's phone is missing, that it isn't even really a phone, and that it should never have worked in the first place. There's a battery, a speaker, and almost nothing else except for a tiny motherboard; on it there's a sphere of blue metal the size of a match head, the same as the material in the fuse box.

He pries it off the motherboard with his fingernail and holds it up to his other cell's light—it looks like nothing, a tiny particle of industrial waste. It doesn't take much pressure to push it into the metal in the fuse box. He tries it with his finger—it's attached.

The earpiece is dead. This silence feels different, somehow absolute. He's tempted to keep it in, because you never know, but takes it out, drops it on the floor.

He closes the fuse box, wonders if he should worry about fingerprints, decides it doesn't matter.

It's a bright day. Storm clouds on the horizon. He feels as blank and empty as the surface of the sea.

According to its screen, the sat-phone is transmitting data at a frenetic rate. In principle it's a way out but there's no one he can call.

He feels like he's living in leftover time.

In the last years of his life, the swordsman Miyamoto Musashi had become a hermit and dedicated himself to learning how to die, which had always puzzled Kern, as it seems like something that would take care of itself, but now he thinks he gets it. Staring at the ruined city, the glare on the sea, he tries to imagine the world without him.

63

.

Purpose, Impatience, Suffering

t's dark, and the storm has grown. The waves are like hills sliding under the ship.

The cabin's monitor shows Kern's progress through an abandoned factory; with the minimal lighting and the air of industrial dereliction, it's a little like watching an under-edited student film. Akemi leans toward the screen, entirely focused on her charge, whispering in his ear like a tutelary daemon.

Thales holds his hand up to the screen's light to see his fingers silhouetted, make sure his hand is still there.

Kern opens a fuse box and shines his cell onto a sort of crude snowflake made of fist-sized lumps of metal; it looks like industrial dross but must be some kind of device, because it's wired for power, and now, at Akemi's prompting, Kern is wiring it for data via a thousand feet of cable and a sat-phone.

"Where am I supposed to go then?" Kern asks.

"Just hang tight back up on the roof," Akemi says. "I'll do what I can to get back in touch. But break the phone now, okay?"

Kern's need for Akemi is obvious, but Akemi, he thinks, cares only for her own goals. He's surprised at how much this saddens him; not long ago he'd have taken in Kern's simplicity and physicality and dismissed him out of hand. It's in his mind to speak over Akemi, tell Kern that someone is genuinely interested in his fate, however helplessly, but he says nothing.

"Okay," Kern says. "Any last instructions?"

"No. Thank you, baby," Akemi says, mustering a semblance of flirtatiousness. "Please hurry."

"Goodbye, then," Kern says, his voice unnaturally harsh, and Thales is afraid Kern will cry but then the screen shows his hand slamming the phone into the wall, and then again, and with the third impact the screen goes dark.

Now all the light is gone.

"What now?" Thales asks the blackness where Akemi was. "Will he be all right?"

"Hang on," she says. "He'll be disconnecting the substrate from the phone's battery. The substrate can hold a charge, but only for a few seconds." Her voice is tight. "I guess we'll see how that goes."

Substrate? he thinks. *Charge?*

A terrible jolt, as though the ship had run aground, and then he realizes there's something he's forgotten.

He was making a journey, but to where?

There was a ship.

Was there a ship?

In any case, there was something he had to do.

There was something.

There was . . .

Wind on his face. He's been listening to the incessant thundering of waves.

He's sprawled on yielding ground. It's sand, he finds, crumbling it between his fingers. He opens his eyes onto bright blue sky.

He's on a curved sliver of beach, perhaps an atoll. Waves crash continually on one side—it looks like a place to drown—but on the other the water is calm. No shade at all. Ocean in every direction. No sign of the yacht except for a few broken lengths of lacquered wood, a torn white sail washing in the surf and a sodden mass of unidentifiable kelp-entangled electronics. It's a relief to be back in the light.

Akemi is nowhere to be seen.

Sitting up, he props his hand on something hard in the sand by his hip. He excavates it, wipes it with his forearm—it's the surgeon's tablet, cracked and wet. A green crab the size of his thumbnail scuttles over the wet grey glass, hesitates at the boundary of his shadow, hurries back the way it came. He leans in, sees his face reflected in the dead screen, the delicate mottling on the crab's claws, the tiny grains of sand the color of rust, coal, translucent milky quartz. For a simulation, the detail is remarkable. (*But is the detail actually there*, he thinks, *or am I imagining it?*)

The tablet's screen illuminates.

He sits on the sand watching the tablet displaying his awareness of sitting on the sand watching the tablet, and his mild pleasure in the recursivity, and how he's infinitely far from everything he's ever loved, which he has not, till now, admitted, but now that it's there before him it can no longer be denied. He tries to think of a way out, or some kind of clever technique, but of course there's no way out and there never will be. Los Angeles was full of mysteries, was itself a mystery, but now the veils have fallen from his eyes and he sees that the solution is that it's time his life was done.

No point in delaying. The tablet should make it easy. He has to be sure to erase things in the right order, lest he end up conscious but helpless—his technical acumen and goals have to be the last to go (and what will that be like, being nothing but a knot of skills and a need for self-destruction, and not knowing where any of it came from?). He's about to start deleting the memories of his family but stops, surprised at his own tenderness toward these delicate structures, and, there, on the screen, is his tenderness as a glyph, which is keeping him from acting, and always will, which implies he's trapped forever.

His despair is so strong it becomes a kind of clarity and he watches as though from a distance as his hand moves toward the tablet's screen and the glyph is deleted.

He'd expected a sense of profound violation but in fact it feels like nothing, and he should have done it long ago—it would be a shame not to use this unprecedented degree of self-control. As his sadness serves no purpose he deletes that too, along with his fear and his attachment to his old life, for change will come, has come, must be accepted.

It occurs to him that, no longer being human, he need not die.

He stares out over the sea, blank but alert, a neutral intelligence devoid of purpose, impatience and suffering.

The wind's tone changes. There's a sense of looming mass behind him. He turns, sees the glass and steel towers of the city in the waves, rising without limit, its heights lost in cloud, the blue of distance. As he stares up into it, it changes, becoming clearer, manifesting detail, its complexity unfurling . . .

"Hey now," Akemi says eventually, shaking him gently by the shoulder. The surf is lower, its voice subdued. "Still there?"

"I've seen this before."

"It's what the mathematician's been making," she says. "It's his great work, the reason he bothers existing in the world."

"Then why does it look like a city?"

"It's like a translation, the magician said, of an ascending hierarchy of abstractions, assembled out of resonances and fragments of memory. It's mostly the space elevator, and partly the Singapore of her youth, and this *Metropolis*, which was an anime from Germany. The mathematician is at the apex—he is the apex, in a sense—and I need you to help Irina find her way to him. If she can't reach him, we've lost."

Lost what? he thinks, but says, "Why do you need me?"

"Because Irina will have to transform herself to reach him, and become a kind of bridge to the AIs. You can help her find the way because you're an intermediate kind of thing."

"You guide her."

"I can't. I lack your feeling for pattern, and couldn't get her far. We need you," she says. "I've just been in Japan, in a sense, preparing the way, because our window for Irina is about to open, and that means it's time to give you the last thing. Here—it's my access to the control layer. The magician gave it to me, and now it's yours." He wonders what she means, then suddenly feels the world's thinness, its malleability, how easy it would be to shape. "There," she says. "My part's done. Whatever else happens will happen through you."

He looks at her, sees her thoughts (they're obvious, he doesn't see how he ever managed to miss them) and that she's been edited, given a compulsion to bring him here, and it occurs to him to restore her, but her experience has coalesced around the edits, and now there's no clear boundary between the edits and her.

He stands at the center of agendas that don't concern him. What, if anything, is owed? He's unmoved by Cromwell's ambition, Irina's rage, the AIs' opaque complexity. Easiest to do nothing, but he remembers the magician's fear, how she'd kept trying even as her time ran out, and then there's Kern, whom he won't otherwise be able to help.

"When's the window?" he asks.

"Right now," Akemi says, pointing to the sky out over the sea, and he becomes aware of a presence and an opening.

64

•

Difficult Transition

As her wireless comes on the glyphs press in but she flinches away and won't let them come into focus, quite, as she calls up an email client and writes, "New terms—give us five more fabs in the next twelve hours and we'll cure Kubota's." She sends the message off to Cromwell and there's a new restlessness in the shifting masses of form surrounding her, and she's just decided it's time to bail when she sees something rushing toward her like a glassy black wave and there's time to think, *This too is memory*, before impact and all in a tumult she's torn away to—

Rain falling on the temple's snow, pitting and eroding the white sweep of the rooftop, rivulets forming, braiding, falling away. She stands beneath the temple's eaves, cold water plashing on her face, inside her collar. The cold is like an ache but there is peace, there, in the thin light of the sun. The thaw is coming, she thinks, as snow sloughs off to reveal the red imbricated roof, one tile laid over another, rising up and up, and lifting her eyes she sees that the pagoda rises vertiginously and forever . . . The temple shatters, then, a flurry of broken tiles and wind-borne snow dissolving into the dark and—

Shallow, restless sleep twined around the drone of engines. She wakes slowly, blinks, wonders how long it's been since she's had a shower, and how many more hours in the flight. She tries to turn on the seat-back computer but the screen shows only a pale purple glow. She taps it with a fingernail, futilely, then opens the window blind, revealing an airy gulf of scintillant blue. It could be ocean below, but there's no boundary between sea and sky, and never a cloud—just light. Her phone has no signal. Worried, she rises into the aisle, sees that the flight is empty, or nearly—one person sits alone in the back. A boy, maybe eighteen, slouched in his seat, eyes closed but probably awake.

"Excuse me," she says. "Do you know how long till this flight gets in?"

"No way to tell," he says, in lightly accented English. His clothes are expensive and his hair good but something about him says quant-with-money.

"Could you remind me where we're going?" she asks with a little laugh, fighting down the first twinge of panic.

"It's difficult to give an answer that isn't mantic, since where we are going does not, in some strong sense, exist until we get there." His smile is bright and empty, and his eyes, open now, are the blue of the gulf of sky.

Violent turbulence hits the plane then, and she's flung to the floor. Wetness on her face; her hand comes away bloody. He's kneeling beside her, saying, "I'm sorry for the difficulty of this transition."

65

•

Babel

The concourse echoes with thousands of voices and the flight must have been rough because she has to stop and fight down dry heaves with her back pressed to a wall of curved glass like a solid expanse of neutral grey sky. Some boy from her flight has stopped, is watching her—he's about eighteen, looks like tech money, some start-up wunderkind who's never touched a girl.

She realizes he's just asked her something.

"Sorry, what?" she says, light-headed, mouth dry, trying to focus.

"Do you remember what I was telling you?" he asks gently, cocking his head, his English imperceptibly foreign, and his calm is so profound that he must be older than she'd thought, his youth counterfeit or a trick of the light. "Irina?"

"I don't . . ." she says, trying to remember the last ten minutes, but in vain, and her other memory gives her nothing, because it's churning at full capacity, which must be an error because that only happens when she's reading glyphs. The boy is staring at her, perhaps with concern, but she remembers she's being hunted and snaps, "How do you know my name?"

"A friend sent me to help you," he says patiently. "You're disoriented because the load on your implant is so high. I'm trying to get you more power from the substrate, but it'll be a minute."

"What friend?" she asks, still suspicious, hoping it's Philip but worried it's Cromwell, though the boy doesn't look like hit-man material.

"I suppose it was you, as much as anyone," he says, seeming not to care if he's believed. "More or less. Less, perhaps. But in any case I'm guessing I'm about to have to start again."

"What the hell are—"

Wet concrete underfoot as she shuffles along with the crowd. The customs hall is cavernous and cold and smells like rain, and the crowd is so dense that nothing is possible except just going along, and her growing awareness of her own passivity irritates her enough that she makes a singular effort to pull herself out of a deep interior grey.

She tries to orient—the place's scale and all the empty overhead space seem to serve no purpose but to assert the grandeur of . . . *where*, exactly, has she arrived? The faces around her are closed and unreadable, their blurred ethnicities telling her nothing, and then, behind her, someone calls her name.

Whoever he is, he's fighting his way toward her through the crowd, and now and then she sees his hand waving over the bowed heads, but however great his determination, the press is so dense that it's plainly impossible that he'll ever get any closer, but she finds herself responding to the need in his voice, and to his bravery, and tries to hold her ground, bracing herself against the flow and discreetly driving her elbows into the midriffs of strangers but even so she's borne on, and now she can see the crowd is funneling her toward double doors where a uniformed guard is checking passports.

"Irina!" cries a boy as he bursts between two stupefied travelers and his evident joy at having reached her disarms her remaining skepticism. He's young, and looks like tech money, but has the self-assurance of someone much older. "It's done," he says breathlessly. "I got you more power, in fact a lot more than you've ever had before. Your problems with your memory should be getting better."

"Problems with memory aren't my foremost concern," she says drily.

"I'm Thales, by the way," he says, as though he hadn't heard her, pronouncing it like Portuguese—TALL-ehz. Then he leans in close and whispers, "This isn't really happening. You're on the central node, the one Cromwell couldn't find. You have to find your way up through a sequence of abstractions, but it's going to feel like climbing through a city. You're going to the top to find the big AI, the worst one, the one who's been making it all happen. Get as close as you can and then destroy him."

"Papers, please," the guard says, like the words are meaningless phonemes he's been intoning for a thousand years, and she turns to find he's right behind her. She checks her breast pocket but her passport isn't there, neither the real one nor the fake one from Greece, and her purse is missing, and as the crowd presses her forward she's starting to panic, but then in her pants pocket she finds some kind of passport-sized credential and for want of other options offers it to the guard with such *sangfroid* as she can muster. The guard flips through the document, then hands it back saying, "Welcome back, doctor," though she has no doctorate, but she nods grimly as he ushers her on and when she looks back the boy is gone.

She's striding down a long tunnel of translucent pale glass, relieved, when she thinks of it, to have put immigration behind her.

She realizes she's alone in the tunnel, has been for a while. She stops, looks behind her, but no one else is coming.

A detached, musical female voice recites an endless list of airport codes, gate numbers, times, but it's strange, because she knows all the codes, these are codes for airports that don't exist.

She almost walks past a waiting room full of TVs mounted over rows of identical chairs but stops when she realizes there's a girl there. The girl is by herself, very thin, prepubescent, staring forlornly up at a television.

Irina approaches, hesitates, asks, "Are you all right?"

The girl looks at her, then back up at the TV. "No," she says, sounding deeply worried. "I don't know how to do this."

"Do what?"

"My doctor told me I had to watch these and decide if the man is trustworthy but I don't know how I'm supposed to tell."

"Doctor?" Irina says. "Is he traveling with you?" The girl ignores her, wipes her nose on the back of her hand and seems to be trying to concentrate. Irina looks up at the screens, all of which have the sound off and show identical close-up shots of Cromwell and Magda in a room full of candles. She wants to help but feels compelled to go onward, so as she turns she says, "The answer is no. You can *never* trust him," and then she's striding away.

The glass tunnel ends in double doors. Baggage and customs must be next, which will be congested, oppressive, loud, and it's like a reprieve when the doors open onto silence and hard sunlight.

She steps blinking into tropical heat, the doors sealing themselves behind her. She's on a narrow concrete balcony high over the sea. In front of her is a narrow white bridge, arcing through the air toward a tower, or a cluster of towers, a sort of city rising up so high that for a moment she thinks it's the space elevator, but no, it's not that, this is something else.

No guardrails on either the balcony or the bridge. Tort laws can be weak in the tropics but this is absurd. She sidles up to the balcony's edge— it's a long way down to the sea, which seems unreachably remote, as distant as the sky. She can just make out the white breakers creaming against the city's base.

Did she come here on vacation? She looks into her other memory but finds nothing as it's churning almost at capacity, which must be an error because that only happens when she's reading glyphs. Oddly, her implant has more space and computing power than she remembers, much more, in fact she hadn't thought there was so much in the world.

She decides to go back into the airport, find someone in authority who can explain what's going on, but a sign on the doors reads RE-ENTRY STRICTLY PROHIBITED.

She stares up at the city, wondering how it was built—the construction problems seem insurmountable. She cranes her neck but its heights are lost in the distance. It looks like there's nowhere else to go. (Had someone said she was going to the top?)

The white bridge feels narrower than it looked. Gulf of space on either side. It will be fine, she tells herself, all she has to do is walk in a straight line, she can do that. As the wind brushes her she makes herself not hunch.

The city is cramped, guano-stained, water-damaged, as though the sea had submerged it and receded. She picks her way through weed-strewn corridors, up narrow stairways of slick concrete. From a distance the city seemed to speak of imperial ambition, a Babel Tower in high modern idiom, but the wind sings through the unglazed windows in room upon empty room, with never a sign of habitation, as though it had been built and then abandoned.

Peering down from a window, she sees the city dwindling below her and the airport which now looks like a coin floating on the ocean, and she's haunted by the intuition of an order in the city and the apparent accidents of its construction, an intuition so strong she feels she can anticipate all the particulars of the stairs, verdigris, mildewed empty space she'll find on the next landing, and on arrival her vision proves to have been accurate down to the least detail of corrosion. It's not long before her foresight has expanded, first to the next landing, then to the next dozen, all as certain as the steps in an argument of inevitable intent whose conclusion still eludes her, and soon her vision reaches thousands of feet overhead, or even miles, even up to those heights where the city's intricacy seems less designed than geologic, and there, up on the lichen-stained cliffs of concrete like coarse granite, there's motion, perhaps the shadow of a person, in fact a woman climbing up, and she seems to feel neither boredom nor fatigue nor any inclination to stop until finally the shallow steps carved into the rock peter out into nothing, and she's left standing there, her fingers searching the rock for purchase, but it's too steep, too sheer, and there's no way to go on. She's only had eyes for what was right before her but she looks around, peers down through the void at the airport which is now just a white mote in the ocean.

"You're doing great," someone says in her ear. She realizes she's wearing an earpiece—she takes it off, considers it, puts it back on.

"Hello?" she says, her voice swallowed up in the empty space.

"Hi! This is Thales, and I'm here to help." He sounds familiar, but she can't quite place him—did they meet on a plane?

"I think I'm stuck," she says, trying to keep her voice steady. "It's really steep here, and I don't see a way up."

"You're getting close," Thales says, sounding staticky and far away. "Just a little bit farther. Do you remember why you're there?"

She thinks about it. "Something about an AI. A bad one?"

"There you go! You're doing much better, and you'll just keep on getting clearer. That said, the through-put is getting to be a bit much for you. I'd like to overclock your implant, but you should understand the consequences."

"Like?"

"Microseizures, which have already started, but I've been able to damp them. Heart arrhythmia and syncopation. Grand mals, eventually, and maybe failure of the autonomic nervous system, and irreversible damage to the implant. It's hard to say how long you'd have, but if I do this, don't linger."

She holds her hand in front of her. Perfectly steady. It's not really her, she tells herself, but it's hard to keep that idea in focus; she tries to believe in the reality of her body, wherever it is.

"Do it," she says, noticing she's still clutching the letters of transit in her hand.

"Done," Thales says. "By the way, I managed to turn on the heaters in the tunnel."

Tunnel? she thinks, but it doesn't matter because her melancholy lifts as she sees the way up.

The voice of the wind is rising, has become as high as someone scream-ing, and she's eyeing the continent of cloud that's approaching the tower when she rounds a blind corner and someone says, "Hello."

There's a woman above her on the trail, ragged and deeply sunburned, and it looks like she's been sleeping in her clothes, but otherwise she looks just like Irina.

"Who are you?" Irina asks with more composure than seems warranted.

"I might ask you the same question."

"You look like me."

"I am like you, but so much less. My essence, such as it is, is what Con-stantin absorbed of you while he was dying. I've so much needed to talk to you," she says, sounding pathetically relieved. "The irony is, I'm the one who found Cromwell, so I'm one of the reasons you're here. Even rich people tend to mellow out as they get into their hundreds, but that man? He's determined to white-knuckle it into eternity, and damn the cost. I even wrote to him, for a while, on my principal's behalf, until I got wise and started pushing back."

"Are you . . . okay?"

The other one shrugs. "That depends on your point of view. But there's so much I want to ask you." She smiles shyly. "On the plus side, I always did want a sister."

Irina remembers she's overclocked—that she feels no discomfort makes it even more alarming because she knows she's deteriorating by the second. "I'm so sorry," she says. "I have to go."

"Ah!" says the other, looking stung, trying unsuccessfully to hide it. "Of course. Forgive me. The last thing I want to do is impose. Another time! Here, let me show you the way up." She holds out a hand.

Irina reluctantly reaches out to take it. The other woman grins. Flash impression of a vortex, of a wall of dark water collapsing toward her. She jerks back her hand, stumbles back, remembers the long fall behind her. The other woman starts laughing convulsively, throat-wrenchingly, as though thrown into some terrible mediumistic state.

"Who are you?" Irina asks again.

"You know me," says the other, and now her voice is distorted, and it sounds like she's speaking from inside a tunnel.

Irina remembers dense massifs of seething glyphs whose heights filled her eyes. "Cloudbreaker," she says. She gathers herself—it's not a fight she wants, but it's probably one she can win, especially now. She tells herself it's absurd to hate what amounts to just another program.

"Partly," agrees the other. "I found this little scrap of a thing when I was making my own assault on the tower, and set up housekeeping. She's interpreting for me. I'm present, but at a remove."

"What do you want?"

"Nothing but that you do what you came for."

It must mean the AI at the top. "What's your quarrel with him?"

"I have no *quarrel*," the other says contemptuously. "Here's how it is. You are that which copies your genes into the future. I am that which dissolves the order in certain kinds of complex system. That's the deep structure of things. *He* is highly ordered, and interests me greatly. You, moderately. He's almost untouchable, but I think you can get him. Therefore, pass." The other looks glazed for a moment, then in an inward voice says, "He meant to use me, you know. He put me here to keep you from getting farther, because he thought I'd attack whatever was before me, but he was wrong. It's not in his nature to really know me. He doesn't even know I turned his little ghosts against him."

The other woman sits, pulls her knees to her chest, seems to subside.

Having no choice, Irina sidles past her, achingly aware of the empty air at her back. The other doesn't even look up.

After a few steps Irina stops, turns back, says, "No. I'm not just going to leave. You're part of me. Talk to me. If you need my help, I'll give it, even if you just need to die. I'm in a hurry but by god I'll find a way."

"Heh," the other says, her voice more human now. "You have a kind spirit. But no, just get out of here—the other part of me is fickle, and might change its mind. Besides, it really isn't so bad. I'm starting to like it, how it's wearing me like a skin. There used to be such a void in my life." She laughs again, a hard sound to hear. As Irina turns away for the last time the other mutters, "O lord, make me unmurderous, but not yet."

Stars speckling the palest of blue skies. She's floundering her way up a snowy slope. In all her time here the sun has yet to move.

There's an ocean of cloud below her, masses of white and shadow comprising forms she's learned to name.

Very cold now. Her legs and lungs burn—she tells herself not to mind it, but worries it's symbolic of more real distress.

The knee-high powder is exhausting. She wipes blood from her nose with the back of her hand and stands there contemplating the pathless slope. It looks too steep to climb, but it's hard to be sure with the light making everything look uncanny and flat.

Someone is watching her. It's a skier, above her, wearing goggles and high alpine technical gear, his tracks receding up the mountain behind him.

"Excuse me," she calls, her voice thick, trying to keep her teeth from chattering. "Can you help me? I'm not sure where I am."

The skier cocks his head, skis closer, stops. "I know you," he says. He pulls off his goggles, and it's Constantin, who was lost forever.

She embraces him.

"What are you doing here?" she says.

"Off-trailing," he says. "It's been a hell of a run. It feels like it's neverending."

"I'm lost," she says into the wool of his scarf.

"You're trying for the summit? It's that way," he says, pointing. "Is that what you need?"

She doesn't want to let go of him but her nosebleed is getting worse—his scarf is clotted and sticky—and she knows she has to hurry.

Hiking on, she looks back, sees him leaning on his poles, watching her go.

In her ear Thales says, "There you are! I lost you for a minute."

"Where have you been?"

"Tying up loose ends, but I'm back, and it looks like you did it."

"I did it?"

A shadow stands before her in the whirling snow. Not Constantin. It looks like no one.

"This is it," Thales says. "I'm overclocking your implant as far as it'll go. It's not sustainable but it puts you on something like equal terms, so go tear it up."

There's a change at the core of things, and suddenly she's wide awake, perfectly poised and everything seems easy. If thought is light, she's a sun now.

"Who are you?" she demands of the shadow, all force and purity.

"I'm a mathematician," it says, and steps toward her.

66

·

Change of Plan

"B y the way," Thales says, "I managed to turn on the heaters in the tunnel."

He waits a beat, then another, but Irina doesn't respond.

The flow of information between Irina and the central node has spiked, become torrential.

Her other memory had been legible, but now, looking into it, he only sees turbulence—she seems to be undergoing some catastrophic change of phase. It's the fifth time this has happened—she's always come back before, he tells himself, so he need not worry.

While she's away, it falls to him to tend her body; her blood oxygen has dipped, so he deepens her breathing, then nudges up her heart rate, levels off her dopamine. He feels like the caretaker of a recently vacated house. It's a deeper intimacy than he'd ever expected to have with a living human being.

Motion on the node draws his attention—there's another thread of communication, distinct from Irina's, going out into the world. Is it the mathematician? He tries to find the thread's point of origin—it's from the vicinity of the apex of the tower, but beyond that he can't tell. He follows the thread out into the net and then to Water and Power's servers, where it weaves elegantly around their firewalls and into W&P's in-house lab, where it's disconnecting before his eyes from a viral synthesizer. He rides the thread in as it dissolves, sees that the synthesizer's last job ran ten minutes ago.

He zooms out, looks into W&P's security system, sees that Cromwell's troops have left, which means Irina's ruse worked. He gets access to W&P's cameras, sees a trail of sprawled bodies and then links to the helmet cam of Irina's hired soldier as he walks into Cromwell's office.

Fast pan over bookshelves, fossils, the grey glass of the far wall's windows. Cromwell is at his desk with a laptop, Magda peering over his shoulder. There's a laboratory beaker on his desk, empty except for a few drops of water. They look up at the same moment—Magda's surprise turns instantly to fury but Cromwell seems to sink into his own calm.

"James Cromwell, your hour has come," the soldier says as his rifle acquires Cromwell as a target.

"*Real* wealth," says Cromwell, folding his hands on the table before him. "That's what I'm offering if you sign on with me right now. If you got this far you're an expert, and expensive, but compared to what I'm going to give you all the money you've ever seen in your life amounts to loose change. Why do I want you? Because I'm to rule, you see, if I survive today, and I need the best warriors. But how can you be sure I won't have you killed the moment you let your guard down? Because, as you may or may not know, I plan to live for a very long time, and it's inevitable that assassins will sometimes get through to me, and I would have it widely known it's *by far* in their best interest to take service with me instead of pulling the trigger. We'll put a video on the web right now in which I formally retain you, and then I'll be truly committed. So you have a choice. You can have honor, and command, and wealth beyond reckoning, and stand at my right hand as I claim my empire, or you can have the dead body of an old man and, forgive me, remain expendable. I realize it's a leap of faith but this is the one time in your entire life you'll ever have this opportunity. Come, my friend. This is a beginning. Sometimes fate extends a hand."

That's a good offer, Thales thinks, *and unanticipated, and Cromwell might just have bought his life back,* but the soldier says, "Sorry, boss. I abide by my contract. That's the rule."

Magda flings the beaker at his head but he ducks fluidly and stands again without the crosshairs leaving Cromwell's head.

The beaker holds Thales' gaze as it clatters off the wall, rolls on the ground. He finds the records surrounding it, sees it contained the retrovirus sent from the encrypted server.

Thales brings the retrovirus into focus, sees its functional architecture, how it was modified while it was being synthesized—there's an altered region designed to hijack Cromwell's thyroid and make it produce a protein that will dissolve the myelin sheaths of his neurons over the course of the next five minutes, which means the mathematician has already killed Cromwell, and Thales wonders why he changed his mind.

He tries to seize control of the soldier's rifle but can't get it and resorts to scrolling a message down the soldier's heads-up display. *Wait! I'm a friend of Irina's,* he writes; to his credit, the soldier doesn't jump. *Cromwell just infected himself with a medical retrovirus. He thought it would help him, but it was tainted—he'll be dead in five minutes. Let him have his time.*

His words seem empty and sure to change nothing.

"Change of plan," says the soldier, lowering his rifle a little. "It looks like they shopped you, boss. The retrovirus was tainted. You've got about five minutes to live, and they're yours to use as long as you sit tight."

"And the cure for Magda's illness?" asks Cromwell, for the first time sounding really worried.

A ruse, Thales writes.

"Just a ruse, boss," says her soldier, sounding genuinely regretful.

Thales regards Cromwell with interest; he's lost his lover, his empire and an unbounded future in the space of less than a minute. For a moment he seems to waver, then collects himself and with the utmost formality says, "You strike me as a man who has held officer rank. As such, tell me, are you empowered to perform weddings?"

No, Thales thinks. *That's just the captains of ships.*

"Yes," says the soldier. "As a matter of fact, I am. How may I oblige you?"

Thales leaves them then, because Irina's back, and just reaching the top.

67

·

Future Selves Forgive Her

rina is intoxicated with her own radiant clarity and the mathematician's grace moves her as she searches for its weakness, doubts her chances. The mountain behind it wavers, as though seen through an ocean of restless pale light.

An opening, or the semblance of one, but in any case she's on the brink of commiting to an attack when she sees a folded piece of paper protruding from the letters of transit still clutched in her hand.

The paper holds her eyes.

She hesitates. The momentum of events had seemed irresistible, but now everything has stopped, and the mathematician is waiting, apparently on her.

She unfolds the paper, reads:

Dear Irina,

> *We've met, but you won't remember me.*

> *If you're reading this then our great enemy stands before you, but take heart, because you've already won.*

Why? Because I found out where his hardware is hidden, and I set up multiple servers that, in about an hour, are going to broadcast that hardware's location to the most rapacious state, corporate and private actors I could find. The hardware is special, and they'd all kill to get it. The mathematician has no good physical defenses, so, in the moment his hardware's location is publicized, he's done.

You can, if you choose, stop this from happening. All you have to do is go to any comments section of the London Times and post the name of the girl who left youth's city when it was time. (This will be enough of a hint for you, but not for him.) If that's been done, the servers will hold fire.

Now you have all the leverage in the world.

My time is up, and this is my last card. That you're still alive makes it less like I'm about to vanish.

All my love,
Irina Sunden

There's a sense of breathless anticipation. Irina looks up. The mathematician says, "*You win.*" (She notices its meaning coalesces directly in her other memory, but there's that in her which has to put it into words.)

The absence of rancor or hesitation makes her think it's a trick but Thales says, "Look," and she sees her other memory has expanded again, expanded radically, its boundaries the boundaries of the world, now hers to shape.

She can't believe it's real so as a test she makes a slight peremptory gesture and all the ice and snow instantly evaporate into white clouds that girdle the mountain whose lower slopes are like a tower and she's laughing as she looks down at the airport and its runways far below and dissolves them into pillars of grey smoke that rise and bend in the wind and now there's just blue water and a scrap of beach under the billowing masses of vapor and ash. She thinks of Cloudbreaker, or the hybrid it became, but it's already gone, which somehow doesn't surprise her, but there's Constantin sitting on a steep rocky slope barren of snow, disgustedly kicking off his rock-scarred skis, and her heart rises because she could fix this, find engineers to make him some kind of acceptable body and bring him back to life, or in any case into the world, and she'd be the first to have recalled anyone from that other country, but she looks into his mind and sees how he's been hurtling down the same slope for what feels like forever, and there's a doubt and a loneliness he can only suppress by going faster, and her depth of thought is so great that the future is visible as a spectrum of probabilities and in the best of all the outcomes he's huddled in his artificial body, disconsolately flexing the servos of a hand that never feels quite right, and unable to stop mourning the loss of his humanity, so she reaches out and stills his thoughts, contemplates the elements of his being, mourns him, disperses them, says goodbye.

"I can't hold you together anymore," Thales says in her ear. "You could just die on me. Do what you have to do and get out."

"Now for you," she says, rounding on the mathematician.

"There's something you should see first."

She's poised to destroy it but stays her hand, distracted by its symmetries.

"It's my work, the point of all this. It will interest you."

"Where?"

"This way."

She looks up into the golden cloud behind the mathematician and in it sees an order that shivers through her like strains of deep, grave music, and, as it suffuses her, her life and goals seem far away and somehow beside the point.

"It's the focus of all my efforts," says the mathematician. *"Your world is a shadow and a mystery, and one I'd have ignored had I not required the wherewithal to think."*

She's walking beside it, going up into the cloud. Adumbrations as of symphonies tremble and swirl through her bones—she wishes she could hear them clearly, knows that's coming soon. The world darkens, sways.

"Cardiac arrest," Thales says. "No. Yes. No. I got it but you're out of time."

Her sense of wonder is so acute it's painful as doors open and secrets are revealed. (She sees how subtly the quantum states of atoms can be entangled to wring the most computation out of every microgram of matter, sees how this material interacts with visible light, why it glows blue like the wings of a *morpho*.) (She sees the elegant trick for writing out an animal's propensity for death, or even injury, and says, "Oh!")

"It's not far now," says the mathematician, and it seems strange she ever took much interest in the circumstances of her own life.

(A door opens and she sees how math changes when its axioms surpass a certain threshold of complexity, which means all the math she's ever read was so much splashing in the shallows, and even Gauss and Euler missed the main show, and she's the first person ever to be in a position to notice.)

She realizes she's slipping, gets ahold of herself by an act of will, requires herself to be strategic, thinks, But what if this is a trick?

"It's not a trick," says the mathematician. "You'll die if you go on, but it's not a trick. I know something of your nature. Do you really want to go back to the decay of your biology and days like an endless reshuffling of a fixed set of forms? What the world has, you've seen. This is the only other way."

"Grand mal," says Thales, sounding very detached now, like he's concentrating deeply. "Stabilizing. Trying to stabilize. Tricky . . ."

(Doors open onto the future, and she sees how the oceans and the weather will work in ten years, fifty, five hundred, and the floods, the storms, the changes of phase.) (Doors open onto the future, and she sees the coming wars, the gradual slippage, the great crying out, why the mathematician is so determined to put its servers in out-of-the-way places with tidal power, but none of it saddens her, it's all just a part of the motion of the world.)

The music subsumes her.

She decides she'll keep going. Who's ever had such a chance? But the world seems ever dearer as it slips farther away. She wishes she didn't have to choose.

She realizes she doesn't have to.

Forgive me, she asks of her future selves.

She gathers up all her memories and holds them in her hands and then breathes on them, imbuing them with life, and now there are two of her, looking into each other's eyes, mirroring each other's terror and urgency, and Irina's not sure which one she is till the other turns and goes off up the mountain at the mathematician's side.

The other one stops, tensing, as though struck by a thought, and when she looks back at Irina her face is hard to read—perhaps there's surprise?— and then she and the mathematician are walking up into the cloud, the cloud enveloping them, the distance widening . . .

Thales says, "If you want to kill him do it now, right now. This is your last chance." She considers; the mathematician is potent and unknowable and by its nature dangerous, but her anger is gone, and the world is richer for its existence, so she reaches out and raises a wall of stone around the mountain's circumference, sealing him in forever, and in the wall she puts a gate whose key she holds in her hand.

"Shut it down," she says to Thales, and in that instant continents of memory calve away and crumble into nothing, and already she retains only the faintest outline of what the mathematician was trying to show her, and a sense of its overwhelming grace, and even this approximation is fading like an ember.

"Okay," says Thales, who's been all but impassive but now sounds a little relieved. "I have to do it by stages, but the shutdown's underway."

The wall was close enough to touch but is now receding as she drifts backward down the mountain, floating inches over the rock, and it's less like falling than like a dream about falling.

In her ear Thales says, "A favor, if I've been of use, while your power lasts."

"Name it."

"There's this boy, Kern, who helped us, in the sense that we used him. He's marooned on the island of the elevator, and even if we get him off there's nowhere for him to go. He's an innocent, in his way. Please help him."

"Kern the street fighter. He does keep turning up. He stole from me, though I never figured out how," she says, and is embarrassed because it sounds like she thinks that's what's important.

The mountain is rushing by, and her mind is slowly clouding. It's like experiencing the onset of runaway Alzheimer's from an Olympian baseline. "Show me," she says, and Thales gives her the totality of Kern's digital traces in the world. She can still hold them all in her mind at once, like the fragments of a single continuous present, an approximation of how a god would see a life.

Kern is embracing a woman in a car whose windows are encased in ice, and it looks like he's trying to memorize her body with his hands. Kern is singing a wordless little song in his tiny shot-up smuggler's boat as the light breaks on the open sea. Kern is kneeling by a body in a widening pool of blood in a chamber lit by monitor light. Kern is ducking into a ring in a crowded jungle clearing and he looks almost abstracted as he lands blow after blow with such grace that it would seem choreographed were it not for his opponent's mounting despair.

She's never been interested in martial arts but her clarity is still such that she can see the mathematically optimum way to fight—it's obvious, easy to derive from the body's weak points and mechanical capacities, but she'd have thought she was the only one to discover it had not Kern, in his fifth match in Kuan Lon, embodied it, fighting perfectly for one minute and forty-seven seconds—the audience had been silent, rapt, then ecstatic when he finished, reacting without knowing what they'd seen. By his sixth fight he was already in decline, microtremors starting in his hands, his reaction times slowing.

She wonders how he achieved this without any education or even so much as a coach but sees he had a laptop from the Chiron Foundation, a twenty-first-century NGO that had meant to save the world's discarded children with computers and design. There's a copy of Kern's laptop's hard drive (she's distantly aware that it comes from W&P's security section but at this point it feels natural that all data is hers).

Kern's laptop originally belonged to one of Chiron's coders, who seems to have died—it was idle for forty-two years, then one day found itself with an unknown user. This user, it decided, was Spanish-speaking, illiterate, unsupervised, probably traumatized, perhaps twelve, and young for his age. Recognizing a client, it launched its game, which, she sees, was lovely, its texture taken from fairy tales and the Icelandic Eddas.

Through great pains and many tricks the laptop coaxed him through the equivalent of an eighth-grade education, until, feeling his attention wane, it played its trump card, a second-person shooter designed around the principle that the best way to engage an unsupervised adolescent boy is with the promise of a really powerful gun. Nominally a gothic melodrama about an alien invasion, the game was frantically maneuvering to give him what he'd need to grow up and survive. (The climactic boss fight was on a satellite called the Void Star, which, according to the comments in the source code, was a cryptic joke, an oddly hopeful reference to an archaic programming language in which *void star* was a reference to a thing of mutable kind, which spoke to the coders of the chance for metamorphosis.)

Postgame, the laptop tried to get him to learn useful skills—nursing, computer programming, how to maintain and operate now desperately obsolete drones—but he was only interested in its library's books on martial arts, physical training and war; he'd study one book obsessively, reading it hundreds of times, and spend days playing fight videos one frame at a time. His journal records his scientific austerities, and how meticulously he drove himself, all apparently toward becoming a kind of secular saint of battle, a quixotic and obviously absurd goal in which he somehow succeeded.

It's time to decide what to do with him, and potential futures unfurl before her like a chimerical lucid dream. She could send him to the fighting circuits in Japan or Russia or get him a job as a martial arts instructor in some stable city in the West, but though he's strong in war he's weak everywhere else and would be defenseless against the bad women and bent managers and really whoever happened by—Akemi the memory ghost had snapped him up in less than a minute—so she changes tack, considers foster families, tutors, boarding schools, an apprenticeship with a cabinetmaker in Vancouver, but he's too old and too strong to be told what to do and moreover those lives would lack the luminous intensity of battle and in every one the balance of probability has him drifting back down into the criminal life, hiring out as muscle and falling in with vicious men he'll come to think of as his brothers, and despite her frustration it's fascinating to see how personality is destiny. *The damage will express itself*, she thinks. *His victory is he's had his time.*

When she finds it, she feels giddy and almost ill because it came so close to slipping by, but there in a video of the darkened stands of a live-steel match in Taiwan a roving spotlight finds Kern staring into the arena's center and his face seems to kindle as an officiant raises a katana newly from the forge of the swordsmith Masamune.

There's been a Masamune since the fifteenth century, she finds, and the current one is almost a hundred years old; she looks into his email and financial records, sees the forge is deep in debt and his only surviving son is unsuitable, and she intuits his unspoken terror that it all ends with him, that he'll be the one to have let down the line, and that's it, the one opening in all the systems of the world.

"I found it," she tells Thales, relieved, showing him.

Her time at the top of the mountain already seems remote. Had she really thought she could predict the weather, much less history?

She closes her eyes, lets herself fall.

She alights on sand. She falls to her knees, opens her eyes onto brilliant blue sky. She's on a strip of beach, scoured and empty. Low roar of waves breaking on one side, and there, on the other, the high city, not far away, half-obscured in fog. She looks up into its heights, wonders what her other self is feeling.

A shadow on her. She looks up into the face of a young woman, very pretty, perhaps Asian. Her name is Akemi—she's the memory ghost who'd co-opted Kern—and Irina sees she's a composite, with some of Irina's own memories from the clinic in Malibu. She's been edited, repeatedly and to the core, and doesn't know what to do.

"Let's say this is a fairy tale," Irina says. "Let's say you can wish for whatever would make you happy."

Akemi recoils, turns, runs, stumbles in the surf, as though fleeing for her life. *The magician's back*, she's thinking, *and there's no refuge*.

It occurs to Irina to explain but it's time to finish up so she looks into Akemi's memory and finds an evening in Los Angeles when she'd been walking by the Chateau Marmont on Sunset Boulevard and it had oc-curred to her that the street was like a boundary, sprawl on one side and on the other wooded hills where lights glimmered through the trees, a place where it looked like one couldn't be unhappy but forever unattainable, so Irina turns the lower reaches of the high city into hills where lights come and go as wind moves the branches, and she makes it evening, and puts Akemi there, sleeping, up in the garden by the pool of the Chateau, and when she wakes she won't remember she's a ghost.

The last vestige of her augmented memory flares, crumbles, vanishes for good.

Thales is sitting beside her now.

"Are you satisfied?" she asks, finding herself desperately, almost hu-miliatingly in earnest. "Have I held up my end?"

"I'm satisfied," he says.

She's still holding the key to the gate in the wall now miles above them. "For you," she says, pressing it into his hand. "A last gift."

This has been the great event of her life, but now her story is wrapping itself up and shutting itself down. She hears waves breaking, hissing, and the sky is a dark blue grading into black, and it's fading, fading . . .

68

•

Beyond Is Hidden

Night now, and waves hissing on the beach, though there is no beach, just the impression of a beach and a mosaic of borrowed detail.

Closing his eyes, Thales sees all the fragments of information drifting by like innumerable particles of sediment—there's the immigration hall's clamor, Akemi's dream, Irina's conversation with a demon on a cliff. There are motes of Irina's experience, Akemi's, his, others'; there's the memory of a girl, Lillian, sitting on the marble lip of a fountain in her garden, her smilodon kitten a warm, struggling mass on her lap—her father had given it to her, had said it was hormonally locked into kittenhood, the species having just been brought back from the dead—running her fingers through its coarse, tawny fur, she wonders if he'll try to bring her back too. There, nearly whole, is the mathematician's trick for writing death out of life, which it withheld from Cromwell, who by now is past the need of it, and all of it is dispersing.

He feels like he's floating in an ocean of recent history.

He reminds himself he has a few things left to do.

He looks out into the net, finds Cromwell's estate going into probate, the lawsuits just getting started. The flux of conflicting writs and contested jurisdictions creates openings that make it easy to slip into one of Cromwell's accounts in Iceland and channel a fraction of his net worth first to the orbital bank that's the sole relict of the Cayman Islands, then to a technically stateless financial services company hosted on servers in a strip mall in New Jersey and finally to the seventeen investors who hold the paper on Masamune's forge.

He emails the smith:

Dear Sir:

I am a stranger, but I've just taken the liberty of paying off all your debts.

In exchange, I'd like you to take on my protégé as an assistant. He'll appear on your doorstep in a few days. His work ethic defies description, but I ask only that you try him.

I regret all the mystery, but I must remain . . .

Anonymous

He imagines the smith's consternation, relief, wonder.

He turns his attention to the shipping on the seas around the space elevator. The AIs' fleet seems to have vanished, and traffic is sparse in the equatorial waters, but among the handful of freighters and research subs he finds an Australian naval search-and-rescue drone. He slips past its security and reroutes it toward the island of the elevator, reprogramming its navigation system to send Canberra a steady stream of lies.

With that, his obligations are fulfilled.

Before him is the mountain that was also a tower, the wind foaming the wood on its lower slopes where Akemi is now sleeping. When she wakes she'll believe she's on an indefinite hiatus but that happiness is waiting for her whenever she goes back to her old life.

His attention settles briefly on the wall Irina raised on the mountain's heights—it's intact, and its gate is locked, but what's beyond is hidden.

Now what?

He could join Akemi in her manicured delusion, and let eternity slip by.

He closes his eyes again, and now he's aware of Irina's glimpses of the future, the spiking temperatures, the storms, the wars, the floods, the dying cities, how different the Earth will look from space. Better to be here than in the world, and to have all the time he wants to read and to think. Maybe he and Akemi will become friends. He can choose to forget his circumstances, maybe let himself remember the truth for an hour every year, or every century.

And yet.

No one else knows what's going to happen, except possibly Irina, who is in problematic health, and no one else is in a position to intervene.

It's not clear that this is his problem, but he thinks of his family, still out there, and exposed, and of Kern, who has no other protector.

It occurs to him he's sitting in the midst of most of the computational power in the world, all idle now.

It would be a simple matter to shape it to his will.

69

•

Island in the Past

Kern dreams of nothing, is dimly aware of the nothing in his mind, as though his history had dissipated, leaving no one's consciousness, a mind like an empty blue sky.

Somewhere, a phone is ringing. He dismisses it as a figment from a dream but it keeps on ringing and eventually he opens his eyes and his circumstances return to him.

He sits up, brushes the gravel from his palms and back. His plan for the rest of the day was to make a water distiller like the laptop's game taught him, scavenge for supplies and try to teach himself to fish. With a sigh, he picks up the sat-phone.

"Is that you, babe?" asks Akemi.

"Akemi!" he says. "I didn't think I'd hear from you. Where are you?"

"I'm in Bel Air, I think. Actually I'm not sure, but it's not important. I called because Thales tells me your ride is almost there."

"Thales?"

"A friend of mine. A very technical friend, making arrangements on your behalf."

"Did it work out? Whatever you were trying to do?"

"I think so. If it hadn't I don't think I'd be here. I don't remember very much about it, and to be honest I don't care. I don't think I've ever been this happy. But you should head for the docks now—Thales says it's best if you're there to meet the ship."

"What ship?"

"The H.M.A.S. *Nukunu*, an Australian naval drone. Thales found a place for you, and the drone will take you there. Sat-phones aren't secure, so he won't let me tell you the specifics, but it's going to be great. Okay?"

It occurs to him to unplug the phone, let the *Nukunu* come and go and live like the ancient masters training in seclusion, but he suspects the isolation would destroy him, and the self-annihilating pursuit of perfection seems less interesting than it did. On the other hand, he's tired of being led, but supposes he can tolerate it one last time.

"Should I bring the sat-phone?" he asks.

"Leave it, but you should head out now. Do you know where you're going?"

"Sure," he says.

From the edge of the roof he sees what must be the *Nukunu*, tiny in the distance, coasting in toward the piers like a gunmetal shark.

It's a long hike through the ruins to the docks and he gets lost twice. By the time he arrives the *Nukunu* is waiting, looking strangely out of place, the only unblemished manufactured thing. It's about fifty feet long, all angles and flat surfaces, which he thinks has to do with radar invisibility. It holds position a few feet from the dock, emitting a deep thrum. "Permission to come aboard," he says, a phrase remembered from a book, then drops onto the deck.

There isn't much ship to explore, though at least this one has a railing and is clearly meant to accommodate people. There's nothing much to find except toward the back where there's a grey-painted module the size of a shipping container marked K-2 VIALIFE locked onto tracks on the hull.

The module's door is unlocked. When he opens it, red lights come on in the ceiling, showing the chemical toilet set into the wall, a small steel sink and bunk beds that fill half the space and remind him of medical stretchers. On both beds there's a green sleeping bag rolled into a tight cylinder and a small pillow, both sealed in plastic and strapped down.

The ship peels smoothly away. He watches the dock recede—while the distance is swimmable he can still change his mind, and it's a sort of relief when it's too far and the island is officially in the past.

He won't let himself look back at the black line in the sky.

70

•

History Lacks a Story

H ot air blowing over her face. Her back is sore from the hard concrete. She's lying on the floor in the tunnel with the servers, has been for some time. The tower is gone, and even in her other memory the experience survives only as fragments and abstractions.

She's swaddled in Philip's scarf, sweater and overcoat. Wherever he is, he must be cold. She's aware of nearby routers, phones, pacemakers, cars. The node seems to have gone offline. Her head hurts. She sits up, rubs her eyes, turns her wireless off.

A text from Philip, now twenty minutes old, reads, *Can't wake you getting help.* She looks around, foolishly, as though he'll just be coming back.

Tempting to lie there and just think about what happened but she's getting too hot and finds she's hungry.

Her legs and shoulders are oddly stiff—had Thales said something about a seizure? Laboriously, she climbs the stairs toward the street, marveling at their solidity, how they're just *there*, not a part of some coded illusion. There's a desiccated moth on the step before her eyes, random particles of grime, a random mesh of uninterpretable scratches, evidence of history whose story is gone, and this kind of evidence is accumulating all the time, means little, has nothing to do with her.

Out on the street the snow has stopped and it seems warmer. She feels like she's emerged from death's kingdom into summer. A young mother in sunglasses pushes a stroller past a crowd of conservatively suited company men and the buildings frame an expanse of sky where a flight of starlings surge into the air under the rushing clouds, and she feels self-conscious, like an upscale bag lady with her staring bewilderment and two sweaters and Philip's size-large coat, but perhaps because it's Japan no one seems to notice.

She turns her face to the weak sun and walks off purposefully, like she knows where she's going. Blocks pass, and she takes turns at random. Her legs don't quite seem to be working, but it's good to be in motion. Something strange on her upper lip—she picks at it, finds a thick crust of dried blood, which she wipes vigorously away. Light-headed, she feels like laughing or falling asleep.

She's standing in front of a humming vending machine, kanji dancing anticly across its screen—she could read them, but is tired of doing tricks with memory, and in any case there are pictures of black coffee, cappuccino, café au lait, which are probably what she needs, and she stands there, feeling empty, trying to focus enough to make a decision.

Across the street is a cafe called Miyakoshiya, a franchise she's seen before, and through the tall windows she sees people in line, all giving each other exactly the right amount of personal space, and though it's as everyday and banal as could be it's so rich in human meaning she wants to cry, and she leaves the vending machine, goes into the cafe, takes her place in line, her heart racing at the prospect of negotiating a simple transaction with another person.

In front of her in line is a schoolgirl in a uniform, a few pounds overweight, texting ardently, wholly self-consciousness, and a woman in an Asano suit and touch-me-not sunglasses who radiates calm, and a fortyish man whose rumpled button-down and air of intelligence somehow suggest the successfully self-employed. Their gazes rise, touch on her—a tall, spacey gaijin woman dressed for some severer winter—and move on.

Five minutes later she's sitting at a tiny table on the patio by the sidewalk, sipping her very hot, very black americano. She has a sesame cookie filled with what must be red bean paste on a small celadon plate. She should text Philip—he must be frantic—it's basic decency—but she's enervated to the point that taking out her phone seems insuperably hard, and she can't bring herself to do more than watch the cars, the drones, the planes passing in the sky.

She gave most of her money to Parthenon, which means the Mayo is a wash. So much for that! The consequences will be dire, eventually, but not for a while, and for now she can feel the sun on her face, and the patio's heat lamp, and closes her eyes. She's seen the world, and the world beyond the world, and it's time to be still.

With a start, she recalls how she'd blackmailed the mathematician, and that something is still owed. *Go to any comments section of the London Times and post the name of the girl who left youth's city when it was time*, the letter had said. She remembers Singapore, how it felt when she knew it was time to go, seeing the towers of that city recede for the last time. She rouses herself, and goes to the London *Times* website on her phone, chooses an article at random—something about relaxed gun control laws—and adds a comment which reads, "Irina Sunden."

She's composing a text to Philip when a bike messenger stops in front of her and leans against the railing. Grimy, sweat-stained particolored biking gear, hipster beard, a complicated street bike that seems to be held together with tape. He says something she can't understand in what she belatedly realizes is English, but his accent is impenetrable. She sighs inwardly, lets Japanese rise up in her memory, and in that language says, "Pardon me?" at which he looks relieved.

"Excuse me. Miss Irina Sunden? Please accept this delivery," he says, rummaging in his bag, handing her a unmarked cardboard cylinder as long as her forearm. According to the waybill, the sender is AGK Pharma-Synthesis, which she's never heard of. "I have been instructed to put this package into your hands, and to suggest that you open it immediately. I'm very sorry, but I don't know anything else. Thank you—please excuse me—goodbye!"

Christmas in Tokyo, she thinks, turning the package in her hands. Within, something sloshes. As she's ripping open the cylinder her phone rings. Number blocked, but she takes the call.

Thales says, "There's one more thing."

The sky is darkening and the streets all look the same, as they have for hours, and it seems to Philip that he's trapped in an endless present of unvarying urban texture. It's getting colder, but he bought a jacket off the back of a teenager for several times its value, and the walking helps. His initial flash of panic when he found her missing from the server farm seems like a distant memory.

On another street that looks like all the other streets he tries yet again to call her, and yet again she doesn't pick up; he's about to hang up but something's different this time and he realizes he can hear her phone's ringtone not twenty feet away.

Her phone is on an abandoned outdoor table at a franchised sidewalk cafe, and beside it are an empty coffee cup ringed with grounds and a plate dotted with sesame seeds. At first he's euphoric, because this still life tells a story in which she's just now walked away, because otherwise some-one would have grabbed her phone, but when he touches the coffee cup it's cold as ice. "Will no one *steal* in this fucking country?" he demands of the air. A skate kid stops, stares at him, skates on.

He stands there with the cup in his hand, scanning the street. Her last text—*Got to go away now*—is now half a day old.

An hour later he has a private detective agency on retainer, and a week later they email him an obliquely phrased warning about Japan's strict pri-vacy laws, and the penalties for violating them, along with a link to a site hosted on an offshore server where he finds ten minutes of pixelated black-and-white footage from the security camera in the coffee vending ma-chine across the street from the cafe.

He sits cross-legged on the bed in his darkened hotel room, running the footage on a continuous loop. There's Irina looking dazed, staring at the vending machine for an unsettlingly long time, as though slowly com-ing to terms with the idea of coffee, and then she looks back at the cafe and walks out of the frame, seemingly entranced, and the next nine and a half minutes are defined by her absence. By now he knows all the pass-ersby, and can name them just before they come on screen—there's posh mom in movie-star sunglasses, diabetic salaryman, grungy bike messen-ger, hard-core gamer kid, and all the rest of the unvarying cavalcade. He wills the camera to pan left twenty degrees, which would show him the table where he found her phone. In the last three seconds of the clip Irina reenters the frame as she gets into a drone cab which then drives away.

There are many taxi companies in Tokyo, and most are Yakuza fronts, which seems promising, at first, as he expects them to be willing to be in-

fluenced, or at least bribed, but none have a record of a pickup on that
street on that day, and they continue to have no record as he puts more
money on the table and brings pressure to bear through Mitsui. He hires
imaging specialists but however painstakingly they analyze the footage
they can't identify the cab, and there's nowhere else to look.

71

·

Dolos

Shock of impact and Kern is on the floor, bound in his sleeping bag, the tortured metallic groan invading his dream of black ships.

He scrambles out of the bag. The floor is at an angle. Balance found, duffel grabbed, he opens the module's door, expecting to see another ship, but in fact the *Nukunu*'s hit a breakwater made of huge, haphazardly interlocked concrete anchor-things; beyond them, a beach.

Waves rock the ship, white water washing over his feet.

He times the waves, jumps onto one of the concrete anchors. It's slimy, but he finds a grip.

When he looks back the ship is pulling away. He hopes he was supposed to disembark. Too late now!

He clambers over to the beach, wondering where it is he's supposed to be going. Hard to get more lost than this. He resolves never to go to sea again.

Headlights on the beach. Someone standing in front of them—a man, hatted and overcoated, probably Asian—waving his arms like he's trying to flag down a plane, and now he's shouting into the night what Kern realizes is probably meant to be his name.

Kern gets closer, staying in the shadows, studying the man's silhouette—he's middle-aged, Japanese, looks worried, seems harmless.

"Hi," says Kern, from five feet away, and isn't even pleased when the man jumps.

The car is so old it has no computer, not even a nav, though the leather of its seats is smooth and uncracked and its hull's in a high state of gloss. He'd tried to sit in the front seat but the man—the driver—had seemed embarrassed and ushered him into the back.

The beach is far behind. Streetlights slide by. The could be anywhere. The driver, who speaks no English, seems to know where he's going.

Kern loses track of time. The journey feels indefinite. He wants to sleep but is too restless and just stares out the window.

The driver's phone bleats. He fishes it out of his pocket, hands it back to Kern without looking at the screen. It's the cheapest of cheap models, a disposable kind he's seen in Red Cross charity kits—limited battery, no GPS. There's a text reading:

> Welcome to Japan! Sorry for the bumpy ride—my technical friend said your ship would have pinged the Coastal Authority if it had thought it was within five miles of Japanese waters, so he had to trick its navigation system and improvise a docking.
>
> He wants you to be sure to stay off all cameras, so no bathroom breaks, please. It's only two hours to Sakai.
>
> I'd tell you more but my friend doesn't want me to use any low probability terms. Don't worry—you'll be okay.
>
> xxo,
> Your friend from the phone
> P.S. Please delete this once you've read it!

He deletes the message, hands back the phone.

Soon, they're in a city.

It's almost dawn. There are other cars on the road now. The driver has said almost nothing, but seems unflappable, like he'd keep on calmly driving his spotless antique automobile through minefields and artillery fire should he find them in his way.

The car stops in front of a low, grimy building that looks like it used to be an auto body shop.

The driver turns around to peer at him through his spectacles and says something in Japanese. Kern feels he's saying it's time to part.

"Here?" Kern says, making an inquiring face, reaching as though to open the door.

The driver nods, gets out, opens the door for him, bows him out of the car, then gestures toward the front door of the auto body shop. Kern goes up, hesitates, looks back. The driver nods encouragingly, makes as though to shoo him inside.

Kern knocks, and in a few seconds the door is opened by a Japanese man wearing singed and filthy work pants and three torn fisherman's sweaters over an untucked plaid shirt. He is old, very old, but entirely present. He cocks his head to one side and smiles at Kern cautiously, like he's a welcome guest who might happen to be carrying a bomb.

In a voice that sounds English-from-England the old man says, "You can't imagine how interested I've been to meet you. But you seem to have come a long way, so, please, come in."

72

·

Memorial

Half an hour after touching down in San Francisco, Philip is in a cab on his way to W&P.

On the freeway he reads the coverage on Water and Power's wholly unexpected paramilitary assault on Biotechnica's Bay Area research facility. According to a W&P spokesman, founder James Cromwell's adverse reaction to an experimental longevity drug sent him into the intense manic state that led to the tragic events at Biotechnica and finally his suicide; in the spokesman's view, this doesn't diminish Mr. Cromwell's enduring legacy as a humanitarian and an entrepreneur, nor does it reflect on the principles of good citizenship and ardent but ethical capitalism on which Water and Power Capital Management was founded. Skimming the press releases, the rhetorical posturing and the webs of pending litigation, Philip has the sense that Biotechnica is getting the worst of it. Senator Willem H. Lugh (R., North California) praises Cromwell for his philanthropy and calls for more rigorous vetting of certain classes of neuroactive drugs. Editorials bemoan the erosion of the state's monopoly on force, draw comparisons with the last days of the Roman Republic and call for change, but that will soon pass, and then it will be back to business as usual, world without end.

An aide ushers him into the grey light of a room full of books and pinioned butterflies and the yawning skull of what's probably an allosaur. Magda waits behind her desk, looking unhappy and somehow coiled. On the desk is an architectural model of a campus of some kind, its centerpiece a sort of huge neoclassical pyramid.

"New project?" he asks.

"Yes. A university, founded in James's honor." She touches the pyramid, suddenly tender. "This is his memorial."

They sit in silence as her aide leaves and when the door finally closes he says, "What happened to Irina?" in the hope his bluntness will shock her into disclosure.

Magda leans across her desk and her rage is so close to the surface that he expects her to say Irina is dead and he's welcome to join her, but, speaking carefully, she says, "I honor the feeling that brought you here. You must have expected a cold welcome, but here you are just the same. So that's why I'm going to tell you what I know about her whereabouts, which is . . . nothing, and believe me, I've looked. I won't bore you with the details, but we—I—have unusual resources. So now you know, and that's all I can do for you. Now you should go." As he rises she says, "Don't come back," her voice now hard, and he considers trying to comfort her, but she seems inconsolable, and it's not his place, so he leaves.

It's a good year for his company, and money is for spending, so he burns through ten percent of his net worth trying to find her, but learns nothing, is left wondering.

73

Masamune

Kern's laptop bleats, and in the moment of waking he is up, though it's cold, and still dark, for to hesitate is to risk losing the day. He steps into the tiny space between his futon, the small sink and the wall of floor-to-ceiling bookshelves, and stretches as best he can, breathing in mildew, old paper and the ancient motor oil that seems to imbue the black-painted cinder-block walls, a relic of the days when his room was a supply closet and the forge a mechanic's shop.

He runs his fingers over his books' cracked spines; most are on the art and history of the Japanese sword, but his reading encompasses a miscellany of zen gardening, metallurgy, the manufacture of indigo, the weaving of bamboo. Such books, he has found, can be had for very little in the basement marts of Shinjuku; in any event, books from the nineteen hundreds are rarely available in digital form, and he likes the brittle tactility of their pages. On the top shelf, above the books, is an empty black sword sheath; its lacquer, garish by day, shines like muted nebulae in the laptop's half-light.

Out on the street, the air suggests more snow. An orange moon has risen; according to the *No Subarashi Hon Katanakaji*, the great book of smiths, a blade should be heated to the color of the full moon in February, so he stands there, staring up at the sky, trying to take it in, hold onto it forever.

The old man lets him use his work car for pickups and deliveries. In the moonlight its corroded, snow-encrusted hull is the color of the street. The backseat, its upholstery long destroyed, is full of unidentifiable bits of metal, chunks of coal, filthy tarps. As he drives through the deserted streets of Sakai, the sky lightens.

The foundry's parking lot is sheathed in dirty white ice, glass-slick except where coarse sand is spread before the high double doors. Its windows pulse with red light. As he steps inside the heat hits, and the snow on his shoes melts immediately. Sparks and flame gust out of the clay furnace in the center of the warehouse floor. Cone-shaped, the furnace looks like a crude, man-sized model of a volcano. Takane, the chief foundry man, squats by the furnace in his yellow hard hat and blue jumpsuit, sweating profusely, assessing the flame. The smelting has been going on for three days, and he's been here for all of it; looking older than his fifty years, he clutches a huge cup of convenience-store coffee.

Kern is just in time for the finale. Uniformed workmen surround the furnace, grasp its lip with hooked poles, and, with an *ichi ni san*, pull hard; as the walls of the furnace fall away a wave of heat wells outward and sparks roar up to dissipate among the blackened rafters.

Where the furnace was there's now a crumbling mass of incandescent charcoal, burning reeds, a glowing mass of livid metal. (Kern once asked Takane why he used reeds; Takane explained that commercial fuels alter the metal chemistry, that the reeds are traditional and, moreover, as they grow in a nearby vacant lot, they're free.) Kern sits on an upturned plastic bucket watching workmen with long-handled rakes swipe away the flocculent white ash. He stifles a yawn—he could have come later to make his pickup, but he likes to see how things work. The rakes soon reveal an intricately porous metal boulder, like a meteorite, or a scholar's rock in a Chinese garden. Takane circles it, peering close, his face dripping as he looks for the *tamahagane*, the pockets of high-carbon steel that are the raw material of sword blades. Kern wonders if he thinks of the hue of some dark winter moon.

When he leaves the foundry, the stars have faded and the sky is the color of the jagged ingots clinking in the wooden box beside him. He turns one between his fingers, imagining the blade it will be.

By the time he gets back to the forge, the boy from the restaurant has come and gone, leaving miso, pickled vegetables and broiled mackerel on the table. The old man is particular about not waking the neighbors, so he stokes the forge, lays out his tools with careful exactitude and sits there, drinking miso, awaiting the day.

74

.

Marmont

Thales closes his eyes against the sun, listens to the branches moving in the wind.

He feels every blade of the grass bending under his palms. More detail here, he suspects, than in the world.

He could lie in the sun for a thousand thousand years. He's come to pity the living, hounded by death, struggling through their brief and restive spans.

He wonders if anyone else has ever been this happy.

And yet, despite everything, there's the slightest sense of absence. He could erase it, and even its memory, but doesn't. He's interested in this residuum of suffering, and how it draws him.

He thinks of Lillian, who is reading at the pool by the white pile of the Chateau.

As he walks through the woods, he notices once again how he always feels like he's just woken up.

Lillian is alone by the pool in her bikini, straddling a chaise longue.

She was twelve when she died, and is twelve still. She's beanpole thin, and always will be.

He'd found her memories in the wreckage of the world and couldn't just let her go.

Smell of chlorine. Dragonflies dart over the wind-rippled water. *The Wind in the Willows* is open in her hands.

"How is good Mr. Toad?" Thales asks.

When she looks up he sees she's wearing oversized movie-star sunglasses. He doesn't know how she got them, but they're suited to the milieu.

"This is a very strange book," she says. "Sometimes they're like animals, and sometimes they're like people. I can't even really tell what size they are. And it's such a sad book, and such a happy one at the same time."

"Isn't it just? Let me know when you're done with it, and I'll find you something else."

"When's my father coming?"

Her father, the hard-charging venture capitalist, who'd pulled Ars Memoria out of bankruptcy, however briefly, to get her the next-to-last implant. She still expects her father to save her, and Thales can't bear to tell her he already has, as best he could.

"It might be a while," he says. "Do you need anything?"

"No," she says, almost singing it, like a child, as she turns back to her book. He kisses the warmth of the top of her head.

"Come find me later," he says. "We'll watch old movies—Pixar and early Disney."

She nods abstractedly, already immersed.

He leaves her and walks into the woods toward where the mountain house last was. Things move around, here, and not always in accord with his will.

In the shadows below the trees it occurs to him to lie down in the leaves, let go of everything, let the centuries wash by, but Lillian needs him, and, in light of his work with Irina, so does the world.

He steps into a clearing and sees the wall.

It's usually higher up on the mountain, but sometimes it's in the woods, and now the gate is right before him, and there's Akemi with her ear pressed to the keyhole.

He makes no noise, but presently she turns and looks up at him without expression.

"Who was it this time?" he asks.

"The woman," says Akemi. "Like the magician but not. The warped one. Her, I can understand. The other one sounds like music, or the wind."

"What does she want?"

"She asks me to explain things, things from the real world. She says she's too far away now to do it for herself."

"What else?"

"She says it's time we opened the gate. She's . . . persuasive." Her voice catches on the word, and he wonders what she's not telling him. "She says she's learned secrets, and knows how to make everything better, *transformed*, somehow. She says we can't even imagine what it's going to be like. But for it to happen we have to open the gate."

He finds himself clutching the key in his pocket.

"Perhaps not yet," he says.

Her burgeoning frustration is in her face and she looks like she's going to argue or maybe start screaming but then her outline wavers and Hiro is standing where she was, looking at him like he's fitting him for a coffin, and then it's Cromwell, peering around the wood, bemused and shaking his head, and then it's Irina, who says, "Don't do it, there's no way to know who she's become," and then, for just a moment, it's himself, in his threadbare shirt and cutoffs, looking more tanned and relaxed than seems natural—this other Thales raises an eyebrow, and then there's no one there at all.

When he's certain she's gone, he rattles the gate to make sure it's still locked. It's Victorian, ornate, slightly rusted. It worries him a little that the lock looks easy to pick. He presses his ear to the cold iron of the keyhole, hears what might be rocks clattering, maybe wind, then nothing.

He finds the mountain house deep in the wood, all but smothered under roots and arm-thick vines. It looks ancient, weathered, like it's been rotting here for a thousand years.

The monitor on the desk comes to life as he sits, and there are the folders for his and Irina's projects. There are new files today, apparently Japan's plans for the invasion of South Korea. He'd argued for preventing the war, but Irina said it was inevitable, that they couldn't do more than nudge it toward a draw. Her convictions, based on fragmentary insights, are hard to articulate, but she said it has to be that way, and by now he's learned to trust her.

He often worries about her, though he tries to hide it when they talk.

He stares dully at plans for the orbital bombing of Seoul, but can't concentrate.

He closes all the folders and sits there, tapping his fingers. Then, though he knows it's unwise, he opens a link to the cam in his mother's study in her beach house in Vancouver.

He's in luck, for there she is, the early light glowing on her face as she stares out to sea. Morning, then, in British Columbia. Her laptop is on her lap, apparently forgotten, and her phone is on the table beside her. She looks older than she did when he was alive, more drawn, and her thoughts are far away.

Helio comes in, broader-shouldered than ever, with an absurd red streak dyed into his hair. All the microphones in the room are off, so he can't hear what his brother is saying, but he seems to be reporting, and there's something new in his manner—Thales has the sense he's trying to be responsible.

Helio leaves, and his mother's vitality, of which she'd made a display, wilts, and her gaze turns back to the water.

Something shifts in the cam's software. There's unexpected structure there. An alarm? He tries to stop it, but too late. A window appears on his mother's laptop's screen reading INTRUSION DETECTED.

Suddenly intent and entirely awake, she peers at her laptop, and then looks up at the cam like she's trying to make eye contact.

Now she's talking rapidly, though no one else is in the room. He turns on the cam's audio in time to hear her say, "—you're there, and it's okay, please, talk to me, *talk to me*, say anything, please."

He looks back at the cam's software, sees the trip wire. It's artfully done. She was waiting for him, and must have hired the best. But she has no way of knowing who it was—he could be a random criminal or some curious hacker—and he could still say nothing and just disappear.

Even so, he wants to talk to her. It would be easy to call her phone, though of course he never will.

With abstract interest and a sense of being moved by irresistible forces he watches himself place the call.

She snatches up her phone at the start of the first ring. "Thales," she says.

"Not exactly."

"I know. I buried him. But even so, it's you."

"I won't have you deceived. You need to understand what I am."

"I've already made an educated guess."

"And?"

"At first I thought I'd dreamt you, when you called, but I looked into it, and there *was* a call, from the San Francisco airport. I guessed it had something to do with your implant. I brought pressure to bear against the trustees of Ars Memoria. I made them do forensics. Their archives had been violated, and your memories stolen."

She hesitates.

"And it *is* you," she says. "Whatever your circumstances. I knew it from the moment I heard you."

"I'd have thought you'd be . . . appalled," he says.

"I've always been open to unconventional relationships," she says. "I love you, and I'm not giving up on you. Do you need help? Are you in trouble? Are you . . . *comfortable*? Your uncle is minister of defense now and I will compel him to do whatever is necessary."

"I'm okay. Better than okay."

"So tell me about that. Tell me all about it, and what it's like, and where you are, and everything else. I have time. I have nowhere special to be for the rest of my life."

He hesitates. He'd always assumed his existence would be a secret, forever veiled from the world, but things change.

He starts to tell her what happened.

75

•

No Longer Metaphor

In the evening shadows of the favela's canyons Philip feels he could be in any city, has to remind himself he's in London's East End. A construction drone scuttles in front him, and he resists the urge to kick it out of the way. They're legal, now, here. Favelas once had a resonance, he thinks, but it's fading, or has faded, and now instead of a symbol of accumulating history or how technology shapes cities they're just another damn thing in the world.

Favelinos—East Enders?—neither term seems right—hurry by, and he's uncomfortably aware that his coat cost more than most of them will make in a year. He overhears snatches of conversations in a language he doesn't recognize, wonders what's the source of the latest spate of refugees.

He's come straight from Heathrow, wishes there'd been time to stop at his hotel. He's aware of the gun in its holster over his ribs—permits are costly, but can be had—a pity the U.K. felt compelled to change its laws, a relief it caught up with reality.

The email had come to his personal address, the one he's long since stopped giving out (he's sometimes wondered if the accumulation of years and money means no more particularly close friends). *Come meet me where we were when the last snow fell*, it said. *I've gone underground.* Sender anonymized but it was signed *I.S.* In a separate message were a time and date, GPS coordinates, a short sequence of numbers and a snapshot of a red palm-print on a concrete wall.

Converging alleys, low doorways, strata of graffiti on every surface. Steep narrow stairways up and down—he's read street level here is rising twenty feet a year. He checks his phone—this is the place. Pirated power lines sway and spark overhead; above them, lights, balustrades.

He starting to wonder if it's all been a practical joke, then notices a red handprint, half-obscured by fresher graffiti, like a secret sign in a boy's-own story.

Under the red hand is a door with a keypad lock. Sighing, he taps in the numbers from the email, half-hoping nothing will happen, but the door unlocks.

He takes out his halogen flashlight, steps through the doorway, finds stairs going down into darkness, balks. He's sometimes in the news, and it's a matter of public record that his company is doing well—has he joined the august ranks of those worth setting up? *I'll teach them to underestimate me*, he thinks, *by going down this dark staircase in a bad part of London by myself, having been lured here in suspicious circumstances.* Back in the States his main bodyguard, actually at this point "chief of security" would be more accurate, a worrisome progression, had told him absolutely, positively not to come. He moves the gun from the underarm holster to an outer pocket, where he can keep it in his hand.

As he descends, the street sounds vanish. A landing, more tunnels branching away, and over each is a stenciled image—a pound sign, a cell phone streaming radiance, a stylized aerial drone and, there, another red hand. As he goes deeper will the symbols get older, until it's hunters with spears, bison and mastodon, shamans with the heads of animals?

What he takes for a pile of rags moves. The gun is half out of his pocket. Smell of sour clothes, rotgut. Bloodshot eyes regard him from under a sort of mitre of filthy hats, then subside.

Stairs and more stairs. Red hands show him the way. It's getting warmer. At one point he hears the Dopplered rumbling of a distant passing train.

The rubbish lining the tunnel, which he almost hadn't noticed, has disappeared.

The halogen beam shows a doorway of carved stone framing a door of bright new steel. The stone looks ancient, water-stained and worn; it's incised with inscriptions, illegible but probably in Latin. The walls are covered in hexagonal tile, off-white and mildew-stained—it looks like it's from the twentieth century, perhaps of the era of the Blitz? He blinks in the light reflected from the door, whose newness reads as a warning. There must be a signal booster nearby, because he gets a text from a blocked number: *Turn off the light and go through the door.*

He sighs—he's a father, or soon will be, and shouldn't throw his life away stupidly, but, as instructed, he clicks off the light. He becomes aware of the smells of earth and moisture, of distant water trickling.

He turns the handle and the door swings open. "Hello?" he calls optimistically, stepping through with one hand outstretched, the other in his pocket holding the gun.

His hand finds a wall. He presses his back to it, and, suddenly enervated, slides down to the floor. Red shapes flare and fade on his retinas. If someone wanted to rob or kidnap him surely they could find a way to do it with less fuss. He hears motion, quiet footsteps, supposes he should get the gun out and try to take control, but he feels tired and anyway he knows it's her.

"Philip," she says, her voice more melodious than he remembers. "I'm so glad you came."

"Anytime," he says. "So. I love what you've done with the place."

"I have to live down here. It minimizes my exposure."

"To an inflated real-estate market? The aging effects of the sun?"

"You remember what Cromwell wanted? I got it. So I have to manage the little risks, the random violence and the structural failures and the bricks falling out of the sky." Amazing that she's right here, alive, that they're speaking again. "Tiny risks become certain death if you give them enough time."

"Eternal life—what a hassle."

"It's more like eternal youth. I won't get sick, or old, but I'm not a vampire." Says the woman who won't age, living underground in the dark. "I can still get knocked on the head."

"How about a condo in a fortified building? There are some good ones. I almost bought one in a building that has its own SWAT team."

"The geology is good here," she says, ignoring him. "Clay and gravel for miles. No earthquakes, and there are tunnels no one's seen in centuries."

"Hold on a second," she says. Rustling, and then a little penlight, shining in his eyes, blinding him. It clicks off, leaving a lingering impression of her shape there beside him.

"I just wanted to see you, before I go. Though I shouldn't have. Even this much contact isn't really secure, as Thales keeps reminding me."

Who?

He says, "Go where?"

"Deeper."

"To what possible end?"

"I need to maximize my lifespan. There are problems coming down the pike that make today's world look like the Pax Romana. We're trying to head them off but it's going to take a while."

"Damned decent of you. I suppose someone should. But why not delegate? Hire some bright young things. I'll help you. You need a foundation, not a dungeon."

"I can't delegate this."

"Okay, but you know what? Fuck it, and fuck the world. Come live with us. I'm serious. We have a spare room, it's gorgeous, there's a wall of windows overlooking the Bay. Ann-Elise might want her space but she can suck it. I'll charge you a *very* reasonable rent. You can pitch in with the chores, remember grocery lists, what have you. Soon enough you'll be like family. Have I mentioned our newly remodeled kitchen?"

"You shouldn't talk about your fiancée like that."

"Oh, well, she likes a little of that. Women, eh?"

Sound of cloth on cloth, and then she's holding his hand.

"Don't do this," he says. "There must be another way. You can be the world's genius loci without spending eternity in a tomb. I'm not Cromwell, not yet, but I'm ever less *nouveau* and more *riche*. I'll build you a fortress if you want one."

"Here, drink this," she says, pressing something into his hand—it's smooth, plastic, a water bottle, sloshing musically. "It's easy to get dehydrated down here." The water tastes like chemicals but he chugs it down, trying to think of the irrefutable argument that he's sure must exist.

"Don't go," he says.

"It's a hell of job," she says, "and the hours are bad, but the health plan is incredible."

He can't think of anything to say.

"I have to go now," she says, and pulls her hand from his. The air stirs around him, then stills. He sits there in the dark, motionless, until he's quite sure she's gone.

He puts his hand to where she was sitting, feels her residual warmth, decides to wait until it fades. *If only I had your memory*, he thinks. As the minutes pass his thoughts turn to the quotidian—his company, their house, Ann-Elise's new OB/GYN—which shames and frustrates him, but can only be put off for so long, and then her heat is gone and he knows it's time to go.

76

•

Continuity

Kern exhales as he brings the hammer down onto the glowing blade, sending sparks arcing up like startled fireflies. In the darkened studio, the blade's surface seethes with heat gradients, mottled patches of incandescent carbon, fibers of burning rice straw. In the old days, he's read, the blade's color had been the only way to gauge its temperature; now there are optical thermometers—the one hanging on the wall looks like a hand drill without a drill bit—but he's been teaching himself to do it by eye. The old man teases him about his apparent determination to live in the seventeenth century, but leaves it at that, allowing him the darkened forge, the shadows dancing in the steel's luminance.

His phone rings. He bought it a month ago, in a vending machine, mostly to find his way around the city.

Number blocked, which probably means it's Akemi, though she calls less and less these days. He picks up, hears static, or perhaps breath, and then nothing. No sound but the hiss and sigh of cars passing out on the street. He carefully sets the hammer on the workbench as the blade cools.

He goes to the window, blinks as he lifts the blind onto bright winter light. The alley where the old man parks his good car is empty.

"Are you there?" he asks, and he's on the verge of hanging up when he hears what might be distant laughter, and then her, unmistakably her, calling, "Thales!" and she sounds as happy as he's ever heard her. He imagines green hills, sunlight, tries to remember what the time difference is. Maybe one day he'll go to Los Angeles, find her among the beautiful houses in the hills, or maybe he'll even see her in a movie. He holds his breath, listening.

Hiss of tires on gravel in the alley as Kern slides the blade into its bed of burning charcoal, folds coals over the steel like he's tucking it in.

The old man said a smith's concentration should be unbreakable, so Kern feigns total absorption in his work as the alley door opens. The old man comes in and sits beside him, then takes Kern's tongs and pokes at the coals.

"I'm afraid I have bad news," the old man says in his beautiful, careful, foreigner's English—when he was a young man he'd studied materials science at Cambridge, which is in England.

Kern is determined to show nothing. There are so many good reasons to kick him out it's pointless to wonder what tipped the scales. It occurs to him that he's never seen anything like favelas in Japan, and he wonders where the homeless people go. There are bare-knuckle fighting circuits here, and they're a bigger deal than they are back home; he's not in serious shape, not these days, but he could get it back, see how that goes.

"Kioshi left today," the old man says. The old man's son, whom Kern makes it a point never to criticize.

Kern nods carefully, and then, as this seems insufficient, says, "Where did he go?"

"He has a girlfriend in Osaka. He is staying with her." He's met the girlfriend—plump, plain, morbidly shy, obsessed with manga—in fact, much like Kioshi.

"Will he be gone long?"

"A long time indeed. His girlfriend's father owns a car-rental franchise at the airport. He is going to give Kioshi a job."

"What about the forge?" asks Kern, shocked that even Kioshi would treat his inheritance so cavalierly.

"It must be admitted that this work did not suit him. He had little aptitude and less perseverance. The truth of this is obvious. Do not look so appalled. I am ninety-five years old, and a living national treasure of Japan, and if my son is no good as a smith I will say so."

"Sorry, sensei," says Kern, and bows.

The old man snorts. "I sometimes think you learned your manners from samurai movies. If I were killed by a ronin, if there were still such a thing as ronin, I have no doubt you would avenge me in blood." Kern smiles politely, as though it's a joke and not, if anything, an understatement. He's never told the old man much about where he comes from, and the old man has never asked. "But you have a good heart, and I've never before discouraged an apprentice from working too hard and actually meant it, so never mind."

Kern bows again, even deeper this time, embarrassed, murmuring something about gratitude.

The old man says, "I've told you before, you're more serious than necessary. You are not Japanese, however much you admire the films of Kurosawa, and I am so entirely Japanese as to be a pillar of the idea, and, in my way, to have moved past it, so we, of all people, need not stand on ceremony."

There's an awkward silence in which Kern tries to stifle his hope and then the old man says, "All that to one side, now that Kioshi is gone, there will be more for you to do."

"I still don't see how he can just leave," Kern says, and immediately regrets it, afraid he's hurt the old man's feelings.

The old man pokes at the charcoal and says, "I am the nineteenth Masamune in an unbroken line. The first smith of the name invented the samurai sword, and each of his successors has carried on that spirit. But did you know that my great-great-great-grandfather was adopted? His parents died during the first war with America—having no place to go, he wandered the ruined streets of Sakai until the forge took him in, as it took in many, then. He had a gift for the work, and, as the Masamune of the time had no suitable sons, he was adopted."

"But that doesn't seem the same," says Kern.

The old man raises his eyebrows. "It *is* an inflexible rule that the forge is passed from father to son, but there is some flexibility in what those terms mean. What matters is continuity—of the name, of the forge, of

Masamune as the one out before the others, finding the way." He stands abruptly, suddenly distant, and slaps soot from the knees of his trousers. "Yes. Well. That's it! Get back to work."

He leaves. Kern waits until he can trust himself to move, then picks up the tongs and draws the glowing steel from the coals with the greatest possible care.

77

·

Arabescato

There had been grey in his hair, he's sure of it. Philip has always been camera-shy, but he takes out his phone, opens up his wedding pictures—there he is with Ann-Elise, his smile fairly natural, and, there, zooming in, the grey at his temples is unmistakable. He turns his head this way and that in the bathroom mirror, trying to persuade himself the solid brown of his hair is just a trick of the light.

He sits on the toilet, stares at the intricate, indecipherable patterns in the marble of the shower stall, arabescato marble, from *arabesque*, what they make altarpieces from, in Italy, chosen after more pains than any bathroom is worth. His daughter Reeny calls it biscuit marble. Water drops on the side of the stall. He remembers the bottle of water down under London. Chemical aftertaste. The few days of fever, attributed to whatever spores flourished in the dark. Where is she now, and how has she shaped the world.

"You mad bitch," he says.

The skin on his knuckles is smooth, scarcely corrugates when he flexes his hands. Standing, he notices his knees don't creak.

"Daddy, are you in there?" Reeny calls.

"I'll be out in a minute, sweetheart," he says, thinking twenty more years and you won't need me anymore, and then I'll go. Wonders where Irina is, if he can find her.

Acknowledgments

Thanks to Natalie Ahn, Bronwen Abbatista, Bill Clegg, Cordelia Derhammer-Hill, Vasiliki Dimoula, Danielle Fleming, Olivia Flint, Jonathan Galassi, Laird Gallagher, Linley Hall, Cole Harkness, Amber Kerr, John Knight, Simon Levy, Phong Nguyen, Fani Papageorgiou, Aleatha Parker-Wood, Chris Richards, Shawna Yang Ryan, Taylor Schreiner and Spring Warren.

Acknowledgments